Ruby
Red
Herring

Also available by Tracy Gardner

Shepherd Sisters Mystery
Still Life and Death
Behind the Frame
Out of the Picture

Ruby
Red
Herring

AN AVERY AYERS
ANTIQUE MYSTERY

Tracy Gardner

NEW YORK

Published in the United States by Crooked Lane Books, an imprint of The Quick Brown Fox & Company LLC.

Crooked Lane Books and its logo are trademarks of The Quick Brown Fox & Company LLC.

Library of Congress Catalog-in-Publication data available upon request.

ISBN (hardcover): 978-1-64385-659-9
ISBN (ebook): 978-1-64385-660-5

Cover illustration by Mary Ann Lasher

Printed in the United States.

www.crookedlanebooks.com

Crooked Lane Books
34 West 27th St., 10th Floor
New York, NY 10001

First Edition: June 2021

10 9 8 7 6 5 4 3 2 1

For Fran

Chapter One

Avery Ayers rushed through the kitchen of her parents' upstate New York home, grabbing a bagel from the spread Aunt Midge set out every morning. She couldn't be late today. Briefcase in one hand, she rounded the corner of the kitchen island and clenched the bagel between her teeth as she poured coffee into her travel mug and replaced the lid one-handed.

She hip-checked her younger sister on the way to the sink. "Tilly. You did send your admissions essay to the conservatory last night, didn't you?"

"Yes! Sort of. I'll do it today, I promise!" Tilly looked from Avery to Aunt Midge, both now staring at her. "I'm having trouble with the closing paragraph, all right? I'll take care of it."

At twenty-five, Avery was seven years older than Tilly, a high school senior. Tilly had definitely inherited the procrastination gene from their mother Anne, just one of several reasons Avery was so glad Aunt Midge lived with them now. Her little sister had better get her admission requirements taken care of, or the London Conservatory of Music would move on to the next voice candidate.

Aunt Midge spoke up. "*We* will take care of it. Right after school, my dear. No excuses." Midge waved a hand covered in sparkling rings at Avery, her long, feathery chiffon caftan billowing around her as she moved. "Go. Give Micah a kiss for me. Be safe," she said, almost as an afterthought.

Avery nodded, meeting Aunt Midge's gaze. It was something they said to each other now, these last several months. *Be safe.* How many times in her life had her parents taken off in their cars without a thought in their heads about staying safe on the road? Would it have made a bit of difference if Aunt Midge— or someone—had uttered those words a year ago when they'd all driven away from Bello's? Would the words have somehow stopped her father from losing control and the car from plummeting into that ravine? Sometimes, when she recalled the crash, Avery still felt the heat that had reached the back seat before she and Tilly were pulled from the wreckage.

She straightened the neckline of her blouse and donned the cropped blazer she'd chosen to go with her slim-fit navy pants. The Museum of Antiquities curator was expecting her in less than an hour. Micah was meeting her there. She knew she was spoiled, usually working from her home office at the back of the house. She didn't mind the trips into Manhattan when she needed to be on-site for an assignment. Lilac Grove was a small, quaint suburb forty minutes or so outside the city. Avery always had the option of taking the train, but she enjoyed the drive.

"Love you both!" Avery put a hand on the front door handle, a plain white envelope on the foyer floor catching her eye. Someone must have slipped it through the mail slot, which was odd, as their mail only ever came to the mailbox at the end of the driveway. "Tilly!"

"I told you I'll do it today—stop nagging me!" Tilly slid into the foyer, followed closely by Halston, Aunt Midge's large black Afghan hound. Tilly's features were scrunched into a scowl under the mass of blond hair piled into a messy bun on top of her head.

"No, I think one of your friends dropped this off." Avery handed the envelope to her sister and pulled open the front door.

"Ooh, what is it?" Tilly tore it open, going silent as she read. The single white paper slipped from her fingers and floated to the floor. Tilly's hand covered her mouth. Her face went pale.

Ugh. Her sister could be so dramatic. Avery bent and picked up the letter, scanning the few typed words across the middle of the paper. "Oh. My God."

Aunt Midge appeared in the doorway. "Another grad party invitation?"

Avery silently handed the letter to her aunt. Her mind was reeling. It couldn't be. It wasn't possible. Was it?

"*Roo*," Aunt Midge read aloud. "*You must decline the contract. Your life is at stake. My love to you and Lamb. —Dad.*" The older woman appeared to have stopped breathing.

"Auntie?" Tilly moved to her side.

Midge looked at them. "What does this mean?"

Avery shook her head. "I have no idea."

"It's him! He's alive!" Tilly beamed, tears rolling down her face. "Dad's alive!"

"I . . . I don't know," Avery said. She took the letter from Midge, studying it. "We don't know that, Tilly."

"What do you mean? He used our names! No one else would know what he called us. Why would someone leave a fake letter from Dad?"

3

"I don't know," Avery repeated. "But we were all there the night it happened. The doctor told us—" She hesitated. The night their parents were killed had been almost exactly a year ago. A year was enough time for it not to still be so sharp, so cutting, wasn't it? Maybe not. Her eyes stung. She spoke the words she didn't want to say, because she had to. She didn't know what the letter meant, but there was no way it was from their father. "You remember. The doctor told us he couldn't save him. We went to his funeral. Their funeral."

Tilly's jaw was squared. She glared back at Avery, the color now high in her cheeks. "I don't care. I don't care! Who else knows he called you Roo and me Lamb? You don't know everything, A. There's got to be some explanation, and I don't even care what it is. Dad's alive!" She was shouting now. She spun around and stormed up the stairs, her bedroom door slamming loudly seconds later.

In the silent foyer, Avery stared at Aunt Midge. She felt awful. She understood—truly, she did. She wanted their father back as much as Tilly did. This house without William in it was not the same. Even with his sister Midge, fabulous, loving aunt that she was, the house had somehow lost its lightness. William had brought warmth and humor into every room, every conversation. Avery would love to believe he was alive.

"She'll be all right." Aunt Midge spoke quietly. "Leave this with me; let me reach out to some of my people, see if anyone has an inkling how we might find out who created this." She took the letter and carefully folded it, sliding it back into the envelope.

Avery nodded. Midge's "people" were vast and diverse. She had a wide network of friends and acquaintances through her travels and her interest in art and culture. At sixty, Margery

Millicent Ayers had lived many lives, as Avery's father used to say. A whip-smart, fiercely independent woman with boundless energy, Aunt Midge had been married once, years ago, but claimed it was the only thing she was terrible at. She'd always been a fixture in Avery's and Tilly's lives, whether it was whisking them away on an impromptu summer trip to Paris or delivering a massive modern-art piece to their Lilac Grove front porch "for the playroom." After the crash, when Avery had left her roommate Brianna and her little circle of friends in Philadelphia and moved back home for Tilly, Aunt Midge had joined the sisters without batting an eye, knowing without being told that she was needed. Her luxurious Upper East Side Fifth Avenue apartment in the city stood empty now except when they all went in for a play or when Avery stayed overnight to focus on an assignment.

"The warning," Aunt Midge said. "Do you know what it means? What contract?"

Avery shook her head. "Not sure. It could mean anything." It *could* mean today's contract. She didn't say that to Midge; there was no reason to worry her further. Antiquities and Artifacts Appraised, her parents' business that she was still adjusting to running, normally had a couple of contracts in progress at once. She didn't see how authenticating a ruby for Manhattan's antiquities museum could endanger her life; the idea was ridiculous. Maybe the letter meant a job they hadn't yet been contracted on yet? Or maybe the letter meant nothing; maybe it was just a cruel joke.

"Well, be careful. Promise?"

"Promise. Thank you." Avery bent and wrapped her arms around her petite aunt in a brief hug before running out the door. Now she was sure she'd be at least a few minutes late for her appointment with Goldie at the MOA—the Museum of

Antiquities. She glanced back at the house in her rearview mirror before turning out of the long, lilac-lined driveway. Aunt Midge stood near the porch swing outside the large craftsman-style house, one hand raised in a wave, Halston at her side. The gray-and-ecru exterior contrasted beautifully with the lush green lawn and deliciously scented purple lilac bushes. Avery knew Tilly would be fine; she was in good hands.

On autopilot for the drive, Avery's mind dissected what had happened this morning. The letter couldn't be genuine. So, who knew their father's pet names for them? Avery had been Roo since seventh grade, when she'd broken the long jump and high jump records at Lilac Grove's middle school. The nickname had been cemented in the next few years as she continued to break regional and state records, eventually transitioning to track, which had been an even better fit. She still tried to run every day; even a quick few miles was better than nothing. And there was no way she was going to finish well in the marathon this fall if she didn't stay on track with her routine.

Tilly's nickname was tied to her attitude rather than a physical trait. She must have been only three or so when William began calling her Lamb, a bit of a sarcastic nod to her boisterous spirit. Tilly was a dynamic force. She had been her own best advocate since before she could form a full sentence, and she made sure everyone around her knew it. William would scoop her up and cradle her when she was small enough to do so, cooing, "Oh, my little Lamb. If only you'd learn to be assertive." Their mother would laugh, saying, "Good Lord, Bill, don't egg her on!"

Of course, the family all knew about the pet names—William's sister Aunt Midge, Anne's brother Warren, the Ayerses' longtime friend and business partner Micah, their other partner,

Sir Robert, and probably Micah's son and Avery's ex-boyfriend Hank. After all, their families spent plenty of time together.

But none of those people had any reason to want Avery to believe her father was still alive. And on top of that, none of them would stand to benefit from forcing her to drop the new assignment with MOA. She hadn't even seen pictures of the potential new acquisition yet, but Goldie had told her the ruby was striking and quite large. She'd hinted that a competing company had been interested in handling the authentication, but she'd chosen Antiquities for this assignment. Goldie had made it clear how highly she'd thought of Avery's parents and of the business as a whole since the museum had begun using them last year.

The business had suffered after William and Anne died. Avery was much more comfortable now in her role as head of the company, but the first few months had been dicey. Her graduate degree in cultural anthropology with an emphasis on gemology made her a perfect fit intellectually, but Avery had big shoes to fill. Micah had been invaluable in showing her the ropes, immediately deferring to her as if she were an extension of her parents. Sir Robert was a bit trickier. She couldn't fault him. Losing the Ayerses had been a terrible blow for all of them.

Antiquities was now finally starting to make enough money to pay the bills again, but they had a long way to go to restore the company's standing in the community. The contract starting today at the MOA could lead to even bigger things if the jewel was as valuable as Goldie had made it seem. There was no way Avery could drop the assignment. Plus, if she even tried, Sir Robert's head would explode. While Micah was Avery's hands-on partner during projects, Sir Robert handled the finances and marketing. He'd already called her this morning, hyped about the MOA job.

Avery made it to the parking structure with only minutes to spare. Micah had called on her way in, saying the trains were delayed—another reason she was happy to be in control of her own transportation—and he'd have to meet her at the shop later. She had already cleared security and sprinted to the elevator up to the third-floor lab by the time she realized she'd left her bagel in the car, barely touched. She groaned; lunch was hours away. She power-walked the long hallway, hoping Goldie wasn't already there waiting for her. She pushed through the door to find two security guards on their way out and the MOA curator, Goldie, smiling at her.

The moment Avery laid eyes on the brilliant, uniquely cut large red ruby on the long marble counter top in the diagnostics lab, she felt a tingle of anticipation. *Possible ruby*, she corrected herself silently. She wouldn't know for certain until she got to work verifying it.

"Impressive, isn't it?" Goldie Brennan spoke as she watched Avery's reaction.

Avery met Goldie's eyes. "It's gorgeous." She turned the black velvet cloth the jewel was presented on, bending down to examine it more closely with her handheld loupe, a ten-power magnifier. "Where did you say the collector acquired it? Nothing about this is a standard cut. And the transparency is incredible."

Goldie took the glasses from atop her shiny silver bob and put them on. At seventy-five, the woman had held the New York Museum of Antiquities chief curator position for over twenty-five years. "Oliver Renell came into possession of the jewel in Munich. The file he sent with the courier doesn't list his purchase price; they rarely disclose that. But he feels certain we'll be interested."

"It can't be." Avery breathed the words as she donned a glove and turned the jewel over. She had an inkling, almost like déjà vu. Was it possible? The gold chain necklace and housing were unremarkable. But the size and cut of the stone . . . She peered through the gold cage on the underside of the setting.

"You know what this reminds me of, don't you?" She looked up at Goldie.

"I do," Goldie said, her expression serious.

"But . . ." Avery scrutinized the jewel again. "How? Oh, my goodness. Could it really be the missing ruby from the Emperor's Twins medallion?" Avery whispered the words, and they sounded crazy as they left her lips.

The Emperor's Twins piece was a priceless medallion at the Museum of Antiquities, the prized centerpiece of the MOA's most valuable display. Avery had first noticed it just a few months ago when she finally took the time to spend a day wandering through the museum as a patron. The striking dragon in the center of the large, eighteen-karat-gold medallion, inlaid with flawless, authentic pearls and jewels, possessed only one of his original two eyes; the fate of the missing ruby eye was the subject of wild lore. Avery could hardly breathe, thinking of the possible implications of what she held in her hand.

"We shouldn't get ahead of ourselves," Goldie said sensibly, Avery's unsolicited reality check.

"Right." Avery carefully set the jewel back on its bed of velvet. "How did Oliver Renell acquire it? Did you say he sent it by courier? *This*? Why on earth wouldn't he bring it in himself?"

"I can't fathom that. I wouldn't let it out of my sight if it were mine. It isn't even ours yet, and I'm not letting it out of my sight." Goldie laughed. "We have a protocol in place that two guards must transport it together at all times."

"Good. I think that's smart. Where did he acquire the stone?"

"Flea market," Goldie said.

"You've got to be kidding me."

Goldie shook her head. "I'm not. The Munich outdoor market is very hit or miss; I've been. Renell obviously had better luck than I've had. If it's real," she added.

"If it's real," Avery repeated. "Thank you, Goldie, for bringing us in on this. Micah and I will start right away, if that's all right?"

"That's perfect, Avery. You'll need to compare the jewel to Emperor Xiang's medallion as well, at some point. Let me know when you're at that stage and I'll coordinate access for you." Goldie slid a check across the counter top. "This should cover your initial costs."

Avery bent down, taking one more look at the jewel before Goldie carefully wrapped it back up and placed it in its locked case, which would then be locked into Acquisitions Pending storage in the north wing of the MOA until Avery and Micah returned in the morning. Today, she had research to do.

Avery accompanied Goldie and the MOA security guards assigned to the new submission during transport as they walked to the elevator. On the descent, Goldie spoke up. "Oh, just so you're aware, the museum's entire south wing and a portion of the basement will be closed off for the next couple weeks. One of those superhero movies is filming some scenes here. It wasn't up to me," she added.

"No worries. Maybe I'll meet a real live movie star or two," Avery joked.

"You might," she said. "You know, if the jewel is real, I daresay this acquisition will be quite a bit more exciting than the Persian textile collection you verified and appraised for us last month."

"Oh, absolutely." Avery laughed, exiting the elevator and turning to head toward the lobby as Goldie and her guards went the opposite direction.

"Grandmother!" Nate Brennan appeared, rounding the corner and catching up with Goldie with his long-legged stride.

Nate nodded in passing at Avery. Goldie's grandson was MOA's associate acquisitions liaison, and Avery still wasn't sure what she thought about him.

Outside on the wide front steps of the MOA, Avery tipped her head back and basked in the warm sunshine, the sky bright blue after days of rain. Today was a perfect seventy-two degrees, her favorite weather to run in. Today's strappy low heels would be replaced later with the pink-and-black running shoes she always kept in her bag—just in case. Running helped her think. It was one of the things she'd never been able to get Hank to understand—running was like solitary therapy for her. Having her boyfriend along defeated the purpose. No matter how she'd tried to explain it, he'd never really stopped taking offense when she refused to let him join her. She'd eventually stopped trying to get her point across.

Halfway through the six-block walk to the Antiquities storefront, her phone rang. *Sir Robert Lane* and his photo appeared on the screen. Sir Robert wasn't actually a sir—that is, a knight; it was more an affectation her parents had used to refer to their partner. Somehow through the years, it had stuck. Robert Lane was Sir Robert to everyone who knew him, and Avery had to admit, he did carry himself with a regal air.

"Good morning!" Avery smiled as she answered his call, still feeling buoyant from handling the jewel that could potentially complete one of history's most important artifacts.

"Good morning to you, young lady." Sir Robert's voice came through the line. "I heard a hot rumor just now."

"Really? I've told you before, Brad and Jen are never getting back together." Avery maneuvered through Manhattan tourists, doing her best to veer toward the right side of the sidewalk. She loved it here. The contrast between the bustling, energizing city and her relaxing Lilac Grove haven made her grateful she had the best of both worlds.

"Funny. No. I'm calling about our new case. Did Goldie give you details? Did you get to see it? What do you think?"

How was he always one step ahead of her? "Nate called you," Avery guessed. She shouldn't have been surprised. Nate seemed to have his hands in everything at the MOA. He was said to have dropped out of art school to mountain bike around Europe, and when his family money had finally been cut off, he had returned to New York and stepped into acquisitions a little over a year ago. Goldie's grandson now sat on the board of directors. The man oozed an unjustified air of confidence and authority.

"Yes, he called me." Sir Robert chuckled. "He asked when I'd be in to take a look at the new bauble."

"Interesting. The great Nate Brennan doesn't trust my expertise?" Nate was such a snake. "That's rich, coming from a trust fund baby who only shows up to work when he feels like it."

"Now, it's not like that. The kid can be a little excitable at times. I believe he's just more familiar with me through Francesca."

"Right, right." Avery rolled her eyes. Sir Robert had been dating the MOA's actual acquisitions liaison, Francesca Giolitti, for the past year. At fifty-two, Francesca was a full ten years older than Sir Robert, but she hardly looked it. She seemed to constantly be working, either trotting the globe or coordinating the museum's rotating collections, and always dressed as if she'd just stepped off a Paris runway. "Does Nate think you'll be taking point on the assignment?"

"Not at all," Sir Robert said. "You know I'd much rather leave that end of things to you. Are you on your way in?"

"Yes. I'll see you in two minutes."

"I'll put the coffee on," Sir Robert said, hanging up.

The door to the shop was sandwiched between the Manhattan branch of Shinola, a chic watchmaking company out of Detroit, and one of the city's many coffee shops. Deep-gold Old English lettering in a curved arc on the glass door read **ANTIQUITIES & ARTIFACTS APPRAISED, est. 2008**, with the phone number and APPOINTMENTS ONLY in smaller lettering underneath. Approaching the shop now, Avery thought of all the changes the past year had wrought. She hadn't been able to walk through this door since the accident without her parents at the front of her mind.

Avery had been the one to organize the family dinner the night of the crash. Despite having a degree compatible with the family business, she had moved to Pennsylvania after college, determined to get some experience on her own. She'd found work with a company that handled insurance claims. She'd made a few good friends among her colleagues, but she hadn't loved the job. Avery wanted to come home. When they met for dinner at Bello's, she'd finally mustered the nerve to ask her parents if she might come work for them. Anne and William were thrilled. They all agreed she would move back to New York as soon as her lease was up. But fate made that happen much sooner than planned.

Sir Robert and Micah kept the business afloat the first couple months after Anne's and William's deaths. Avery was nearly incapacitated by grief and guilt: If she'd left well enough alone and stayed at her job in Pennsylvania, there wouldn't have been a family dinner. If there had been no family dinner, there wouldn't have been a car crash, and her parents would still be alive.

Aunt Midge found a wonderful therapist for her and drove her to the first appointment.

In the past year, Avery had lost her parents and her boyfriend—her parents through tragedy and Hank through anger. Avery hadn't been able to see anything clearly ten months ago when Dr. Singh began treating her. Now she saw that she'd lashed out at Hank, though he'd only been supportive and concerned; her anger had needed an outlet, and even in her grief-fueled fog, she'd kept Tilly and Midge in a bubble of protection. The demise of her relationship with Hank was the collateral damage of that awful night.

But she was doing better now. Avery entered the little shop, and the bell over the door jangled pleasantly.

Sir Robert stood waiting for the coffee to finish brewing at the buffet on the far wall. Micah Abbott was buried in paperwork at his desk, which faced Avery's, a design they'd both decided worked well for collaborating on projects. The bare red-brick walls and slightly uneven hardwood flooring gave away the building's age, which—appropriately—infused the shop with a historical authenticity. The entryway and small reception area where she or Micah typically met with clients was an elegantly decorated space with a vintage brown leather Chesterfield sofa and chairs placed around a substantial old-world coffee table on a red-and-gold Oriental rug. More valuable items had rested on the coffee table at Antiquities and Artifacts Appraised than Avery could count.

Avery took her seat, tucking a strand of chestnut-brown hair behind her ear. She'd inherited her mother's long, graceful limbs and deep-brown eyes, while Tilly took after their blond, fair father. On the flip side, Tilly possessed Anne's verve, her energy and habits, while Avery's calm demeanor and endless motivation mirrored her father's.

"The assignment?"

Avery looked up at Micah, jolted back to the present. "What?"

"Tell us about the assignment. Nate told Sir Robert that a collector submitted a ruby as big as a golf ball!"

Avery laughed. "Not quite! But it is stunning. If it isn't genuine, it's a pretty good fake. I don't know anything yet. Nate told you what Goldie and I are thinking, right?"

Sir Robert and Micah stared blankly at her.

"Or not?" She looked from one man to the other. "This will sound crazy, but the jewel bears a striking resemblance to the Emperor's Twins ruby."

Sir Robert gasped, his hand flying up to cover his mouth. Micah sat up abruptly in his chair, feet coming down off his desk.

"The Emperor's Twins? The missing ruby?" Micah was the first to speak.

"Well, honestly, I hardly had a chance to look at it. We could both be wrong. I probably shouldn't have said anything yet."

"How—" Sir Robert began. "How did it come to the MOA? Who submitted it?"

"A private collector, Oliver Renell," Avery said. "Do you know of him?"

"I don't. Amazing. This is simply amazing."

"You'll want to see it," she said. "Even if I'm wrong, it's still a stunner."

She could see Sir Robert's wheels spinning. "The lost ruby from the Emperor's Twins medallion," he mused. "Can you imagine? The exposure it would bring, not just for the MOA but for us as well . . ."

He was lost in his dreams of fame. Avery could read his mind with no effort. "Or it could simply be a spinel," she said, bringing him crashing back to earth. Spinels were much like rubies but far less valuable.

He frowned at her. "Or it could be the ruby. You don't know yet."

"It's highly unlikely," she admitted, feeling a little guilty she'd even shared the supposition. "It's much more likely to be a well-done spinel. It's happened before—of course you know of Henry the Eighth and the crown jewels. The Black Prince's Ruby set in the front of the Tudor Crown was eventually proven to be a spinel."

"Of course," Sir Robert said, "everyone knows about that. It took three hundred years for experts to discover that the jewel wasn't a real ruby. But this isn't some poor copy of the medallion showing up with two sparkling dragon eyes. It's a large, seemingly good-quality gem that resembles the missing ruby, found in—where did you say the collector came to acquire it?"

"The open-air flea market in Munich."

"Fascinating," Micah said. "I've always wished to be the one discovering priceless artifacts at those places. The finds can be amazing."

"I'm just so happy Goldie brought us in on this," Avery said.

"When do we start?" Micah asked. He shoved some of the papers on his desk to the side, clearing a portion of his large desk calendar. His desk was as cluttered as Avery's was meticulously neat. Whereas the surface of Avery's was bare except for a laptop in the center and a few small color-coordinated boxes along one edge, organizing various items and mirroring the setup in her home office, Micah's held stacks of folders, a bowl overflowing with a mix of paper clips, pens, and sticky notes, his own large dinosaur of a computer that he refused to replace, and torn scraps of paper with scribbled notes tucked everywhere. But Micah maintained that he knew right where everything was; he had a system, even if it didn't look like it.

"I told Goldie we'd start tomorrow morning. Sound okay?"

"Absolutely." Micah was already writing it down on his calendar.

"Sir Robert, could you deposit the advance, please?" Avery handed him the check from Goldie. "You don't mind holding down the fort here without Micah?"

"Not at all. I've got to work on my pitch for the Barnaby's meeting—it'd be great for us to land that auction house contract. And either way, rubbing elbows with that crowd is good for our reputation."

"It's not a bad idea at all," Micah spoke up. "Going for the Barnaby's contract helps us, whether we win it or not; it increases our visibility, and if we get it, it's guaranteed steady work."

Avery looked from Micah back to Sir Robert. He was right—they both were. She spoke to Sir Robert. "You're right; go do what you do best. They'd be crazy not to give you the contract. Do you want to test your presentation on us?"

Sir Robert handed a steaming cup of coffee to Avery, moving back to the buffet to make one for himself. "I would prefer not," he said haughtily.

Avery couldn't help laughing. "Oh really! It's that good?"

He threw her a glance over one shoulder. "It will be."

Avery scooted her chair in and powered on her computer. "I have no doubt." She smiled, exchanging amused looks with Micah.

Chapter Two

After dinner, Avery and Tilly sat across from each other on the family room floor, a Scrabble board on the coffee table between them. The contention of the morning was gone. Tilly had been waiting on the front porch swing with two lemonades after Avery's evening run and informed her that she'd submitted her admissions essay. Neither of them acknowledged the elephant in the room, but that didn't diminish the thoughts of William in the air between them now. The furry, elegant Halston snored next to Avery, his head propped on her leg. Aunt Midge peered around her newspaper at Tilly's tiles; Avery saw one immaculately arched eyebrow twitch.

Midge sipped her perfect Manhattan, plucking the Luxardo maraschino cherry from the top. "I wonder if anyone feels like a nice slice of baklava."

Avery frowned at her. "We don't have any."

Aunt Midge used the toe of her feathered, kitten-heeled slipper to tap Tilly's leg. "Yes, but still, some baklava would be delightful, wouldn't it? Who doesn't love a good, sweet piece of baklava?"

Tilly gasped and quickly gathered up tiles, assembling them on the board in front of her. *B-A-K-L-A-V-A.*

Avery pursed her lips and glared at Aunt Midge, then at Tilly. "Cheating! How is that fair, you cheaters?"

Aunt Midge folded her newspaper and set it on the table beside her. She smoothed the hem of her bejeweled orange-and-beige tunic, rings sparkling in the light, and murmured, "I have no idea what you mean. This damn sweet tooth of mine."

Avery laughed, giving up. "You're just lucky she's facing your tiles, you snot," she whispered to Tilly.

Her younger sister smiled sweetly at her. "Your turn."

Avery shifted, studying the board. "Well, now I want baklava. You're winning anyway."

Aunt Midge stood abruptly, and the Afghan woke, slowly stretching his large, lanky frame and standing as well. Aunt Midge on her feet this time of evening inevitably meant a walk, and Halston knew it.

"It is a lovely night for a stroll, girls, don't you think? We might luck into the last few pieces at the White Box before they close." She left the room, returning moments later having swapped her slippers for her leopard-print Belgian soft-soled casuals.

Aunt Midge slipped an arm through Avery's as they set out on the ten-minute walk into town. Tilly walked ahead of them with Halston at her side. Lilac Grove's best and only bakery, the White Box, had a little of everything. Since Avery had returned home from Pennsylvania, she'd already gained five pounds, due mostly to the bakery's cannoli and lemon cake. Her tall, lithe frame could fortunately handle the extra weight, but she knew she should start setting limits on her sweet tooth.

"MOA is looking at acquiring the largest ruby I've ever seen," Avery told her aunt. "Well, I'm not sure yet if it's a genuine ruby. But if it is, it's going to make headlines. It must be at least sixteen carats. The cut is unique—it gives the jewel this brilliant sparkle—and the deep, blood-red color is stunning."

Aunt Midge stopped walking. She stared at Avery for a moment before resuming her pace. At just five foot one—five three with her hair properly coiffed—the older woman had to tip her head up to look at her nieces now, something that seemed incongruous to Avery and Tilly, given petite Aunt Midge's booming, Broadway-worthy voice and commanding presence. Avery had always thought Tilly had inherited her beautiful singing voice from Aunt Midge.

"A sixteen-carat ruby? Oh my. That would be incredible," Midge said, making a whistling sound.

"We start the authentication process tomorrow. There's a chance that it's even more valuable than we think. Aunt Midge," Avery said, lowering her volume now without even meaning to, "do you remember the Xiang dynasty display? It centers around the Emperor's Twins medallion, with this fierce, gorgeous dragon with a missing eye."

Aunt Midge's pace quickened. Avery glanced at her and noticed her brow was furrowed.

"I know that piece," she said.

"Goldie thinks—we both think—that this jewel might possibly be the missing ruby, the dragon's other eye." She looked at her aunt as she stopped in her tracks again. "I know," Avery said. "It would be a groundbreaking discovery."

"Yes," she said slowly.

Tilly had stopped now, half a block away from the bakery. She turned back toward them. "Hello? We *are* going to get baklava, aren't we? They're closing in a minute!" Halston had halted at her side, standing stock-still in his place.

"My dear, impudence is quite unattractive," Aunt Midge said, her tone pleasant.

"Yes, Auntie. Sorry." Tilly huffed out a sigh and turned, continuing on.

Midge resumed walking, her grip on Avery's arm a little tighter. "Your parents worked on that piece. Did you know that?"

"The Emperor's Twins? My parents were involved in that acquisition? How—when? The exhibit at MOA is striking. I assumed it had been there for years."

"The exhibit went up sometime last year. Probably shortly after your parents were finished with the authentication process," Aunt Midge said, pulling the bakery door open for Avery.

* * *

"All right, Auntie," Avery said, setting the brown paper bag on the coffee table back at home. "Would you please go through this again for me?"

Aunt Midge took her seat. "Of course."

Tilly carried dessert plates, forks, and napkins in from the kitchen. She left and returned a second time with Aunt Midge's authentic carved Yixing tea set, which they'd brought back from China on their last trip. Tilly served up three pieces of baklava and cups of tea while Aunt Midge and Avery talked.

"I just can't believe Mom and Dad worked on the Emperor's Twins medallion." Avery shook her head. "Goldie hired them? And Sir Robert and Micah knew about the job?"

Midge nodded. "They all probably assumed you knew, that your parents told you about it. But you were in Pennsylvania then, at least until the night of the crash. They never mentioned it to you?"

"No." Avery frowned. "Which is strange. It's an exciting piece; it must have been a very involved assignment. I mean, maybe they didn't want to say anything until they knew for sure that it was the real Emperor's Twins medallion?"

"I'm not sure. I'm afraid I don't know a thing about what you all do," Midge apologized. "Your father tried sometimes to explain the process to me, but my mind just gets caught on the pretty words: *gold, flawless, clarity, carats, brilliance*." She smiled, fanning out one hand to admire the rings she'd collected through the years.

Tilly laughed. "I know exactly what you mean. I could feel my eyes glazing over when Dad and Mom and Avery got into all the science-y stuff. Snoozeville."

Midge widened her eyes at Tilly. "I didn't quite say that, Matilda Marie. Don't be cheeky."

Tilly scooted to Aunt Midge's side and gave her a peck on one cheek. "Sorry, Auntie. I'll be more mindful of my manners."

Aunt Midge gave Tilly a one-armed hug. "Lovely, my dear. And thank you for so graciously handling our refreshment."

"Anyway," Tilly went on, "I just meant, I never really knew what pieces Mom and Dad were working on. But a dragon? Isn't that what you said, A, that the ruby could be the missing eye of a dragon? What kind of dragon? Is it like a big statue at the MOA?"

"It's a dragon medallion about the size of your hand," Avery said, opening her hand, palm up, with her fingers splayed out. "I went and took a good look at the exhibit today after talking to Goldie. The necklace was thought to be from Chinese Emperor Xiang's private collection, given to him as a gift around 1755. As the story goes, upon seeing the two beautiful, fiery red ruby eyes of the striking dragon, he dubbed it the Emperor's Twins.

The medallion disappeared after he died and is believed to have had various owners since. By the time the necklace made it to MOA, one of the rare ruby eyes was missing. You should see it, Tilly; you'd never forget it. The dragon design and inlaid jewels are striking. Even the Bismark link necklace the medallion was acquired with is genuine eighteenth-century gold."

"Wow," Tilly breathed, her usual sass subdued for the moment. "I want to see it."

"I'll bring you," Avery said. "Anytime, just let me know when."

"I think I'd like to take a look at the Xiang display myself," Aunt Midge spoke up. "We'll make an afternoon of it soon. I do recall Anne stressing about that blessed medallion. It was such a high-profile artifact. The *New York Times* ran a piece about the find when the display opened. I wonder if I saved the article. It included such a nice write-up about your parents, in memoriam," Aunt Midge said.

"Why was Mom stressed? They handled valuable artifacts all the time. Was there something about the medallion that concerned her?"

Midge shook her head. "No, not that I recall. But she spoke about the importance of the discovery. Even she and your dad were a little awed by the intricate jewel-and-pearl inlay. There was a lot of to-do over the Emperor's Twins artifact surfacing and the MOA being the one to acquire it. You know how your mother was—normally nothing ruffled her. But she was so intent on making sure she covered every detail of the medallion and its history. It was quite an involved case."

"Do you think we have that article somewhere? Or anything from that assignment? It would help, going forward, as we compare the characteristics of the new jewel to the existing one in the Emperor's Twins display."

Midge sipped her tea. "I know we cleared out the inactive files and paperwork last year from the Manhattan shop and the home office, when you were acclimating to running the business. I'll go up to the attic tomorrow and see what I can find." She paused. "We should talk about the letter."

Avery's breath caught in her throat. She'd been trying not to think about it. Had Aunt Midge learned something from someone in her circle? "Did any of your friends have suggestions?"

She sighed. "Not really. But I'm not so sure we should disregard the message. Have you thought any further about what contract the letter refers to? No work assignment is worth your safety, Avery."

"I know, don't worry. I don't feel as if I'm in danger. We started that ruby case today, but so far I don't know anything about it. And I don't see how anyone could even know we're on that case, besides us and Goldie."

Midge was uncharacteristically pensive, nodding and thinking before replying. "Did you feel at all unsafe today while you were at MOA? Or even going to the shop?"

"I really didn't." Avery met Tilly's gaze. "I honestly think it must be a prank or a terribly cruel joke. Everything went fine today, nothing out of the ordinary."

"All right. Please be extra careful until we know for sure."

Avery nodded, standing to head to the kitchen. "I will, I promise. More tea, anyone, before I go to bed?"

Aunt Midge was always the last to turn in for the night, though Avery and her aunt often crossed paths again by chance in the kitchen around three AM when they came to grab a glass of milk or some small snack. Avery remembered her father also having the same habit when she was growing up. She was apparently just like them. Somehow she always slept better after a middle-of-the-night trip to the kitchen.

Tonight, Avery stopped in Tilly's doorway before heading down the hall to her own room. Her sister would be away at college in London this fall if things went the way Tilly hoped. Avery wondered how she and Aunt Midge would adjust, what would change. Would Midge return to her apartment in the city, or would she stay in Lilac Grove? Avery was content here. She hadn't been ready to move back home, but she'd truly missed it—the town, the house and yard, the people. The way the shop owners here treated townsfolk like family. Faye, owner of the White Box, had packaged up not only the remaining baklava for them but the last few cannoli, doughnuts, and croissants as she was closing for the night.

"Are you nervous about your voice audition?" Avery asked her sister from the bedroom doorway.

Tilly looked up from her vanity, where she was braiding her hair so it would be crimped in the morning. "Nope. I can't wait. Five more days! I wish you could come." She spun around on her stool, making a pouty face at Avery.

"I know. I wish I could too. But Auntie promised to send me a zillion photos and videos, and you're going to love LA!"

"I wish I could just audition in London so we could go now. I can't wait to see the school."

Avery shrugged. "Don't worry. You'll be in school there soon, homesick and whining that you miss us. Or at least Halston," she said, teasing.

"Never," Tilly said. "I know I'll want to stay there. You and Auntie and Halston will just have to move there with me." She flounced onto her bed, kicking three fluffy yellow-and-pink throw pillows off the edge, and picked up her remote. "Come watch *Friends* reruns with me before you go to bed. It helps me sleep."

Avery couldn't argue. Soon everything would change; for now, she snuggled up with Tilly and watched half an episode of *Friends* before they both fell asleep.

* * *

True to his word, Micah Abbott was waiting for Avery in front of the MOA the next morning. Always impeccably dressed, he wore a hunter-green pocket square that matched his tie, his close-cut brown hair was freshly trimmed, and his expression held anticipation.

He handed her a cup of coffee as they climbed the steps. "So do you really think this could be the missing Emperor's Twins ruby?"

Avery showed her badge to the guard, and they went through the turnstiles. "I'm not sure," she said, turning to glance at Micah. "We were talking about it last night. You worked on the original evaluation and appraisal of the medallion with my parents, right?"

Micah nodded. "Yes and no. We were swamped around that time, and I was dealing with a few other cases. I wasn't involved in the medallion authentication; Anne and William handled all of it. But I knew they were working on it, since it was a high-profile assignment."

"Ah. Okay. I'll have to ask Sir Robert what he recalls." They were alone in the elevator now, on the way to the third floor. "I'm going to see if there's anything in my parents' files about the medallion that might be useful."

"Oh, perfect," Micah exclaimed. "That's good thinking. I do remember your mother carrying around pages and pages of notes."

Avery's interest was piqued. "Really?" They exited the elevator, and she showed her badge to the guard at the door to the lab.

He addressed Avery and Micah. "I'll have the submission brought to the lab now if you're ready, Ms. Ayers?"

"Yes, thank you."

She and Micah moved about the lab, setting up the equipment they'd be using. The first order of business would be to remove the jewel from its mounting, and that would require some precision, depending on whether the setting really was eighteenth-century gold or just gold-plated steel.

While they waited for the guard to return, Goldie Brennan came through the doorway. "Well! I hardly slept last night," she said, dropping her own disposable cup in the trash can. "And I don't think this coffee is a good idea. I'm too excited as it is."

"We're excited too, Goldie. You know the process takes a while, though," Avery said gently.

"Oh, of course. And especially with an item like this. Take your time. If we know, one way or another, in time for the charity gala in two weeks, I'll be one happy curator. But no pressure."

Micah pulled a chair out for the older woman. "Please, sit." He gestured.

"No, that's all right. No one needs a little bird watching over their shoulder. I'm not staying. I just—" She broke off as two guards returned, carrying a locked case.

"Right here is fine." Avery touched the long marble counter top in the center of the room. She pulled thin tortoiseshell glasses from her purse and put them on.

The taller guard set the box down and inserted a key, unlocking it.

"I'll leave you to it!" Goldie reached over and gave Avery's arm a light squeeze. "My goodness, you remind me so much of your mother."

That warmed Avery's heart. "Thank you, Goldie," she said. She paused for a moment, struggling with emotion, then returned her attention to the business at hand. "Are you able to put us in touch with the collector who submitted the piece? I'd just love to clarify how he came to find it, hear his description of the discovery, anyone he might have dealt with in purchasing it, you know?"

Goldie nodded. "Of course. I'll reach out and have him contact you. I'm sure he won't mind." She turned to follow the guards out, stopping to call back over her shoulder, "Let me know if there's anything else you need—you remember, just pick up the phone and dial twelve to get me."

"We're all set, Goldie, but thank you." Avery smiled.

The door snapped shut, and she and Micah were alone in the lab. Avery carefully removed the package from the lock box and set it on the counter top, unwrapping the black velvet to reveal the large, sparkling, red jewel.

Micah sucked in his breath, an odd sound in the quiet lab. He met Avery's eyes.

"Wow. Just"—he bent to peer at it—"wow."

"I know," she whispered. "I mean, Micah, this is the kind of artifact we could spend our whole careers waiting to see. Right in front of us."

"You're right." He matched her whisper.

"If it's real," she added, taking a little wind out of Micah's sails.

"If it's real," he repeated, nodding. "Yes, *if* it's real. We have seen some amazing forgeries."

"We have," Avery agreed. "So, I think, we first evaluate it as is before freeing it from the setting, and then we work just on the verification and appraisal of this jewel. *If* it's real, then we request access to the Emperor's Twins medallion so that we can start the process of learning whether it might be the missing dragon's eye."

Sometime before lunch, the door to the lab whooshed open, and Avery was startled out of the almost trancelike state she'd lapsed into while staring at her laptop across from Micah. She was perusing online resources for any mention of a ruby or red spinel that had been reported missing. They had to make sure they weren't dealing with a jewel that had been illegally acquired by the collector. She was also scouring the internet for some type of provenance for a jewel of the gem's description, with or without its current setting. Provenance was basically a chain of custody for an item, tracing it all the way back to—ideally—its creation. Finding a provenance for a mysterious piece like this one would be huge, as it would provide proof of what exactly the jewel was. Avery had come up empty-handed after all her research—no sign that someone had reported the piece missing, but no sign of a provenance either.

Francesca came through the door, along with Sir Robert. "Oh my, this looks serious." Francesca moved around the counter top with her hands clasped behind her back, peering over Micah's shoulder at the gem. Her tall, fine-boned frame moved fluidly in a lavender silk pantsuit, which flattered her svelte figure. "It's breathtaking, isn't it?"

"I thought you were working on your presentation," Avery said, looking at Sir Robert. "But I'm so glad you'll get a chance to see it."

"Francesca and I are going to lunch," he said, by way of explanation. Sir Robert made no secret of the fact that he was quite proud to be dating Francesca, and Avery understood why. The woman was as kind as she was lovely; it was no wonder people were drawn to her.

Micah was flanked now by Sir Robert and Francesca. He raised his gaze to Avery, cocking an eyebrow and pausing in his motions as he worked with calipers to capture the details of the cut on the exposed surface of the jewel. It was a painstaking process.

"Give him a little space," Avery said, standing and turning her laptop toward Sir Robert. "So this is what the ruby is estimated to look like in a three-sixty view if we were able to see all of it—that is, if it wasn't in its setting."

Sir Robert assessed the picture on the screen, then looked back at the jewel in Micah's gloved fingers. "It's striking. And enormous."

Francesca nodded. "It's an amazing find."

"Just based on this"—Sir Robert gestured at the laptop—"and the gem itself, I think it's got to be a real ruby. And we've all seen that poor, gorgeous dragon missing his ruby eye—this certainly looks like a match to me. Why don't we just have Goldie send the medallion up to the lab so you can compare?"

"Oh no," Avery said. She always used a methodical approach, and she had the plan nicely laid out in her head. Sir Robert's optimism was great, but Avery wasn't certain the jewel was even authentic yet. "It's far too soon for that. First things first. But I hope you're right. I hope we're all lucky enough to be involved in the discovery of the missing Emperor's Twins dragon eye."

Francesca nodded, moving away from Micah and flipping her long, silky black hair back over one shoulder. She stopped to look at the photo on Avery's laptop, running a fingertip across the mouse pad to rotate the picture into its 360-degree view. "The collector seemed quite startled himself to have come across the jewel. I think *lucky* is the right word; I was lucky to be the one he reached out to. But we should leave you to your work. Robert?"

Sir Robert moved to her side. "I'll be back at the office later if you need me, team. We're off; lunch at Andiamo won't wait." One hand rested on the small of Francesca's back as he escorted her toward the door.

"Have fun," Avery called.

"We will!" Sir Robert said, grinning over his shoulder at Avery.

Before the door could close again as they left, Nate Brennan entered.

"Oh, for Pete's sake," Avery muttered, looking up from her laptop at Micah. "Seriously?"

"Shhh," Micah hissed, his voice low. "Be nice to Goldie's pet."

"How's everything going?" Nate's voice boomed in the quiet room.

At least Francesca and Sir Robert had had the decency to observe the atmosphere and keep their intrusion to a minimum. "Going great," Avery said quietly.

"Grandmother says you might be done looking at it before the benefit? Does it look real so far?" He reminded her of a clueless, spoiled, oversized puppy; he was a pain in the ass.

Avery snapped her laptop closed, glancing at the clock on the wall behind Nate. It was almost lunchtime, and there was no way they were getting more work done with him here. "Let's go to lunch," she said to Micah, leaving Nate's question unanswered for the moment.

"Sounds good to me," Micah sighed, removing his gloves. "I'll call the guard."

"Our job"—Avery focused her attention on Nate—"isn't to *look* at the jewel. Anyone could do that. You could do that." She could feel Micah's gaze on her, but she couldn't help it. Nate Brennan rubbed her the wrong way; he had since she'd met him. "My partner and I take a scientific approach, which involves investigating and proving whether a piece is original, researching the provenance or documented history of the piece, verifying that the documentation is genuine, and examining the piece in terms of characteristics and distinct features. Once that process is complete, we begin the task of valuing the worth of the piece, using authenticity and current market value. And if this jewel makes it through all of that and turns out to be what your grandmother and I believe it might be, the assignment gets even more complicated."

Micah cleared his throat. "It's a bit of a long and time-consuming procedure. Not something a layperson would have any reason to know about," he told Nate, his tone much kinder than Avery's. "But it'll take us a little while, I suspect. There's a lot involved, especially with this piece. It's pretty exciting. Have you seen it?"

Avery sighed loudly and rolled her eyes at Micah, bending to pack up her notes and laptop in her case.

Nate moved a little closer, looking chastised. "Sorry," he said, looking at Avery and then Micah. "I got to take a look in Grandmother's office when it first arrived. It's really huge—the biggest jewel I've ever seen, for sure. It's pretty heavy."

Micah nodded. "I'll agree with that, and we've seen our share of dazzling artifacts." He stepped aside. "It's quite brilliant, especially when seen through the loupe. Go ahead, check it out." He watched while Nate bent to get a closer view.

"It's really beautiful," he said. "What would it be worth if your appr—the verification process and everything else—shows it's real and belongs to the dragon medallion?"

"That's impossible to say," Avery spoke up, softening. "We don't know anything yet. But we'll keep you updated, Nate. I know it's a fascinating acquisition."

"Thank you. I know you're experts in this. I'd love to watch your process, at least some of the time, if you don't mind."

He was staring at Avery, which she appreciated. Micah was always more tolerant, and she knew she should try to adopt his attitude. "I suppose that'd be fine. Once in a while," she added.

Nate nodded vigorously. "Sure. Okay. Well, maybe I'll stop by tomorrow and see how it's going then."

Two guards entered the lab and moved to the counter top to transport the jewel. "Going to lunch?"

"Yes! Ready?" Avery tugged Micah's sleeve. She was more than ready to get out of there. "Thank you. We won't be long," she told the guards as they followed Avery, Micah, and Nate out.

When they all exited the elevator, Avery and Micah headed toward the café. Nate had gone in the opposite direction. As they stood in line for the daily special, a chicken fajita bowl with rice, Avery voiced her thoughts. "Micah."

"Hmm?"

"What do you think of Nate?" She kept her voice low.

"I think he's a little green and immature, but he doesn't seem like a bad kid."

"I don't think he's a bad guy," she agreed. "But he's definitely Goldie's blind spot, don't you think?"

Micah frowned at her. "You mean, because she gave him the job even though he had no qualifications?"

She chuckled. "Well, yeah, you're making my point for me. But no, that's not what I meant. Francesca and Sir Robert stopped by to see the jewel and then went on their way. Why does Nate feel it's okay to just hang over our shoulders all day asking questions? How does watching us have anything to do with his actual job in acquisitions? And did you catch what he said about getting to *handle* the jewel in Goldie's office when it first got here?"

"I did catch that. I think he's just excited. It's a major acquisition."

"Maybe you're right. But I don't want him in and out of the lab constantly. It bothers me that he doesn't have any boundaries, and Goldie seems to think that's fine."

Micah nodded. "Well, Goldie may not impose boundaries on Nate, but we certainly can. Don't worry," he said, his tone reassuring. "Nate Brennan is manageable."

Chapter Three

When the phone rang at four thirty in the afternoon, Avery's eyes were beginning to cross from looking at her laptop. As Micah was handling the imaging of the jewel, she had taken the opportunity to learn more about the Emperor's Twins medallion. She'd always been a little superstitious and would never want to jinx their progress, but she was dying to know if they might have a headline-making discovery on their hands. Best to be well versed in the known and rumored history of the Emperor's Twins medallion, just in case.

After the death of Emperor Xiang and speculations regarding the fate of the dragon's missing ruby eye, the last documented date that the medallion had been observed intact and complete—with both rubies—was 1818, roughly twenty years after the emperor's rule ended and his subsequent death. A whole lot could have happened to the ruby in two centuries.

Interrupting Avery's research now and then was a pop-up notification on her screen alerting her that another image was available; Micah was uploading them one at a time to Avery from the other side of the lab. MOA's lab held the newest state-of-the-art equipment, and Micah was using hyperspectral imaging as part of their verification process. Even though the transparency of the ruby seemed striking, there was so much more the hyperspectral images would show than could be seen with the naked eye or simpler equipment. Antiquities and Artifacts Appraised did possess its own traveling lab equipment, from tools as rudimentary as a loupe magnifier and handheld dichroscope to high-end instruments—stereo microscope, refractometer, spectroscope—but the MOA equipment was excellent as well and didn't need to be carted around.

Avery wasn't familiar with the type of setting that held the jewel, and she had yet to identify the era it was from. There was no hallmark stamp visible, but she hoped to know more when she and Micah removed the ruby from its housing on Monday. It was impossible to tell what they'd find under the setting, especially as so far it appeared to be eighteen-karat gold but with odd wear patterns on one side. In some circumstances, precious metals were known to have a hallmark stamp—the identifying stamp placed there by the maker, often denoting location and year and even specific creator. If they found a hallmark on this piece, it'd be an amazing game changer in their appraisal and certification.

"Hello?" She spoke into the phone. "MOA lab," she said uncertainly.

"Ms. Ayers, this is Security Officer Woodson. We're just letting you know we'll be up shortly to collect the jewel. The museum closes at five PM."

"Thank you, Officer. We're just finishing up for the day." She hung up and returned to Micah's side. "We're done for now, right?"

He glanced at her. "I wish we could get the setting off tonight. But I've got to pick up Noah from the train station. Back here Monday morning, right?"

"Monday morning," Avery confirmed. "How exciting Noah's coming home! How long is he staying?"

"He's got a week off before his internship starts," Micah said. "Lehigh set him up with an engineering internship at DeSouza Corporation. But the boy's got nothing in the way of proper attire, so we have a little prep work to do next week."

"Oh, how fun," Avery said, moving to the door to tell the guard they were ready to send the jewel back and close up for the night. "I'd be happy to help. Tilly and I both would. You know she lives for that kind of thing; makeovers are her specialty."

Micah laughed. "I'm not so sure he'll go for the idea, but better you two than me. Obviously." He made a sweeping motion from his head to his feet.

Avery patted his arm. "Micah, you're the pinnacle of fashion. Midcentury modern fashion, at least. You're always put together." She smirked at him, knowing he wouldn't take offense. Micah's whole style was a throwback, definitely not what a nineteen-year-old college student should wear for a Fortune 500 company internship.

The duo of guards returned and secured the ruby, and Avery and Micah finished packing up and headed for the elevator. Avery stepped in, scrolling through an article on her tablet, and crashed right into a man already in the car. Her tablet slid out of her hands, and she grappled for something—anything—to stop the slow fall she could feel herself in the middle of. The man caught her around the waist, steadying her as she got her footing.

Mortified, Avery stared at him. "I'm so sorry! Totally my fault!"

The man's blue eyes crinkled with a smile, and he shook his head. "No harm done."

Avery glanced quickly at Micah as he handed her tablet to her; thank goodness she'd had the case on it. The doors whooshed shut and she took a step sideways, knowing she was invading this man's personal space, first falling all over him and then him having to catch her. She read the badge on a lanyard around his neck: *Tyler Chadwick, Action Entertainment.* Wasn't that . . . Avery racked her brain. This guy had to be part of the movie being made in the south wing. His perfectly combed hair was three shades of blond, there was just a hint of five-o'clock shadow over his chiseled jawline, and his V-neck shirt stretched nicely across his broad chest.

"Are you all right? Miss—" He tipped his head, reading the name tag clipped to her lapel. "Miss Ayers? Or is it Mrs.?"

"Miss. Avery."

"Ah. Good to know." His mouth went up at one corner, and he met her eyes. "I'm a little lost, but I'm thinking I don't mind so much now, Miss Avery."

Micah cleared his throat beside her. Avery's cheeks burned. "It's just Avery," she said, and her voice came out sounding ridiculously girlish. For Pete's sake, put one movie star in her path and she turned into a teenager. "You're . . . are you in the movie they're filming here? You must be." She pointed to his lanyard and badge.

"I am. I have no clue how I ended up on the wrong side of the museum—though I'm glad I did. Could you direct me to the south wing?"

"Of course," she said, as the car came to a stop on the main floor.

Chadwick allowed Avery and Micah to exit ahead of him.

"All right," she said. "So you're just going to take that hallway there, all the way to the end, and then make a left. Go through the set of double doors with the guard stationed outside, and that will take you right onto the film set."

"Perfect. Thank you. Maybe I'll see you again? Do you work for the museum?"

"Oh," she said, taken off guard. "I, ah. No. Well, sort of."

"We're privately contracted," Micah said. For the second time that day, she could feel him looking at her. Micah was probably the closest thing she had to a father figure, and this whole interaction was making her feel squirmy.

"Hmm." Chadwick took a few backward steps toward the hallway Avery directed him to. "Well, maybe I'll see you around anyway. I'd like that. And you know where to find me." He gave her the sexiest wink she'd ever seen before turning and heading away from them.

She finally turned and looked at Micah. "Stop it."

Micah looked surprised. "I'm not doing anything."

She groaned. "Well, don't. I'm sorry. He just kind of surprised me." She dropped her voice. "He was flirting with me, right?"

Micah chuckled. "If you want to call it that. He was fairly obvious."

"Okay, that's enough. Let's go. You've got a son to pick up."

Goldie was coming toward them from the opposite end of the atrium. She waved a hand. "I have news."

Avery raised her eyebrows at Micah. "Think she got ahold of the collector for us?"

When they met, Goldie shook her head. She looked exasperated. "I heard back from Oliver Renell. I cannot convince him to come in. I honestly don't understand what his concern is. I've assured him the MOA has ample security, if that's what he's concerned about."

"That's odd," Avery said.

"Yes. Listen, the bottom line is, he told me to pass his email address on to you. I think that's the only way you're going to be able to ask him questions. I've never run into this situation before. Normally the collectors are proud to present their acquisition in person—they want to be acknowledged. Not Renell."

Avery shook her head. "That's definitely odd."

"I'll forward you the email he sent me," Goldie said. "Let me know if there's anything else you need. I've got to run."

Micah spoke on the way out. "Avery, about Noah's internship wardrobe, I actually would appreciate your help. We both would. Cicely was a much better shopper than I am. Without her, I'm afraid Noah will buy one pair of slacks and a white dress shirt and consider it taken care of. Maybe we could go before his internship starts?" Micah's wife, Cicely, had passed away two years ago.

Avery gave his arm a squeeze. "Absolutely. Aunt Midge and Tilly are out of town midweek for Tilly's voice audition in LA, but they come back Friday. Maybe next Sunday?"

Tilly would be excited to hear of the shopping trip with Noah; she'd nurtured a little crush on him for years.

Avery walked with Micah out onto the wide front steps of the MOA. "Give Noah our love. Have a great weekend!"

He nodded. "I plan on it. You too, and tell Midge she owes me a game of bridge."

Avery kissed his cheek as they parted. "I forgot—that was from Aunt Midge yesterday. Monday we get some answers," she called as he flagged down a cab and climbed in.

He raised a hand as the car pulled away, and Avery headed for the parking garage.

Next weekend was the Ayers family annual summer barbecue, and Avery couldn't wait. All of their friends would be in attendance, even Goldie and Sir Robert. Croquet set up on the expanse of green lawn, the smell of grilled corn on the cob, the crackle of the fire in the evening—it all sounded wonderful, especially with the commute and long hours she'd been working lately.

Arriving at home, Avery went right up the wide staircase to her bedroom, intending to change into her running gear, and nearly did a somersault over the small tower of bins stacked just inside her doorway. Aunt Midge had been busy while she was at work. Avery's compulsively organized mother had labeled them:

Avery baby
Tilly baby
Lilac Grove office archive

Midge came around the corner in the long hallway from the attic and deposited another bin next to the stack, labeled *Manhattan office archive*.

She raised her eyes to Avery's.

Aunt Midge came close and planted a kiss on her forehead. "I thought it'd be fun to see what's in these, from when you were babies. And there's one more, but it looks to be household finances, appliance warranties, that kind of thing. We don't need that brought down, do we?"

"No." Avery pushed the bins out of her bedroom into the hallway. These were items her mother had saved with the idea that maybe one day she or Tilly might want to go through them. Two things ran through Avery's spinning thoughts: she couldn't do this without Tilly, and she wasn't sure she could do this at all.

Midge adopted the same stance as Avery, possibly without meaning to—arms crossed over her chest, looking down pensively at the bins now stacked in the hallway. "The nice thing about these boxes," she said, "is that every secret they've kept for years, they'll continue keeping until you're ready."

When Avery had asked to have a look through her parents' belongings, it had seemed like such a routine task. And this was just—what? Baby clothes and work stuff. There was no reason she should have this heavy stone in her chest all of a sudden. But she missed her parents. More than she usually let herself admit.

Avery slid down the wall until she was sitting crossed-legged on the hardwood floor and pulled a bin over to her from the deep-red-and-gold carpet runner that split the hallway down the middle. She looked up at Aunt Midge.

"I'm twenty-five years old. I should be able to handle this."

"I'm sixty years old, and there are still things I'm afraid to do."

"I'm not afraid."

She nodded. "I know that. Would you like me to leave you alone? Or maybe you'd like to wait for your sister?"

"No. I'm fine, and please stay," Avery said quietly.

Midge pulled the padded hallway bench away from the wall and sat next to Avery and the bins.

She lifted the lid off the first one, labeled *Avery baby*, and it was exactly that: articles of hers from twenty-five years ago. Little footed sleepers, a rattle, a worn stuffed bunny, and a priceless find buried at the bottom: a baby book. Avery leafed through it too quickly, unwilling just yet to linger and read words her mother had written about her. She packed everything back into the bin and pushed it to one side but set the baby book against the wall next to her.

She stood, picking up one of the two boxes labeled *office archive*. "Let's take their work papers down to the home office.

I want to start going through the files down there along with these."

"Good idea." Aunt Midge bent to lift the other box, and Avery stopped her.

"What are you doing? I'll come back for it."

"And why would you do that? Do I look incapable? How do you think these boxes made it down here from the attic, young lady?" She picked up the second work box, the thing dwarfing her small frame. "Let's go. Don't treat me like an old woman again, or I'll have to ground you for a week."

Avery laughed. "I believe you. I'm far too busy to be grounded. Sorry, Auntie." Midge certainly didn't appear to be struggling with the box. Avery led the way downstairs.

In her parents' office at the back of the house, Avery removed the lid from the box labeled *Manhattan office archive*. Inside were file folder organizers with countless files and papers, each one labeled differently, and in both her parents' writing. "Wow." She glanced at Aunt Midge and then back at the files. There didn't seem to be a method of organization, not by month or by alphabetization. The titles in each tab ranged from a word or phrase (*Stonehenge dig, Russian tapestry, Princess Sofia's hairbrush*) to simply a year or years (*1742, 1964–1965, 1893*).

The front door snapped open and shut, and Tilly called out, "Hey, peeps! Wilder's here, and he brought dinner!"

Avery put the lid back on the *Manhattan* box. "Later," she said, standing. "I don't even know where to start."

Aunt Midge stood with her. "We'll help you. I'm sure we'll find something related to that medallion your parents were working on. Don't worry."

Avery and her aunt joined the other two in the dining room, Midge's best friend Wilder putting out place settings for each of them. Wilder Mendelsohn and Midge had been inseparable since college in the 1970s. For years, Avery and Tilly had both assumed Wilder was their aunt's boyfriend, until it became clear that, though Wilder would likely always carry a torch for Midge, she valued her independence much more than the idea of romance. Wilder was a professor at Columbia University, twice divorced, and as tall and broad as Midge was small and petite. Quiet and calm, with a dry sense of humor and an air of parental affection toward the girls, Wilder was always a welcome addition to their trio.

Over a dinner of Chinese takeout, Avery filled Aunt Midge and Wilder in on the elusive collector, Oliver Renell. "So now, on top of trying to prove provenance for this new ruby—possible ruby—I also feel like we should look into Renell. Something seems off about how he came into possession of the jewel. I asked Goldie to reach out to him and see if we might set up a meeting; Micah and I have questions about the acquisition. It's strange. Goldie says he won't meet in person; he sent the jewel in by courier. She's only ever communicated with him over email. So that's the only way we're going to be able to get more information from him."

"Oooh," Tilly spoke up. "Maybe he's on social media. I bet he is!" She began typing on her phone screen.

"Tilly." Aunt Midge tapped the table with her fingers, looking sternly at her niece. "No phones during dinner."

Tilly rolled her eyes and touched the phone screen, scrolling. "Auntie. You know it's the twenty-first century, right? Staying connected is like air to my generation!"

Midge's expression didn't change. "I suppose it's all a matter of how long one wishes to go without air, then. Half an hour, or all night?"

Wilder set his fork down and exchanged glances with Avery, the two of them silently watching the volley.

Tilly stared Midge down and lost. She slid the phone into her back pocket. "Fine. I'll send you anything I find later," she told Avery.

"Thanks." Avery smiled.

"I wonder if Barnaby's has heard of your collector," Wilder offered. "Might be worth looking into. I doubt this tentative transaction with MOA is his first such deal in New York."

"Yes!" Avery pointed at Wilder. "Great idea. Sir Robert has cultivated a relationship with one of the auctioneers. I'll have him check. Thank you for that."

He shrugged, picking up his fork again. "It's just a thought. Not that I know much about antiquities. But ask me about Nietzsche and I'll give you the full ninety-minute lecture."

"I'd love to hear it," Midge told him. "No one expands my mind the way you do, Professor."

Calm, cool, and collected Wilder Mendelsohn blushed—Avery saw it just before he used his napkin, covering part of his face for a moment. He cleared his throat and speared a piece of chicken, keeping his gaze on the plate in front of him. Did Aunt Midge have a clue how enthralled he was with her? Avery truly couldn't tell.

"Oh! Avery." Midge handed a slip of paper across the table to her. "I found this today in my files upstairs. I'd nearly forgotten it. It's an evidence intake receipt. You should check in with our police department. They should still have some of your parents' documents. A detective came to the house asking questions after the accident. He took some papers from your father's study—work-related items, I think. I never thought to try to get them back, but maybe they'd be useful to you now."

"Perfect, thank you." Avery's memories of that night were still patchy. She was working with Dr. Singh on getting clearer details. With the trauma of the crash and the aftermath at the hospital, Dr. Singh was certain Avery had been in shock for hours.

After dinner, the group of four moved into the family room. Tilly brewed tea and made the rounds, pouring for everyone and then heading back into the kitchen. A loud bark came from outside. Avery jumped up, hurrying through to the back door. "How did we forget Halston outside?"

She pulled the door open, ushering the dog inside. As the large Afghan passed her, the scent of lemons and cedar struck her, adhering to her senses. William's aftershave. Avery dropped to her knees, wrapping her arms around Halston's neck, and buried her face in the dog's fur. He smelled just like her father.

Chapter Four

Tilly stopped on her way back through, a tray of cookies from the White Box in one hand. "A? Is he okay?" She gave Halston a scratch behind one ear.

"Smell him." Avery let go of the dog.

"Um." Tilly stared at her, wide-eyed. "No thanks? Not if a skunk got him again! I don't smell anything, though."

"No," Avery said. She stepped out onto the patio, calling back over her shoulder, "Smell his fur, Tilly, right now!" She sprinted across the grass and down their gravel driveway, head whipping in both directions up and down the long dirt road. Two pinpoint red lights receded in the distance to the left; she quickly lost them, even when she squinted. Who was that? It couldn't be William. It just couldn't. If their father was somehow alive, he wouldn't be torturing them this way.

Tilly caught up with her, Halston running in excited circles around the two of them and barking. "Shh!" Tilly patted her thigh twice, and the large hound immediately heeled obediently at her side. "Did you see him? I told you he's alive!"

Avery shook her head. "No. There's nothing out here." The taillights down the road had to have been a neighbor. The Ayers home sat on ten acres of land, and the house was set back off the road a bit, which meant there were no visible neighbors. Avery normally loved it, as her parents had. Tilly despised the quiet seclusion. If it was up to her, they'd have moved into Aunt Midge's luxurious Manhattan apartment and sold the house after losing Anne and William. Avery still hoped Tilly might grow to love having the best of both worlds, the bustling city and the peaceful country.

Right now, though, Avery wished they weren't so isolated. "It's not Dad. I'm sorry; it's just not. Someone is messing with us."

Tilly kept her cool. "I think you're wrong. There's no reason for anyone to try to make us think Dad's still alive. And how would they even know what aftershave he used? Why would Halston let whoever it was get close enough to touch him?"

Avery tipped her head, skeptical. "Really? This guy?" She patted Halston's head. "Everyone's a potential best friend to him; you know that. I don't have any explanations for the rest. I just can't make sense of it. Whether we try to assume it's Dad or not." She couldn't remind Tilly again of that night in the hospital. That would be cruel.

"Whatever." The girl spun and started back toward the house. "I'm texting Miss Jennie to ask if she saw anything weird."

Miss Jennie—Jennie Langmore—was their childhood babysitter who lived next door, on the other side of the pine trees. "Okay. Maybe she did. Good idea." Avery doubted Miss Jennie had seen anything other than a car passing by, if she'd even noticed that.

Aunt Midge and Wilder were on the porch waiting for them. "What happened? Was he after a deer again?" Midge scowled down at Halston.

"Avery forgot Halston outside, and when she let him in, he smelled just like Dad, but she thinks it's just a weird coincidence or a conspiracy or something." Tilly's voice dripped with satisfaction at tattling on her older sister.

Their aunt bent, putting her face close to the dog's fur. "Hmm. Possibly. It's hard to say for sure. You know, I just had him at the groomer yesterday. I wonder if they're using a new shampoo."

Tilly stood, hands on her hips, gaze going from Midge to Avery. She kept her voice level. "You've got to be kidding me. The simplest explanation is usually the right one."

"Occam's razor," Wilder murmured.

"Quite," Aunt Midge agreed. She took Tilly's hand between both of hers. "But what is the simplest explanation, Matilda? That your father is alive despite all we know from that horrid night? Or that the groomer switched to a citrus-scented shampoo?"

Tilly pulled her hand away. She opened her mouth to speak but didn't. She pushed past Midge and Wilder and slammed the screened front door on her way inside.

Aunt Midge sighed. "I'm not an unreasonable woman."

Wilder shook his head. "No, you're not. You're using logic. Tilly's thinking with her heart."

"Yes," she agreed. "Are you coming in, Avery?"

"In a minute." When her aunt and Wilder had gone in, Avery took a seat in one of the rockers on the porch as Halston sat beside her. She'd been planning to squeeze in a quick run after dinner, but now she was having second thoughts. If their dad truly had been here, that was one thing. If there was something more sinister to the mysterious note yesterday morning, followed by the notable aroma on Halston tonight, that was something else entirely. Maybe a night run just now was a bad idea.

Avery leaned forward and rested her cheek against the Afghan's black fur over his shoulder blades. The dog leaned into her. She hadn't exaggerated; he loved anyone willing to give him a few ear scratches. She closed her eyes and inhaled deeply. It wasn't basic citrus. It was lemons, not oranges. But now she wasn't positive at all that she smelled cedar. Had it been her imagination? They'd all petted Halston in the last few minutes; was the scent fainter now, or had her brain simply paired cedar with the lemony smell when it first drifted to her in the foyer? Was that possible? Scent was the strongest tie to memories. Maybe her senses were playing tricks on her.

But if the simplest explanation was indeed the right one, could the simplest explanation be that their father was somehow alive? Because the alternative meant someone was going to great lengths to make them think he was. The idea made Avery shudder. Who had known the specific scent of William's aftershave or cologne? Her mother Anne, obviously. Micah, she assumed, as he was more an uncle to her than a colleague. He'd known William for years. Maybe Sir Robert, if he paid attention to that sort of thing? William's sister, Aunt Midge. And perhaps any of his friends or acquaintances who had taken note of it.

But what would someone have to gain by leaving a forged note and then planting William's scent on Halston's coat while he was out in the yard? Why risk being exposed? The warning to decline a case the very morning Avery had first laid eyes on that striking ruby, in light of her current knowledge that her parents had handled the dragon medallion's appraisal and now this scent on Halston, seemed all too personal.

Or was the note a cruel prank and the scent on the dog's fur a wild coincidence? Maybe the groomer *had* begun using a lemon-scented shampoo and Avery's mind had done the rest. That was almost more believable than the other options. She gave Halston another quick hug and tried to put the mystery away for the night as she went into the house. She'd skip tonight's run, and she'd let Tilly find out if Miss Jennie had seen anything. Tomorrow she'd visit the Springfield County Sheriff's Department.

* * *

Lilac Grove marked the eastern edge of Springfield County. The Sheriff's Department was one town over in Dogwood Heights, a twenty-minute drive southwest. The next town after that was Begonia Bend. Every town in Springfield County was named after some type of flower, but Avery felt her little town of Lilac Grove had the best moniker. She stood in front of the desk sergeant, a stern-looking middle-aged woman in blue-rimmed glasses. The brass name plate declared her to be Sergeant Lynn Tunney.

"Excuse me, Sergeant. I have this." Avery produced the evidence receipt from Aunt Midge. "I think some of my father's files might be here? I came to retrieve them."

"Your father will have to sign for them himself," the woman said, without looking up.

Avery placed the receipt on the desk in front of the sergeant. "He's dead. The files were collected from our house by one of your men the night he died last year. We were told they'd be released when the case was closed."

That got her attention. Lynn Tunney met Avery's gaze over the top rim of her glasses. "I'm so sorry." She tapped her keyboard, reading the several-digit receipt number. "Yes. We have the files. That case is still open. I'm afraid the detective on your father's case is the only one who can release them."

Avery frowned. "What? Why is the case still open? It was a car accident. Can I speak with the detective?"

The sergeant scrolled and looked up again. "He's not in today. I can have him call you. Or I can give you his number and you can leave him a message today." She picked up a pen.

"Yes, that'd be great. When is he in next?" Avery looked down at the phone number on the orange sticky note Sergeant Tunney handed her. Had the detective just forgotten to close her parents' case?

"Monday morning. Shall I let him know you came by?"

She shook her head. "No, thank you; I'll call him." She had turned to go when Sergeant Tunney spoke again.

"My deepest condolences on the loss of your parents, Miss Ayers."

* * *

Sitting in her car outside the station, Avery waited through the detective's voice mail greeting, her mind racing. The recording was simply an automated announcement with his badge number and options for reaching someone for those who didn't want to leave a message. The system beeped loudly in her ear, startling her. "Uh, hello, Detective. This is Avery Ayers, William and Anne Ayers' eldest daughter. You handled their, uh, case, almost a year ago. I tried to get the files back that were taken into evidence the night of the accident, but Sergeant Tunney says the case is still open? And that you're the only one who can turn those over to me. I'm looking specifically—"

An abrupt click interrupted her. Avery pulled the phone away from her ear. The call had disconnected. Nice. She called back a second time. "Detective, I'm not sure if my first message went through. This is Avery Ayers. I need you to please call me back about my parents' files that were collected the night of the accident last year—oh, this is regarding William and Anne Ayers. My number is 518–97—"

Avery growled at the second click she'd just heard. She glared at the CALL ENDED screen. What the heck.

She called back a third time and waited through the boring recording again. This time, after the beep, a computerized voice informed her, "This voice mailbox is full."

She threw the phone onto the passenger's side floor, cringing when it bounced off the mat and hit the underside of the dash. "Great. Nice to know my county's detectives take weekends off and are completely unreachable. Perfect." Her movements crisp and angry, Avery turned the key in the ignition, buckled her seat belt, and jerked the car into reverse, grinding the clutch. She turned to back out of her parking space and found a young police officer not ten feet from her car, staring at her. He'd been about to cross behind her.

Avery's cheeks flushed. That could have been disastrous. She shifted the car back into first and set the parking brake, opening her hands on the wheel. She mouthed the word *sorry* to the officer. He hesitated a moment more, then adjusted the visor on his cap and continued on his path behind her car. When he reached his squad car a few vehicles over, he stopped and frowned at her before getting in.

Avery forced herself to take a deep breath, slowly in through her nose, slowly out through her mouth. And again. She quietly recited ice cream flavors, as one did. Dr. Singh had suggested street names of her childhood or favorite dog breeds, but she knew more ice cream flavors than streets and dogs combined. "Superman, mint chocolate chip, death by chocolate, moose tracks, orange sherbet, cookie dough." She checked to her left and found that the officer she'd nearly run over was gone.

"Strawberry, Neapolitan, pralines and cream, Oreo, Mackinac Island fudge." She felt calmer already. It was ridiculous to get so aggravated over something as dumb as a full voice mail. Her parents' files had been at the Springfield County Sheriff's Department for nearly a year; they'd keep for another couple days until she could reach the detective.

When she pulled into the lilac-lined driveway back home, Avery had completely recovered from her little fit and now wanted ice cream. She felt better knowing her next therapy appointment was only a few days away. Halston greeted her on the porch steps, and she gave him a few pats, noting that he smelled like his usual doggy self.

She found Tilly upside down on the couch, feet propped where her head should be, chatting with a friend on a video call. Upon seeing Avery, she flipped around and sat upright, telling Eve she'd call her later. "So?"

Avery shook her head. "Nothing. We'll have to wait until Monday or Tuesday when I can talk to the detective who worked Mom and Dad's case. He wasn't in."

"But what about the files?" Tilly's eyes went to Avery's bag.

"No files. He's the only one who can release them, apparently. What are you doing right now?"

Tilly slouched back onto the couch cushions. "That sounds like a trick question. If you're about to bug me about doing the dishes, I already told Aunt Midge I'd take care of them."

Avery laughed. "That's not why I asked. We brought down those boxes yesterday, full of information about the cases Mom and Dad worked on. I thought you might help me start going through them."

"Sure. For a while, anyway. Eve and I are going to the movies later."

Avery moved to the kitchen for the raspberry cheesecake ice cream she knew was in the freezer, and Tilly followed her. She set two antique Russel Wright Iroquois bowls on the cherry hardwood counter top and ran the scoop under hot water. The kitchen had been their father's favorite room in the house; he'd chosen the unique, gleaming counter top material, the white Shaker cabinets, and the bronze-pendant light fixtures himself a few years ago when they'd renovated. It was money and effort well spent at the time, as he was the chef of the family. "What movie are you seeing?"

"It's a choice between that animated teddy bear movie and the newest Batman. So we're seeing Batman."

"Good choice." The Lilac Cinema had only two screens. They were probably lucky they even had a movie theater in their little town. She handed Tilly a heaping bowl of ice cream. "Did I tell you they're filming some superhero movie at the museum?"

Tilly grabbed the chocolate syrup and poured a generous serving over the top of her dish. "No way. What movie?"

"I'll find out. I should have thought to ask."

"I bet it's the second Firefly movie." She passed the chocolate syrup to Avery and pulled out her phone. "I think I read something about it filming in Manhattan. Oh my God, I love Solana Davis so much. Have you seen her? Can you get me an autograph?" She glanced up from furiously tapping her screen. "A. You have to get me in to meet her. I'm the hugest Firefly fan."

Avery laughed. "You must think I have a whole lot more power than I do. I don't even know who you're talking about. I'm not big on superheroes."

"It *is* the Firefly sequel! Look! Ugh, you're so lucky!" Tilly turned her phone screen, and Avery glimpsed a pretty blond actress at an awards show.

"I did meet an actor the other day on the elevator. I almost knocked him down," she said. "I can't remember his name, but he was so cute. Tyler something. Micah might remember."

Tilly frowned. "A Tyler who was cute? There are a bunch of those. Tyler Wade, maybe? I'll look up the cast and figure it out. See, so if you've already met one, you'll meet more. You have to at least try to get me in to meet Solana. Promise," she demanded.

"Okay, okay. I'll try. I'll talk to Goldie." Avery led the way to the office at the back of the house. She set her ice cream on the blotter on her father's desk—her desk now. Though it would always be her father's desk to her. She stood between his desk and her mother's desk, staring down at the boxes she and Aunt Midge had set on the large, oval, russet-brown rug in the center of the room yesterday. Where to begin? "I guess we need to start by finding either paperwork directly related to the medallion, or at least files they were working on in the months before the accident. What do you think?"

Tilly was somehow balancing her bowl of ice cream in the crook of her elbow and spooning it into her mouth while also stopping to tap her phone screen every so often. She stood between the two boxes, oblivious to Avery's question.

Avery sat on the plush rug, took the lid off the box labeled *Lilac Grove office archive*, and lightly smacked a preoccupied Tilly's leg with it. "Hello?"

"What? Chill for a sec. I forgot to show you what I found last night." She sat cross-legged on the floor next to her sister. "Your collector guy, Oliver Renell? He's on social media."

"Really? Let me see."

"He has a Twitter account, and he's also on Network'd. That's all I can find on him. Twitter is kind of a super-crowded, fast-paced Facebook, but with shorter posts and fewer pictures—"

Avery nodded, cocking an eyebrow at her sister. "Um, yeah, I know what Twitter is. I made a Twitter account for Antiquities and Artifacts Appraised last year—@AveryAyers_AAA. You should check it out sometime. Sir Robert and I run it."

"Really? Huh. Okay, so here's your guy's Twitter profile."

Avery took the phone from Tilly. "There's no photo of him. It's just the placeholder thing." On the screen next to Oliver Renell's name was the gray-and-white outline of a person where a photo was normally uploaded. The self-created bio was equally bland and uninformative: *Collector, Antiquities Expert; London, New York, Amsterdam.* "Is it weird that he hasn't added a photo?"

Her little sister shrugged. "I mean, kind of, but I don't think he does much with this account. He only has a handful of followers. It shows right here that the account was created less than a year ago, and he's only tweeted a few times." She took the phone back for a moment before handing it over to Avery again. "This is his Network'd profile. Network'd is more for business connections."

"Networking," Avery said. "I get it. I've heard of this platform, but I don't use it." She frowned down at the screen. "No photo again. He doesn't seem very active here either. I'd think a collector like Renell would get a lot of use out of these sites. But Sir Robert will probably know more, with his connections . . . I'll see what he thinks Monday. And maybe Renell will have answered my email by then."

Tilly took the lid off the other box, labeled *Manhattan office archive.* "Oof. Wow. This is a *lot.* So what exactly are we looking for?"

"Anything pertaining to the Emperor's Twins medallion." Avery groaned inwardly as she looked at the jumble of files and papers in her own box; this would truly be a needle-in-a-haystack search. "Separate anything you see about the MOA, the Xiang dynasty, a dragon, a ruby eye, even a Bismark link gold chain. Oh, or dates. We know Dad and Mom were working on the medallion sometime in the early part of last year."

"Um." Tilly paused in her perusal. "MOA is mentioned in like every other job in these."

Avery sighed. "I was afraid of that. All right, then just look for notes or documents with any of those other key words that catch your eye."

Halston wandered in and stretched out on the cool hardwood floor beside the rug as they worked. Among the files of organized papers, copies of provenances, and printed records were other odds and ends strewn in the bottom of the boxes: business cards for various contacts, paper clips and receipts, a few ring-sized boxes in floral print that were Anne's trademark for storing and organizing small items, scattered bits of colorful scrap paper with handwritten notes. Anne had an entire drawer in her desk and another in the kitchen just for the squares of paper she cut up to be used for notes, whether to jot down a few grocery items, send a note to William reminding him she'd be out with friends for dinner, or record bits of information about an artifact. And she'd collected little floral boxes for as long as Avery could remember; her desk here and her dresser upstairs were neatly lined with sets of them.

"Ha!" Tilly exclaimed, startling Avery.

"What'd you find?"

Tilly extracted a manila file folder from the center of her box and handed it to Avery with a flourish. XIANG ERA MEDALLION was printed in William's block lettering on the tab. "Jackpot, right?"

Avery smiled at her sister's triumphant expression. "Yes! There's more in mine too." She produced a pink scrap of paper with the words *Dragon medallion lost by Emperor, track locations via silk road?* scrawled across it. Underneath that, she grabbed a photocopy from a pile of pages and held it up for Tilly to see.

" 'Factors in Differentiating Eighteenth-Century Rubies and Spinels,' " Tilly read aloud. "What's a spinel?"

"Spinels are similar in appearance to rubies and sapphires but have different chemical makeups. A spinel isn't quite as hard as a ruby, and it's also singly refractive, which means when you view it from different angles, the color remains consistent, whereas a ruby shows changes in color from different angles. Spinels were first discovered in the eighteenth century, as they were often passed off as rubies. There are a few really famous pieces that were originally thought to be set with extremely large rubies that turned out to be spinels."

"Really? So a spinel is kind of a fake?"

"Kind of. It depends," Avery hedged. "Spinels are recognized for their own value now, as they offer more affordable options and can still be quite stunning. But yes, especially centuries ago, they were considered great impostors."

"Oh! So, the dragon's ruby eye, right? What does that mean—were Mom and Dad thinking the dragon's eye was a spinel?"

"Maybe at first. I mean, they certified and appraised it, it's on display at MOA, so it must be real. But that's always a primary task when looking at gems. Micah and I have to verify our new red stone is an actual ruby, too, before we even get to the point where we can compare it to the existing dragon's eye."

"And that's where the chemistry and all that comes in, right?"

Avery nodded. "The composition and other factors. So much of what we're looking at isn't even visible to the eye."

Tilly groaned. "No way. Not for me. Too much math, for one thing."

"I'm excited for you to see the medallion," Avery said. "Did Aunt Midge say which day might work?"

"She's not sure yet. You've seen her calendar—it's always full!"

"True," Avery said, smiling. "She likes it that way. I wonder," she mused. "Maybe Micah would want to show Noah the exhibit too. We could all go next Sunday."

"Noah? We're going to the museum with Noah?"

She nodded. "If Micah thinks it sounds like a good plan. I told him we'd go shopping with them Sunday. They'll be happy to see you." Micah Abbott and his wife and son had been in their lives since before Tilly was born. He'd gone to school with William and was the girls' godfather. "Noah needs a little help with his wardrobe—he got an internship with a Fortune 500 company. Micah and I thought you might come along and help him find a couple nice suits—if you don't mind?"

Tilly's eyes widened. "Are you for real? Do I *mind*? Will I go with Noah Abbott and watch him model different outfits while I decide what looks good?" She leaned back on her palms, grinning. "I will do that any day he wants. For as long as he wants."

"Perfect." Avery laughed. "And you can't just tell him everything looks good, you know."

"I know. It's cool. I'll help him. I think it'll be fun. A . . ."

Avery was thumbing through the documents in the box again. "Yeah?"

"Does he have a girlfriend at college? Do you know? He's been away a whole year—maybe he does."

"I'm not sure. I didn't think to ask—Oh my God," Avery said. Her breath caught in her throat as she reread the print on the yellow carbon copy she'd just pulled from the box. And then read it a third time. She wasn't seeing things.

"What is that?" Tilly leaned forward, reading upside down. " 'Certificate of authenticity and approximate value.' What does that mean? Is that for the dragon medallion?"

"Yes, it is. It's a summary, the final form that's submitted to a client—or in this case, the Museum of Antiquities—to confirm a piece is genuine. It can sometimes stand in for a missing provenance. It's done in triplicate; this is the second page, under the original. This form always marks the end of an assignment." She turned it around so Tilly could read it more easily. "It's faint, but look at the date of Mom's signature."

The color drained from Tilly's rosy complexion. "June sixth."

"The day they died."

Chapter Five

"I'm going for a run." Avery stood.

"What?" Tilly nearly shrieked the word. She jumped to her feet, facing her older sister. "Now? What is wrong with you?" She snatched the packet from her older sister's fingers, reading it herself.

Avery grabbed the file folder Tilly had found, labeled XIANG ERA MEDALLION. She flipped it open, spreading the pages out on William's desk. There must have been twenty or thirty papers: originals, copies, printed emails . . . She riffled through quickly; she'd need to sit down with all of it later and compile her own notes. The file held the intake form for the assignment; initial notes on the location of the medallion and the collector; the acquisition confirmation, signed by Nate Brennan; the MOA purchase offer, notarized by Francesca Giolitti; messages to William and Anne from Goldie; a transcript of a meeting among the collector, Sir Robert, and William; a third-party valuation from a gemologist; a certification from a government official in Persia dated 1932, when, it seemed, the medallion had resurfaced; Paris newspaper clippings from 1934; emails back and forth among Micah, Anne, and William speculating on the medallion's whereabouts after that . . . this was an in-depth assignment. In all of this, where was her parents' full appraisal and verification report? That always accompanied the original of the authenticity certificate and was typically three or four pages long, detailing defining marks, micrometer measurements, chemical composition, a history of the object, and several other factors.

She straightened up, sweeping everything back into the folder. She took the yellow form from Tilly.

Her younger sister faced her, hands on her hips. "This doesn't make sense. Mom wasn't working that Saturday. Remember? We were in the city all day. You met us in Manhattan for lunch after Mom took me and Eve to get our hair and nails done for the choir concert that night. We barely made it home in time, and we went straight from the concert to dinner."

Avery studied the yellow carbon copy more closely. It was fuzzy but legible. Everything on the certificate was complete. And Goldie had signed under Anne Ayers's signature, verifying receipt, two days later on Monday, June eighth. "But she did sign it that day. Maybe she and Dad took care of it that morning, before you left for the city?"

Tilly was quiet, thinking. "I don't know. I don't remember that. We left the house pretty early. The whole day was rushed, from breakfast until we got to Bello's for dinner after the choir concert. Besides, if she really did sign that ahead of when it was due, how is it here? Wouldn't the triple form have gone to MOA where Goldie is? Her signature is right there under Mom's."

"I'm sure it did," Avery said. "Micah brought all the archived files here to the home office last summer, when I finally started doing my share for the business. There's no space at the office. That's not the mystery; it makes sense to me that our yellow copy would have gotten filed away after the job was done, and now it's in storage with everything else. But . . ."

"But the timing . . ." Tilly said, her voice quiet.

"The timing," Avery agreed. "I have to admit it's odd that Mom signed it the day she died. Like she knew. Of course she couldn't have known," she added hastily.

Tilly stared at her. "How could she have known? Why would you even say that?"

She shook her head. "Obviously she didn't know the car was going to go off the road. It's just weird timing, that's all. I need a break. My eyes are crossing. We can get back into this tomorrow; I really need a run." Avery carried the boxes over to William's imposing desk and began stacking the file folders on the blotter.

"What are you doing?"

"I don't want all of this out in the open, not until we know what's really going on. Could you get the keys, please?"

"Ugh!" Tilly's features scrunched into a pout. "Why can't we try to get through this today? Maybe it would make sense. You can get Micah to come out, and I'll cancel my plans with Eve." When Avery didn't reply, she stormed over to one of the bookcases behind William's desk. She bent and pulled *The Great Gatsby* from the bottom shelf and dumped a hidden key out into her palm, handing it to Avery. She then moved to the end table by the couch in front of the window on the other side of the room and lifted the lid of a small porcelain box detailed with miniature pink chrysanthemums, an arched green stem acting as a handle. Anne had circulated her key among the small porcelain boxes in the office, much like William had alternated his hiding space among dummy models of several classic novels.

Avery and Tilly had believed their parents were secretly government spies for much of their childhood, mostly because of these hidden keys. William had been putting his desk key away one afternoon when thirteen-year-old Avery burst into the office. He'd looked up, frozen with his hand poised over the cut-out rectangle inside the pages of *The Odyssey*. "What happened to knocking?"

Avery had stood in the doorway, staring wide-eyed at her father. She was at his side in an instant, feeling the edges of the hollowed-out section of the book and then looking up at William. "Just like in the James Bond movies!"

Tilly came sliding into the office, never far behind Avery. Precocious and energetic even at six, she'd been tuned in to every little thing her older sister did. "What's that?"

William snapped the book closed and moved to put it back on the shelf. "It's just a book, Lamb."

"That is not just a book! I saw a book like that in Scooby-Doo! Show me!"

Instead of deflecting or flat-out lying to the two of them, William had explained that he and their mother sometimes brought their work home from the Manhattan shop in the course of certifying and appraising items. As some of those items were worth a lot of money and didn't belong to them, they needed to keep them safely locked up. Looking back, Avery saw how impactful that moment was to her and Tilly's lives. In the next few years, Tilly had developed a deep and obsessive love for all things Sherlock Holmes. She was the resident expert—if it had happened in a Sherlock Holmes story, cartoon, or movie, she knew about it. And it was no mistake Avery had become fascinated with discovering the hidden stories and long-forgotten secrets of society's artifacts. She was sure stumbling across her father's cloak-and-dagger hidden-key habit had factored into her pursuit of a career similar to that of her parents; it was all so exciting and mysterious, and the scientific end of it fascinated her.

Now she took the first key from Tilly and used it to open the deep bottom-right drawer of her father's desk. She put the stack of files into that drawer and then added three of the little floral boxes before she ran out of room. Tilly wordlessly dropped the second key into Avery's open palm and helped her carry the boxes over to the gilt-edged mirror on the wall, which opened to reveal a wall safe. They turned both boxes upside down into the open safe, leaving all the loose newspaper clippings, envelopes, and notes on scrap paper and the last two tiny floral boxes to be gone through later.

When it had all been locked away and the keys had been put back in their hiding spots, Avery finally faced her younger sister. "I'm not quitting, I promise. But I need to think. We can't possibly get through all this in one afternoon." She kissed the top of her sister's blond head. "Just a quick run. I'll be back shortly. Okay if I take Halston?"

"I want him here."

Avery was already on her way out of the office. "Okay . . . ?" she said, her inflection turning the word into a question at the end. It was strange, Tilly wanting Halston to stay. She usually complained that he was underfoot too much.

"A, I'm already creeped out with the weird things going on. Especially with you feeling the need to lock everything up. I don't want to be here alone. Let me keep him with me. Make sure you take your phone with you."

Ugh. Avery felt her adrenaline draining. "I can stay." She really needed to go. She had to get her thoughts sorted out, and she couldn't do it standing still.

"*Go*," Tilly said, irritation obvious in her tone. "God. Just go. Come on, boy," she said to the dog, patting her leg. She marched past Avery and up the stairs, Halston following obediently.

Avery gritted her teeth. Where was Aunt Midge when she needed her? Should she just stay? She didn't see why Tilly was being so dramatic. She dug her thumbnail into the side of one finger, vacillating between being a doting sister and exercising her own self-care. Aunt Midge should be home soon, and Halston would serve as protection—if barking at everything that moved outside counted as being a good watchdog.

Three minutes later, Avery reached the end of the lilac-lined driveway and turned right onto the dirt road, her pink-and-black running shoes kicking up dust. They were overdue for rain.

Avery's mind always seemed to work best when she was running. It took a little while; she had to get that first mile under her belt, and then the endorphins kicked in. The loop through town all the way to the orchard and back home was almost exactly three miles. She'd been doing four loops every other day since December, with a quick one-loop run each day in between, until Thursday morning when they had gotten that letter. It had thrown everything off. And then Halston's fur last night . . . that still didn't make sense.

There was no way her dad was still alive. There were fuzzy spots in her memory the night of the crash, but that surgeon coming through her hospital room door at Springfield County was clearer in her mind than she could bear sometimes. He'd stopped and stared at the three of them—her, Tilly, and Aunt Midge—from the doorway. His head had dipped, his hand on the back of his neck, as he came over to them. That was when she knew about her dad, before the doctor even reached them.

Ruby Red Herring

A few hours earlier, her dad had been stealing frosting from the wedge of chocolate cake Avery and Anne were sharing, having already polished off his own piece of carrot cake. Tilly was guarding her ice cream sundae with elbows on the table and both arms in front of it. Bello's wasn't far from Lilac Grove. They should've arrived home with plenty of time for a game of Farkle. Instead, they'd ended up in their Lincoln Town Car upside down in a ravine four miles away. Tilly was entertaining Avery in the darkened back seat with her best impressions of her high school teachers, the two of them laughing so hard they had to keep stopping and catching their breath; she'd meet Tilly's gaze, and Tilly would transform her face into another impression, triggering another outburst. Avery remembered wishing she'd never moved away to Pennsylvania; she missed her little sister so much.

And then Tilly's shoulders pressed into Avery as the car swung hard to the left. She'd thought they'd just turned too quickly. The car swerved back the other direction, she and Tilly were jerked forward as the brakes squealed, the car spun, and suddenly the world flipped and nothing in Avery's line of sight made sense anymore.

She had clutched Anne's hand over the front seat, not letting go, even when Tilly shrieked for help with her seat belt. She felt her mother's hand go slack—Avery's mind twisted reality and tried to convince her that her mother had only fallen unconscious. But Avery knew she was gone. Anne had been squeezing her hand, her eyes wide, her voice a whisper. Her mother was with her, and then she wasn't.

William had been trapped behind the steering wheel, suspended upside down by his seat belt. He never opened his eyes. After the firemen had pulled Avery and Tilly to safety, she sat on the metal perch on the back of the ambulance with her sister and watched while first responders worked to get their dad free. The night air was filled with yelling, orders being shouted, a loud, crunching, metallic sound from the Jaws of Life or whatever that machine was that cut William loose, and then there was silence— a hurried, urgent silence that seemed somehow deafening when the underside of their Lincoln Town Car burst into flames.

She had no memory at all of what happened after that until she saw the blue-scrub-clad surgeon with a hand on the back of his neck. Tilly told her later that they'd gone together in the back of one ambulance to the hospital; Tilly never saw what happened to their mom after that, but William's gurney was loaded into a different ambulance that sped away before theirs even got going.

Tilly had sustained a broken tibia and two fractured ribs. Avery's right arm was broken in two places, and the side effects of her concussion lasted for days. Or longer, if you counted the patchy areas of her memory that still persisted. The surgeon told them that night that their dad's internal injuries were too severe. The team had done everything in their power to help him, but he couldn't be saved.

Tilly collapsed and was kept overnight for observation in the same room as Avery.

Avery didn't speak until the next day. She didn't cry until weeks after the double funeral.

Aunt Midge wailed. Avery had never heard such an awful, heart-wrenching sound; she hoped to never hear it again.

The possibility that William might be alive and sending them messages was abhorrent. It would mean their dad had deliberately caused them the worst pain of their lives. She couldn't reconcile that with the man she knew.

Which meant the scent on Halston must have been placed there by the same person who'd slipped the cryptic note through their mail slot. The lemon-and-cedar scent wasn't a new shampoo at the groomers. Avery did believe in following the simplest explanation; in this case, that meant that if Halston had smelled like their dad, someone had wanted him to.

Why? Putting that warning message together with the first day of the MOA ruby assignment and adding to that the new knowledge that her parents' own assignment involving the Emperor's Twins medallion had wrapped up right before they died, all of this must somehow be about the gem. Or the medallion. Or both.

Her gaze was caught by the large red barn on her left that meant she was a quarter mile from home; this was her fourth lap. Letting her thoughts carry her away while running was the equivalent of driving on autopilot; she could barely remember the last two loops. When she turned into the driveway and saw Aunt Midge's powder-blue 1957 Thunderbird parked there, relief washed over her. She'd told herself Tilly would be fine, but she was still grateful that Midge was home with her.

She needn't have worried; Tilly was already gone for the evening with Eve. Aunt Midge suggested a bite in town at the Old Smoke, and it was the best idea Avery had heard all day. She was starving. "I've been craving barbecue ribs. Let me jump in the shower, and we'll go!"

"Don't jump; that's dangerous!" Midge called up the stairs after her, and Avery heard her head toward the kitchen, chuckling at her own joke. Aunt Midge had taken over the bad dad jokes in their household without any effort at all.

Avery left her hair damp; it dried stick straight whether she blew it out or just left it. She pulled on a pair of slim dark denim jeans, a sheer pink blouse and cami set, and ballet flats. She glanced in the mirror before heading down to Aunt Midge. She rarely wore makeup, but she applied a few strokes of mascara and a swipe of pink lip gloss.

Seated at an outdoor table on the patio at Old Smoke, Avery breathed in the delectable aroma of the eatery. They had the best ribs and steak in New York, hands down. Behind the restaurant was an enormous wood smoker. It was no wonder Avery was in the mood for barbecue; she'd just run four times through town. Small globe lights were strung in a crisscrossing pattern overhead, and the band at the other end of the space played an eclectic blend of Jimi Hendrix, Johnny Cash, and Bonnie Raitt classics.

Their server, a smiley, middle-aged redhead named Candy, brought their drinks: a red Burgundy for Midge and an unsweetened iced tea for Avery. She'd have loved her usual mojito but wasn't drinking anything except water, coffee, and tea until after the race.

She and Midge had specifically asked to be seated in Candy's section; she'd been the Ayerses' favorite server here since they'd started coming when the girls were small. Candy pulled her notepad from her short black apron; like all the staff here, she wore a black polo with the Old Smoke logo. "Are you lovely ladies ready to order?"

"I think we need a moment," Aunt Midge said. "Catch us on your next time around, why don't you?" When Candy left, Midge raised her glass and Avery did the same. "To mystery and intrigue," she said, winking at her niece. "Your sister filled me in on the activities of the day."

"I figured she would. Was she all right when you got home?"

"She was fine. She was raiding your closet for a purse to match her outfit. I'm sure you have thoughts about everything you stumbled upon today? I know running helps you think."

"I do," Avery said. "I'm going to try to get through the details of at least some of what's in the Emperor's Twins file tomorrow. And I've already let Micah know I'm coming in late on Monday. I'm going back to the Springfield County sheriff's office first thing. I don't see why anyone would still need whatever they took into evidence after the accident; it's been a year. If that detective isn't in, I'll go over his head."

"Well! There you go." Aunt Midge closed her menu. "I can't decide between the porterhouse and the mahimahi. So I'm getting the combo. Let me help with your efforts, Avery. What can I do?"

"Since you asked," Avery said, "I was hoping you'd walk me through exactly how it went when the police came and collected Mom and Dad's files. I've never really understood why they did that over a car accident."

"I never have either. And every time I tried to get answers, I was told they were simply dotting *i*'s and crossing *t*'s. I dealt with a Detective Freida Klein. She and her partner came to the house that night." She shook her head. "That awful night. You know I tried to stay with you girls at the hospital; do you remember that? I wasn't going to leave you, but the nurses wouldn't let me stay."

Avery placed a hand on Midge's forearm as it rested on the table. "I remember. Don't worry. You've gone so far above and beyond, Auntie."

The woman waved away the compliment. "Ridiculous. You're family. Anyway, they were waiting for me when I got to your house that night—it was almost midnight. They were kind, but I've never understood what they wanted with your parents' files. After Detective Klein reassured me several times over the new few weeks that they were closing out the case, that your parents' deaths were accidental, I stopped calling her. I haven't thought about those files in months."

Candy reappeared and took their orders. Aunt Midge waited until she'd gone, then went on. "I'll come with you Monday morning. I'll make them turn everything over to us. Did you know I used to date the commissioner?"

Avery laughed. "I'm not even surprised. But it's okay, I can handle it. Don't worry. Oh . . . how did the detectives know what files to take? Did they just go through the office?"

Midge's eyes grew wide. "Oh no. Not a chance! I had Micah come over and sort through things to give them only what they thought they were looking for."

"That same night?"

She nodded. "Yes. He was a peach. Took him until around one in the morning to drive in from Harlem, and he didn't bat an eye. I was not about to let those detectives rifle through your parents' hard work. They drank coffee with me while we waited for Micah, and then he arrived and took them into the office. When they left, they seemed satisfied with what they took."

"I had no idea," Avery said. She'd already planned to pick Micah's brain on Monday when she saw him, with everything she and Tilly had discovered today. Had Micah neglected to tell her all of this in an attempt to shield her from the events of that night? Had he assumed it wasn't important?

Avery ate too much; she always did here. Aunt Midge had enough of her steak wrapped up for an entire second meal, but Avery's plate was nearly clean. They'd paid the bill and gotten refills of their iced tea and wine, and Avery was slouched in her chair, one hand resting on her belly, when her ex-boyfriend took a seat at the table right beside theirs. What was he doing here? Hank lived closer to Manhattan than to Lilac Grove. He spotted her before she had a chance to compose herself.

Self-conscious now, she sat up and whipped her napkin off her lap, dabbing her mouth to make sure the barbecue sauce was gone. She looked down to find she'd just dragged the end of the napkin through the thick, sticky sauce on her plate and transferred it to the front of her pink blouse. Brown splotches decorated her chest, embedded in the fabric. Great. Aunt Midge held out a towelette for her, meeting Avery's gaze and then following it over her shoulder, where Hank was approaching.

"Hey, Avery," he said, smiling. Of course he was smiling; he'd just watched her wipe Old Smoke Flaming Hot #3 all over herself. "Thought I should come say hello. Hi there, Ms. Ayers," he said, addressing Aunt Midge. "Having a nice evening?"

"Mr. Henry Johansson." God love Midge. "You look well. Your hair—" Her hand went to her own coif. "You've had it all cut off. I recall saying to Avery you always reminded me of a young Kenneth Branagh with all that hair. It's quite a change, isn't it?"

Hank laughed and then stopped abruptly, obviously caught off guard. "Well. Yes, I guess it is." He glanced over his shoulder. Two beers in frosted mugs had arrived at his table. The man he'd come in with was chatting with two pretty young women at the table on the other side of theirs.

Avery finally found her voice. "You look great, Hank. How've you been?" Hank was one of Avery's many regrets from the past year. Not Hank himself; the relationship was one she would always cherish. But the way it had finally died still needled her. They'd dated off and on for years, having met Avery's senior year of college. They'd tried the long-distance thing for a while when she'd moved, Hank twenty minutes north of Manhattan and Avery in Philly, but they'd let it fizzle out . . . until Hank showed up at the funeral last year and they'd begun seeing each other again. She knew now from Dr. Singh that rekindling the relationship with Hank on the heels of her parents' death had not been the smartest move. She was a mess. Hank was wonderful. Present. Supportive. Which all translated to far too healthy and nurturing for Avery's state of mind at the time. It lasted, miraculously, eight months, until Avery had snapped during an argument and called him a clingy, controlling underachiever and he'd left. She didn't blame him at all.

Hank signaled to his friend that he'd be there in a minute. He faced Avery again. "I'm good. Here with a buddy from work—Scott. He lives in town. You really look great. Have you . . . how are you . . . are you doing all right?" He was nearly squirming with the awkwardness of the situation.

"I'm okay. I'm doing a lot better." She sucked in air. She needed to just say it; she might not get another chance. "I'm—" She couldn't, here in front of Aunt Midge, in front of the entire restaurant and Hank's friend Scott. "I hope you have a nice dinner," she finished. Lame.

He nodded once and backed away. "Sure. You too. Nice seeing you. Both of you," he said to Midge. He turned back toward his friend.

"Hank." Avery gritted her teeth. He looked at her. "Hank," she said more softly. "I'm sorry. About how things—how I ended things. I'm sorry for the way I treated you." Her cheeks burned.

His eyebrows went up in surprise. They were so blond they were nearly red, darker than his close-cropped hair. "That's . . . okay. Thank you for that. I'm sorry too."

He was always such a nice guy. Probably why she'd felt like utter trash for lashing out at him in such an ugly way four months ago. She felt marginally better, having apologized, but she still felt queasy over her part in their breakup. For the second time today she was thankful she'd be seeing Dr. Singh this coming week.

Aunt Midge, quiet and absorbed in setting the time on her fine gold watch the whole time Avery and Hank had been talking, now raised one eyebrow at her niece as Hank rejoined his friend. "Ready?"

"Oh yes," Avery said. She was about ready to bolt out of here.

On the walk home, Aunt Midge linked her arm through Avery's elbow. "I've told you before about people, haven't I? About their roles in our lives?"

Avery looked down at her fabulous little aunt. "No."

"No? Well, I'm sure you've heard it before. Reason, season, or lifetime. People come and go in our lives for a reason, a season, or a lifetime. Perhaps your time with Hank served its purpose."

"What do you mean?"

"You rekindled things at a pivotal time. He offered something you needed just then. It ended. But look how you've changed from when you met him until now. Don't wish your time with him away or regret it happened. You've both grown and now can move on."

They walked the rest of the way in silence. As with so many other things, Aunt Midge was right.

Chapter Six

Monday morning, Avery squared her shoulders and pushed through the Springfield County sheriff's office door. She was determined to leave there with her parents' papers. The same woman from Saturday looked up at her.

"Good morning, Sergeant Tunney," Avery said. "We spoke the other day. I came back to retrieve William and Anne Ayers' things."

The sergeant turned to her computer screen and tapped the keys. "If you'll just—"

Avery rested a hand on the sergeant's desk. "Look. I know you said I'll have to wait for the detective on the case to release the file. But it's been nearly a year. My family and I need those documents. I didn't have any luck getting through to the detective, but I don't see why he needs to sign off."

Lynn Tunney cleared her throat. "I was about to say, if you'll just wait a moment, I'll get the file for you." She met Avery's gaze over the rims of her glasses, her stoic expression unchanging. "The detective did receive both your messages."

Avery was sure she shrank two inches as she stood there in front of Sergeant Tunney. She stepped back, feeling appropriately chastised. "Oh."

Tunney's chair rolled out behind her and hit the wall as she stood and left the reception area. She returned a few minutes later with a fresh, steaming cup of coffee in one hand and a file folder in the other, which she handed to Avery. "Is that all?"

She nodded. "Yes, ma'am. This has been a difficult time for me. But that's no excuse for rudeness. I'm sorry."

"Of course," the woman said. "You have a good day, Ms. Ayers."

Her stop at the sheriff's office added an extra twenty minutes to her drive into Manhattan. After a quick call to let Micah know she'd be at the MOA lab by ten, Avery hit the Caff-N-Go drive-through just before the expressway for a large mocha latte. Her therapy appointment couldn't come soon enough. She'd come a long way in the past few months, but she needed to do better about keeping her foot out of her mouth. It only ever happened when her hackles were up from some perceived injustice or slight—but that seemed to happen far too often. Not everything needed to be a fight. She was getting tired of having to apologize for her own behavior all the time.

She glanced at the unassuming file on the passenger seat beside her. There were so many things she didn't know about that night. She'd known there were holes in her memory from the concussion, but she hadn't realized she was missing details that could be important.

Yesterday had marked the one-year anniversary of the accident. By some unspoken agreement, she and Tilly and Aunt Midge had spent a quiet Sunday at home together doing nothing. They'd cooked breakfast, read, and then napped before making Avery's dad's lasagna for dinner. It was an odd sort of feeling, simultaneously wanting to mark the date while wishing it gone. Avery had been relieved to wake up this morning with it behind her.

She exited the elevator on the third floor of MOA as two guards were leaving the lab. They must be up here dropping off the jewel, which meant her partner was already there. "Good morning," she said as they passed. The shorter guard met her gaze and nodded, returning the nicety, but the taller one pulled his visor lower over his brow and kept his focus forward. Not a morning person, obviously.

"Perfect timing!" Micah smiled at her, the potential ruby in one white-gloved hand while he poked at it with a pair of calipers in the other. "Grab the dichroscope, would you? I need the specs from this angle . . ."

She never had a chance to jump in and pick Micah's brain about what she and Tilly had found over the weekend. They worked until just past noon before breaking for lunch. A different set of guards came to lock the jewel away until they got back. In the sunny MOA cafeteria, Avery chose a table near the courtyard that was dappled with light from the block glass set into the vaulted ceiling. She was dying to get Micah's thoughts on the strange timing of the completion of the Emperor's Twins job, but she dug into her salad and let him get a few bites of his Reuben before she began. She pulled out the file Lynn Tunney had given her and set it on the table. "I have questions, Micah."

"Hmm?" He looked at her curiously and set his sandwich down.

"Aunt Midge brought me up to speed this weekend on some of what happened the night my parents died. She said you drove all the way out to Lilac Grove in the middle of the night to help sort through their office for the police. And Tilly and I discovered that the Emperor's Twins assignment was completed on June sixth, the day our parents died in the car accident—Mom signed the certificate of authenticity that day. Did you know that?" She heard her own tone, and it sounded accusatory. "I mean, did you remember that when we started making comparisons between this job and the medallion?"

Micah's gaze went from the manila folder to Avery. "Was it the sixth? That very day?"

She nodded. He looked genuinely surprised.

"I guess that's possible. We were in the middle of things with the Emperor's Twins right around that time. She signed it the actual day you were in the accident?"

"She did," Avery confirmed. "Goldie countersigned two days later, on Monday, presumably when the report and certificate were submitted. We just thought it was strange Mom signed it that Saturday . . . I wasn't at the house, I was on my way in from Philly, but Tilly says it was a crazy day. I met Mom and Tilly and a friend in the city, then rushed home to Lilac Grove for the choir concert and dinner at Bello's. I think we're surprised Mom would have squeezed in finalizing the certificate that particular day. Why not wait until Monday?"

Micah was frowning. "I don't know. But now you're jogging my memory. I got a message from your dad."

Avery inhaled sharply. "When?" She leaned forward across the small round café table.

"It was a day or two before the accident, I think. On my house phone—your dad knew how I felt about these things," he said, tapping his dated flip phone in his breast pocket. He steadfastly refused to upgrade to a smartphone.

Disappointment washed over Avery. She'd thought for a second he'd meant recently. "What was the message?"

Micah looked up toward the skylights as he thought. "He just said he wanted to . . . go over something or show me something about the Emperor's Twins piece. Ugh, I can't remember

81

exactly. It didn't seem pressing; we'd send emails or leave phone messages whenever we needed to communicate something about a job. You know we were hardly ever all in the same place at the same time, between the shop, on-site jobs, this place." He gestured around him.

"Did you ever end up connecting with him?"

"I don't think so. I don't think I saw him after that; it must have been the Friday before . . ." Micah's voice trailed off. He looked at Avery, the corners of his mouth drawn down. "And then it was the furthest thing from my mind when we came back to work Monday."

She nodded. "I get that. Do you know who submitted the certificate and report to Goldie that Monday? Was it you or Sir Robert?"

"Sir Robert took care of it. What exactly are you getting at? Do you think the final report was tampered with?"

"I don't know. I guess I have no reason to think that. Mom signing ahead of time is strange, that's all, on top of the timing—the medallion job coinciding with losing them. And then getting our current assignment. I haven't told you this, but there have been some odd things happening at the house." She filled him in on the letter and the scent clinging to Halston when she'd let him inside Friday night.

Micah's eyes were wide. He opened his mouth to speak but then didn't.

"I know. And now Tilly thinks Dad is alive."

"Oh no. Oh, poor thing," he said, his brow furrowed in concern. "There's got to be an explanation. Let me help, please. Keep me updated if anything further happens, will you?"

She nodded. "I don't need any extra excitement in my life, so hopefully nothing else will happen. Oh. And what about these?

I just picked this up this morning from the Springfield County sheriff's office."

"Why are they just now giving them back?"

"Because I asked for them." She leaned forward on her elbows. "I don't understand why they even wanted information from my parents' office. I thought it was just an accident. Did the authorities initially think it wasn't? That it was connected to one of their cases? The medallion must have been the most high-profile case at the time. Certainly the most valuable."

Micah frowned, thinking. "We were swamped. I was handling a couple jobs Robert had gotten us through Barnaby's auction house, and your parents were dealing with the medallion on top of a porcelain doll trio from a private collector. Sir Robert and I had pitched in a little with historical research and coordinating with the collector for the medallion assignment, though it was mainly your parents' case. The two detectives that night asked for basic information on all active cases the business was working on." He slid the file folder over and flipped it open. "Have you had a chance to look through this yet?"

She shook her head. "I just got it this morning. This all started because I was looking into Mom and Dad's notes on the medallion; the further into this ruby assignment we get, the more I wonder if it could be the missing dragon eye."

"I'd love to think that. You know we've got to follow the process through first. But as long as the gem is authentic and once we're able to value it, I'm intrigued at the idea of comparing it to the existing ruby and the empty eye socket." He turned the folder around to face Avery. "All right, so all I did that night was make copies of the intake forms for each case that was still active the date of the accident."

She lifted the first few pages, scanning them. "That's all?"

He nodded. "The only thing I could figure at the time was that they were looking into the cause of the accident. Now you know, that in itself has always seemed a bit strange. Dry roads, minimal traffic that time of night—it's not surprising the police wanted to make sure it was really an accident."

"I suppose. I didn't get to speak with the detectives when I picked up the papers. I'd still like to—" She stopped talking as a shadow fell over their table.

The actor from the elevator the other day stood looking down at her. "I thought that was you." He flashed his thousand-watt smile. "Avery, right?"

"Yes," she said. "It's nice to see you, Tyler." *Chadwick*, she read on his badge. She'd have to remember to tell Tilly.

He pulled up a chair beside her, nodding briefly at Micah. "Do you mind if I join you?" He rested a hand on the back of Avery's chair and trained his intense blue-eyed gaze on hers. "I was hoping I'd bump into you again. I've been hanging out by the lunch counter waiting to spot you."

She laughed. "You have not."

He raised one eyebrow. "You took off the other day without giving me your number."

Avery glanced at Micah and then back at Chadwick. As she recalled, he was the one who had taken off. She'd given him directions back to his movie set in the south wing and he'd fol-lowed them. "Um."

He sat back, letting go of her chair. "I'm sorry, Avery. Maybe I misread our little meet-cute?"

She felt heat flood her cheeks as she smiled widely. Had he really just said *meet-cute*? He was a movie star. She spent most of her time behind a microscope staring at molecules. He watched her, waiting. She didn't have a tenth of the willpower needed to resist this man's flirtations. "No, I think you read it perfectly," she said, lowering her voice. Lord, what was she doing? She had a sudden flash of Saturday night at Old Smoke and a very different gentleman at her table. She'd promised Dr. Singh she was going to work on herself for now; she was in no shape to start some kind of fling with a movie star.

Visibly more relaxed, Chadwick put his hand back on her chair rail. He lowered his voice a notch as well and tipped his head toward her. "I'm glad you feel that way. Are you free tonight for dinner? I'd love to take you out."

Avery took a deep breath. Dinner. That's all it was. She'd need to eat dinner, whether it was by herself or with him. "That sounds great."

He stood, looking triumphant. He swung his borrowed chair around and pushed it back in at the other table. "Does eight o'clock work?"

"Yes. But—" At eight o'clock she'd be home in Lilac Grove. Unless . . . "Let me give you my address." She pulled one of her mother's dozens of neon scrap papers from her purse and jotted down the number and street name, handing it to him.

Tyler Chadwick grinned devilishly at her and pressed the paper back into her hand. "Not so fast. Your phone number too, please, Miss Avery." He winked with the *miss*.

She did as he said and had a thought as he took the paper. "Tyler. I need yours too." Had she seriously just demanded a movie star's phone number?

The man took the pen from her, capturing her hand in his and turning it palm up. He wrote his digits across her palm and gently folded her fingers over them, closing her fist. "I'll see you at eight, Avery." He backed up, glancing over at Micah. "Sorry for my intrusion, Mr. Abbott."

When he was gone, Avery finally met Micah's gaze. His expression was every bit as skeptical as she'd expected it to be. "I know, okay?"

Micah shook his head. "That guy . . . all that attitude and arrogance. You're really going out with him?"

"I am." She speared a chunk of lettuce and cheese and popped it in her mouth.

Micah made no further comment. He used his napkin and then smoothed it out, setting it beside his plate. His silence was louder than anything he could have said.

"It's just dinner."

"You don't know him at all. He could be an ax murderer."

She stared at him. "I doubt he's an ax murderer. It'll be fine, Micah."

"You don't know that. How did he even know my name?"

Avery looked pointedly at Micah's MOA badge clipped to his shirt.

"All right, well, where is he picking you up? Did you give him Midge's address?"

"Yes."

He nodded. "At least there's a doorman. They don't miss a thing. Keep your cell phone with you, and for God's sake don't give him your Lilac Grove address until you get to know him. You can't be too careful, Avery."

"It's just a date! He's an actor in a movie being shot here; it's not like he's some unknown entity who's going to ax murder me and then disappear into thin air. And in case you didn't already know this, Micah, I'm not exactly the damsel-in-distress type. I'm trained in jiujitsu."

He didn't crack a smile. "I know that. I just worry. Someone's got to look out for you. I don't care if you're Tilly's age or twenty-five or forty-five. Your parents would have cautioned you when going out with someone you don't know; I'm just trying to do the same. You'll check in with Midge too, right, so she knows you're staying at her apartment?"

Avery took the tray from him. "I will. Thank you for worrying, Micah, but please don't. Okay?"

They took a detour before heading back to the lab, making their way to the east wing of the main floor. The Xiang dynasty exhibit was one of three at MOA that was a major draw for the public. As they walked, Avery's phone dinged with an email notification. "Renell answered us! There's an email from him." She turned the screen toward Micah and then read aloud:

Hello Ms. Ayers,

I appreciate you reaching out. I'm happy to provide any necessary information you require during the course of your appraisal and certification. I'm quite pleased the task will be handled by Antiquities & Artifacts Appraised. My deepest condolences on the passing of your esteemed parents, Ms. Ayers; a great tragedy, to be sure.

In response to the questions you've asked, I acquired the ruby at a flea market in Munich approximately a month ago. The gem was in a child's wooden keepsake box with a jumble of costume jewelry and beads; it was being sold at a booth as one lot. I'm sorry I can't explain how such a valuable gem came to be in this odd collection. The woman running the booth spoke a German dialect I'm not versed in, unfortunately. She was quite certain, though, as I perused the contents and noted the gem, that she still wanted to make the sale.

I believe MOA to be the best fit for the gem. Following my initial discussion with acquisitions liaison Ms. Giolitti, my only point of contact at Museum of Antiquities has been Mrs. Goldie Brennan. Mrs. Brennan did utilize the services of her grandson Nate, who I understand works in acquisitions, to deliver the contingent contract to me, though we did not meet in person. I then had the gem couriered to MOA, care of Mrs. Brennan, on Wednesday, June 2nd, at which time it was signed into custody by Mrs. Brennan herself. I respectfully request to limit my communications strictly to Goldie Brennan and yourself. Ms. Brennan is aware and has agreed to honor this request. It should be stated on record that the gem never left my sight between Munich and the moment I gave the package to my private courier. Suffice it to say, I guarantee you are working with the gem I acquired in Munich.

I look forward to learning the outcome of your investigation. I do feel there is more to this piece than you might at first deduce.

Please let me know if I may offer any other information. I prefer to handle my affairs remotely. I'm always reachable through this email address.
Thank you for your interest.
Oliver Renell

"Well." Micah had slowed his pace to the point that they were barely moving down the long hallway. "Interesting."

"He puts a whole lot of focus on the fact that he was in possession of the gem until it arrived here." Avery frowned. "Odd. One more oddity, I guess, though maybe we shouldn't be surprised. I've never dealt with a collector more reluctant to meet or speak in person, you know?"

Micah agreed. "Yes, I'm not sure what that's about. Maybe it's just his own little quirk?"

Avery raised one eyebrow. She hadn't thought of that. "Hmm." She glanced down at the email again. "I know how we can find out. Let me answer him." She typed a few quick sentences and hit send.

"How can we find out?" They'd resumed walking, and now the Xiang dynasty exhibit came into view ahead.

"I just asked Renell if we could chat over the phone. I said it'll be easier than going through email. At least that way we'll know whether he even has his own number or is using the hotel phone, plus I think I'll be able to gauge things better if I can speak with him."

As they approached the exhibit, Nate Brennan rounded the corner into the large room, talking to himself—or looking like he was talking to himself. He had a Bluetooth device in one ear. He wove in and out of small clusters of patrons, immersed in his conversation.

Avery sucked in her breath and glanced at Micah. "I have an idea." She stepped into Nate's path. He stopped short, face breaking into a grin.

"I'll call you back," he said, and tapped his earpiece. "I'm so glad I ran into you. I was talking to Grandmother this morning, and we wondered if you're close to verifying the ruby. Do you need the medallion to compare the two rubies yet?"

"Not quite," Micah replied. "I expect we'll have the gem out of it's housing this afternoon, and then we'll know more."

Avery spoke up. "We did tell Goldie last week that it'd take a handful of days before we could verify if the jewel is authentic, and there's no point in doing the comparison to the ruby in the dragon medallion if it's not. It's only our second day working on it, Nate." She cringed inwardly. She was fully aware of the hierarchy here; Nate was Goldie's grandson and Francesca's right-hand man. Her tone bordered on disrespect, but she didn't mean it to.

Nate's gaze went to Micah and then back to Avery. "Got it," he said, his reply clipped and terse. He stepped to the side as if to go.

She tried to soften her attitude; she needed a favor from him. "We'll make sure to let you know right away, as soon as we get to that point, okay? I'll call you directly."

"That'd be great," he told her. "Thank you."

"Nate," Micah began. "We've got a quick question for you about the collector, Oliver Renell. We've been emailing with him, and he mentioned you'd hand delivered the tentative purchase contract to him, of course pending what we find."

He nodded. "Yes, I did."

"Did you meet him?" Avery asked. "You got to speak with him?"

"No, I had to leave the documents with the concierge. He wouldn't let me come up. Grandmother warned me he's a little eccentric, very private."

"Concierge? So . . . a hotel? Is he only in town temporarily?"

He shrugged. "I don't know. Grandmother wanted the contract hand delivered to him at Beckworth Suites, but I might as well have just emailed it. The guy's a little off, if you ask me. None of us has actually ever met him. The concierge promised to get it to him."

"Ah," Micah said. "Eccentric indeed. That helps more than you know, Nate. Thank you."

"Sure." He headed in the direction they'd just come from, stopping to call over his shoulder, "Get ahold of me as soon as you know something!"

Avery and Micah moved to the display where the Emperor's Twins medallion was illuminated on a pedestal inside its shatterproof alarmed glass case.

"I'm positive Goldie didn't ask Nate to check on our progress," Avery grumbled. "Just for the record."

Micah chuckled. "No. That was all the great Nate Brennan. He's kind of chomping at the bit over this."

"He's probably planning his statement for the press release." Avery stuck her jaw out and squared her shoulders. "Be sure to get my good side, boys," she said in a deep voice.

"And I'd better see my name in bold print," Micah added to the imitation. "Shall I spell it for you?"

Avery laughed and smacked Micah's arm lightly. "Terrible. We're both terrible."

"Oh, it's all in jest. His heart's in the right place."

She shrugged. "I guess." She leaned closer to the medallion. Twenty-four-karat gold, at least seven or eight centimeters in diameter, the creature at the center was surrounded with inlaid pearls and jewels. The one large red gem sparkled back at them above the dragon's toothy roar, catching the light, making the empty setting beside it that much sadder. "It's stunning. Truly. And can you even imagine it with both the dragon's ruby eyes intact? If this all pans out, it'll be well worth our efforts."

Avery replayed the conversation with Nate in her head that evening on her way out to the parking garage. She knew she was too hard on him; of course he was excited at the possibilities surrounding the jewel. She resolved to silently list her favorite ice cream flavors the next time he irritated her.

When she arrived at her car, her thumb froze above the unlock button on her key fob. She bent and peered through the window. On her dashboard inside the locked car was a plain white envelope with her name on it.

Chapter Seven

I nstantly on guard, Avery spun around, searching the empty fourth level of the structure she'd parked on. The elevator and stairwell were a sprint away. She felt as if she was being watched, but she saw no one.

She clicked the unlock button on the key fob and then shifted the key ring in her hand so that her finger was on the trigger of the pepper spray canister she'd kept with her since freshman year of college. Would it even have any potency left to it after six or seven years? She really didn't want to find out. She put her nose to the window and checked the back seat before hurriedly yanking the door open to get in; once inside, she locked the car again. Not that that would do a bit of good, seeing as how someone had clearly gotten inside her car to leave this note—or whatever it was—here for her. A chill ran up her spine; there was no explanation. Her car hadn't had a spare key since last year when she'd gotten aggravated with Hank during a hike upstate and thrown her car keys off the edge of a rocky ledge.

He'd simply stood and stared at her; she really hadn't thought that through. Tilly had had to call off work to bring her spare set to her. She couldn't even remember what she'd been so mad about, or how pitching her keys was supposed to make her point. But one thing was for certain right now; no one could have gotten into her car besides her. She had the only key. Which had been in her purse all day in the museum.

Avery tore open the envelope to find another plain white slip of paper, just like the first message at the house. In the center were handwritten only a few words: *Find Art at MOA. He's an ally.*

He. At first, she'd thought the message was redundant—the museum was full of art. But apparently she was being directed to get in touch with a man named Art. An employee, presumably . . . among the dozens or more Museum of Antiquities employees. On a whim, she tapped the screen of her smartphone and opened the MOA website. Perusing the menu and the other tabs, she was disappointed to see there was no listing of employees, only the names and profiles of the board of directors. None were named Art.

She whipped her head around, the feeling of someone watching her suddenly strong. An older couple was walking from the elevator down her aisle, but that was all. She needed to get moving.

On the way to Aunt Midge's Upper East Side apartment, Avery called home and got Tilly.

"Auntie's not here. She went to lunch with Colin and Prince Ivan. I'm making spaghetti for dinner. Are you on your way home?"

Midge and her friend Colin had been engaged for a brief moment back in the 1990s, long before he'd met his future husband, Prince Ivan. Avery could never remember what country he was prince of. They were a delightful couple. She hoped they'd make it to the barbecue next weekend. They always brought the most delicious pasta salad. On the heels of that reflection, Avery thought of Tilly making spaghetti and cringed. That made this difficult. "I'm so sorry for the late notice, but I'm not going to be home for dinner tonight. I was actually thinking of staying in the city—" She stopped abruptly as Tilly raised her voice, interrupting.

"Tonight? Why? You're supposed to help me pack and figure out my hair! We leave tomorrow night, and I'm not even close to being ready!"

"I know, I'm sorry. It just can't be helped." Should she mention her date with Tyler Chadwick? That'd make her sister understand. "I kind of got asked out to dinner."

"Oooh! A date? With who? It's not Hank, is it? Where are you going?"

"That actor I mentioned, Tyler Chadwick, is picking me up at Aunt Midge's. I don't know where we're going yet." She turned the Bluetooth volume down as her sister shrieked.

"Oh my Gawd, A! Yay you! Okay, I forgive you. What will you wear?"

Avery glanced down at her tweed slacks and plain white blouse. If only she'd known a movie star was going to ask her out! "Um."

"No. Oh no, you are not wearing your boring work clothes on a date with Hollywood. Tyler Chadwick. I'm looking him up right now. Let's see. Okay, yes, he plays a cop in the Firefly sequel. This says he's twenty-nine, perfect for you! He's super cute for an old dude. Nice snag, sis."

Avery burst out laughing, alone in her car. "Thanks. What's old, anyone over twenty? I'll check and see if I've got anything to wear at the apartment. Maybe from when we spent the night after that concert last month, though it might not be dressy enough. I'll figure something out, don't worry."

"You could always wear one of Auntie's dresses, and it'd be a scandalously short micromini. When will you be home to help me pack?"

"I'll be home early tomorrow, I promise. Micah's busy in the afternoon, so we're taking a half day. We'll have plenty of time to strategize your hair and get you packed, don't worry. And you remember we're shopping with Micah and Noah on Sunday, right?" Aunt Midge and Tilly were flying out Tuesday night for her sister's voice audition in Los Angeles. Midge had pushed to make it a mini vacation for the three of them, but between Tilly's senior year commitments and Avery's current assignment, it just wasn't feasible. They'd be back home Friday.

"I can't wait," Tilly said. "I'll be so much more relaxed after the audition."

"Tilly," Avery said, "I have a small favor you could help me with." Should she tell her sister about the second mysterious note? Perhaps not. She didn't want to worry her, especially not right before her audition. And despite the notes being mysteriously delivered and quite cryptic, there was really nothing ominous about them. But she could get Tilly's assistance in a roundabout way; her younger sister was the most tech-savvy person she'd ever met. "I need to get ahold of someone who works at MOA, but I don't want to bother Goldie. The problem is, I only have a first name. Is that something you think you might be able to find online somehow? There's nothing on the website."

"I'm sure I can do that. What's the name?"

"Art."

Tilly laughed. "Too funny. What's his position there?"

"I have no idea. But I don't think there are a ton of employees. And Art is not a common first name."

"Even if it's Arthur, that's still pretty unusual," Tilly mused. "I can handle a challenge."

"Thanks so much. I have faith in you! I'm almost to the apartment; I'll call you after the date. And Tilly?"

"Yeah?"

"Make sure you keep the house locked, all right? I know we have differing opinions on this, but I'm still not sure what that note or Halston's scent was about."

"Everything's already locked," her sister said. "I'm fine, and Halston's here."

Midge Ayers's seventeenth-floor apartment was plush and pristine, just as Avery had left it the last time she stayed over. Midge had the southwest corner of the luxurious high rise on Fifth Avenue between Eighty-Fifth and Eighty-Sixth Streets, with a view overlooking Central Park and the Met museum. Today Avery spied the spire of the Empire State Building against the clear evening sky. The formal dining room and twelve-foot marble table accommodated large dinner parties, which spilled over into the open living room and terrace. Both rooms were devoid of window treatments, allowing plenty of natural light in to nurture Aunt Midge's beloved plant collection. Upstairs, both bedrooms held floor-length paisley-print blackout curtains, as Midge couldn't sleep well unless it was completely dark. The entire apartment encompassed every shade of white, with splashes of color—a red chintz chaise longue, velvety red couches, a peacock-blue tapestry on the wide stairway wall.

Avery sat for a moment at Midge's baby grand near the stairway, tapping out chopsticks. She'd snuck out of her piano lessons each week, whereas Tilly had begged their parents for guitar lessons on top of piano, and then it was violin, then cello. Once she'd discovered her voice was her instrument of choice, she and Midge became the holiday entertainment each year, Midge sitting straight-backed at her baby grand playing the classics while Tilly sang. Avery's meager rendition of chopsticks mocked her lack of interest in learning to play. She finally stood and ascended the stairs to see what she could find in her aunt's wardrobe.

She met Tyler Chadwick on the sidewalk in front of the building; he'd had the night doorman, Dustin, call up for her at exactly eight o'clock. Tyler's driver—of course he had a driver—stood beside a sleek platinum Lexus LS holding the door open. She could hardly have told they were moving if not for the tall buildings rolling by, the ride was so smooth. Tyler turned toward her in the back seat and flashed his wide, movie-star grin. "How does the Silver Spoon sound?"

"It sounds unlikely," Avery said. "I've been dying to try it." Silver Spoon had opened just last month in Greenwich Village and immediately become a reservations-only hot spot that was impossible to get into.

"No worries, it's not worth life or death. We have a table at eight thirty."

Avery was impressed. She was about to ask how but thought better of it. Because she was on a date with Hollywood, that was how. The little black dress she'd left at Aunt Midge's when she and Tilly had last slept over was perfect, and her aunt had even had it dry-cleaned and hung back in her closet. She'd luckily left her burgundy suede heels in the foyer closet over a year ago when she and Tilly and Midge had gone out to a play, and between those and a few sparkly bangles on her wrist, the ensemble worked nicely.

Seated at a cozy table in the corner, Tyler took the liberty of ordering for both of them—the mixed grill sampler, an assortment of steak, shrimp, and scallops with very pretty but miniscule servings of the side dishes accompanying it. She speared one of the three garlic-and-lemon-pepper pan-seared brussels sprouts on a small plate, closing her eyes as she enjoyed the flavor.

"So how did you get into acting? Was it something you always knew you wanted to do?"

Tyler's eyes lit up. "Always. I was forever putting on skits and plays in the living room. I started a neighborhood theater group when I was nine, and we got one of the dads to build us a stage. But I was the only one who went on to pursue acting. I think, looking back, it was when I won the lead in my high school play that I really knew it was my calling."

Avery nodded. "Wow. That's wonderful, and that you were able to break into that world. I'm sure it wasn't easy."

"Oh, that's an understatement. It's definitely a commitment."

"How's the filming going at MOA? It all seems very secretive. I've seen some of the crew members on their way in when I arrive in the morning, but that's it."

He nodded. "It's a closed set. I'm surprised I was even allowed to wander away that day you bumped into me."

"That was embarrassing," she said, smiling.

"But lucky." He was most definitely super cute, as Tilly had said. With his black dress shirt under a slim-cut Italian jacket, she could imagine him as a James Bond type in some spy movie.

"My sister looked up the movie being filmed—she says it's Firefly two? She's a huge fan of superhero movies. She was practically bouncing off the walls when she found out. Oh! I just remembered. I'm sorry, but I have a bit of an awkward question for you."

Tyler raised one eyebrow. "Shoot."

"I promised my little sister I'd ask . . . do you know Solana Davis? I guess she plays Firefly, right? Tilly thinks she might have a chance at meeting her." Avery touched Tyler's arm lightly. "I know filming will be finished soon—the museum curator said it's only for a couple weeks. I doubt it'd even be possible, but I promised I'd ask."

Tyler Chadwick's expression shifted, and for a moment Avery thought he looked worried. No, not worried, but something. Caught off guard? That was probably it. Then it was gone. "Solana's great. She's always busy, but that's a good problem to have. You know, it doesn't hurt to ask, right? Let me talk with her tomorrow. You can tell Tilly I'll work on it; how's that?"

"Oh, that's fantastic. Thank you!"

He shrugged. They sat back as the server cleared their dishes, and Tyler ordered two slices of tiramisu. It was a little disconcerting, having her date make all the decisions for her. She wasn't sure she enjoyed it. She and Hank had dated off and on since college, and the few men she'd seen besides him had either gone dutch or at least assumed she'd order for herself. Tyler raised a hand in the air and snapped his fingers as the server walked away. "Waitress!"

Avery pressed her lips together, watching him.

"Two coffees with the tiramisu."

Avery registered the lack of a *please* or *thank you* for the umpteenth time that evening, and she saw from the young woman's face that she did too. "Of course, sir," she said, through what sounded like clenched teeth.

"Thank you," Avery told her. Tyler was beginning to remind her of every rude customer she'd ever waited on when she'd worked as a server in college.

He was blissfully oblivious. "So, Avery. I'm fascinated with what you're doing at the museum," he said, leaning toward her.

"Your job must be thrilling, working with priceless jewels and artifacts."

"It can be. More often than not, it's a lot of lab time, studying flecks of metal and molecules and measuring fractions of millimeters on angles. But it can be really interesting."

"Well, especially when you get a case like your current one, right?"

She tipped her head, frowning. Had she told him about the assignment?

"Oh." His eyes widened. "That's why you're up there where all the science-y stuff is on the third floor, isn't it? Am I not supposed to know?"

"Um. What have you heard?"

He lowered his voice, leaning toward her. "I heard it's a ruby the size of a walnut and it might be the long-lost dragon-eye jewel in some priceless legendary necklace at MOA. Is that true?"

Avery laughed in spite of herself. "You make it sound like something out of a movie. But we aren't really sure yet what exactly we're working with. Who did you hear that from? I'm just curious."

Tyler looked caught off guard again. He quickly recovered. "I don't want to get anyone in trouble. The acquisitions guy came out to have a smoke this morning while I was out there—Ned? What's his name? I'm bad with names. He's got kind of a surfer look?"

"Nate? Wait, he smokes?" Tyler smoked? Avery was surprised; she hadn't seen him smoke yet tonight. And she'd had no idea Nate smoked. The more she learned about Goldie's grandson, the less she felt she knew about him.

"Nate. That's it. And not really; I think they were clove cigarettes. He was just talking. He said if you can prove it's real and it's the missing ruby, it'd be the most important acquisition the museum's made in decades. I figure he's probably not exaggerating; I've seen how they bring the ruby back and forth to your lab with the guards and everything. They don't mess around."

Avery rolled her eyes. As if Nate knew anything about MOA's history. "He's a little ahead of himself. It's a bit of a long process. We don't even know yet if the ruby is authentic, and then if it is—"

Tyler was listening, rapt. She supposed there was no harm in chatting about the assignment. As Tyler himself had said, it was no secret that the piece was under lock and key and required two armed guards to transport it at all times. "Well, if it is authentic, then we'll have to evaluate the dragon medallion that's part of a popular exhibit at MOA, so we'll want to time things to avoid the heavy crowds. I mean, you wouldn't want the focal piece in one of the biggest exhibits to be missing on the one day you decide to tour the museum, you know? So there's the timing issue."

"Ah, I didn't even think of that. But listen. Here's what I really want to know." He kept his voice low and moved his chair around the small table to sit beside her. "How much are we talking? Like, *priceless* is such a relative word, right? Do you know yet? What it'd be worth, if it's the real deal? And then how much if it really *is* the dragon's missing eye?"

She met his gaze, the subtle scent of his cologne drifting to her. She and Micah hadn't even discussed the actual worth of the piece. In assignments for MOA, even though her job was to certify and value artifacts, the dollar amount an item might be worth seemed like a moot point. These items were truly invaluable pieces of history. "I honestly don't know. We aren't nearly that far yet."

"I'll bet you have an idea of whether or not it's real." He tipped his head toward her, running his thumb along her forearm. "I wish there was a way I could see it. I bet we could convince the night guard to let us in and get it for you. Between my film set badge and your work with MOA, they'd probably do it. Now *that* would be an incredible first-date story for us to have, wouldn't it?"

The hair stood up on Avery's arm where he'd touched her. As exciting as Tyler Chadwick's attentions were, an uncomfortable feeling was needling her. "I'm pretty sure they're sticking to exactly what Goldie has told them about keeping it under lock and key at all times. Even if they did let us in, it'd be a great way for me to lose any future MOA jobs if anyone found out."

He looked disappointed. "I can't convince you to live dangerously? You're sure?"

She shook her head. "Yes, I'm sure."

"Well. Worth a try, right?" He gave her a wink and that crooked smile that had done such a great job of reeling her in at MOA. It hit her differently this time.

The server arrived with their tiramisu and coffee, giving Avery a much-needed moment to collect her thoughts. No one, not even Goldie, had said the assignment should remain a secret, but this entire conversation had made her uncomfortable. Thankfully, Tyler dropped the subject as they enjoyed the delicious dessert.

Back at Aunt Midge's building, he walked her to the door. He leaned in to kiss her good-night, and Avery turned slightly so that he kissed her cheek. It wasn't planned; she simply reacted. The jovial, flirtatious Tyler Chadwick she'd met at MOA was the more attractive version of the man she'd just spent the last two hours with; this Tyler was a little elitist, a little nosy, and a little pushy. She wasn't looking forward to breaking the news to Tilly that her date with Hollywood hadn't been all that fantastic.

Avery settled into Midge's red chintz chaise longue, a steaming cup of tea beside her on the round tray that sat on an oversized round ivory ottoman. She'd changed into comfy fleece pajamas and now smoothed the white chenille blanket over her lap and called her sister.

Tilly's frowning face appeared on the video-chat screen. "It's only ten thirty. Why are you home already from your date?"

Avery chuckled. "It's a school night. I have to be up early tomorrow."

"Ugh. You're so boring. What did he say about Solana Davis? Did he think I might be able to meet her?"

"He said he'll work on it. He said he'd call me, so I'll let you know."

"That's a good sign," Tilly said. "He wants to see you again."

"I'm not positive that's a good thing," she said. "I'm not really sure what to think of him." She filled Tilly in on the date, pulling the phone away from her ear when she mentioned they'd gone to Silver Spoon; her sister's high-pitched shriek could have shattered glass. Tilly's take on the little things that had irked Avery was that Tyler was nervous. She supposed that was possible, though unlikely; after all, *she* wasn't a famous movie star.

"But maybe he doesn't care about that. Maybe he was awed by your beautiful brain."

"Oh, you're cute," Avery said, laughing. "All right, I've actually got to get to sleep. I want to get to MOA first thing tomorrow and see if I can get one of the docents to let me borrow the staff directory. They're both really nice, and they know more about the exhibits and staff than almost anyone besides Goldie."

"Oh! I almost forgot," Tilly said. "I found a back door into the museum's personnel files. I can't see anything personal, just names and hire dates, but there's an Arthur and an Art on staff at MOA."

"No fricking way," Avery said. "That's kind of scary. How the heck did you hack into their system? What else can you see?"

"Not much," Tilly said. "It's literally just, like, human resources–type stuff. Nothing juicy like how much Goldie's paid for pieces or what exhibits are worth or anything. But I wanted to cover all the bases, so I looked at any employees or board members with the name Art or Arthur anywhere in their name. I found two others, one with the middle name Arthur and a board member named Samuel Arthur the Third."

"Wow. I hope you only ever use your powers for good, Ms. Superspy. Okay, I actually know that one. Samuel Arthur is a board member, but he's been in a nursing home since last year, sadly. So we know it's not him."

"How do we know? What are you trying to find an Art for?"

Avery pursed her lips. She'd meant to keep things vague. "No, I just meant the Art I'm looking for should be on-site at MOA. Working."

"A, what's going on? What are you doing?"

She took a deep breath. "All right. But you can't freak out. I got another letter."

"You what? When? You weren't going to tell me or Auntie or anyone?"

"Well, I guess I'd planned to tell Art, if we could find the right Art. I would have told you. I'll show you the letter when I get home tomorrow."

"What did it say, exactly?"

Avery groaned but didn't argue. She fetched the note from her purse and read it aloud to Tilly. *"Find Art at MOA. He's an ally.* It was inside my locked car."

"What? And you didn't think that was a big deal?"

"Yes, it totally creeped me out! But there was no one around. And if anything, the note seems like a tip to help me."

Her little sister was quiet on the other end of the line.

"Tilly?"

"You only have one set of car keys. You should have told someone right away." The screen suddenly spun upside down and then went dark, the sound muffled. Avery heard Tilly call out to their aunt, "Avery's just telling me about her date." A pause. "Love you too, Auntie. Good night."

Midge must have stopped outside Tilly's bedroom door on her way to bed. She'd created the habit her first night in the Lilac Grove house, stopping outside each of their rooms to call good-night. Aunt Midge would have made a great mother, but Avery suspected she thoroughly enjoyed being eccentric Aunt Midge.

"Sorry." Tilly was back. "Okay, put up your pinkie. Right now." Her scowl was prominent in the video chat.

Avery did as she was told.

"Pinkie swear you'll tell me immediately the next time a mysterious note—a mysterious anything—shows up. Do it."

"I swear. I promise. I just didn't want to worry you." Avery lowered her hand. "I'm sorry. But if I can find the Art in the note, I think that'll help ensure we're safe."

"I still think I'm right. I think Dad is connected to all of this somehow. It's the only thing that makes sense."

"I want to believe that's true," Avery said. Though if it was, she certainly couldn't see how.

"Be careful, A. For real. Do you want the deets on the other three Arts?"

"Yes, shoot. I've got a pen."

Avery's phone dinged just as she turned out the light. She rolled over and fought with the fluffy comforter to get an arm out, grabbing her phone. Oliver Renell had already sent a short reply to her email.

Dear Ms. Ayers,

I appreciate your desire to be thorough, but I'm afraid I'm not available to speak by phone currently. I eagerly await further news on your investigation of the jewel.

There is an important matter we should speak about after the authentication is completed.

Regards,

Oliver Renell

Avery sat up in bed and reread the short message. What important matter? And why couldn't he talk to her? It couldn't be that he was otherwise committed; she hadn't even suggested a date or time for a phone meeting. She scrolled up to his original message and read that all the way through as well, an eerie, unwanted thought creeping into her mind. It couldn't be; she must be wrong. But . . . what if she wasn't? What else could explain the refusal to meet or be seen, even the refusal to speak on the phone? And what about the lack of any presence or profile photos online? Avery dropped the phone and scrubbed both hands through her hair, blowing out through pursed lips. Micah was going to think she was crazy. She didn't even want to mention her theory to Tilly. If she was right, it'd be unforgivable.

What if Oliver Renell was William Ayers?

Chapter Eight

A very was on the front steps of the museum at 8:59 Tuesday morning. She and Micah had agreed to meet at the shop in an hour. She still wasn't sure whether she should say anything to Micah about her suspicions. She needed more than a couple mysterious notes and an antisocial collector, but she couldn't just dismiss the notion either. Her father had been dealing with the Emperor's Twins medallion right before the fatal car accident. If something had happened a year ago during that assignment, something to do with the existing ruby or even the authenticity of the medallion, perhaps it was now being brought to the surface with the new jewel. What if her dad had faked his own death, then located the jewel and submitted it? What if Tilly was right and their father was alive, but somehow working covertly as the collector?

Avery shuddered involuntarily. It was too crazy. Her dad would never have put her or Tilly through the trauma of losing him. There'd been a double funeral. The whole thing had been horrific. It didn't matter how much any artifact might be worth. The William who'd raised her would never do that.

Unless he had no choice. And that train of thought led nowhere, because of course he'd have a choice whether to tell his girls he was alive and well.

She decided not to decide until she saw Micah. She couldn't take her partner looking at her with pity, and that's what would happen unless she'd worked out some sort of plausible explanation for how and why William was masquerading as Renell. Either way, she and Micah had to meet with a client at the shop to go over the findings on her antique watch collection, the assignment she and Micah had been working on prior to the potential ruby. They'd get back on top of the MOA job Wednesday and finish up the last few specs, which would tell them for certain whether the jewel was authentic. Assuming they cleared that hurdle, they could move on to the heart of the assignment and begin comparing the ruby to the jewel in the medallion. Examining the empty eye socket in the gold dragon, along with both rubies, would finally answer the question of what they were dealing with—a real ruby that couldn't possibly be the missing dragon's eye, or a ruby that was an exact match for the missing eye, restoring the Emperor's Twins artifact to perfection. There was still the possibility they'd discover the stone was a very pretty spinel, worth a fraction of the value.

She found Emily, one of the museum's docents, organizing pamphlets and facility maps at the welcome desk. Avery set a steaming mint mocha latte in front of the perpetually cheerful woman and was greeted with her biggest smile.

"Emily, I'm going to be completely honest with you," Avery said, putting both hands, palms down, on the desk and speaking in a low conspirator's tone. "I need a small favor."

The sixty-something's eyebrows went up, disappearing underneath her short, curly gray bangs. "Really? I'd help you without the coffee, you know that."

Avery smiled. She and Emily had struck up a friendship these last few months as Avery struggled to learn her way around the museum. In return for what Avery felt was an excessive amount of navigational assistance, she'd made a habit of bringing the woman goody packages from the White Box in Lilac Grove. She hadn't planned ahead enough to do that today, so coffee would have to suffice. "I'm hoping I might run a few names of employees by you, and you'll tell me if you know them at all."

"Of course! Go ahead."

She consulted her notes. "Arthur Dansby."

Emily nodded. "Yes, Arthur's a friend of mine. I'm sure you know him; he runs the sandwich counter in the cafeteria. Very sweet man, close to my age, a little shorter than I am," she said, holding a hand at about temple height, palm down.

Avery jotted that down. "Perfect, perfect. Do you ever call him Art? Does anyone?"

Emily's eyes widened. "No. I wouldn't; that's a little familiar. He's just Arthur."

"All right." She had to assume the note specified the name Art intentionally. "Okay, the next one is John Arthur Smith."

Emily frowned. "John Arthur Smith," she repeated.

"Art. He probably goes by Art Smith." She loved that the older woman apparently had no interest in why Avery was asking about men named Art.

"Oh! I think I know." Emily pulled out her staff directory and flipped through it. "There's a security guard named Art Smith. He must only be part-time, as I don't see him often. I'm sorry I can't recall much of what he looks like. He's tall, I know that. Tall and kind of brooding, maybe in his early thirties."

Avery was furiously scribbling in her notebook. "Good, good, thank you. And the last one is Art Wychoski."

"I know Mr. Wychoski. He's one of the exhibit supervisors, a stocky, muscular man in his midforties, I'd guess. He's a little, ah . . . difficult to approach." Emily ducked her head toward Avery. "He's sort of crabby, at least whenever I try to talk to him."

"You're the best," Avery said. "Seriously." Her mind was racing. She did know of the sandwich-counter Arthur, and he was, as Emily had said, very nice. But her money was on one of the other two. "Last question. Is the security guard Art working today?"

"One moment," the docent said. She tapped the keyboard on the computer in front of her. "As a matter of fact, he is. He's at the east entrance until three today. Do you remember how to get there? I'm happy to walk you over."

Avery shook her head. "I actually remember, thanks to you! What about Art Wychoski? Is he here now too?"

"The schedule says he comes in at one this afternoon."

Avery thanked Emily again and was walking out the museum's east entrance a few minutes later. She'd start with the security guard, and if he seemed not to be the Art in the note, she'd stop back here before leaving the city to track down the exhibit supervisor.

She approached the guard stationed outside the doors. "Excuse me, sir." He towered over her, even in her black chunky heels.

He met her gaze, his expression cool and unreadable. She recognized him now as one of the handful of rotating guards handling the ruby and other artifacts she'd worked on here. He apparently didn't recognize her.

"My name is Avery Ayers, and I'm contracted with MOA. My company certifies and appraises pieces before the museum acquires them. I think I've seen you upstairs at the lab." She pulled the note from her purse. "I have a question for you . . . It's probably easier to explain with this. I received this last night."

The man read the brief message—*Find Art at MOA. He's an ally*—and stared at her. He looked shocked. "Did you see who sent this to you?"

Avery was taken aback. This had to be the Art she was looking for. "Um, the note was in my car when I came out after work yesterday. I don't know who put it there. As a matter of fact, it was in my *locked* car, and I'm the only one with a key."

Strangely, that added information didn't seem to surprise him further; his expression didn't change. He looked down at the note again and then back up at Avery. "I know who you are. You need to drop your current assignment. Tell the curator to find someone else." He handed the slip of paper back to her.

She stood looking up—way up—at him with her mouth hanging open. Literally. She finally shook her head, trying to make some sense of this, and pushed him for more information. "I can't do that. Who are you, Art? How do you know anything about my assignment?" All she could think of was the first note that had come through the mail slot in Lilac Grove. This guard had just much too closely mirrored the sentiment in that first warning.

He shook his head. "I can't tell you that. But I know what it's going to take for you to be safe."

"Art. Officer Smith." Avery crossed her arms and moved a step closer to the guard. "Tell me what's going on. Who are you working with? What do you know about this note? Who sent it to me?" She waved it in the air, frustrated.

The man took a deep breath, exhaling slowly. "I know you want answers. But I'm telling you, the best thing you can do at this point is drop the ruby assignment. Seriously, Ms. Ayers."

Avery could feel her temper simmering. She didn't have the time or patience for this. She stepped back, looking at his name tag, which read only *Art Smith, MOA security officer*. "I'm not dropping it. But maybe I will talk to the curator about why an MOA guard is warning me off certifying the ruby that she hired me to evaluate. *John* Arthur Smith." She turned to go back inside. She wasn't bluffing; Goldie should know exactly who this man was, or at least why he was advising her on her job.

"All right!" He spoke sharply, and Avery whipped her head around at him. "Okay," he said, scowling. "Listen. I'm aware of the potential surrounding your assignment. That it could turn out to be the missing Emperor's Twins dragon eye. I have good reason to believe you'll be at risk of being harmed or worse if you continue your authentication."

"How—what makes you say that? What do you know? Do you know Oliver Renell? William Ayers? Do those names mean anything to you?" she demanded, openly angry now at this cloak-and-dagger ruse. "Who are you, really?" She repeated the question, her volume louder now as she ignored a family of museum patrons brushing past her, exiting the building.

"You need to calm down," Art said, challenging her intently with his dark-eyed gaze and making her even angrier. "Avery. I'm someone who can help. As your note says." He pointed. "Please, consider getting the case reassigned. Surely there are other companies who do what you do."

"Tell me how you're involved in this and I'll consider it."

A muscle in his jaw pulsed. "I can't do that."

"Then I guess the note is wrong," she said, shoving it back into her purse. "You're not an ally." She turned to go, and this time he didn't stop her.

Avery didn't remember her trek back through the museum to the front entrance; she was fuming. Art, the completely unhelpful security guard, had just highlighted how in the dark she felt about too many things. By the time she passed Emily's desk and was nearing the front exit, her heart was racing, her palms were sweating, and she wanted to yell at someone.

"Have a great day, Avery." Emily's voice broke through her fog of rage.

Avery slowed her pace and took a deep breath. Orange sherbet. Chocolate chip cookie dough. Superman. Birthday cake. Pumpkin spice cheesecake. Her heartbeat was slowing; she could feel it in the pulse at the side of her neck. She produced a small smile for the docent. "Thanks, Emily, you too. I appreciate your help." Her voice sounded pinched and quiet to her own ears.

On the front steps of MOA, she abruptly sat down and took her pink-and-black running shoes from their compartment in her bag; days like today were the exact reason she always kept them with her. She swapped her heels for the runners and stood, pulling her hair into a high ponytail with an elastic from her wrist. She looked down. The shoes looked ridiculous with her nice cropped slim pants and brown plaid blazer. She folded the blazer, stuffed it into the mesh bag, and hit the pavement. Running was the only thing that was going to snap her out of this dark mood. But she'd made it only as far as the corner—the end of the MOA compound—when she spotted Francesca on the side of the wide concrete steps into the south wing talking with someone. Avery slowed her pace. The man had his back to

Avery, but from here she was able to pick out the artfully high-lighted blond streaks in his hair. As she passed, the man turned slightly, confirming for her that it was Tyler Chadwick. He and Francesca appeared to be immersed in an intimate conversation, their heads close together and Francesca's hand resting on Tyler's upper arm.

Avery picked up speed, facing forward. She should mind her own business. Perhaps Tyler was chatting Francesca up for details about the ruby just as he'd pushed her. Judging from their body language, though, Avery suspected it was something a little more personal. She couldn't really blame Tyler if it was. Francesca was gorgeous and intriguing; it'd be tough to ignore her attentions. But for Sir Robert's sake, she hoped it wasn't what it looked like.

It took Avery two blocks to decide not to mention what she'd seen to her partner. She didn't know what she'd witnessed, and it would only upset Sir Robert.

By the time she'd completed the six-block run to Antiquities and Artifacts Appraised, she'd come up with a plan. She'd prom-ised Tilly she'd be home early today, but she was going to put her wild theory about Renell being William Ayers to rest before she left the city. She'd stop at Beckworth Suites and refuse to leave until the collector came down to meet her, even if only for a minute. She'd tell him why if she had to. If he truly was Oliver Renell, he'd have to come down and prove her wrong.

The bell over the door jingled, and Avery was surprised to see that the little shop was crowded. Normally it was a rotat-ing combination of the three of them, Sir Robert, Micah, and her, but Micah was just sitting down with Mrs. Weber and her daughter in the reception area to discuss the woman's antique watches she'd hired them to appraise.

Avery said hello to Sir Robert, who was engrossed in something on his tablet, and carried her fresh, steaming coffee over to join Micah and their client. "We were so impressed with this collection, Mrs. Weber. My colleague," she said, glancing at Micah, "and I rarely see so many family generations of an item. The fact that you've been able to gather seven generations of your ancestors' watches is pretty amazing in itself, no matter their value." She and Micah had mixed news for the woman, and she always tried to tamp expectations when that happened.

Micah took his cue from Avery. "You do have one quite valuable timepiece here. Your great-great-grandfather's watch from his boyhood appraised higher than any of the others." He opened a file folder with printed results of their findings and turned it around on the table to face their client.

When they'd finished, Avery moved to her desk to wrap up a few tasks before heading out. Sir Robert stopped beside her and stuck a yellow sticky note to her computer. "A call came in for you. I'm off; I've got a lunch date with Francesca. And I wanted to let you know, something's fishy with your collector Renell."

"What?" Avery stared at him. "How do you mean?"

"My contact at Barnaby's has never heard of him. You must have had an inkling something's not quite right there. Is that why you asked to me to see if he's on the books with the auction house?"

Avery nodded. "Who's your contact? Barnaby's is the largest auction house outside LA. How's it possible they have no record of Oliver Renell? This can't be the first item he's submitted."

"Well, I didn't say all of Barnaby's has never heard of him," Sir Robert hedged. "But my contact handles a lot of the incoming pieces. Shouldn't he know of him?"

Avery frowned, thinking. "Renell doesn't have a physical address in the States, at least not that Goldie was aware of. She sent Nate to his hotel to drop off paperwork last week. And Nate wasn't able to actually see the man." She looked at the note on her desk, not really seeing it. Should she say something about her suspicions? She'd hoped to run things by Micah alone. Though both men had been part of her parents' business since the beginning, she'd never really gotten to know Sir Robert as well as she had Micah. Where Sir Robert tended to rub elbows with Manhattan's social set, intent on widening his circle of important friends and acquaintances, Micah and his wife and son had never missed an Ayers family barbecue or event. Micah's having a child close to Tilly's age had also helped cement that bond.

Avery kept her mouth shut; Sir Robert would think she was crazy.

"A reclusive collector," Sir Robert scoffed. "You'd think he'd want to reap the rewards of submitting such a valuable item. Or, uh, potentially valuable. Is it?" He tipped his head and raised one eyebrow at her. "What are you thinking about the ruby?"

Avery shook her head, glancing at Micah, who was still on the phone. "We aren't quite at that point yet."

"Oh." Sir Robert's voice betrayed disappointment. "Well, I don't know about that collector. Something's off; we'll have to keep that in mind as you move forward, in case you run into any issues."

"Right." She leaned back in her chair, looking up at him. What on earth did that mean?

"All right. I'll see you tomorrow." He checked the antique clock on the wall in the reception area. "It's never good to keep a beautiful woman waiting!"

He'd never said who his Barnaby's contact was, she realized, watching him hail a cab out front. How odd that the auction house—or at least Sir Robert's acquaintance there—had never heard of Oliver Renell. Renell himself wasn't making any of this easier, if he really was Renell. He still hadn't answered her last email, asking him what exact matter needed to be discussed after the appraisal was finished. She picked up the sticky note Sir Robert had left. *Edward Johnstone 212–555–7289.* It would have helped to know what the call was about; she'd take care of it later. She hoped to spend most of her afternoon basking in Tilly's excitement over her Wednesday voice audition in LA, helping her pack and figure out what she'd wear. For now, she turned to some business housekeeping items on her computer.

An hour later, Micah walked back to MOA parking with her, and she summoned her courage and shared what she was thinking about the collector. To her relief, he didn't think she was crazy. Or at least he entertained the idea that Renell might be William Ayers. But he strongly discouraged her from following through on her plan to visit the hotel and demand that the collector see her.

"Avery," Micah said sensibly, "if you're right and by some miracle your father is masquerading as Renell, then there's got to be a very good reason he needs the world to believe he's gone. You could end up endangering him or yourself. If you're wrong and the collector is agoraphobic or eccentric, you're going to alienate him and invade his privacy. There's no reason you can't simply wait a few more days until we have our findings on the ruby, and then we can go through proper channels via Goldie. You see?"

She no longer had time to execute her plan of trying to see Renell by the time she pulled out of the parking garage. Her therapy appointment was at noon. Dr. Singh was midway between the shop and Lilac Grove, in Roseville. The therapist worked out of her home in a beautiful home office decorated in whites, ivories, and pale rose tones. Avery always chose one of the big overstuffed armchairs, though she imagined Dr. Singh had clients who stretched out on the comfy-looking couch.

When the appointment began, Avery tattled on herself, bringing up her irrational anger at the Springfield police desk sergeant and then mentioning that she'd actually gone on a date.

"Let's talk about that" was Dr. Singh's way of pushing Avery to explore her feelings. When Avery admitted that she'd been surprised and disappointed at not connecting well with Tyler Chadwick, the therapist made an observation that forced her to look at her own participation in her life since coming home last year.

"Have you considered that you were disappointed in the lack of connection for other reasons?"

Avery frowned. "What other reasons?" Sometimes she wished Dr. Singh would just say what she meant.

"Maybe your disappointment has nothing to do with your date."

Avery always left therapy feeling like she understood so much and yet not enough about how her own mind worked. Dr. Singh was the best.

Her sense of calm was shattered minutes later. Tilly's voice was frantic over the car's Bluetooth as she demanded that Avery come home immediately.

Chapter Nine

Tilly was nearly yelling and difficult to understand. Midge took the phone from her. "Tilly would like to know when you'll be home, but we both want you to know that everything's *fine*." Avery heard Tilly in the background, but Midge spoke over her. "A man came to the door claiming you'd sent him to collect some files for the museum. But—"

Avery interrupted at that point, alarmed. "What? I did not! You didn't let him in, did you?" She turned toward the expressway, her only focus now being getting home to Lilac Grove.

"Of course we didn't let him in."

"We're not stupid!" Tilly shouted from a few feet away.

"What did he do? Did he argue, or just leave?"

"When I told him he'd have to wait until you were here, he tried saying he knew you through work. He did finally leave without much protest when I insisted he leave a card. Which he didn't," Midge said. "And as you know, dear, I wasn't born yesterday. Halston and I followed his car out to the road and watched him go."

"We got photos of his—" Tilly took the phone back from Aunt Midge, her voice becoming clearer. "We got photos of his car and his license plate."

"I'm hanging up. Call the police right now and tell them what you told me." Avery waited five minutes and then called Tilly back, but the phone only rang and rang. She tried Aunt Midge's phone, and it didn't even ring but went straight to voice mail. She spent the remainder of the drive worrying and calling and getting no one.

Halston greeted her at the front door, full of wags and kisses. He pawed at the door to go out, but she kept him in, calling out for her aunt and sister. Nothing. Tilly's suitcase was open in the middle of the tiled foyer, clothing spilling out of it, and a few other items lay on the stairs as if waiting to be packed. The house was too quiet. She climbed the stairway to the bedrooms, telling herself that if something was horribly wrong, Halston wouldn't be his usual excessively happy self. "Hello?" she called again. She followed the dog down the hall and was flooded with relief when she heard her sister and aunt in Midge's room. She opened the door and gasped.

Tilly was standing on the hope chest at the end of Midge's king-size bed wearing an elegant black floor-length gown with tiny flutter sleeves, her blond waves pinned up off her face and cascading down her back. "Oh my," Avery whispered. How could she be mad? Aunt Midge was kneeling on one of her plush red-and-gold throw pillows on the floor, sewing the hem. "Tilly. Mom would cry if she could see you. Wow."

Her sister turned glistening eyes toward her. "Thank you. Auntie did it."

"Why didn't you answer your phones?" Avery had an odd sense of whiplash with the abrupt switch from being anxious and worried to sentimental. "When we hung up, you were about to call the police. What did they say? They didn't come? Where are your phones?"

"Oh no, I'm so sorry," Tilly said.

Aunt Midge chimed in at the same time. "We must have left them in the kitchen after we called the police station."

"So you did call?" Avery sat down in the center of Midge's high bed and admired her sister. Tilly was growing up. Suddenly it didn't seem as if there were seven years between them, seeing her in this beautiful evening gown.

"They said they'd send someone if we thought we were in danger. As it was, they just had Tilly email the photos we took to the precinct, and they said if there was any sign of the man returning or any other odd happenings, we should call again," Aunt Midge finished.

"I told Auntie about your note, A. We told the police about it too." Tilly's tone lacked the singsong lilt it usually held when she had exclusive information on Avery. "I don't know anymore if it's Dad. Not after that man came to the door. Someone is messing with us."

Avery sighed, leaning forward with her elbows on her knees. Aunt Midge continued her stitching without comment, but Avery knew the older woman was taking in every word. "You're right," Avery said. "And I think it's related to this ruby we're working on. I think it's connected to the Xiang era medallion, and maybe also to Mom and Dad's death. I just don't know how."

Avery told Tilly she'd found the Art from the note, though he certainly didn't seem to be an ally. She filled Aunt Midge in on her less-than-stellar date with movie star Tyler Chadwick, including the fact that, besides being rude to waitstaff, he'd seemed just as intrigued with her current assignment as everyone else was right now. She mentioned that Sir Robert's connection at Barnaby's had never heard of Oliver Renell and finished with the news that, the night of the car accident, Micah had merely given the police a copy of the intake form for each active case they'd been working on. "And Micah promised to check and see if he can find his old answering machine. He remembered Dad calling and leaving a message on his house phone Friday before the accident. But he said it hadn't seemed urgent; he recalls thinking he'd talk to Dad Monday if he didn't get him by phone."

Aunt Midge let Avery and Tilly hash over the details of the last few days while she finished the hemline of the gorgeous gown. When she finally stood, she arched her back and stretched her arms up over her head. "Off you go." She helped Tilly down. "That's about enough of you being twice my height. Wilder will be here for our early dinner in an hour. You've got some serious packing to finish before we leave for the airport tonight, Matilda Marie."

When Avery began to follow Tilly to her bedroom to help, Aunt Midge stopped her with a hand on her arm. "I'd like a word." Tilly shot a worried look over her shoulder and hastily entered her bedroom, shutting the door. When Aunt Midge said she'd *like a word*, it typically meant she was unhappy with one of them.

"Auntie, I'm sorry—" Avery began. It was always a good idea to get in front of it.

"Hmm," Midge interrupted, shaking her head. "You know I try not to interfere." She placed a hand on each side of Avery's face, gently forcing her full, silent attention from several inches lower. "But you are my beloved niece. You and Tilly mean more to me than my own life. I do hope you realize that? Your parents entrusted me to keep the two of you safe and healthy. That's not easy to do if you're working against me."

Avery nodded. "You're right."

"No more secrets between us, Avery. Not one more. Please, if not out of concern for your and your sister's lives, then for my own sanity."

Avery's eyes widened. "Auntie." She bent, pulling the woman's small frame into an embrace. "Tilly's safety, all of our safety, is my greatest priority. I'll absolutely tell you if anything strange happens again, I promise."

"Wonderful." Midge loosened her hold. "Now go ahead; I'm glad you're home early. Your sister needs some assistance packing. She's had her suitcase at the foot of the stairs since nine this morning, and I believe all she's got in it are your mother's floral scarves."

Avery lugged Tilly's suitcase back up to her room. Why on earth had she thought it made sense to pack like that, trips up and down the staircase? By the time Wilder arrived to take them to dinner, Tilly's and Aunt Midge's bags were neatly waiting by the front door and Avery had even put together a little carry-on package with miniature Snickers bars, a small blank journal, mint chewing gum, a compact coloring book and colored pencil set, and fuzzy pink socks with pictures of kittens all over them. Tilly's audition was at eleven tomorrow morning, and if it went well, she'd have the opportunity to be part of a prospective student showcase tomorrow evening. Avery had a momentary pang, wishing she was going with them; but then Halston would have to be boarded for two days and she'd fall behind on the MOA job.

At the O'Shannahan, Lilac Grove's pub and the best seafood place around, Tilly perused the London Conservatory of Music's website, reading little tidbits of information aloud to the group at the table. The school had been founded in 1928 and had concert facilities in London, LA, and Nashville, though only the London site had an education center. If Tilly was accepted for a callback based on her audition, Avery would be able to watch her in the live-streamed showcase.

"I can hardly believe you might be away in London this fall," Wilder said, smiling at Tilly. "Do you remember being there as girls? You must have been only eight or so, right? Your aunt and I tried to make sure we hit all the major attractions in that brief trip." He looked at Midge.

"Good memory," Midge told him. "Tilly was seven and Avery a squirrely fourteen when we took them. What a lovely trip," she said, reaching across the table and giving Wilder's outstretched hand a quick squeeze.

Tilly spoke. "I can't wait to see it again. *If* they accept me. I don't remember much."

"I remember," Avery said, swallowing a bite of deep-fried butterflied shrimp. "You sucked up all our time at Buckingham Palace trying to make the guards smile. Or laugh, or even just react. You wouldn't budge when we had to leave; you threw yourself down on the pavement and pitched a fit until Aunt Midge said she wasn't going to let you feed the pigeons unless you stopped."

"I have no memory of that," Tilly said. "It must not have been that bad."

Wilder chuckled.

"Oh, it was bad," Aunt Midge said. "Now's your chance at a do-over."

Tilly nodded. "I know I can get a reaction out of one of them. I'll try harder this time."

Laughter erupted among the foursome at the table. "I don't think that's what she meant," Avery said. "But I'd love to see you try. You're going to get in, Tilly. I'm sure of it. You've got Aunt Midge's talent for singing."

At the airport after dinner, Wilder unloaded the luggage from the back of his Subaru Forester. They all said their good-byes, and he and Avery stood and watched Midge and Tilly head toward security and the gates beyond until they weren't visible anymore. On the way back to Lilac Grove, Wilder asked Avery if she'd thought much about the Emperor's Twins dragon itself in terms of what made the medallion so important.

"From Mom and Dad's notes, and everything I've learned about Chinese culture around the time of both the Xiang dynasty and the Han dynasty, which preceded it, dragons embodied good fortune and luck for those who were deserving. In Emperor Xiang's case, my guess is the medallion was additionally significant because dragons convey imperial power."

Wilder nodded. "Interesting. And aren't rubies important in Chinese culture as well?"

"Yes, rubies are one of the most valued gemstones. They're said to originate from Buddha's tears. Which makes the absence of one of the medallion's eyes a great loss, whether you look at it purely from a financial value standpoint or from a historical standpoint."

"Well, you've taught me something," Wilder said. "The whole case sounds fascinating."

"My parents would have agreed with you," Avery said. "It is pretty cool that I get to pick up where they left off. Micah and I hope to have the medallion on the lab counter in front of us by the end of this week."

Wilder turned into the driveway to drop Avery off, and it struck her that he'd spent the last couple decades seeing Aunt Midge in the city, and now, since Avery's parents had died, he'd been making the long trek all the way up here to Lilac Grove without a word of complaint. He lived on Riverside Drive on Manhattan's Upper West Side, near the university where he taught. It hadn't been necessary for him to drive Tilly and Midge to the airport tonight; Avery could have done it. But Wilder had insisted.

"Fingers crossed you'll find you've got a long-lost dragon eye on your hands," Wilder said, putting the car in park as Avery gathered her things.

She leaned across the front seat and kissed his cheek. "That's the hope!" She got out and leaned down, peering through the window. "Thank you so much, Wilder, for dinner and for taking them to the airport. You're the best. We're all lucky to have you." Maybe it was unnecessary to say so. But since losing her parents, she'd been trying to do better at telling the important people in her life what they meant to her.

He cleared his throat and shrugged. "Your aunt filled me in on what happened today . . . and on all the odd occurrences since you took this assignment. I'm not sure it's safe for you to be here alone. Is there a friend you could call to stay the night with you?"

She shook her head. "No one close by." It wasn't exactly true. Hank was twenty minutes from here, south toward Manhattan. Not that she'd consider calling him. And her best childhood friend, Rachel, lived in Lilac Grove. Avery thought about her every time she ran through town past Mixed Bag, Rachel's little secondhand shop. But she'd lost touch with her friends here when she moved to Philly, and she'd been consumed this past year with just getting through losing her parents as well as the reunion and then ugly breakup with Hank. She'd dropped the ball in the friendship arena in both states. She missed her old friend and roommate, Brianna, but she hadn't reached out since she'd moved back. And she hadn't seen Rachel since the funeral. She'd have to remedy that.

Wilder frowned. "Midge didn't have any qualms about you being here on your own while they're gone?"

She smiled. He was so sweet; she was twenty-five and he still worried about her—and about doing right by Midge. "I don't think it crossed her mind. She did say, when she and Tilly spoke with the officer who took their call, he was going to pass everything on to the same pair of detectives who handled the accident last year. Aunt Midge said the officer didn't seem to care much about the guy who came here today until she brought up the strange notes we've gotten and Halston smelling like Dad. The officer said they'd send someone out here right away if anything else happened."

"Well, I suppose it's all right then. I think I should still like to see you inside." He exited his side of the Subaru and walked up the porch steps with her. "Did Midge or Tilly give the police a description of the man who came here?"

"They tried. They disagreed on some details. I guess he had a slouchy hat on and a scarf pulled up around his neck and chin; not much of his face was visible to describe. Probably on purpose," she said, shuddering. She unlocked the front door, and Halston greeted them excitedly the moment they stepped into the foyer, his furry body dancing between them. The Afghan loved company. "I've got the best organic alarm system around," she said, laughing.

Avery kept the promise she'd made Wilder. She and Halston went room to room and checked all the locks. The rich fried-seafood dinner and the nighttime drive to and from the airport worked like a drug on Avery. She'd been knocked out for what seemed like hours when Halston's loud, jarring bark startled her awake. She sat up in bed, hearing the dog growl his way down the hallway toward the stairs. For a moment she was frozen. Should she get up? Where was her phone? What time was it?

"Hey," she hissed. "Halston!" She kept her voice a loud whisper. She couldn't hear the dog anymore. She didn't hear anything at all. Heart pounding in her throat, she silently swung her legs out of bed, feet flat on the floor. She crept to her open doorway and then realized she hadn't grabbed her phone from the nightstand. Once she'd tiptoed back and gotten it, she looked frantically around her bedroom for something else. Something to wield as a weapon. If someone was downstairs, what was she going to do? Creep down there in the candy-cane pajamas she should have put away after Christmas and nicely ask the intruder to please leave?

Her gaze rested on the gazelle sculpture her mom had given her on her twenty-first birthday. Wrought iron and with its legs outstretched midsprint, it'd have to do. Avery wrapped her fingers around the hind legs, surprised at how heavy it was. It had sat on her dresser the last four years, untouched except for when she pushed it around to dust. The gazelle represented Avery's speed.

She peered out into the hallway from her bedroom, chest rising and falling quickly. She dialed 911, and when the dispatch operator picked up, she whispered, "Someone's in my house. Nine-three-oh-eight Maplewood."

"Ma'am? I can't hear you. Can you repeat that? Can you get to a safe—"

Avery frantically hit the volume-down button, but she couldn't silence the operator completely and she didn't know how far down the hallway the woman's voice on the other end of the line would carry. Her finger hovered over the red hang-up button, but then she thought of every mystery Tilly had ever made her watch. Could the police really trace a call and send help, like in movies?

Halston yelped from downstairs and Avery jumped, the phone flying out of her hand and hitting the floor with a thud. She sucked in her breath, eyes enormous, her fight-or-flight instinct kicking in and logical decision-making on hold. Halston half barked, half yelped again, an ear-piercing, dread-inducing sound, and Avery raced down the hallway, iron gazelle in her raised hand.

Chapter Ten

Avery took the stairs so fast she skipped the bottom four, crouching into her barefoot, silent landing and then running toward the office, where she could hear the dog's muffled, distant barks along with scratching, scraping sounds. She stopped short as she reached the open office doorway, stunned to see a figure in dark clothes hunched over her mother's desk, throwing papers and items out of the drawers. The intruder even had the gall to turn on the desk lamp so he could see better! Avery clenched her teeth together as she realized he thought no one was here. He thought he had the house to himself, except for the dog. Halston!

The scratching noises were coming from the closet door on the far wall, past William's desk. Avery's gaze darted back to the man at the same exact time he realized he was being watched. He made eye contact, registering shock. Avery couldn't move. Her body was paralyzed, her limbs frozen. The man came straight for her.

Her body unfroze a split second before he barreled into her like a train. Avery threw herself into the doorjamb and out of the way. He brushed by her and her right hand swung round, the weight of the gazelle leading and hitting him hard on the back of his neck and shoulder before it slipped from her grip and struck the wall. She was already pushing off the doorframe and moving toward the closet as she heard him bellow in pain and slam onto the hardwood with a thud that shook the floor under Avery's feet. Without thinking, she hoisted her father's desk chair and heaved it at the window, relief washing over her for a moment when it shattered the glass and went through. She threw open the closet door, not allowing herself the split second it might've taken to hug the dog or look for injuries but instead shouting at him, terror smoldering around the edges of her command. "Halston! Come!"

The dog initially lunged straight toward the doorway and the man groaning and getting to his hands and knees in the hall just beyond. *"No! Halston! Now!"* She grabbed at his fur, grasping his collar, and he turned, whining but coming to her side. She climbed through the window, the glass shards catching and tearing her pajamas. As she balanced with one leg out the window, finding a foothold on the siding eight or ten feet from the ground, she saw the man get to his feet in the office doorway. Her heartbeat thudded wildly in her temples. She couldn't pull the dog through with her; she had to trust that he'd obey. "Halston!"

She dropped to the ground, the dog came through almost on top of her, and they ran, Halston so close at her side that his fur brushed up against the skin of her leg through her torn pajamas every few seconds. Avery ran full throttle toward the nearest neighbor's house, trying not to think about how long it'd take to cover the ten-acre distance between her house and theirs. The unsolicited thought that Halston normally trotted ahead of her, could easily outrun her, floated through Avery's mind, and she pushed it away. He was with her and they were okay. That's what mattered.

She chanced a look back and spun around, facing the house and slowing down. The figure was coming down the front steps toward a car he'd pulled right up onto the lawn by the porch. He threw something in, across to the passenger side—probably everything he'd just stolen from the office. It looked to be just one person. She hadn't seen anyone else. Encased in the dark along the tree line and finally feeling her pulse begin to slow, Avery watched the car speed down the driveway. It turned left onto the road, away from town, kicking up gravel and dust. The taillights receded, and Avery and Halston began walking back toward the house, sirens breaking the night air from the direction of Lilac Grove and heading her way.

So it was true. They'd been able to track her location and send help. Her cell phone must still be connected somewhere upstairs in her room.

Avery made it back to the front yard, but the wide porch steps seemed impossible. She sat down in the cool grass, noodle legs collapsing beneath her. Halston leaned against her and awkwardly, slowly, lay down beside her. She put a hand on the side of his face, stroking his muzzle, and the big dog let out a forceful sigh and rested his head on the lawn. He was hurt. He must be. She'd heard him. What had that horrible person done to him to force him into the closet? Hot tears streaked down Avery's cheeks, and she struggled to calm herself as police cruisers pulled into the driveway. The more she worked to breathe deeply and calm down, the harder she cried and the worse she shook.

Two officers and a paramedic surrounded her, asking her questions: what happened, are you hurt, who broke into the house, what was taken, did you recognize the intruder, is the dog hurt.

At that she was finally able to speak, to get a few words out. The sound of her own voice scared her. The last time she'd sounded this way was the night of the accident, in their upside-down car. She focused on the paramedic in front of her. "I think he's hurt." She kept one hand lightly on Halston's side, feeling his fast respirations, her stomach making a sickening, lurching motion at the knowledge that the dog would never normally remain lying down with all these people around. Halston unharmed would have been bounding to each one, soaking up the attention.

The paramedic—Bev, according to her name badge—was perfectly suited to her job. Her sympathetic expression calmed Avery more than she'd been able to calm herself so far. "He does seem to be pretty subdued. We'll check him out. Tim?" she called over her shoulder.

A fellow paramedic joined her, carrying a large red bag. He crouched down beside Bev.

"Now, hon," Bev spoke. "My friend Tim here is going to help this big fella, if you'll let me check you over? Can I get your blood pressure?"

Avery nodded, and Bev went about unpacking items from the bag to get Avery's vital signs. Avery gently stroked Halston. She wanted him to know she was there and would help him, the same as he'd done for her. Tim set a bright electric lantern on the grass, casting a circle of light around them. He gently ran gloved hands over Halston's body, then began checking each leg.

"Can you tell us what happened?" One of the police officers spoke at Avery's left. She looked up and saw the man wasn't wearing Lilac Grove uniform blues but dark denim jeans and a brown leather jacket. He bent one long leg and knelt on a knee, which looked a little difficult for a man of his height, bringing him closer to eye level with Avery.

She blinked, frowning. It was Art Smith from this morning. Had that only been this morning? It felt like days ago. What was he doing here? She didn't need a museum guard! She needed the police! She shook her head. "What—?"

"I'm Detective Smith. Art Smith. With the Springfield County Sheriff's Department. I'm going to help you."

Avery stared blankly at him. "I don't understand. You're not. I need to speak with the police. You're them?" She was incredulous. She knew she sounded idiotic. "You work for the police too? Detective Smith. You're the detective I've been leaving messages for. Right? Are you?"

He nodded. "I had to make sure your loyalties were in the right place, Ms. Ayers, before we spoke. I'd planned to call you tomorrow, but then dispatch sent us out tonight."

"It's the leg." Tim the paramedic spoke from Avery's other side. His brows were furrowed in concern. "The left front, here." He moved his hand over the damaged area, hovering an inch above the dog's lower leg, which Avery now saw was deformed.

"Oh my God." She bent and rested her forehead against the Afghan's ear. "I'm so sorry, buddy. Good boy, Halston. We're going to help you." She echoed Art Smith's promise.

A police radio crackled from somewhere outside the circle of light, and a woman Avery took to be Smith's partner came over to them, updating them on the team clearing the house. "The officers inside say point of entry was the patio door, broken lock. There are a few kitchen cabinets and drawers open, papers scattered. The perp was looking for something; he must have found his way to what appears to be a study or den. Small pool of blood in the hall outside the doorway and office window broken with outward impact, likely point of exit. Blood visible on the glass shards. Tire tracks on the front lawn there and over there." Holy hell. The entire chaotic race to save her own life and Halston's all neatly tied up in a twenty-second summary. Sounded like they'd already figured it all out. Avery hoped they were as adept at finding out who'd done it.

Detective Smith was nodding, listening. "Thanks, Klein." He addressed Avery. "What I'd like to do is this. Let's get you into the ambulance—"

Avery's eyes widened at this, and she saw that there was indeed an ambulance now adding to the collection of first-responder vehicles in her driveway.

The detective continued. "Springfield County Hospital will check you over while we get your friend here loaded into the back of Officer Perry's patrol car and take him to the twenty-four-hour vet clinic in Dogwood Heights. They take emergencies." He raised an arm over his head, motioning for two additional officers Avery hadn't even noticed. Smith leaned over toward Tim. "What do you think? He's a pretty large breed, but I think Afghans aren't typically aggressive. Maybe three or four of us can do a sheet lift of the dog? In case of any other injuries."

"No!" Avery blurted. "No. No you aren't sending me to the hospital; I'm fine. I'm a hundred percent fine. I'm going with my dog. Check me out here, do what you have to do, but I'm going with him. And please," she said, swallowing hard, "please be careful with him."

"Now listen, hon," Bev said, getting Avery's attention. "Look here." She pointed to Avery's thigh, visible through the torn pajamas. "You're bleeding. Here, and here, and also your arm." Bev lifted Avery's right arm. Long cuts were scattered over Avery's legs and the underside of her right arm, and as she looked closer, a triangle-shaped shard of glass jutting out of her forearm caught the light.

"Oh," she said, recoiling. "I think I'm going to be sick."

Bev produced an emesis basin for her and calmly held it at chest level for her. "That's all right. Take some deep breaths for us."

"Ugh." She chanced another look at the glass shard, the nausea passing. "That's disgusting. Can you take care of it here? Please, Bev? It hardly hurts."

"I cannot," the paramedic said firmly. "You've got little pieces embedded in your thigh here too. It'll go much quicker and smoother in the ER. You've really got no choice, hon."

Avery looked down at Halston. The dog's eyes rolled up toward her and he wagged his tail against the lawn, whining. "I can't," she murmured. She couldn't just send Aunt Midge's dog—their dog, as Halston had become part of the Ayers family since Midge moved in—to the emergency vet by himself. He'd be terrified. And what if it was something worse than a broken leg? What if the doctor had to speak with someone about decisions or treatments? Whom could she call? She thought of Wilder. "What time is it?"

Tim answered her. "It's two fifty-five AM."

She closed her eyes. She couldn't call Wilder. And she couldn't send Halston without a familiar face. She just couldn't. "I'll go to the hospital," she said, still keeping a hand on the Afghan. "But I have to make a call. Could someone get my phone? It's upstairs on my bedroom floor."

* * *

Detective Art Smith rode in the back of the ambulance with Avery and Bev. From up front, Tim gave them an update.

"Officer Perry says to tell you your dog is doing fine. They're five minutes out from the clinic."

"Thank you," Avery called. "Detective, why, again, were you at MOA? What was that about?"

"I've been moonlighting there a couple shifts a month. I schedule them for when I know you'll be on an assignment. I tried to keep a low profile; I wasn't at the hospital long the night of the accident, but I was concerned you might recognize me."

"Sounds a little creepy," Bev said, raising an eyebrow at Avery and making her laugh.

"I suppose it does," Art Smith said. "But it's not. I've been keeping tabs on you since last year."

"Oh," Bev exclaimed, winking at Avery, "now, is that supposed to make it sound less creepy? Because . . ." The paramedic let her voice trail off, her expression skeptical and cracking Avery up.

The detective scowled at the two of them. "That's not helpful. Shouldn't you be trying to keep her blood pressure down or something?"

"Laughter is the best medicine," Bev stated. "And this girl's blood pressure is perfect, even after a race for her life across her front lawn."

"Nice," Avery said. Maybe she'd fare better than she expected in the marathon. Assuming she lived that long. She and Micah needed to finish authenticating the damn gem, get their hands on that medallion, verify that the ruby either was or wasn't the missing dragon eye, and be done with it. Sheesh.

"Anyway." Art hadn't cracked a smile yet. "I've felt—no, I've known—ever since I handled the accident report last year that something was off with that case. With that night, the way it happened. I can't give you all the details yet, but I have reason to believe the crash may have been intentional, and the same person or persons are now stirring up trouble for you. And from everything you've said, I do feel it somehow involves the ruby you're in the middle of evaluating at MOA."

Avery was speechless. She'd thought when she lost her parents that there was no worse grief. But now, to be told that it hadn't been an accident? That her parents might have been killed, and over one of the antiques they had been working on?

Oblivious to the activity in the back of the ambulance, Tim called back to them. "All right, Avery, they've just carried your dog into the clinic, and your boyfriend was already there waiting for them. He's planning on staying until Halston gets released."

Avery closed her eyes, taking a deep breath and exhaling slowing. What a relief. Halston knew Hank well. At least he'd know someone was there with him. "He's not my—" She interrupted herself. What did it even matter? No one in this ambulance cared who Hank was to her. She was just so grateful he was such a good guy. "Tim," she called. "Please thank Officer Perry for me and ask him to thank my boyfriend."

"I take my cat to Dogwood Heights Vet Clinic," the detective told her. "Don't worry, they're good. They'll take care of your dog. Of Halston. Perfect name for him, by the way." Art finally smiled.

"Oh good. Detective, can you tell me what those notes I've been receiving are about? Who directed me to find you?"

He shook his head. "I can't tell you that."

She sighed. She'd guessed as much. "Can you tell me anything at all about why I was warned off the case? Is it something to do with the collector?"

He looked curious. "The collector?"

"Oliver Renell, the collector who submitted the current gem we're verifying and appraising with the hope that it might possibly be the missing dragon eye. I thought possibly Renell could be . . ." She paused. She couldn't bring herself to say it; he'd think she was crazy.

He watched her, waiting expectantly.

"Never mind. You've never heard that name before? Renell? He's a little mysterious, won't meet in person or talk on the phone with us, wouldn't come to MOA to meet with the curator."

Art was writing in a tiny spiral notebook he'd just pulled from his inside chest pocket. "Spell the last name. Where's he from? Do you have a home address for him?"

"*R-E-N-E-L-L*. And no, we don't. All we have is his hotel information. Something strange with him. He sent the jewel by courier to the curator when he submitted it. This thing is greater than ten carats. If it's real, it'll be worth hundreds of thousands or more."

The detective's eyes grew big. "Oh wow. That is odd."

The ambulance rolled into the receiving bay at Springfield County Hospital, and Bev got out to speak with the nurses who'd take over Avery's care. Avery put a hand lightly on Art Smith's arm. "Listen," she said, keeping her voice low. She hadn't wanted to tell anyone but him, in case the items somehow hadn't been stolen. "My sister and I had been going through some of my parents' files from around the time of the accident. We had everything locked up in the home office. I ran through there so fast, I have no idea what the thief took. Could I tell you where to look, if you're going back to the house?"

He nodded, leaning forward with his elbows resting on his knees. Close up, without the standoffish attitude or the low visor of his MOA security guard cap, Art Smith was a good-looking man. His eyes were a hazel-ish shade of brown, under prominent dark eyebrows that complemented his Johnny Depp cheekbones and chiseled jawline, which was only minimally visible under some serious five-o'clock shadow. "Yes," he said, in answer to her question. "I'm headed back to your house as soon as they take you in. Listen, we'll get to the bottom of this. This isn't the right time or place to discuss it, but I do believe your parents were the victims of foul play. There's evidence suggesting the car was sabotaged that night. You need to be careful. It's a good thing the perp tonight thought the house was empty. You said something about your sister's suitcase being in the foyer all day?"

"Yes." Through the ambulance doors, she heard Bev say the word *dog* and then, a minute later, *dead parents*. What a sweet woman; she was letting the hospital staff know a few important details before she handed things over. Avery knew they were almost out of time.

"The man who tried to get your aunt and sister to let him in earlier must have seen the suitcase. And then with your aunt's friend driving all of you to the airport and your car put away in the garage, I can see how they drew the wrong conclusion," Smith said.

"Well, for Halston's sake, I'm glad I was home."

Bev threw open both ambulance doors. "All right, hon, ready?"

Art Smith tucked a business card into Avery's small purse, which his partner had fetched for her along with her phone. "Send me details about your parents' things. I'll be in touch soon."

Avery picked up her phone and put it back down several times while waiting alone in her curtained area in the emergency room. She so wanted to talk with Aunt Midge or Tilly. But she didn't dare let them know what was going on, not right before the voice audition.

By seven AM she'd been released from the hospital, the new proud owner of sixteen stitches. She instructed the Uber driver to take her to Dogwood Heights Vet Clinic. On the way, she called Micah at home in Harlem and told him there was no way she could come in today. She knew she was letting him down, as they were so close to finishing the authentication of the ruby and moving on to the medallion phase. But her house was torn apart, her arm where the glass had been was now throbbing, she had to find someone to come install a new office window, and she didn't even want to think about whether or not the thief had found the items she and Tilly had locked up to be gone through another day. Micah chided her for apologizing and said he'd be at her house in a couple hours to board up the broken window until it could be repaired. She loved that man.

True to his word, Hank was sitting alone in the empty lobby of the vet clinic when Avery came through the doors. She was acutely aware now of her appearance: bedhead, torn red-and-white candy-cane pajamas, pink high-top Converse sneakers because they were what Detective Klein had grabbed for her to wear when she'd gone in for Avery's phone. Avery joined her ex-boyfriend on the bench and hugged him, pushing the nagging voice in her head away that cautioned her against getting personal.

"I owe you," she said. "Big-time. I'm so sorry I had to wake you and ask you to come."

Hank shrugged. His bedhead looked much sexier than Avery's. His pajamas were just plaid bottoms and a black tee that had no business looking as good as they did on him. "You know

I love Halston. He's a great dog. The nurse—vet tech—came out ten minutes ago to say the doctor was closing up, whatever that means."

"Ugh." Avery cringed. "It sounds like closing up an incision. Poor dog. I can't believe that asshole did this to him. The police had better catch the guy. I want a minute or two alone with him when they do." Hank had phoned her once the veterinarian had had a chance to assess Halston, while Avery was being stitched up in the people ER. He'd gently broken the news to her that the dog's leg was fractured in two places and would have to be surgically pinned. Any surgery posed a risk, especially to a senior dog, and Halston was eight.

"Yeah, anyone who'd do that to an animal should serve jail time," Hank said. "He was only doing his job, trying to protect you."

Avery felt her bottom lip quiver. Hank was right. She hoped Halston would pull through. It wasn't even eight AM and she was thoroughly exhausted. All she wanted to do was collect her dog, go home, and crawl into bed and sleep until everything made sense again.

Hank put an arm around her and pulled her into him so that her head rested on his shoulder. "I'm sorry this happened," he said. He touched his lips to the top of her head, a light kiss through her hair. "Halston will be okay, don't worry."

Avery closed her eyes. She couldn't remember at all why they'd broken up.

The snap of a door closing jarred her awake, and she looked up to see a doctor in blue scrubs and a lab coat walking toward them. She rubbed her eyes, noting that the wall clock now read 9:22 AM. Holy cow, she'd slept on Hank on this hard, uncomfortable bench for over an hour.

"I'm sorry, I didn't mean to fall asleep," she said, looking up at Dr. Morgan. He was smiling.

"Halston is a very strong dog," Dr. Morgan said. "The bones came together fine with the hardware. He'll have a cast, and he should be able to come home this evening. He just needs some time and rest and he'll recover nicely."

Chapter Eleven

Micah and his son Noah were sitting in the rocking chairs on Avery's front porch when she and Hank pulled into the driveway. Micah met Avery halfway across the lawn and folded his fatherly arms around her. The short nap at the vet clinic had helped her state of mind; she felt at least capable of handling what had to be done now.

Micah let go of her so she could give Noah a hug too. Both men's expressions reflected worry. Avery glanced down at herself. "I'm a mess. Let me change, and I'll get coffee going. I'm so glad you're both here. Thank you."

Avery had grown up babysitting Noah and Tilly anytime the Abbott and Ayers families got together. Tilly and Noah were only a year apart, and now somehow Noah was set to begin an important internship next week and her little sister might end up in London this fall for school. In the two years since Noah's mom had died, he and his dad seemed to have become a close-knit team of two. It was just the two of them now in their Harlem brownstone, when only a handful of years ago they had been four. Micah's sweet, elderly mother-in-law had lived with them until she passed, and then Micah and Noah had lost

Cicely only a year later. Avery's heart swelled with pride at how focused and driven Noah was, even with all he'd been through.

"Are you okay?" Noah asked, eyeing her arm and leg.

"Yeah, pretty much," she said, touching the bandage on her throbbing right forearm. The numbing agent they'd used to extract the glass and stitch it up had definitely worn off. "I got a few cuts from the broken glass. I think I was lucky nothing worse happened. I'm more tired than anything."

"You're very lucky," Micah said. "Noah and I brought breakfast." He pointed at the carry-out boxes on the porch table. "Pancakes and bacon and a carton of hot coffee. You'll feel better after some food."

"Oh, guys. Wow. Thank you. Go ahead inside, maybe put everything in the dining room if nothing's torn up in there. I'll be right in." Avery turned toward Hank, still standing by his car. "Hank, will you join us for pancakes? It's the least I can do."

Hank shook his head. "Thanks, but I've got to get to work. You'll be all right here?" His gaze moved from Avery to Micah, who was now following his son up the porch steps. "Do you want me to bring Halston home later today, when he's ready? You know I work near the clinic."

Avery bit the inside of her cheek, thinking. She could feel the line blurring between amicable exes and something more. She couldn't let him take care of picking up Halston. "No," she said, coming back over to him. "I should pick him up; the vet probably has instructions for me. And you've done plenty already. You must be tired. I'm sorry you've got to go to work instead of back home to bed." She frowned. She shouldn't have mentioned going to bed. That was one part of their relationship that had always been pretty great.

He shrugged. "It's no big deal. Get Micah or his son to stay here tonight, will you? Or maybe you should just stay with me."

"Oh." She had a panicked moment as she realized she hadn't thought about being here alone tonight. At the same time, her cheeks burned as she thought of a sleepover with Hank. She couldn't go down this road again; she'd done a lot of work since they'd ended things. She was over him. Wasn't she?

"Or someone," Hank said. "You shouldn't be alone."

Well, she'd certainly misread that. "I'll make sure someone stays with me. You're right. Um . . . thank you, seriously. For everything."

In the house, Avery skipped the pancakes for the time being and headed for the office. Whoa. She stopped short in the hall. While she'd been at the hospital, a full crime scene investigation had taken place. Yellow police tape was strung across the doorway. A small pool of blood had collected on the hardwood in the hall, where the intruder had fallen after she'd hit him. A yellow plastic number marker sat beside the blood, another one next to the wrought-iron gazelle on the floor ten feet or so away, below a large dent in the wall. She peered into the office and then gingerly ducked under the yellow tape and took a few slow steps inside. More yellow number markers were scattered around the office. The sheer curtain had been dragged through the window and was caught in jagged sections inside the frame, eerily billowing up and down in the breeze. The closet door stood open against the lilac bushes her mother so loved outside the window. Rows of scratches from the dog were visible on the door and floor inside. The sight made her cringe; he'd been frantic to get out and protect her. She turned and saw the gilt-edged mirror on the wall in place and intact.

She exhaled and closed her eyes, relieved. She grabbed a tissue from an end table and used it to peek behind the mirror, finding the safe still locked and untouched. The thief hadn't found the keys, thank goodness. Of course he'd never think to look in the odd places they were stowed. She knew she shouldn't be in here, beyond the crime scene tape. But it was her house, and this was her business. She had one more thing to check and then she'd go. Careful to avoid going anywhere near the debris or yellow markers, she moved through to her parents' desks, almost afraid to look. When she did, her heart sank. Every drawer was pulled at least partially out, papers, notebooks, pens, and other items lying around the desks, and the deep, lockable drawer on the right side of her father's desk had been pried open, the wood splintered around the lock. The folders and her mother's little boxes inside were gone.

"It looks like the desks have been cleared out." A deep voice spoke from the doorway, and Avery jumped a mile, spinning around. "Don't do that!"

It was Art Smith—sheesh, he'd scared her. "I was hoping I interrupted him before he got to the files." Her tone sounded as frustrated as she felt. The detective had never gotten back to her after she'd texted him, asking him to let her know if the mirror and her father's large maple desk had been tampered with. She ducked under the yellow tape and moved along the wall to avoid the blood in the hallway. "What do I do about that? About all of this? Can I start cleaning everything up?"

"Yes, my forensics team has finished in here. I'm hoping the blood sample will tell us something, but he'll have to already be in the system for that to pan out." He pulled a card from his breast pocket and handed it to her. "This is a cleaning crew people sometimes use after an incident like this. It's up to you.

Homeowner's insurance will usually cover the cost; make sure you include that in your claim."

Avery sighed. "I hadn't even thought of that. I've got my work cut out for me today. They went through the kitchen too, I saw. I haven't walked through the rest of the house yet. God. I can't believe they took every single file we had on the Emperor's Twins medallion. And a couple of my mom's organizing boxes; I don't even know what was in them." She was so aggravated.

"The rest of the house looked fine to us. And the kitchen didn't seem to have much damage, just a couple drawers and cupboards opened and papers pulled out before the perp made his way through the house and found your office. I thought I'd let you see for yourself what was taken. I'm sorry about the files. You said there are some things behind the mirror too though, right?"

"Yes," she said. "The safe was still locked when I checked."

Noah appeared from the dining room. "Is it all right if I get into the garage to cut the wood for your window, Avery? Dad and I already got the measurements. It's going to rain soon."

"Yes! Please, Noah, that'd be great." She turned back to Art. "My colleague's son. They brought breakfast, if you'd like some, Detective."

"Art. Please. I've eaten, thanks. I just came by to check and make sure you and the dog are all right. I see they got you squared away." He motioned to her bandages. "How's Halston? My partner was a little worried; she didn't know what the outcome was after dropping him off at the clinic."

"He's still at the vet, sleeping off the anesthesia from surgery. He'll get to come home later today. They had to set the leg with pins and put a cast on." She winced, thinking about it. "When you catch the guy who did this, I hope you'll charge him with abuse for what he did to our dog on top of the break-in."

The detective nodded once. "That's my plan. Speaking of catching him, how would you feel about giving a description to a sketch artist to supplement the statement you gave last night?"

Avery's eyes widened. "I could try. I'm afraid I only saw him for a second. You might be better off getting my aunt and sister to describe him. It only makes sense it was the same guy."

"Our composite artist will benefit from all three of your descriptions. Let me grab her, and she can start with yours for now."

The detective went back outside and returned with the artist. Avery was surprised he'd brought her with him, but he explained that the sooner the victim gave a description, the more accurate it typically was. She didn't like him referring to her as *the victim*. But she supposed that's exactly what she was.

Avery sat with the artist, doing her best to recall details of what she'd seen, from the first moment he'd made eye contact across the room to when she'd been halfway out the window and seen him get up. It was harder than it looked on television. Dark hair; very dark eyes, almost black; a knit cap pulled low over his ears. No identifying marks such as tattoos, a mole, scars; the man had been covered except for his face and hands. When the woman turned her sketch pad toward Avery, it was as she'd expected: the vague figure of a dark-haired man in a cap. She hoped Tilly and Midge would have more to offer when Art put the artist in touch with them later today via video chat, well after Tilly's audition. She made the artist promise to hold off until after she'd had a chance to talk to them herself first.

Art passed on one more piece of information before he left. He rested one hand on top of the open car door while the artist put her things in the back seat. "Listen, Avery. I dug around a little this morning for anything I could find about your collector Renell."

"Oh! What did you find?" *Is he real?* she wanted to ask, but it sounded so dumb. Nevertheless, she held her breath, hoping, wishing, she might be right about Renell and her father.

"Well, you're right. There's definitely something odd about him. I pulled phone records and a credit check on that name. Of course he's not the only Oliver Renell, but I've got him pegged, based on him being in New York this past week. Your guy has almost no credit history since 2013. Prior to that it gets hard to track. No cell phone records either. It gets weirder. I can't find any residence connected to him. No history of paid utility bills. No credit cards."

Avery's stared at him, rapt. "What does all of that mean?"

"Generally, it means he doesn't want to be found. He's using cash for everything. He must have a burner cell phone that he discards every few weeks. Without having any bank account information, I have no clue where he gets his cash. I do know I'm tracking the right guy, because Renell purchased a couple flights using cash. The FAA won't let anyone fly without proper identification on record, even though he used cash. So Renell did fly to Munich around the time he told your curator he came into possession of the jewel. And I have him arriving back in the city at LaGuardia two days prior to submitting the jewel to MOA."

"Do you know what he looks like?" Avery blurted the question out before she could think about it. "Okay, I know this is crazy. But how do you know for certain that Renell isn't an alias? A pseudonym for William Ayers? My dad."

Art Smith drew back a bit, giving Avery an assessing look. "How would that be possible? I'm sorry. I'm sure you're hoping that might miraculously be the case. But how?"

"I don't know," she said, disappointed. What had she expected? For Art to say her dad was alive and living at Beckworth Suites?

"I wish I could tell you that Oliver Renell was your father. I'm sorry."

She nodded. "Yeah. It was a crazy idea."

That afternoon, against Micah's advice to act sooner, Avery called Aunt Midge. She'd gotten a call from Tilly a little while ago that she'd let go to voice mail. She went outside and sat on the front porch to get away from her cleaning efforts on the bloodstained floor while Micah and Noah worked on getting kitchen cupboards and drawers back together. Four PM Avery's time was one PM West Coast time. By now, Tilly should know if she'd made it through the first round of auditions, and there'd be a little downtime before the prospective student showcase. Avery was positive her little sister had done well.

She was proven right. Tilly answered Midge's phone, her face on the video-chat screen lit up the way it always was on Christmas morning. "I did it, A! Oh my God, it was so fun! You wouldn't believe that stage; I've never seen one that huge. The instructors and vocal director weren't scary at all—everyone was super nice. I screwed up my first line, and they even let me start over. We had to wait for results—we were going to call you as soon as we knew, but you beat us to it!"

Avery smiled widely into her phone. "I knew it! I'm not surprised at all! Congratulations, Tilly, you deserve it."

"I know! I mean, thank you!" She laughed at her faux pas. "I'll send you the live-stream link, but you should be able to find it in search too. They still have to review my transcripts and essay and all that, but I am *so excited*!" Tilly bounced a little on the screen, making Avery laugh.

"Good! You should be!"

"Auntie said Wilder was so worried about you last night when he dropped you off. Everything's all good? Put Halston on—I want to give him a video smooch."

Avery's stomach dropped. "Uh. Is Auntie around? I need to—"

"Yeah, yeah, she's here; let me boop my puppy's nose and I'll give her the phone, okay? I need to take another shower before tonight; I spilled salsa on my dress, and it got in my hair."

Neither of them was especially coordinated around food, especially when they were nervous. "No! Not your black gown?" She knew she was delaying the inevitable.

"No, the blue dress I wore for auditions. Dude, is he outside or something? Here, talk to Auntie and let me talk to Halston when you're done. Gotta go." The view on Avery's phone screen tilted to the white ceiling of the hotel room before Aunt Midge picked it up.

Midge put her face a couple inches away and peered into Avery's eyes. "Your sister is bouncing off the walls."

Avery pulled the phone away, stretching her arm out. "Auntie, just hold the phone normally. I can see you fine."

"Ah. That's right. These silly things," Midge said, fussing with the phone. It finally went still, and her face came on-screen. She appeared to be sitting at the table in their suite. She'd propped the phone up on something. "She's showering, and then we've got to get some food in her before the showcase. I've never seen her so keyed up. It's fabulous, Avery; she's thrilled. Your parents would be so proud."

"Yes, they would." Ugh. *Just rip off the Band-Aid, Avery.* "Auntie, I'm going to tell you something, but I need you not to freak out. It's all under control. Someone broke into the house last night." Midge's face had gone pale on Avery's screen. She barreled forward. "I called the police, and they came right away, and they're working on finding the person who did it. I think it was probably the guy who came to the door yesterday, saying I'd sent him."

It took a moment before Aunt Midge spoke. "You're all right?"

Avery nodded vigorously. "I'm totally fine." She was suddenly mindful of the white bandage on her forearm and arched her elbow slightly, making sure to keep her arm off-camera. Midge would be home soon enough, and she'd deal with that little white lie then. "The house is mostly okay too; whoever that man was wanted information on the Emperor's Twins medallion. Nothing else was taken. I've just got some cleanup to do, and Micah and Noah came to help." Should she mention the office window? She might be able to get that replaced before Midge and Tilly got back Friday.

"Let me hang up and call the airline. We'll get a flight home as soon as Tilly's done with the showcase tonight."

"No!" She'd been afraid of this. There was no reason they needed to rush home. "Auntie, Tilly has dreamed about this audition and trip for so long. Let her have it. Please. I swear to you, everything will be okay here. The detective that worked on my parents' case is handling this, and he's great. Micah and Noah will stay here with me tonight, and I'll call a friend to come stay tomorrow night, and then you'll be home. And the police are going to have cars drive by and check in every so often, too, until they catch the guy." She'd thrown in the thing about Micah staying on impulse, so now she'd have to ask him, and she had no clue what friend she'd thought she was going to ask for tomorrow; she'd figure it out. But Halston. The dog was front and center in her mind. She had to tell her aunt.

Midge was silent, her expression drawn and pensive. She turned and looked over her shoulder as Avery heard Tilly call out from the shower—something about a tour the next day.

"What'd Tilly say?" Avery tilted her head, wishing she'd heard.

Aunt Midge closed her eyes for a moment and then opened them. "She's asking if Zac Efron's house is on the Hollywood tour we've booked for tomorrow. As if I know." She mustered a tiny smile. "Avery, I'm not comfortable staying here knowing you're in danger."

"I'm not. I'm really not. The break-in was never about hurting me; it was to get the files they wanted, and they got them. It's over. But, um, there's something . . . Auntie, Halston was super brave; he ran right toward the commotion last night. And . . . he got hurt." She frowned and looked down. "I'm so sorry. I couldn't stop him. He's okay," she said quickly, seeing her aunt put a hand over her mouth. "He's going to be fine, the vet said. But he's got a broken leg. He'll have a cast."

Aunt Midge was visibly choked up. She didn't speak.

"Auntie," Avery said softly. "I'm so sorry. I did get him out of the house and away from the guy. He was such a good dog; he listened and followed me out. The vet seemed very confident he'd be just fine. I know how much you love him. I'm sorry."

"I love all of you," Midge said firmly. "Of course I love that dog. He's been with me through thick and thin. All right, my dear, I'll compromise. I won't change our flight yet. But you have to keep me updated. If anything at all changes—with you, the house, Halston—we're coming home. And stop apologizing," she added. "None of this was in your control. It sounds like Halston did his job."

"Yes he did. I'm staying home from work until you're back Friday, so he won't be alone here. So don't worry about him, all right?" Now she had two things to discuss with Micah. Though she didn't see how it could be helped; she couldn't leave the dog alone in the house with a cast and pins in his leg.

"No." Midge shook her head. "No. You've got to get this thing wrapped up, one way or another. Go to work. I'll call the dog sitter and get her to stay at the house during the day while you're gone. I'll have her there by eight tomorrow morning. Listen." She looked over her shoulder again. "Your sister is shouting now about plans after the showcase tonight. I'd better go. Love you. Keep me updated," she stressed, before hanging up.

Avery came in from the porch to the delicious aroma of Micah's famous stew. She was so thankful to have him—it was almost as good as having her parents here. He and Noah had reassembled the kitchen, repaired the couple drawer fronts that had gotten damaged, and somehow made her bright, inviting kitchen even cleaner than when she'd left it yesterday.

As it turned out, they'd come prepared to stay overnight. Noah had nailed the board up over the broken window, and the glass company would be out after work tomorrow to put the new one in. Avery had taken care of calling her homeowner's insurance and making the claim, she'd gotten the locksmith out earlier today to install new locks throughout the house, the kitchen and office looked great, and she'd thrown a rug over the repeatedly scrubbed and treated bloodstain on the hardwood floor outside the office doorway. By the time Aunt Midge came home, nothing would really be amiss except for Halston in a cast and the broken bottom drawer of William's desk. She'd pushed getting into the safe to the end of the day, anxious to see what was left of the possible trail to her parents' work on the medallion, but it was after midnight before she finally sat down on the couch. Her eyelids snapped open again an hour later and she stumbled up to bed, secure in the knowledge that all was safe with new locks and Micah and Noah in the house.

* * *

Halston's sitter, Stefanie, was on the front porch at seven forty-five the next morning. Under one arm was a brand-new plush leopard-print dog bed, a large bag hanging from her hand with the Pampered Pet logo on the front.

Avery led Stefanie into the family room, where Halston was set up like a king on his perfectly fine old dog bed, surrounded by pillows and toys and his water bowl and snacks. "I'm so glad you were free today," she told the girl, who looked to be close to her own age. "He's getting around on the cast without much trouble, and he doesn't act like he's in pain. He tried to chase a squirrel this morning. I'm sure I wouldn't be doing as well."

"I'll swap out the beds when he gets up to go out later," Stefanie said, smiling. She unpacked the bag, setting out several new toys and treats and a new, handsome red collar. "Your aunt had all of this paid for and ready to be picked up last night; she insisted he needed it. Hi there, boy! How's my buddy doing?" Without a word to Avery, the girl pulled couch cushions onto the floor beside the dog, building a makeshift little couch for herself near Halston, careful to avoid the blue cast on his leg. The daughter of one of Aunt Midge's many friends, Stefanie was halfway through veterinary school and had been Halston's exclusive sitter for the last three years. He loved her.

Avery had no qualms at all about leaving the dog as she rode with Micah and Noah into the city. Noah dropped Avery and Micah at MOA on his way home to the brownstone in Harlem.

Francesca was at the elevators, waiting, when she and Micah arrived.

"I was on my way up to see you! The elevators are taking forever today." Francesca changed her large Chanel bag to her other arm and flipped her long, shiny black hair over one shoulder. "Are you okay, Avery? Goldie said you had a break-in. How awful."

She nodded. "Yes, I'm fine, thank you." She'd explained just a little of what had happened when she'd called yesterday to let Goldie know she and Micah wouldn't be in as planned but would be back to MOA Thursday.

"Good! Well, I'm excited you two are back. Oh! Finally," Francesca said as the elevator doors swished open. Once their trio was in, she pressed the third-floor button and continued. "Goldie says today might be the day? She's so hoping the gem Renell submitted will be a perfect match for the eye socket in the medallion. Have you finished the appraisal yet on our potential ruby?"

"Almost. We have a little more to finish on the gem, but we should be looking at the medallion by this afternoon."

"Wonderful! Fingers crossed for an easy task once you're at that point," Francesca said. "I'll come up with you. I'd love to see the gem without the gold housing on it."

The elevator car stopped on the second floor and they shifted, making room. The doors opened and Tyler Chadwick stepped in, registering surprise as he saw them.

"Well! Hello there," he said, smiling. "Oh no, are we going up? I keep getting lost in this place; it's like a maze."

"You all know each other, right?" Avery asked. She had mixed feelings about the man, after their date and then seeing him speak so closely with Francesca the next morning.

Francesca glanced at Avery. "Oh! Um—"

Avery looked at Tyler, who was studying his coffee cup.

"We do," Francesca said, sighing. "Please don't say anything to Sir Robert, Avery. I know how he'd feel about this."

Avery's eyes widened. *Holy wow.* She'd half thought she'd been overreacting, wondering what they'd been talking about, but now it seemed she hadn't. Poor Sir Robert!

Francesca went on. "I'm secretly an enormous superhero fan. I collect the Firefly comics, I've seen the first movie four times, and then when I found out *the* Tyler Chadwick was at *my* museum, well . . ." She looked sheepishly at Avery and Micah and then rolled her eyes over to Tyler. "I couldn't help asking for an autograph. I know it's silly. Sir Robert won't watch anything except French art films and documentaries. He'd judge me so harshly if he knew I went all fangirl on a movie star."

Avery chuckled. "His movie tastes are a little pretentious. Don't feel bad."

"Thank you," Francesca said, relief in her tone. "And you were so great," she told Tyler.

He flashed his gorgeous movie-star grin. "No big deal. I love what I do."

"He even took a selfie with me," Francesca said sheepishly.

"Nice," Avery said.

Tyler stayed on when their trio exited at the third floor. "Have a good day, all," he said as the doors closed.

"He must have to deal with fans all the time," Francesca said. "He was so gracious about it, even though I'm sure it gets old."

She nodded. "He really doesn't seem to mind." That exchange she'd witnessed sure made a lot more sense now, especially knowing that Francesca felt self-conscious about being mildly starstruck.

"Not a word to Sir Robert, please," she reiterated. "He'd never let me live it down."

Avery smiled at her. "Don't worry, your secret superhero crush is safe with us."

Chapter Twelve

Francesca had left for her office after marveling at the striking red jewel, all of it now fully visible. Avery and Micah had been focused and relatively silent, working, when Micah sucked in his breath and straightened up. "We've got it. Check this out." He pointed at the screen on the laptop that was connected to their Raman spectrometer, a lab tool used to show the molecular structure and chemical composition of material. "There's virtually no iron or lead at all in this stone. We know that lead, even in trace amounts, can point to a lab-created ruby. And when we're searching for growth lines, curved lines that can betray a synthetic, there just aren't any. And look at these readings."

Avery bent and scanned the screen more closely. "The iron content—or lack of it." She pulled cotton jeweler's gloves on and lifted the ruby using the locking tweezers, peering at it through her handheld loupe. "I've never seen this level of fluorescence. It's so much more apparent now that it's out of the gold housing. This can only mean one thing. This is a Burmese ruby, isn't it? Oh my God, Micah."

He nodded. "I know." His eyebrows were raised in excitement, mirroring Avery's. "But I'm not jumping to conclusions.

We still have to get the exact cut dimensions and angles and do a full comparison to the existing ruby and the empty medallion setting to know for sure if this is *the* ruby."

"Yes. But this." She looked at him. "This is a sixteen-carat natural Burmese ruby. I mean, that in itself is incredible. I'd say the odds are pretty darn good that it's the missing dragon's eye."

Twenty minutes later in the lab, Avery and Micah explained their findings to Goldie Brennan, who stood between them, hands pressed together palms to fingertips in a prayer position at her chin. The septuagenarian looked from Avery to Micah and back, grinning widely.

"I knew it," she whispered. She shook her head before either of them could speak. "I understand you've still got to evaluate the medallion. But what a find. Goodness."

"I expect our collector's going to be pleased," Micah said, glancing at Avery.

"Oh yes," Goldie said. "I'll notify him today. Our tentative contract wasn't contingent on it being the dragon's eye. I believe he'll accept the generous MOA purchase offer."

There it was—her shot. Avery widened her eyes at Micah and jumped in. "Goldie, Oliver Renell and I have been emailing back and forth quite a bit. He's an interesting man. Relatively new as a collector, at least here in the States." She was winging it a little too well, her tongue running on before she could reel the lies and half-truths back in. "It'd sure be great for us, for MOA, to work with him again sometime. I mean, look at his first submission."

"Absolutely. Impressive, to say the least. I agree."

"Right. Did you know I literally go right past Beckworth Suites where he's staying every single day?" That wasn't a complete lie. She passed it whenever she was going to Midge's Fifth

Avenue apartment. "Why don't I stop by today and give him the good news in person? Judging from our correspondence, I highly doubt he'd agree to come here in person to sign the purchase contract."

Goldie turned toward her. "Hmm. That's a nice idea. Much better than an email or phone call. Yes, if you don't mind, I think that'd be perfect. We've already sent over the boilerplate terms, so he'll be familiar with the details. I'll draw up the contract for you by this afternoon. You're a third-party contracted appraiser, so you'll be able to sign as a witness. Are you comfortable with that?"

"Of course. I'll stop by your office before we leave today and pick it up, along with his contact info—room number and phone number. And," she rushed on, to keep Goldie from thinking too much about releasing that information to her, "I'll shoot him one more email and let him know I'm stopping by to discuss some good news."

"Perfect," Goldie said again.

The guards arrived to take the ruby; Avery had called for them so she and Micah could go to lunch. She looked up hopefully when the door opened, expecting to see her new friend Art, but she was disappointed. Well, he'd said he worked minimal hours there, and it was basically to keep tabs on her. She should hear from him eventually; he'd promised to update her on the break-in investigation.

They might as well not even have gone down for lunch. Neither she nor Micah could focus on eating. Twenty minutes after taking the ruby away, the same two guards brought it back, along with the Emperor's Twins medallion. Avery donned her gloves and carefully took the medallion out of its case and set it on the thick black velvet jeweler's cloth. It was heavy with the weight of not only the twenty-four-karat gold but also the many jewels and ornate design. She stepped back and stood with her hands clasped behind her, taking in the large, striking medallion, inlaid pearls and small sapphires and jade gemstones surrounding the ferocious dragon looking back at them with one beautiful ruby eye. She was at a loss.

"How do we begin?" she asked Micah. He'd been in this line of work a lot longer than she.

He also stood back a bit from the medallion in reverence. "Not sure I know. I've never worked with something this intricately designed before."

Nate Brennan came through the door. "Grandmother told me! Oooh. Let me see." He joined them at the lab counter top, standing between them to look at the piece. He rocked back on his heels and then forward, peering more closely at the medallion and the possible missing ruby eye. "Dang. Sure looks like it matches to me! This should be easy, right?"

Avery rolled her gaze past Nate toward Micah.

"It really does!" Micah read Avery's mind with no effort at all. "Let me show you how we determined for sure this morning that we've got a sixteen-carat natural ruby on our hands here."

It worked like a charm. Nate followed Micah to the laptop still connected to the spectrometer. While Micah launched into explanations about chemical makeup and molecular structure, Avery gently handled the medallion as she put it through preliminary tests, including weight, dimensions, dimensions of the raised dragon, and dimensions of the empty eye socket, entering each value into her own laptop as she went.

Nate finally got bored with the science end of things and came around the counter, pulling up a stool to watch Avery's process. She glanced at him. "Tyler Chadwick said you two bonded in the smoking area the other day. He was almost as excited about the ruby and medallion as you are."

Micah cleared his throat loudly. "It's fascinating, I agree." He frowned at Avery.

She didn't care that Nate was Goldie's grandson. If he was going to work in this job for the long haul, he needed to take it seriously. She turned back to the medallion.

"I, uh . . ." Nate became still on the stool, quieting his bouncing knee. "Should I not have mentioned it to him? I don't think I gave him any secret details. I don't actually know any secret details about all this." He chuckled.

"Goldie typically likes to keep things close to the vest while we're in the middle of the appraisal process, that's all," Avery said. What *was* it about this guy that just pushed her buttons?

"Oh. Sure, that makes sense." He was quiet for the next minute or so. "What do those measure?" he asked, eyeing the calipers in her hand.

She closed her eyes and breathed in deeply, then resumed her work. "These are vernier calipers. They measure distance between points on the gemstones down to point-oh-two millimeters."

"Wow." He fell quiet again.

Avery could tell he was making a concerted effort not to irritate her. Keeping her eyes on the medallion, she spoke. "Your grandmother probably has something big planned to announce the restoration of the medallion at the charity gala, if we're able to confirm this is the long-lost dragon eye." To be fair, Goldie seemed just as excited as her grandson. But she was nowhere near as annoying.

"She does!" Nate leaned forward on his stool. "She's already talked to several potential advertisers for when she does the press release. She wants to add a silent auction to the event, with a pair of annual all-access passes to MOA and exclusive viewing of the Xiang dynasty exhibit when the medallion is unveiled."

Avery stopped working and turned to look at him. "Oh. That's um . . . a lot. I hope this all pans out," she said, looking at Micah on the opposite end of the lab. That had gotten his attention as well; he was already staring at her.

"I think it will. She doesn't seem worried, anyway; it's not like it's her money she's working with. It's all marketing and advertising dollars or whatever. Oh. Sorry," he said as his phone rang. He jumped off the stool and answered it as he walked to the door. "Hey. No, I don't have it all yet, I told you. Just go ahead and do it; you know I'll come through."

Nate was quiet for a moment, listening. He spoke again into the phone as he opened the door. "Not until, uh, hold on." He stopped talking, and the door to the lab swung shut behind him.

Micah moved to Avery's examination area. "That makes me a little nervous," he said.

"What does? Goldie planning an unveiling of something we haven't even verified yet? Setting up advertising and a silent auction for tickets to an exhibit that could very well end up being no different than it's been the whole last year? Or *that*?" She moved her head in the direction of the door Nate had just exited through, her hands still full with the calipers and medallion.

"All of it. And that phone call—I'm sure I'm reading too much into it, but it sounded like he owes someone money." Micah raised his eyebrows at her.

"It sure did. What was the *you know I'll come through, just do it* about? I mean, we don't really know Nate at all," Avery said.

"True."

Nate came back through the door, off the phone. "So sorry about that." He returned to his stool beside Avery's work area.

"You don't mind, do you? If I hang out for a bit and watch? I'll try to be quiet."

By four PM, Avery could no longer say she didn't know Nate Brennan. She was now an expert on all things Nate. She knew, for instance, that he'd been raised by his nanny while his mother climbed the social ranks and his father did something or other in stocks. He was sent away to boarding school at age fourteen. The rumor about him dropping out of art school to travel Europe was only half true; he'd graduated from Cambridge University with a fine arts degree before embarking on his two-year trek through Europe. The expedition was a soul-searching effort to discover his path in life, and he thought he found it at the age of twenty-four in Monte Carlo. For three straight months, Nate seriously entertained the idea of becoming a professional blackjack player. He was on fire, his winning streak the stuff of legends—until it ended. He'd wound up back in New York, broke, tan, a string of broken-hearted girlfriends left behind in Europe (as Nate told it), and in need of a reboot. His father had put him on an allowance and his grandmother had installed him as assistant acquisitions liaison. "I'm not like my dad; I'm just not smart when it comes to money. And I don't know anything about acquisitions," he said candidly. "Francesca is teaching me."

In addition to the detailed history of Nate Brennan, Avery and Micah now also knew his favorite color, food, cocktail, vacation spot, and designer. Surprisingly, she liked him a tad better than she had before. And she had finally pinpointed what she didn't like about him. He'd been handed everything. Which gave him very little appreciation for anything. Plus, the man had no clue how to be quiet.

What should have been accomplished with the Emperor's Twins medallion in three or four hours of lab time was pushed to Friday. Avery picked up the contract for Oliver Renell from Goldie and headed out to Beckworth Suites once she and Micah had finished for the day. She had the most nauseating combination of anticipation and dread, making her stomach do flips; she was about to see either her father, after a year of believing him dead, or Oliver Renell, who'd said there was something important they needed to discuss once the ruby was certified.

Micah had pushed her for details on how she thought she was going to see Renell, but she'd just said she had a plan. She did, sort of. And she hadn't emailed Renell to tell him she was coming; it was crucial that she arrive unannounced.

Avery pulled down the visor in her car and generously applied the makeup she'd stopped and bought at CVS on the way to the hotel. She took her hair down from the ponytail and mussed it, back-combing and then smoothing the crown and fluffing the long strands around her face. Shedding her tan blazer, she reached into the back seat and grabbed Aunt Midge's sparkly pink cardigan with feathered lapel. Midge kept a sweater in both their cars for whenever they were out to dinner or a movie; she tended to get chilled. On Avery's long limbs and frame, the cardigan was transformed into a trendy, cropped shrug, perfect over her all-black ensemble today. She checked the mirror once more. The look was more date night and less antiques expert. Now for the finishing touch. From the inner zippered compartment of her purse, Avery took out her dummy cubic zirconia engagement ring. She hadn't worn it since her last girls' night out with Brianna and Jenna in Philly. It always came in handy toward the end of the night. That diamond ring on her left hand spoke a thousand words to any overly persistent guy she just wasn't into.

She crossed Beckworth Suites' ultra-contemporary three-story lobby to the elevators, making a spectacle of digging around in her oversized purse. Producing nothing, she walked over to one of the console tables behind a couch and dumped out the entire contents of her purse, digging through it, sighing and huffing in frustration.

The concierge approached. "Ma'am? Might I help?"

Avery scrunched up her face, drawing the corners of her mouth downward as she looked at the man. "Probably not! It's classic Zoey, you know? I always forget something!" She wrung her hands, looking down at them to draw attention to the obnoxiously large "diamond" ring. "Mr."—she read his brass name plate—"Summers, you've got to help me."

Mr. Summers, a middle-aged man with thinning hair, had a kind face. His brow furrowed in concern. "What is it?"

"I'm surprising my husband. I mean, I was." She shook her head, trying to muster tears. Halston. She conjured poor, sweet Halston lying on his dog bed this morning with the clunky cast on his leg. She blinked as her eyes filled with tears. "It's our one-year anniversary. He's such a good man, he does so much for me, and I was going to surprise him. We're staying here while our kitchen's being redone, and I had to leave to take care of my mom. I was going to miss our anniversary, but she's doing so much better! He has no idea I'm even back. I've got champagne about to be delivered and I was lucky enough to get a dinner reservation at Silver Spoon—is that crazy or what? He's going to be so surprised! And now I can't find my stupid room key!"

The concierge listened, his expression reflecting sympathy and then changing as she finished. He looked immensely relieved. "I can help you with that! That's no problem. Do you have the card or the card number the room was reserved with?"

"Oh." Avery stared at him, wide-eyed. "Ollie handles all of that. I just mostly carry cash."

Mr. Summers nodded. "All right, no worries. We can just give him a quick call to confirm we're giving you an extra key. What's his full name and room number?"

She put a hand on the man's arm. "Oliver Renell, room eight twenty-two. I really wanted to surprise him. Please . . . how about if I leave you my ID, and I'll bring him down with me later to collect it?" She dug in her bag for her wallet. She had half a mind to pull out a fifty along with her license, but something about the man's demeanor told her not to try that. She tipped her head just a little closer to him. "Are you married, Mr. Summers?"

"Yes, fifteen years," he said, smiling.

"Oh, how wonderful. Then you know. You *get* it."

He raised his eyebrows. "What's that?"

"That you have to celebrate the little things." She wiggled her ring finger. "This is the second time around for both me and Ollie. You really have to appreciate the little things to make a relationship work. Make it all count. Right? I really wanted to surprise him." Avery looked down sadly.

Mr. Summers turned and went to the registration desk without another word. Two minutes later he pressed a key card into Avery's hand. He covered it with his other hand. "I know it shouldn't be necessary, ma'am, but I do need to hold your ID until Mr. Renell can call or come down. Do you mind?"

"Oh, I could kiss you!" Avery smiled at the man. She really could have. She handed him her sophomore-year fake ID. "He's going to be so surprised. Thank you, Mr. Summers!" She spun on her heel and headed for the elevators.

"Ma'am," he called out as she was about to step into the elevator, the ID in his hand.

Avery turned around, holding her breath. Was he about to mention her last name not being Renell on her ID? She'd say she hadn't had a chance to change it yet, or she'd kept her maiden name. She should have gone easier on tonight's makeup. She hadn't been thinking about how young she looked in her Zoey Stone photo. Yikes. "Yes?"

He smiled. "Happy anniversary."

She relaxed. "Thank you!"

Avery knocked on the door of room 822. The whole ruse to get the key was simply so she could make the elevator work. She remembered from a couple years ago during a gemology convention here that the elevator control panel required a room key to be inserted in order to press the floor buttons. She had no intention of invading Oliver Renell's privacy any more than necessary.

When there was no answer, she knocked harder. She pulled out the purchase contract for the ruby and scanned it, finding Renell's phone number on the third page. Not sure if she'd be calling his hotel room, a cell phone, or a house phone somewhere else, she dialed. She heard the room phone ringing in the distance, but no one picked up.

She hadn't planned for this. The man was so reclusive, it had never occurred to her that he might be out. Or possibly he'd seen her through the peephole and wouldn't answer. Which would make sense, too, if it was her father on the other side of this door, not wanting to be found. Much as she couldn't imagine her dad refusing to see her, Avery also realized she was missing several pieces of this particular puzzle. But she knew her happiness at seeing her dad alive and well would far outweigh how upset she'd be at him.

She shook her head. God. She was getting as bad as Tilly. All she was doing was setting herself up to be disappointed. *Stop it, Avery.* She knocked extra loud, one more time, with no result other than a grouchy woman down the hall sticking her head out of her room and yelling, "Get a clue, no one's home." Sheesh.

On impulse, Avery put the room key card in the slot, and the light turned green. She shot a furtive glance up and down the hallway as she entered Oliver Renell's room.

Chapter Thirteen

The man was dead.

Avery clapped a hand over her mouth to cover her scream. The man who had to be Oliver Renell had been shot in the center of his forehead and was lying faceup on the floor by the bed. If not for the gory bullet hole in his head, he would have looked as if he'd decided to take a peaceful nap on the floor. His navy-blue pajamas with white piping were still creased on the seams, and his slippers were on his feet. His complexion was the same shade as the pale-gray hotel room walls. He had to have been dead since at least this morning.

She stepped out into the hall, looking both directions and spotting a housekeeper pushing her cart. "Help! I need help, please! A man's been shot!" Despite his awful skin color, Avery darted back into the room and knelt by the man's side, reaching out a shaking hand to check his pulse at the side of his neck. His skin was cool and unyielding, that give, the softness under the surface that indicated life, missing. There was no pulse, no movement from his chest. She recoiled, pulling her hand back and standing. This was very much not William Ayers. The weight of disappointment was crushing. Avery closed her eyes, drawing in a hitching breath. She hadn't wanted to get her hopes up; she'd tried to prepare herself for this, for learning her father was really gone, but real tears now seeped from under her eyelids, and she covered her face with both hands. Some part of her had believed she'd find her dad when she opened that door.

Half a dozen people crowded into the room at once, talking, giving orders, going through the motions of verifying there were no signs of life. In need of somewhere to look that wasn't the dead collector, Avery's gaze rested on the small corner table. The hotel notepad, pen, and Renell's laptop sat on the tabletop, perfectly neat and perpendicular to each other. The bedside table held Renell's phone, two equal stacks of quarters, and a small dish with a tie tack and cuff links, all tidy and in their place. There wasn't even a jacket slung over a chair. The hotel manager moved out of the circle of people surrounding Oliver Renell, letting paramedics and police close the gap. She gently put an arm around Avery's shoulders, leading her away from the body.

"You shouldn't have to see this, ma'am. Are you all right? Are you the one who found him?"

Avery nodded. Oh no. She shouldn't be here. Not as Zoey Stone, Renell's fake wife, and not as Avery Ayers, who'd conned her way into a room key. Her mind whirled with the horrible possibilities . . . but she couldn't be held accountable if Renell had been dead for hours, could she? Plus, she'd yelled for help.

"Are you his wife? Daughter?"

"Wife," she murmured, moving slowly backward in the direction of the elevators.

"Let me find a chair for you. You look peaky. We'll let the first responders do their job, and I'll sit right here with you until one of the officers comes to talk to you, all right?"

No! She had to get out of here. "Okay," she replied, and the hotel manager sped off down the hall in search of chairs. Avery took her chance and ducked into the stairwell, descending two flights before suddenly imagining the hotel manager telling the police that the dead man's wife had fled toward the stairs. She exited the stairwell and grabbed an elevator from the sixth floor to ground level. The concierge had his back to her, but that might not last. She went the opposite direction through the elevator alcove down a long hallway to the right, scanning the brass plaque on the wall: BANQUET HALLS A, B & C. She hazarded a quick look behind her, but the hallway was empty. Maybe there was an exit at the end of this godforsaken unending hallway?

"Wait! Stop!"

Avery's heart lurched, stopped, and then took up a wildly rapid pace high in her chest. The voice could be Mr. Summers or a cop. She wasn't sure, but she didn't look back. She ran. She pushed through the heavy, twelve-foot-high wooden door of Banquet Hall C and raced across the ballroom to the staff area, which thank heavens had an exit door on the opposite wall. The banquet hall door clapped closed on the other side of the staff door. Avery stumbled through the exit and found herself outside in bright sunlight. She looked left and then right, trying to get her bearings, and kept running.

Thank goodness she hadn't wanted to pay the exorbitant parking garage fee and had instead used metered parking two blocks away from Beckworth Suites. Ten minutes later she was on her way out of Manhattan.

Her entire body seemed to be vibrating, she was so unsettled. A call came in through her Bluetooth and she instantly answered, somehow sure it must be Micah checking on her. It wasn't.

"Avery, it's Art Smith." He sounded out of breath.

"Art?"

"You shouldn't have run."

She gasped. "That was you? Yelling at me to stop? You could have said so!"

"I didn't think I needed to. Avery. You just fled a crime scene you were the first to discover. Using an alias."

"Ugh! What was I supposed to do? There's no way I could explain why I had to lie to get up there! They'd have thought I was making it up, about him being so secretive and reclusive."

"Listen, I can't talk now. You're heading home?"

Avery glanced in her rearview mirror, sure he was following her. It'd be impossible to tell in this traffic. "Yes."

"All right. Go straight home; we've got round-the-clock surveillance set up at your house now. I do need to go over what happened this afternoon and get your description of what you saw. Do you mind if stop by for a few minutes around seven or so?"

When Avery hung up, she left a quick message for Stefanie at the house, letting her know that if she saw a car out front, not to worry; it was the police keeping an eye on things. She then called Micah and told him she'd just discovered Oliver Renell dead in his hotel room. She called Sir Robert after that and repeated the same details. Sir Robert did that thing he did when something surprised or perplexed him: a long, low whistle, typically followed by scratching his chin between his thumb and forefinger. She could almost see him doing it now.

"And you're fine? Did you see any sign of who might have done it?"

"No. I mean yes, I'm fine, but no, there was no sign, or at least I didn't see anything. I wasn't really in the room long enough to see much other than Oliver Renell dead of a gunshot wound to the head. I think he'd been dead several hours, or maybe even since yesterday. I don't know."

"Have you told Goldie yet? What about Francesca?"

Avery shook her head, even though she was alone in her car. "No. Why would I tell Francesca?"

"I don't know," Sir Robert said. "I could tell them, if that helps. Shall I call Goldie for you?"

"Yes, actually, please." All Avery wanted to do was get home.

"Oh," Sir Robert said before hanging up. "That Johnstone fellow called again for you. He won't say what it's about. You never called him back?"

Avery smacked her forehead. "I totally forgot." No wonder. The last few days had been a blur. "I'll call him right now. Would you read me his number?"

Edward Johnstone picked up on the first ring. "Hello?"

"Mr. Johnstone, hello. This is Avery Ayers. My colleague said you called for me?"

"Thank you so much for the call back, Ms. Ayers. I was calling to inquire about the large ruby you're working with currently. Have you verified yet whether it's a genuine Burmese ruby?"

Avery's voice caught in her throat.

"Ms. Ayers? Did I lose you?"

She cleared her throat, recovering. How on earth did this person know the exact type of ruby she and Micah were dealing with? "I'm here. You took me a little by surprise, I'm afraid. Who is your point of contact, please? Do you work for the museum?"

Now Johnstone took a moment before replying. "I've been . . . intrigued with the Emperor's Twins piece. I understand the recently submitted ruby is quite possibly the missing eye of the dragon. I was simply hoping for an update on your findings, if you might be able to share that with me."

Avery frowned, looking up to see that she was about to miss her exit to Lilac Grove. She quickly got over two lanes and merged onto the smaller highway that would take her the rest of the way home. "I'm sorry, Mr. Johnstone. I'm not in a position to release any information about our assignment. I suggest you get in touch with MOA's chief curator, Goldie Brennan, regarding any questions you might have."

"I understand." The man's voice betrayed a smidge of disappointment.

Avery had expected an argument but got none. "All right then," she said. "Have a good evening." She reached out to press the end-call button on her car's touch screen just as Johnstone spoke again.

"Don't let the ruby out of your sight."

"What did you say?"

"The ruby and the medallion should be under your eye alone or locked into Acquisitions Pending at all times. Trust no one." The line went dead with a click.

What in the world? Of course the ruby and medallion should be locked up at all times. Who was this Edward Johnstone, and how did he know about the ruby—that it was indeed a Burmese ruby and possibly the dragon's eye? And why was his name so familiar to her? She'd heard it from Sir Robert twice this week, but she didn't think that was it. Where had she heard the name Edward Johnstone before?

The last twenty minutes of her drive seemed to take forever. She burst through the door of her house, intending to head straight for the safe behind the mirror in the office. She'd already planned to go through the rest of those items tonight anyway, but she wanted to dive in right now. Halston greeted her in the foyer, Stefanie following close behind.

"He's feeling better!" The girl smiled at Avery. "He's actually had a good day. He's eaten three times, he took the pain pill with no problem, and he's obviously happy to see you! He got up when he heard your car at the end of the drive."

Avery knelt down and hugged the sweet dog gently around his neck and shoulders. "Good boy, puppy. I'm so glad you're feeling better!" She handed the dog sitter the folded bills she had ready; Stefanie was worth every cent. "I'm so grateful you were free today." Stefanie agreed to come back tomorrow and stay until Aunt Midge and Tilly got home in the afternoon.

After Avery and Halston had had dinner together in the family room, where Halston was nice and comfy, Avery emptied the safe behind the mirror in the office, carrying everything into the family room and spreading it all out on the coffee table. She glanced up, suddenly very aware of all the windows and open curtains in her house. She went room to room, closing window coverings and triple checking all the locks. Settling back down in front of the coffee table, Avery slowly perused the scattered items. Her mom had been a bit of a pack rat; she never threw anything away if there was the slightest chance it could important. Avery figured that was why she'd built a substantial collection of small decorative boxes.

The floral boxes from the safe varied widely in size from tiny enough to hold a ring to large enough to house a teacup, and there were miniature envelopes as well, and scraps of colorful paper with notes jotted down, a few newspaper clippings, several pens, and a few photocopies from what were probably library books. The collection was organized chaos. The first small box held around a hundred tiny multicolored paper clips. That was all. The next one Avery opened contained one lone bottle of Wite-Out. The third held a tiny set of highlighters. In the remainder, she found a combination lock, two watch batteries, two keys, and a red-and-black loupe.

As she sorted through the scraps of paper, two in particular jumped out at her. One was the article she and Tilly had seen that covered information about spinels, and the other was a square of orange paper with math figures in her father's narrow, slanted handwriting scrawled all over it. But not just any math. Avery recognized the numbers as an expression of chemical composition and refractive index, listed as 1.712 to 1.736. The number on the opposite margin, 3.59, was circled. Given the context, that number had to be the magnitude, also known as the specific gravity. Holy cow. Was she looking at her father's findings on the medallion's ruby?

But these numbers did not reflect the chemical composition of a ruby. It might seem insignificant to some, but tenths and hundredths were critically important in gemstones. Genuine natural rubies' specific gravity was slightly higher at 3.99 to 4.0, and the refractive index was also higher by hundredths. Had her father jotted these figures here as a context for the difference between a natural ruby and a spinel? Or was this the actual makeup of the dragon's existing ruby eye? She had to show Micah.

The doorbell rang at the same time Avery's phone did, making her jump and Halston bark, though he did it from his lounging position on his new dog bed rather than trying to get to the door. She patted his head to reassure him. The phone call was Art telling her he was at the door. She led him through to the kitchen, part of an open floor plan and separated from the cozy family room by the island counter top and stools. Halston watched them warily for a bit and then settled his head on his bed.

While Avery made tea, Art sat at the kitchen counter and opened a notebook in front of him, pulling out an iPad as well. "How are you feeling?" he asked.

"Like someone in one of Tilly's Sherlock Holmes mysteries. And not one of the cool, in-the-know characters. More like the clueless neighbor who keeps stumbling onto bits of information too late to do much about it. I'm so frustrated and angry about all of this!" She set the tea down in front of him and leaned on her elbows on the counter top.

"That's fair," Art said. "How about your cuts?" He pointed to her arm.

Oy. When the detective had asked *how are you feeling*, he'd clearly meant physically—how was she recovering after the break-in and trip to the hospital. "Not too bad. They sting, but as long as I stay busy, I don't think about them. Art, am I going to be in trouble? For leaving after I found Renell?"

"I took care of it."

"What does that mean?"

Art took a sip of his tea, cocking his head sideways at her. "Just that you don't have anything to worry about. Though you should probably avoid Beckworth Suites for a while. They do have you on camera, Zoey Stone." His expression remained deadpan as he slid her fake ID across the counter top to her.

"Listen, all I wanted to do was meet him. I just . . . a little part of me wanted to believe it was possible he wasn't really Oliver Renell. I know it's crazy to even entertain the idea that my dad is still alive."

"I talked to a friend of mine who's part of the investigation into Renell's murder. It was obvious the poor guy had been dead for a while before you discovered him. I don't think they plan to pursue the mystery woman who found the body. If he has questions, I'll deal with him—but seriously, Avery, at least involve me before you devise your next elaborate plan."

"How were you even there? Does your friend have any leads?"

"I told you I've been keeping tabs on you," the detective said, as if Avery should just get past it. "And I'm not sure yet about the direction of the investigation. They'll get into any points of contact he's had recently, to begin with. The scene didn't give them anything."

Avery's spinning thoughts quieted, images of the hotel room playing in her mind. "Renell's hotel room was definitely neat. Everything was in its place, even after someone came into his room and shot him. There was no struggle. What does that mean? Maybe that he knew his killer?"

Art raised his eyebrows. "Not bad. No struggle at all. You're good at this, but let's hope you don't have to play again."

"What does that mean? Should I warn my colleagues? Are we all in danger?"

He shook his head. "I wouldn't assume that. I'll keep you updated if I hear anything you should know, okay? And we're going to keep an officer parked out front until there's some progress on Renell's case."

"Thank you."

"I'm glad to see your friend is feeling better," he said, moving to Halston's area and tentatively offering a hand for the dog to sniff. Smith's gaze moved to the cluttered coffee table while he was stooped down, petting Halston. "What's all this?"

Avery joined him. "That's all that's left of my parents' things that we were going through before the break-in." She moved a few of the items around. "There's just so much I don't understand. Like, what are these keys to? Why are they in with all of these notes and articles? And there are notations from my dad that I need to show my partner, suggesting that the ruby they were working with may have been a spinel—a synthetic ruby. But I don't see how that's possible, with the medallion on display at MOA and my mother having signed off on the certificate of authenticity."

Art nodded, looking over the items and notes. "You're sure she signed off on it?"

"Yes. Tilly and I both saw the yellow carbon copy of the form, before it was all stolen. Mom's signature is very faint, understandably. It's dated two days prior to the paperwork being submitted to MOA and countersigned by MOA's curator. We thought her signing early was a little odd, but she was very busy this time last year. Tilly and I figure she signed in advance just to be sure it got taken care of. She was very organized. Anyway, the original copy stays on file at MOA. We would have gotten the yellow copy filed back in with our records as soon as Goldie signed, and then our inactive case records were eventually collected from the Manhattan office to be stored here."

"That might be something I could help with," the detective said. "We could at least request a viewing of the original document to make sure it jibes with what you and Tilly both saw before the break-in."

Avery stood at the front door and watched Art Smith stop and speak with the officer in the patrol car before he got in his own car and left. Something about his serious, calm demeanor made her feel less worried, more relaxed. He listened, he didn't minimize any of her concerns, but somehow he was able to put her mind at ease over them. Avery finally felt like she wasn't alone in this race to uncover what had really happened to her parents.

* * *

Early-morning and late-evening runs were the best for clearing Avery's mind, and she got a long one in at the crack of dawn Friday morning after going to bed at an unprecedented nine PM. Her four loops through town that day constituted the first time she'd ever run twelve miles with the police tailing her, an odd sensation. On her fourth trek down Lilac Grove's Main Street, most of the storefronts still darkened and sleepy, she spotted her friend Rachel sweeping the sidewalk in front of her eclectic secondhand shop, Mixed Bag. Forcing herself out of her comfort zone, Avery broke her own rules and slowed, jogging in place so she could say hello. Dr. Singh's words from the last therapy session played loudly in her head. They'd touched on why Avery hadn't seen anyone besides Hank and her coworkers since coming home a year ago. Her therapist's insights were quite often spot-on. *Reconnecting with friends here doesn't have to signal backward progress; you could view it as a step toward committing to a new life in Lilac Grove.*

Rachel graced Avery with a tentative smile. Avery didn't blame her for her hesitance. Her best friend from high school had sent her friendly little messages several times this past year since she'd been back, suggesting a quick lunch or coffee to catch up, and Avery hadn't even replied to most of them. It was about more than committing to Lilac Grove, she realized. Committing to a new life here would mean admitting her parents were really gone.

"Good morning, Rachel. Wow, you sure get started early, huh?" What a dumb way to begin such a long-overdue conversation. "I'm so sorry I've been out of touch." There. Better.

Rachel's folded-down apron layered over jeans and a loose, ruffly blouse lent padding to her already generous curves. She stood a few inches shorter than Avery. Her red hair was piled into a wild bun atop her head, tendrils escaping everywhere. She stopped sweeping and came to stand on the grassy strip between the sidewalk and Main Street. "It's okay. I understand, really." The woman shifted her grip on her broom. Her face was painted with thinly veiled concern. "How are you?"

"Doing better, I think." She smiled. "Maybe we could plan lunch sometime next week?"

Rachel's face lit up, and she bounced on the balls of her feet. "I'd love that."

Avery impulsively stepped in and hugged her friend. "Me too."

She felt lighter than she had in months on the drive into Manhattan later that morning. She should do that more often—push herself outside her comfort zone. Dr. Singh had better not be too smug when Avery filled her in at their next session. Avery had even invited Rachel to their barbecue tomorrow, and she couldn't wait to catch up with her friend.

She was relieved Aunt Midge and Tilly would be back that afternoon. They'd have to hustle to get everything ready for their annual summer party Saturday, but Avery had a grocery order coming later that day and was ready for the distraction of the party. The yard was freshly mowed and the patio just needed a little attention—cleaning up flowerpots and putting out all the new, brightly colored furniture cushions Midge had purchased for the occasion. She and Tilly and Midge would be busy that night making homemade potato salad and coleslaw, seven-layer dessert bars, and Aunt Midge's famous raspberry lemonade and marinating the chicken and ribs. It was exactly the kind of busy Avery needed right now.

Avery arrived in front of the Museum of Antiquities Friday morning to find it bustling with people—and not museum patrons. Several news media outlets and police officers were milling about in clusters. Another large group of people, some in varying stages of being costumed in spandex superhero garb and makeup, had gathered, and a pair of detectives were speaking with them. Strips of yellow police tape covered every one of the entry doors at the top of the wide concrete steps. A police radio crackled nearby, and Avery heard the words *security breach in the north wing*.

Chapter Fourteen

Micah picked up on the first ring. "Where are you?"

"I'm at the front entrance—well, as close as I can get. Where are you?"

"On my way." Micah hung up and spotted her a few minutes later, Sir Robert with him. They stood side by side, staring up the steps at the police tape behind the crowd.

Sir Robert spoke first. "A friend of mine at News Four says there's been some kind of possible break-in in the north wing. That's all I know."

"Goldie Brennan's office is in the north wing," Micah said.

"So is Acquisitions Pending," Avery added. Both men looked at her. "What if they took the ruby?"

Micah closed his eyes and shook his head. "No. I don't even want to think about that."

"The Xiang exhibit is in the east wing," Avery mused. "Yesterday, after we examined the medallion, they put it back in the exhibit, right? We shouldn't worry it was locked away into the pending area, right?"

Micah stared at her. "No! Why would you even say that?" He looked up toward the sky. "For the love of Pete, Avery. Take it back."

"Okay!" She laughed nervously. "I take it back. Of course the medallion's fine. I hope the ruby is fine."

"Okay, gang," Sir Robert said, standing between them. "Let's not get ahead of ourselves. This could have absolutely nothing to do with our MOA assignment. Francesca says there are always items coming and going here. We really know nothing at this point."

"Call Francesca," Avery said, looking at Sir Robert. "She'll know something."

He looked taken aback. "I can't just call her and ask her that. Our relationship is about so much more than our mutual interest in artifacts and antiques." His tone indicated hurt, as if her simple suggestion had insulted him.

"I'm sorry, Sir Robert," Avery said. She slipped her hand through the crook of his elbow and patted his arm. "Of course it is. I only meant it as a way for us to learn if we should make other plans for the day. She might know how long the museum's expected to be closed."

He nodded. "Yes. That's true. All right." He pulled out his phone, going to his contacts. Hesitating, he separated himself from Avery and walked up the sidewalk away from them to make the call.

She shook her head, looking at Micah. "He's so easily offended when it comes to her," she murmured.

"I noticed that too," Micah said. "They've been together a little over a year. I'd think that would be improving by now."

"Seems like he'd be more confident after a whole year," she agreed. "But you have to admit, there's kind of an odd dynamic there."

Francesca appeared and greeted Sir Robert with a quick kiss, the two of them rejoining Avery and Micah. She was quite obviously in conversation via her Bluetooth earpiece, simultaneously texting something on her phone screen as she shifted her purse from her elbow to her shoulder. "I believe that's it, yes. Please keep me updated. Kisses!" She yanked the earpiece out and dropped it into her Louis Vuitton Neverfull bag. "Ugh! Can you believe this? That was Goldie just now. I told her not to bother coming in; this will just upset her."

"What happened? Do you know anything?" Avery asked.

"Nate's the one who discovered it. You know the whole lower level at the north end of the building, where we have Acquisitions Pending, transfer items awaiting shipping, the shipping and receiving docks? It's just below Goldie's office."

The three of them nodded. Avery held her breath.

"Nate was down there and found a heating duct panel broken off. He thought it was suspicious, so he showed one of the guards, who called Goldie. She called in the calvary, I suppose just to be prudent." Francesca's tone and expression told them what she thought about the hullabaloo taking place on the front steps of MOA.

"Oh. Well, I guess it's lucky it wasn't anything serious," Avery said. "We can finally get caught up on some research for that coin collection we just got. Are you heading to the shop?" She looked from Micah to Sir Robert.

Micah nodded. "I'll walk with you."

"Great," Avery said. "I've got a couple things to run by you both, about the medallion," she said.

"I'm afraid I'm out for the day," Sir Robert said, looking over his shoulder now at Francesca, who'd wandered away to speak with one of the museum guards. "Francesca says it's the perfect time to do the botanical gardens tour, and I have to agree. But we'll see you tomorrow!"

Avery set out beside Micah, hoping he'd speak first. He didn't. "If Francesca said it's the perfect time to get hit by a bus, Sir Robert would gladly jump in front of one."

Micah laughed, looking at her in surprise. "That might be going a bit far. He's smitten, not suicidal."

"I've seen smitten." Wilder popped into Avery's head. "That's not smitten. I'm sorry, but that's a little beyond what I'd call a healthy balance in a relationship."

Micah tipped his head to one side and then the other. "Yeah. Well. You're not wrong. Though watching them makes me miss Cicely something fierce. I hope Noah eventually begins socializing in college, maybe goes on a few dates with someone nice. So far, he's so focused on his studies, he's never really dated."

"Aw. Give him time. The first couple years of college are a big adjustment. It sounds like he's doing amazing. He's such a kind, respectful kid, Micah. You and Cicely did a wonderful job." She started to say something about Tilly's crush but thought better of it. She'd hate for Noah to hear something Micah might accidentally let slip. If anything ever came of it, best for it to happen naturally. "I'm sorry you're missing her. Now, that was a relationship to aspire to," she said, giving him a small smile. Micah and his wife had been *that* couple, the kind who truly enjoyed each other's company. Avery hated that he now had to live without her.

"I appreciate that." He spoke for a bit about Noah's upcoming internship, and Avery reminded him of their shopping date on Sunday.

They were a block away from the shop. Avery dug around in her purse. "I'd hoped to get the three of us together to go over what I found in Mom and Dad's things, from when you all worked on the Emperor's Twins. Dad has some interesting notes; I brought them to show you. Where is it?" She frowned and peered into her purse.

"I meant to tell you, I did find my old answering machine, and the message from your dad is still on there. Remember, he'd left me a message a day or two before the accident?"

"Yes. What did he say?"

"It was nothing, just him reminding me about the medallion paperwork. I brought the machine in to give you." He patted his messenger bag. "Maybe you'd like to hear his voice again. Or maybe not. If that's a terrible idea, then please just get rid of it." His eyebrows were furrowed with worry.

"It's a sweet idea, Micah. I'd love to hear his voice."

Micah unlocked the front door of Antiquities and Artifacts Appraised and held the door open for Avery.

She filled him in on what she'd found in the archive boxes, pulling out the sheet of note paper with her dad's handwriting and numbers jotted here and there. "Were you in the lab together when he wrote down these figures? What do you think this is?" she asked.

"Let me see." He took it from her and moved to his desk, setting the answering machine out on an uneven stack of papers piled on his calendar.

Avery started the coffee and pulled her chair over to Micah's desk. She didn't know how he was ever able to find anything at all in this mess. He studied the slip of paper with William's handwriting on it while Avery searched for an outlet to plug in the answering machine.

"You found these calculations in with the other notes from the assignment?"

"I mean, generally speaking, yes. It was all kind of thrown in together. But look how he circled the specific gravity here."

She pointed. "These aren't the right readings if it was a natural ruby."

Micah stared up at Avery, frowning. "Right. That'd reflect the specific gravity of a spinel. Why would your dad have written this, unless he was suspicious the ruby in the medallion was a fake?"

"Well, I'm glad you said it. I was afraid to," Avery said. "But they must have ruled that out or redone their calculations prior to it being certified. Mom never would have signed on to the authenticity if the ruby wasn't real."

"Absolutely," Micah said, nodding. "She did sign, though. So it's got to be real."

There was too much that didn't add up for Avery. The odd date her mother had signed, the stolen files from the home office, the strange, cryptic messages, and now these numbers. "I'm not so sure." She finally spotted an outlet behind her desk and plugged in the answering machine.

William's voice rose into the air from the little speaker, and Avery's eyes instantly filled with tears. She hadn't been prepared for that. Even through the tinny answering system, it was still her dad.

Micah glanced up from the paper and quickly put an arm around her shoulders. "Oh dear. I'm sorry, honey."

She shook her head, smiling and wincing at the same time. It always surprised her that grief could still sneak up like this after a year. The so-called stages didn't always present themselves in an orderly fashion or stay gone once they'd passed. Dr. Singh said sadness marked progress from anger, but anger felt more tolerable to Avery, in spite of the way it wreaked havoc in her life. "No. No, it's okay. It's all good." She took a deep, shaky breath in. "I really miss him. Let me listen this time; I'm sorry. I didn't hear what he said." She pressed stop and then play again, breathing through the bittersweetness.

Micah, William here. I'm leaving the office now, but we should sit down before the Emperor's Twins document is turned in Monday. There are a few things on the, uh, paperwork. To discuss. All right.

That was it. Her dad had never signed off correctly. Ever. Even in a phone conversation, he'd rarely said good-bye. When he did, it wasn't actually *good-bye*; it was a *see you later, talk soon*, or something similar. But that wasn't what she was supposed to be paying attention to, was it? She looked at Micah. "He sounds awkward. Stilted."

"I noticed that this time around too. I think I was too over-whelmed, hearing his voice, when I listened at home."

"And you never had a chance to talk again after this?"

Micah sat back, frowning, staring through the papers on his desktop into the past. "Did we? I don't think we did. This message came in Friday night. I called him back but got his voice mail. He probably figured we'd catch up on Sunday. Now, in light of these numbers," he said, tapping Avery's scrap of paper in front of him, "I'm not so sure what we're going to find when we're back in the lab on Monday."

Avery stood abruptly, pacing. "Ugh. I don't want to be the one to tell Goldie her Emperor's Twins exhibit is centered around a fraudulent ruby. This sucks. I have so many questions and so few answers." Which made her think of another. "Edward Johnstone. Does that name ring a bell? He called here the other day and Sir Robert gave me the message, and then I missed another call from him before we connected. When I finally phoned him back, he said the strangest thing."

"Edward Johnstone was the collector who submitted the Emperor's Twins medallion to MOA last year," Micah said.

Avery stared wide-eyed at him. "What?"

He nodded. "Why did he call you? Why would his name have seemed familiar to you, I wonder?"

She smacked the desktop, scattering papers. "In those files Tilly and I found, with the history of the piece originally being submitted. I knew I'd seen his name somewhere. Yes, I remember, he was listed as the submitting collector. But what does that mean? Micah, he asked me about the status of the ruby we're currently working on. And then he gave this warning that was like something out of one of Tilly's mysteries. He said, 'Trust no one.' He told me to make sure we never let the ruby and medallion out of our sight or that it had to be locked up when it wasn't with us. But that's not new advice; it's standard protocol."

"That is very odd. There was nothing else in the archived items mentioning Johnstone or anything about an item not being handled correctly, was there?"

"No. There may have been something in the files that were stolen, but we'll never know now." She couldn't keep the frustration out of her voice.

The phone rang, and Micah answered it while Avery poured their coffee. The rest of the day dragged; it was tough to concentrate, knowing her sister and aunt were on their way home and knowing there were a plethora of things that weren't adding up, the latest of which being her father's cryptic phone message and the weird warning from Johnstone.

When Avery's phone rang on her way home that afternoon, from a private number, she answered it, expecting to hear Edward Johnstone's voice again. Instead, a muffled, deep, man's voice came on the line through the speakers in her car. "Use the key." The line went dead.

Avery hit the steering wheel, accidentally grazing the horn and startling herself when it blared. "Ugh! What? What key? Use what key? *Who are you?*" She didn't recognize the voice, but that was the point, wasn't it? To keep her guessing and off balance?

She was still fuming when she turned into the driveway, past the police officer stationed there. No number of ice cream flavors could cool her aggravation with whatever was happening. Halston was on the front porch, lying in the sun, and Stefanie's car was gone, which meant Tilly and Aunt Midge were home. Thank God.

Halston's happy greeting and the aroma of butterscotch and chocolate drifting to her the moment she came through the front door began to work their magic on her mood. She found Aunt Midge and Tilly in the kitchen, nearly hidden behind the biggest, most beautiful bouquet of pink roses she'd ever seen. Avery crossed to the counter where they stood and pulled them both into a tight hug.

"My girl," Aunt Midge said. "You must have been terrified. I still think we should have come home right away."

Avery shook her head. "No. I'm glad you stayed. I'm super excited for you," she told Tilly. "Who sent you flowers? They're gorgeous!" She reached out and turned the little white card so she could read it, and her breath caught in her throat.

Never stop at enough.
So proud of you, Lamb.
Love to you and Roo.

"They're from Dad," Tilly said softly. Her blue eyes were wide and hopeful, and Avery couldn't utter a single word of disagreement.

She nodded. "Yes. They must be."

Her younger sister's expression immediately relaxed, and Avery knew she was remembering the last time a message had come to the house. But how could Avery crush her sister's hope over this? She didn't have the heart to. No matter who the flowers were from—and Avery mused that they might even have come from a well-meaning Micah or Sir Robert or Wilder—the sentiment was just as perfect as the arrangement.

"I know Dad sent them. No one else would know about Billie."

When Tilly turned ten, she'd decided she wanted to sing. And not just in the shower. Church choir wasn't enough. A part in the elementary school play wasn't either. So Anne and William had found a voice instructor, and Tilly fell in love with song, and with jazz in particular. Avery still remembered William coming home one day with a rolled-up black-and-white poster under one arm and handing it to Tilly. Tilly made Avery take her to the big Crafts and Cloth store in Forsythia Hollow, a half hour away, so she could spend her allowance having it matted and framed. The image of Billie Holiday singing her heart out beside the quote on the poster still hung on eighteen-year-old Tilly's wall. The full quote from Billie read *Somebody once said we never know what is enough until we know what's more than enough.*

Avery put her face near the gorgeous roses and inhaled, closing her eyes. She smiled at Tilly. "You deserve them."

As they were clearing dinner dishes later that night, Midge spoke. "I saw the floor by your office. I can't even imagine what you went through."

"I can't get the blood out. The cleaning company gave me some stuff to use every time we do the floors, but it's not coming all the way out."

"Good," Tilly spoke up. "Who cares about the floor? I'm glad you hit him. The stain just proves how badass my sister is." She gave Avery one more quick hug and went back to squeezing the lemons for lemonade. Leave it to Tilly to lend some perspective to the situation.

"I'm glad you're home," she told them both. "So is Halston. He was the really brave one. He got himself hurt trying to protect me."

Aunt Midge made a kissy face at her still-regal Afghan hound, now sprawled out on the cool tile. "Of course he did. And he'll be fine, especially after he sees the hero's dinner I'm making him. Steak and liver."

*   *   *

Each summer, the Ayers family barbecue was a casual afternoon event, often stretching into the evening, that included the small Ayers family along with their closest friends. Last summer the party had been skipped entirely, as it had been scheduled for the weekend after the accident. Avery and Midge had discussed skipping it this year as well, but the get-together was needed more now than ever. Midge's core group of friends would attend, which meant her four closest girlfriends and their plus-ones, her long-ago fiancé Colin and his charming husband Prince Ivan, and of course Midge's good friend and wannabe suitor Wilder Mendelsohn. Avery had extended an invitation to Art on a whim, and Micah, Noah, Sir Robert, and Francesca, and even Goldie Brennan were coming. In a moment of weakness she'd even invited Nate yesterday, as they were leaving the lab. Tilly would no doubt have her close friends in attendance as well.

Avery, Tilly, and Aunt Midge worked tirelessly into the night Friday, preparing all the food, sweeping and sprucing the patio, and setting up croquet and the volleyball net on the back lawn. Tilly turned on the small globe lights they'd strung through the trees, and Avery went along and replaced the four bulbs that were out. The evenings were still cooler than the days this early in June, which meant perfect weather for a cozy fire when it began to get dark. Avery stocked the firewood nearby and set out a few extra candles, finally collapsing on the new, super-soft cushions on the patio swing beside Tilly. She tipped her head back and breathed in the scent of the lilac bushes all around them.

"I invited Rachel," Avery said. She wasn't going to mention Art, as he'd seemed a little caught off guard when she'd asked him.

"Awesome!" Tilly grinned. "Rachel was always your most fun friend. I've missed her. Eve and Mindy are coming, and maybe Chase."

"Really? Chase?" Tilly had dated Chase a few months ago, but they'd both agreed after a couple weeks that they were better off as friends.

"Sure. He and Mindy are a thing; it's cool. You said Noah will be here, right?"

She nodded. "Yes. He sounded excited to see you. Well, as excited as a nineteen-year-old boy can sound." Avery chuckled.

Aunt Midge spoke. "I called and thanked them both this morning before our plane boarded. It would have made your parents happy knowing Micah and Noah rushed out here to help you."

"I can't believe he spent the night here and I missed it. You could have told me. Maybe we would have come home early," Tilly grouched, making Avery and Midge laugh.

"I'm sorry," Avery said. "I assure you, after he'd helped me clean up the broken glass and repair the kitchen drawers and boarded up the office window to keep the rain out, then cleaned up after the glass company, we all went to bed early. We were a very boring group. You didn't miss a thing. You'll see him tomorrow and then all day Sunday when we help him find a few nice suits."

"I can't wait. If I can ever get him to look at me like a girl and not some kid he grew up with and ask me out . . ." Tilly addressed Aunt Midge. "I'm allowed to go out with him, aren't I, Auntie? He's not that much older."

"You'll be eighteen by end of summer, and Noah just turned nineteen, isn't that right? I believe I can live with that. Keep in mind that, as it is the twenty-first century now, it's entirely possible for a young lady to invite a young gentleman out on a date as well." Aunt Midge winked at the two of them on the swing and stood. "I'm off to bed before I fall asleep right here. I love you girls." She blew them kisses and whirled around toward the French doors to the kitchen, drawing her chiffon shawl in a circular swoosh around her as she went.

When Tilly had gone up to bed too, Avery sat on the family room floor with Halston by her side. She rested her elbows on the coffee table, holding up the two keys she'd found yesterday in the archived collection. *Use the key.* Which key? And use it for what?

Chapter Fifteen

Before going to bed, Avery spent over an hour trying both keys in every keyhole she could find, even the ones that were hidden. She rummaged around in the basement and found a locked box inside one of the cupboards under the tool bench. *This is it*, her mind told her. But she was wrong. The larger key did indeed open that box, but it was a collection of hundreds of baseball cards in protective plastic sleeves. Her father's key must have been inadvertently tossed in when they were clearing out closed-case items from the home office last year. As disappointed as she was that she hadn't unlocked some supersecret item that would answer all her questions, her heart lifted when she saw the baseball cards. The ones right on top were her dad's favorites; she'd heard him talk about the greats whenever they went to games. In pristine condition inside their plastic sheaths were Detroit Tigers Al Kaline and Lou Whitaker and New York Yankees Mickey Mantle and Mariano Rivera. Her dad must have had some of these since he was a boy. Avery didn't know much about baseball, but this was quite a find. She hefted the box under her arm and carried it upstairs. Aunt Midge would be thrilled to see her brother's baseball card collection.

She set it on the kitchen table and put the key on top of it for Midge to find in the morning. Avery racked her brain, trying to think of anywhere in the house she hadn't searched for a lock to check with this other blasted key. She turned it over in her hand, trying to make out the inscription. One side was smooth and blank; the other had a few numbers and letters stamped into the metal. In the home office, Avery picked up her mother's antique loupe with the beautiful mother-of-pearl handle and read the inscription on the key: *LEX1073*.

She sat behind Anne's desk. She normally used her father's desk, but her mom's chair was infinitely more comfortable. Avery only had to pull one drawer open to find a scrap of paper, this one lavender. She wrote *LEX1073* on the paper and folded it completely around the key, then locked both into the safe behind the mirror before going to bed. She'd tell Aunt Midge tomorrow about the phone call and her subsequent late-night key quest. That inscription should lead her to whatever it was she was meant to *use the key* on, once she deciphered what it meant.

When Avery joined Midge in the kitchen for coffee the next morning, she was warmed to see William's baseball collection spread out all over the table and Midge reading the back of one of the cards.

"Where did you find these? I haven't seen them since we were kids! I can't believe how many he added!" Aunt Midge was beaming.

Avery refilled Midge's coffee and explained. She retrieved the key and lavender slip of paper from the safe and set it in front of her aunt. "Have you ever seen that key before?"

Her aunt unwrapped it, turning the silver key around in her palm. She shook her head. "Never. So this has got to be the key your mysterious phone call referred to. The phone number was hidden? Do you think it's from the same source as the notes?"

Avery nodded. "I'm thinking it must be. The voice was altered somehow, so I couldn't recognize it. I've been racking my brain since yesterday trying to think what this unlocks. Whatever it is, it's not in the house. Which I think leaves either the Manhattan office or a safe-deposit box somewhere." She slid the key back toward herself across the table and picked it up. "I'm going to show it to the detective as soon as I get a chance."

Aunt Midge nodded. "That's a good idea. I really don't like the fact that someone is still contacting you, especially after the break-in and now your collector turning up dead. I'm glad we've got a Springfield County patrol car sitting out front. It makes me feel a little safer."

"Yes, for sure." Art had warned her it was a bad idea to have a whole bunch of people in and out of their house right now. She'd argued that it was only friends and family, and he'd countered by asking her how sure she was she could trust each of them. None of that was worth sharing with Aunt Midge; it would only worry her.

Avery chose dark denim jeans turned up at the ankle and a sleeveless red blouse with a wide satin ribbon around the fitted waist. She'd first tried on a couple sundresses from her mother's closet, as she and Tilly hadn't had the heart yet to clean everything out, but they just didn't look right. She'd never been a dress person, much as she admired them on Tilly and her aunt. Silver hoop earrings, a little mascara, and her new bright-white Vans finished the look. She was the first one downstairs and ready before the party.

Tilly emerged from her room as Avery was setting out hors d'oeuvres. "Oh! You look so pretty," Avery exclaimed. Tilly's blue sundress was perfect on her, with her white canvas high-top Chuck Taylors lending a nice ultramodern vibe to the outfit. Her long blond hair was loose, and Avery could see she'd taken extra care in placing a solitary thin braid to hold it back on one side.

"Thank you," Tilly said, smiling. She twirled around and lifted the hem of the short dress, revealing blue-jean short shorts underneath. "Pretty and functional. I'm not losing at volleyball just because of this dress!"

Two of Aunt Midge's friends arrived first, around three PM. Colin carried in a huge bowl of his out-of-this-world pasta salad and set it in the designated spot Avery had left cleared for it. Sir Robert arrived next with Francesca, who handed her an expensive bottle of white wine bearing a pink bow. The remaining guests trickled in over the next couple hours, Tilly's friends included. The Ayers annual summer party typically went late into the evening—plenty of time for everyone to eat, mingle, play a round of croquet, have a cocktail, eat again, and relax by the fire.

Sometime between first dinner and second dinner, Avery spotted Art Smith coming around the house on the green lawn between two stands of blossoming purple lilac bushes. She didn't know if it was seeing him in sneakers, jeans, and a black polo shirt or catching the slightly intimidating detective ducking under an errant lilac bush branch that made him seem so out of place. She met him halfway across the backyard near the patio, aware that he knew no one else there. She spotted him before he saw her and he looked uncomfortable, like he might just disappear the way he'd come.

"Don't do it," Avery said. "You'll miss the most amazing food."

"Don't do what?" he asked.

"Leave. You've got this look, like maybe you wandered into the wrong backyard," she said, smiling. "I'm glad you came."

"Thanks for the invitation." He bent down just a bit toward her, something Avery wasn't accustomed to men having to do at her height. But Art must be at least six four or so. He lowered his voice. "It should be a great opportunity for me to get a feel for the people you associate with. Most crimes are committed by someone the victim knows."

She felt the wind leave her sails. They hadn't known each other long at all, but she enjoyed being around him, so she'd invited him. Apparently Art viewed the party through a completely different lens. Fine. She'd have to adjust her own view. She'd probably overstepped, inviting him to a family-and-friends party. "I've heard that's true. Though I really don't think you're going to find a criminal here in my backyard. Are there any leads yet on Renell?"

"Nothing I can share while the investigation's active. But my old coworkers are on top of it, don't worry."

Avery led him into the momentarily empty kitchen and gave him the rundown of all the delicious dishes set out on the island, some sitting in ice and others on warmers. She handed him a plate to get started. "You said your former coworkers? You used to be NYPD in Manhattan?"

Art looked up at her, a large spoon of potato salad in the air on the way to his plate. "Uh. Yeah. Didn't realize I said that. It was a long time ago."

"What happened?"

He visibly bristled, frowning. "I moved. And I believe cops should live where they serve." He moved down the counter, heaping his plate with pasta salad, ribs, garlic rolls.

Good to know, Avery thought. That was clearly a touchy subject for him. She held out a second plate. "Need another one?" She tried not to react to the startling amount of food about to spill off Art's plate.

"No thanks. I'll just come back." He caught her eyeing the food he held. "Everything looks good," he said, the corner of his mouth threatening to tip upward into a smile. "I should have warned you, I'm sort of a bottomless pit."

Avery laughed and was pleased to see Art give in to a slow, embarrassed grin. "That's all right. I'm glad you're hungry. Follow me. I saw an empty spot at Micah's table."

She introduced them officially. Micah had met Art Smith a year ago in Avery's parents' home office the night of the accident, an upsetting memory for all involved, and since then Micah had only unknowingly crossed paths with Art a few times at MOA.

"Art is a security guard at MOA; that's how we met," she told Micah. She bent down so only he could hear her whispered instructions. "He asked me not to share with anyone his connection to my parents' case, all right?"

Micah nodded. "Of course, understood." He shook hands with Art. "Good to meet you," he said loudly.

Avery cringed and left them to jog back toward the house, where she'd just seen Rachel arriving.

"Rachel! It's so good to see you," she said, happy when her old friend folded her into a hug. "I'm glad you came."

"I've missed you," Rachel said, letting go. "It was good luck, me being at Mixed Bag so early the other day and spotting you! I see you run by at least a few days a week. I could never do it; I hate exercise."

"Oh, it's not exercise," Avery said. "I mean, I guess it is. But it's always helped clear my mind; it's kind of my therapy. That and actual therapy."

Rachel's eyebrows went up. "Oh? Well . . . I think that's smart, to talk to a therapist after all you went through. I'm sure it's helped with you two adjusting. How is Tilly doing?"

"She's all right. She insisted she didn't need to see a therapist, but she really likes Dr. Singh now. We both still have nightmares sometimes, though. I—" Avery cut herself off. Holy cow, where had her filter gone? She put a hand on Rachel's arm. "I'm sorry. I don't know what's wrong with me; talk about oversharing. Tilly is doing a lot better. We both are."

Rachel shook her head, frowning. "Don't do that. You aren't oversharing. I've known you since we were six. If you can't share with me, then that's pretty sad. I wouldn't have asked if I didn't really want to know how you both are!" She took Avery's hand and squeezed it.

Avery got them both moving, pulling Rachel toward the kitchen. "I'm glad you're here," she repeated. "I promise I won't let us lose touch again. I want to hear all about you and how the shop's doing."

Tilly's friend Eve burst through the kitchen door, breathless. "Avery!"

Avery stared at her. "Eve? What's wrong?"

"Tilly just told me what happened to Halston! Where is he? I need to give him hugs! Can I see him, please?"

Avery smiled apologetically at Rachel. "Go ahead and make yourself a plate, and there are a million drink choices in the fridge. Aunt Midge is just outside to the left; she'll be thrilled to see you. I'll find you in a bit. Eve," she said, motioning to the excitable girl.

"Come on, Halston's chilling out in my room for the afternoon, until things settle down later. I'll take you to him."

An hour later, when Avery circulated back around to check on Art, she found him chatting with Micah and Wilder.

"Speak of the devil," Micah said, glancing up at Avery. "We were just saying how your parents raised you girls in the best of both worlds, didn't they? Peace and quiet here in your little Lilac Grove, and time spent at shows and the apartment and shop in the city."

She pulled up a chair, knowing she needed to replenish drinks and put out new portions of the salads. She couldn't sit for long. Thank goodness Sir Robert had agreed to man the grill. Tilly looked completely engrossed in some story Noah was telling, the two of them sitting on the grass near the ongoing badminton game, and Aunt Midge was in her element, laughing with her friends. Avery agreed with Micah's sentiment.

"I feel very at home whether I'm on the subway headed to your place in Harlem or on my front porch swing watching the hummingbirds," she said. "I'm sure that was their intention."

"I remember the spring they bought this place," Wilder said.

Avery was surprised. "You do?"

He nodded. "Oh, your poor aunt was heartbroken they were leaving the city. You were just a toddler. Tilly came a few years later. Your mother was determined to give you a yard. She wanted to find a bit of her own midwestern upbringing, even though your dad and Midge were born and raised in Manhattan. And your dad's primary goal was always to make his family happy. Now here we are." Wilder smiled at her. It was more than he ever typically said at once.

"I never knew that," Avery said. "And I had no idea it affected Midge . . . my dad must have been torn."

Micah spoke. "He was. To be fair, they both were. But then Anne and William never really left the city, what with the shop. I think Midge came to see that. And you remember long weekends with her and Halston visiting, here in Lilac Grove. She learned to drive for you, you know."

"What?" Avery looked from Micah to Wilder. "Seriously?"

Wilder chuckled, nodding along with Micah. "Margery Millicent Ayers never once sat behind the wheel of a car until you were four years old and demanded she'd better visit you every day at your new house. Well. She didn't visit every day, obviously, but she made me teach her to drive beginning the day you figured out how to use the phone to call and make your demand. She had her license two weeks later. She was determined."

Avery turned and looked toward the patio, where Aunt Midge was reclining on the wicker love seat alongside her best friend, Lucille, the two of them sharing some private joke. "I never knew. I've always wondered if she regrets being here with us this past year instead of her plush Fifth Avenue apartment. She doesn't seem to."

"She's exactly where she wants to be," Wilder confirmed.

Avery stood. "Thank you for that." She was surprised Midge hadn't ever shared that story herself, at least the part about learning to drive. Avery had a pang, wishing her dad could somehow know how easy his sister had made it look, fitting herself into their lives full-time now, lending the support she and Tilly needed. Avery was too busy with work to be a good parent substitute to her sister. Midge had stepped up at a crucial time in both their lives.

She stopped by the grill, where Sir Robert was finishing the next batch of ribs. He and Francesca were discussing destination options for their summer trip to Europe, with input from Nate Brennan.

"I bet Avery will agree," Nate said as she approached.

"With what?"

"I was telling them about Monaco. Francesca's been, but Sir Robert hasn't. They've just missed the Monaco Grand Prix, but there's Monte Carlo and so many other things to see and do."

"Aunt Midge took me and Tilly to Monaco for the international yacht show a few years ago. I'd agree it's a fabulous place. But personally, I'd choose Romania." Avery swiped a bit of sauce to sample. "The countryside is so beautiful this time of year." Granted, she'd been only once, but it had made an impression.

Francesca smiled. "Thank you! Sir Robert is on the fence, and I've been trying to tell him we've got to check out Romania."

As she left them to drift over to Goldie's little group, she heard Nate say, "Avery's right. I crashed at my buddy's place in Brașov on the way to Paris, and man oh man, the view is sick." She smiled to herself. She'd never really know how much of Nate's demeanor was real and how much was for show.

"May I freshen your drinks?" Avery asked, holding a hand out for Goldie's empty glass.

Goldie was seated with, to Avery's surprise, Colin and Prince Ivan. "I'm sorry," she said. "I'd make introductions, but it looks like you've already met?"

"We attended the MOA gala last year," Colin said. "We spotted the intrepid Goldie Brennan just now and had to come say hello. We've got our tickets for next weekend!"

Goldie beamed from the compliment. "There are big things in store!" She winked at Avery.

Colin reached up and placed a hand on Avery's forearm. "Avery, this is a lovely party. You must have Midge bring you and your sister over for dinner sometime; we'd love to return the hospitality."

She patted his hand. The stunning ring on Colin's left hand caught her eye, and she held it lightly in her own for a moment. "Oh my. What a gorgeous ring!"

Colin held his hand out at arm's length, displaying a unique, gold-embossed band inlaid with small, tasteful diamonds. "Thank you! We just got them, our anniversary bands. Show her yours," he said, tapping his husband's knee.

Prince Ivan leaned forward and displayed his ring proudly. His was the converse of Colin's, a brushed titanium band, but with the same pattern and set of sparkling diamonds.

"Wow," Avery breathed. "Those are gorgeous! Did you design them yourselves?"

"Oh no," Prince Ivan replied. "We found the set at a really great jewelry shop below the High Line. It's called Rizzolo's."

"Really?" Goldie spoke. "I believe that's the shop that handles some of the independent appraisals our collectors have gotten. Nate would know for sure."

"They've got so much unique stuff," Colin said. "If you're ever in need of rings . . ." He raised an eyebrow at Avery.

She laughed. "I think it might be a while. My closest contact at the moment is quite possibly my aunt's dog."

Colin pulled a sad face at her. "I have lots of amazing friends, Avery. Some are even straight. I'll set you up anytime you're ready."

Avery's eyes widened. "My God, what has Aunt Midge been saying about me?" She shook her head, smiling.

Colin sat back, putting his hands up. "Nothing! Not a thing. And maybe you don't need any help. We saw you chatting with that one," he said, tipping his head toward Art.

"Oh, ah, he's a friend of mine though the museum," Avery said. "Goldie, I'll be right back with your drink."

Moose tracks. Pralines and cream. Blueberry. Birthday cake. Pistachio. Why had that upset her? Avery rinsed out Goldie's glass and poured the wine at the kitchen counter. Maybe because she'd developed a tiny crush on Detective Art Smith and Colin's comment highlighted the fact that it wasn't mutual. Butter pecan. Superman. Death by chocolate. All right, that was probably true. Still no cause to get mad.

Walking out to return Goldie's drink, Avery was surprised to find she really wasn't mad. She was embarrassed. She handed the glass to the curator and put a hand on Colin's shoulder. "I didn't mean to be short with you. I guess it's a bit of a sensitive subject."

Colin patted her hand. "No worries. I've been told," he said, glancing at his husband, "that not everyone loves a matchmaker."

Prince Ivan rolled his eyes skyward and looked apologetically at Avery. He shook his head. "I can't control him. He shows our rings to everyone, and somehow it always leads to trouble."

"Well," Goldie said. "I personally believe the best gift of jewelry is the kind you buy yourself."

Avery smiled at her. "Aunt Midge would agree with you there. Is anyone getting their second wind for round two? Sir Robert's almost finished with the ribs, and there is still so much food!"

She was finally able to relax by the fire later that evening, after everyone had been amply fed and some of the early crowd had trickled out. The fire pit was situated at the far side of the patio, surrounded by chairs and a few benches. In the gathering darkness, the globe lights strung over the patio through the trees lit the backyard with a warm glow. Avery sat back and watched Aunt Midge circulate with a pitcher of frozen margaritas, filling cups here and there for the adults. Noah, Tilly, and her trio of friends had claimed the side of the fire nearest the lawn and were taking turns roasting marshmallows. Someone had changed the music playlist, and Avery liked the eclectic mix of contemporary and alternative soft rock.

The detective took the empty seat next to her and handed her a fresh beer; he must have noticed what she'd been drinking earlier.

"Hi," she said, surprised. "I wasn't sure if you'd left."

"Nope. Just finishing a game of croquet in the dark back there with Nate and Sir Robert."

"I won," Sir Robert said, he and Nate coming up behind them and finding chairs a couple yards away. Francesca came from the kitchen carrying a platter of dessert bars. She handed them to Wilder to pass, and Sir Robert captured her hand, pulling her toward him. "What's my prize?"

Francesca perched on his knee. "For winning at hitting a ball through a little wire hoop? You think you deserve a big prize, do you?" Her dark hair brushed Sir Robert's face as she planted a kiss on him.

"That'll work." Sir Robert grinned.

On Avery's other side, opposite Art, Micah leaned toward her. "I'm sorry, Avery, but I should get going. Long drive and all that."

She nodded. "Of course. Listen, I wanted to show you something I found. Remind me tomorrow, all right?" It was one more thing to add to the growing list of concerns surrounding their work. She was thankful they'd been able to get through most of the party without discussing any of it.

"Will do. You and Tilly are coming to the house first? What time are you thinking?"

"Hmm. How about around eleven? Have you had a chance yet to see if you've still got any of the initial notes from the medallion case? Any kind of communication with that collector who called me?"

Micah groaned. "I completely forgot. I'll get into my storage after Noah leaves tomorrow night, I promise. It might take a little digging. My, uh, organizational system leaves something to be desired. But I'm sure I've got copies of at least the basics; we all did. I'll bring what I find to the office Monday."

Avery was well aware of Micah's organizational system. But even with his chaotic desk, he did seem to always know where everything was. She stood to walk him out. "Sounds good. Whatever you've got. I don't know what exactly I'm looking for, so anything helps."

Micah motioned for her to sit down. "We can find the car just fine on our own. You must be exhausted. Nice meeting you, Art."

Art shook Micah's hand. "Safe drive back to the city."

Others slowly began saying their good-byes, and Avery tried to keep Art engaged in conversation as much as she could, hoping he'd stay longer. She'd been waiting all night to show him the key.

Chapter Sixteen

A rt Smith was the last to leave the party.

Avery kept expecting him to say it was late and he should go, but he seemed truly relaxed on the patio by the fire. She and Aunt Midge took turns getting up now and then to bring out more snacks or help folks gather their things to leave. The other boy in Tilly's group left shortly after Noah and Micah did, and Tilly and her girlfriends went upstairs to make popcorn and find a horror movie to watch. When Avery came back outside to the patio after saying good-bye to Colin and Prince Ivan, Art had put the wire-mesh cover over the fire pit and was clearing cups and party debris.

"You don't have to do that," Avery said, surprised.

"It's no big deal. You and your family did most of it already." He pushed the chairs in around the table opposite the fire pit area.

She went over to him. "Really. Thank you for cleaning up, but you're off duty." She smiled. "From this and your real job."

"You throw a great party. I almost didn't come."

"But you had to, to check out my people. Right?" She'd been reminding herself of his words all night. He was doing his job, even off duty.

He frowned at her. "Well, sure. It was helpful in that respect."

She raised her eyebrows, curious. "Really? How so? What did you learn?"

"Ah. I learned that your friends and family think very highly of the three of you. You've got a nice circle."

"That's all?" She felt deflated. She didn't know what she'd expected, but that wasn't it. "No suspects, no thieves or murderers in the bunch?"

Art sat back down by the fire, resting his elbows on his knees and turning to look at her as she joined him. "You make it sound as if I spent the evening studying each of them."

"You didn't? I figured that's why you stayed so long."

He stood abruptly. "Sorry. I'm, ah, not the best at reading social cues."

"Oh no. Please. Art, sit down. That's not at all what I meant." She looked worriedly up at him.

He sat. "All right, maybe I came looking at this as an opportunity to flush out a suspect. But that's not why I stayed." He was staring straight ahead into the fire.

"Oh," Avery said, her voice quiet.

"I don't go to these things. I haven't . . . in a long time. This was nice."

Feeling bold, Avery leaned toward him and bumped his shoulder with hers. "That's nice to hear. I'm really glad you stayed."

He turned his face toward hers, his half hidden in shadow. Then he stood again. "I should go. It's late."

She was trying to keep up. "Okay. I'll walk with you to your car." She suppressed her natural inquisitive urge for about as long as it took them to reach the lilac bushes at the side of the house. "Have you lived in Springfield County long? What made you leave the city?"

Art let his breath out in a long exhale. He ran a hand back across the top of his head. "I had to."

Avery swallowed hard. "Why?" Oh, she hoped she wouldn't regret asking that.

"I made a critical error on a case, and it almost got my partner killed. I was put on leave, but when the suspension was over, I decided I'd be better at my job in a setting that wasn't a pressure cooker." He kept up his pace, not looking at her.

"Oh. That's awful. I'm sorry. But I'm glad your partner was okay." His explanation had told her everything and nothing about why he'd left Manhattan. By now they'd reached his car.

He rested a hand atop his car. "I appreciate that. Springfield County is a better fit."

Avery nodded. She couldn't begin to know what it felt like to go through all of that. "Well, for my sake, I'm glad you chose Lilac Grove," she said quietly.

He started to speak but then stopped. He cast a quick glance over his shoulder to the midnight-shift patrol car that had replaced the afternoon officer. When he looked at Avery again, his guard was back up. She hadn't realized it before, but now that she'd just experienced both versions of Art Smith in the space of a few seconds, she got it. For just a moment she'd been talking with the exposed, raw Art Smith. Now Detective Art Smith was back. He opened his car door. "You said earlier you had something to show me? What was it?"

Avery sighed. She really liked this man. But she was totally in the dark about anything he thought or felt about her. No matter what he felt, she knew she was safer when he was around, and she'd enjoyed his company tonight. She'd kept the key all day today on a chain around her neck. She had been about to lock it back into her parents' safe when she realized there was nowhere safer than right with her. She'd removed an old, costume-jewelry unicorn charm from a long silver chain she'd rummaged in Tilly's jewelry box and threaded it through the key, throwing away the lavender scrap of paper. She'd memorized the inscription without even meaning to. Now she pulled the chain from inside her blouse and held out the key at the end of it.

Art bent down to take a look, raising his gaze once to hers. He pulled out his phone and shined the light on it, narrowing his eyes.

"It says LEX1073," Avery told him. "Yesterday on the way home I got an anonymous call that said, 'Use the key.' And this was in my parents' office—it's got to be the key the caller meant. I don't know yet what it unlocks."

Art snapped a photo of it. "Let me work on it. The call came in yesterday? Why didn't you tell me?"

"Um. I don't know, I didn't really have anything to tell. I still don't know anything."

Now he looked aggravated. "You've got to keep me in the loop. Otherwise I can't help you. All right?"

She nodded. "Yes. Sorry. I told you about Edward Johnstone, right?"

He blinked once, slowly, and stared at her.

"Oh. No?" She brought Art up to speed on the call from Johnstone as well. "I promise to let you know the very second anything else happens from now on," she swore.

"I'll find you in a day or two, once I know something," Art told her as he left.

*　*　*

Avery had never seen Tilly quite so animated. She and Micah watched from a distance at Armand and Sons while Noah modeled business attire. A football player in high school, nineteen-year-old Noah was the perfect menswear model size. The garments fit him well and would need no tailoring. The salesman stepped in every few minutes with a helpful word about shoulder room or inseam length, but it was clear that Tilly's opinion was the only one that mattered.

"They're adorable," Avery said quietly to Micah. "They're both still about twelve in my head. I can't believe he's a sophomore and Tilly will be a freshman."

Micah nodded. "I'm sure the last couple years have felt like a long road for both of them."

Avery hadn't thought about it much before, but she wondered if the shared experience of losing parents had brought Noah and Tilly a little closer. They seemed to have the sort of long-standing friendship that was easy and comfortable, no matter how infrequently they saw each other. She wasn't sure if or how it might transition to anything more, as Tilly hoped, but perhaps it would.

Avery called to make sure MOA had been reopened after being shut down Friday morning, and after a quick lunch, they found themselves in the Xiang dynasty exhibit. Aunt Midge had planned to take in the exhibit with them, but she'd changed her mind that morning, saying she needed a day of rest. Avery didn't blame her a bit. The pace over the last several days had been tiring, even by Midge's standards. Avery and Tilly had left her on the couch with her current book, a cup of tea, and Halston curled up on his new dog bed by her feet.

The Emperor's Twins medallion was the prized focal point of the exhibit, but the installation itself was much more than simply the medallion. Avery enjoyed being the tour guide as she walked Tilly, Micah, and Noah through each display, offering bits of information about the gold thread woven into the tapestries during that period, the meaning behind the ceremonial garb worn by Chinese royalty, and the techniques used to create a piece as intricate as the medallion.

She let the trio drift away toward the next exhibit, staying behind to scrutinize the dragon and his striking ruby eye. The piece sat under a spotlight in a display case. The jewels and pearls surrounding the dragon's head looked just as genuine as the eye itself. She bent closer, pulling her pocket loupe out and peering through it. It didn't give the same view as having the medallion free from the case, but even up close, Avery couldn't say that this enormous, sparkling ruby wasn't the natural Burmese ruby it was purported to be. It was stunning. And at this level of magnification, there was nothing to tell her it wasn't real. She couldn't wait to get back into the lab tomorrow. She and Micah would know before the day was out whether MOA had acquired a fake.

Avery and Tilly dropped Micah and Noah off at their Harlem brownstone before dinnertime. Micah had to get Noah on the train back to school later that night. They climbed the steps to the porch, Avery handing over the bags she'd helped carry up. Besides Armand and Sons, they'd hit a few other stores, finding shoes and other necessities for Noah. Tilly had come away with a new luggage set for her London adventure this fall. Avery hugged Noah good-bye, suddenly overcome with emotion at the thought of doing the same in August for Tilly.

"Your mom would be so proud of you, Noah," she told him. "I know we are. You'll do great." She smiled, swallowing hard. She let go and trotted down the steps, raising a hand to Micah. "See you in the morning!"

Avery waited in the car, buckling and looking down at her phone, trying to give Noah and Tilly a moment to say good-bye.

She peeked through her hair up at the house and saw that Micah had had the same thought; he'd gone inside.

Tilly was quiet most of the drive home to Lilac Grove. Avery put music on, and Tilly finally opened up when they were approaching town, just a few minutes away from home.

"I'm really going to miss him. Everyone. I'm gonna miss everyone!"

Avery looked sharply at her sister; her tone was so forlorn. Tilly met her gaze with tears in her eyes. "Oh, Tilly." Avery took her hand, squeezing it.

"What if I don't want to go to London? What if Noah meets someone at his fancy internship? What if she's this badass engineering intern like him but with stilettos and big boobs and a genius IQ and he totally forgets about me?"

Avery laughed and then stifled it, trying not to smile at the image. "I think that's highly unlikely. Noah's known you since you were tiny. He loves you. And he doesn't strike me as the kind of kid to be wowed by stilettos and, uh, all that."

Tilly shook her head, looking out the window. "Maybe he just loves me like a sister. I mean, he hugged me good-bye, and he said he'd miss me. But it doesn't even matter, because we'll be a million miles apart, and I know this is stupid, but I've crushed on him forever, and it's not fair—"

Avery lifted her sister's hand, squeezing it harder. "Hey! It's going to be okay. Really. I promise. Noah's doing what he needs to do for now, for the future, and so are you." She paused. "And you know, if you really decided you truly didn't want to go to London, no one is going to make you. It's your future. It's all up to you."

Avery took a deep breath, taken aback by her own little speech. She felt so out of her depth in trying to give parental advice. She had this deeply ingrained memory of sitting down and talking things over with their parents. Anne and William would help lead Avery and her sister to the answers. But Avery was supposed to know the answers now. She hoped she'd given her sister the right one.

Tilly sniffled. "You mean it?"

"Um. Which part?" She glanced at her sister from the corner of her eye.

"The part where you said I don't have to go to London?"

Avery clenched her jaw, pushing away the fish-out-of-water feeling. There was no one to answer to now but themselves— and Aunt Midge. "I mean it."

Tilly was quiet.

They turned onto the road to their house. Avery spoke. "I do think you should wait a while before making any firm decision on it. Sleep on it, talk it through a little more. But it's always up to you."

Her younger sister drew in a hitching breath. "Well, I don't want to miss out on London," she said softly.

There it was. Maybe she just needed to know the choice was hers. "I don't blame you there." Avery pulled into their driveway, now accustomed to seeing the patrol car sitting there. Art expected to have answers this week, between getting a look at the original copy of the Emperor's Twins certification from the MOA records department, tracking down the collector Edward Johnstone, and also finally learning if the DNA from the blood outside the office doorway was a match for anyone in the system. She was sure Springfield County didn't have the budget to cover twenty-four-hour surveillance much longer.

The aroma of pot roast and fresh biscuits assaulted them in the foyer along with Halston, almost back to his usual happy, waggy self, only slightly hindered by the cast. They found Midge setting plates at the island, where they normally ate only breakfast. Dinner was almost always at the big dining table between the kitchen and family room in the open floor plan. But the dining table was covered with a map.

Avery went to the table and saw that it was a map of Manhattan, a pink highlighter line drawn down the middle of it. She peered more closely, squinting to read the street name: *Lexington Avenue.* "Of course!" She grabbed Aunt Midge and pulled her into a hug. "The key. It opens something on Lexington Avenue."

"I got a little farther than that," Midge said. She tapped the screen on her tablet on the adjacent countertop. "One-oh-seven-three Lexington Avenue was the home of Bennington Bank. The branch closed for renovations"—she consulted a yellow scrap of paper—"it closed in November of last year for renovations. Then I had to quit and get the roast out of the oven."

"I could kiss you. This is huge, Auntie. The key must be to a safe-deposit box. If that particular branch closed, they had to have relocated the boxes somewhere. I'll take it from here, I know I can figure it out."

Aunt Midge appeared to have fully recovered from her fatigue, even though—judging by the delicious dinner and newly cleaned downstairs, no trace of the party present—she hadn't rested much.

"Did you get much reading done? Looks like someone spent the day cleaning. You didn't have to do that. I'd planned to finish that tonight," Avery said. She dipped her biscuit in gravy and took a bite.

"I actually did get some reading in. And Halston and I caught up on our reality television too." She smiled. "I enjoyed tidying up, my dear. It was a wonderful party, and I'm so glad you girls had a day in the city. Did Noah find some handsome business attire for DeSouza?"

Tilly spoke. "We found three nice pairs of pants, two suit jackets, five shirts and ties, and a pair of dress shoes that Micah said better last Noah until he's old and gray."

"It was not a cheap afternoon for the men," Avery added. "But Noah contributed; he wanted to. He'll definitely look the part now at DeSouza. He'll stand out among all the dull, unattractive engineering interns," she said, winking at Tilly.

Midge frowned. "Well, that's not very kind. I'm sure they'll each have their positive qualities. Though none quite so much as our Noah."

Their aunt never failed to surprise Avery. Midge had caught on to the topic without any explanation. Avery would fill her in on the conversation with Tilly in the car; she wanted to make sure Aunt Midge felt she'd done all right with how she'd handled Tilly's cold feet. They needed to prepare for the possibility that she might change her mind about voice school in London. There were plenty of great options in the States too.

While Tilly and Aunt Midge settled in the family room to read, Midge with the paperback of one of her favorite Blue Ridge Library Mysteries and Tilly on her Apple Books app, Avery brought her laptop to the dining table where the map was. She searched through Bennington Bank's website, eventually finding a page with customer notifications of changes happening. It was from seven or eight months ago, and there was a lot of rhetoric about maintaining the highest standards for clients as the bank went through reorganization and growing pains, information on whom to contact regarding unanswered questions, and assurances that Bennington's mission statement remained the same, as they hoped to continue to inspire confidence in their banking solutions. Ugh.

She found the contact information for some of the higher-ups in the system and sent a very sweet and polite but urgent email to the CEO, the CFO, and the assistant CEO, inquiring how she might learn where her parents' safe-deposit box had been relocated. Everything she could find on the website made reference to hard-copy letters that had been mailed to banking clients with details on the branch closing. Avery was mentally preparing for a deep dive into her parents' personal and household files when she spotted it. Simple. At the very bottom of the webpage were the underlined words ***Find your new neighborhood branch here***.

She clicked the hyperlink, and the browser opened a new window with a short form to complete, reading:

Enter current or former Bennington Bank address or branch number in the box below.

So she did, typing in *1073 Lexington Avenue, NYC, NY*, and hit the enter key.

A pinpoint on a map of New York City appeared. Avery zoomed in. Oh for goodness' sake. Her parents' branch had moved three blocks south and one block over to Third Avenue, just a handful of blocks from the Museum of Antiquities. She'd go tomorrow and find out what the key opened.

* * *

Avery called Micah on her way in to the city Monday morning. She hoped he might know what her parents had stored in the safe-deposit box that was so secret. She'd never come across any record of it, not even in their Emperor's Twins files where she had found the key. When she didn't get him, she tried his house phone; Micah really hated cell phones. Half the time when she couldn't get ahold of him it was because he'd silenced the ringer or his phone was turned off. She left a message on both phones and then tried Sir Robert, who picked up on the first ring.

"Good Monday morning, Avery Ayers! What are you up to today?"

"I see someone's had their coffee! Good morning, Sir Robert. How are you?" She knew she'd answered a question with a question, but Sir Robert didn't really want to know her plans for the day. He was always this jovial in the mornings.

"I'm great. I've already been to the gym, and I've got an appointment at Barnaby's at ten. Then Francesca's coming by the shop with lunch, and I'll be holding down the fort for bit while we go through our French Riviera cruise itinerary. A perfect day," he said. "And you didn't tell me what you've got on your schedule."

Avery told him about the key with the LEX1073 inscription and finding the bank that her parents had apparently stored something at. She assumed it was related to the Emperor's Twins. She'd had that strange phone call and the key had been in their files, though come to think of it, so had the key to the baseball cards. "Anyway, that branch of Bennington is just over on Third, so I'm going to run over there when we break for lunch and collect whatever is in the safe-deposit box. Do you have any idea what it could be?"

"Not a clue," Sir Robert said. "But I wasn't really involved in the Emperor's Twins assignment."

"I'll let you know what I find. I'm almost to MOA; keep your fingers crossed Micah and I can confirm the ruby is the missing dragon eye today."

"Fingers crossed. Call me when you know!"

Avery waited for Micah at the MOA elevators, surprised he wasn't already here. When he hadn't shown up yet by 9:05, she went down the hall to buy coffee, iced this morning instead of her usual hot. It was surprisingly warm today, despite the early hour. Her car thermostat on the way in had read the outside temperature as seventy-eight degrees. Several members of the film crew were in line for coffee ahead of her, speculating over what had been stolen that had lost them a whole two days of shooting. Avery hadn't realized the museum had stayed closed on Saturday as well. That was unheard of. Saturday was the busiest day of the week. None of the movie folks seemed to know what had happened. Avery recalled Francesca's explanation and disdain; she'd given the impression that a heating duct cover had fallen off and that Goldie or the powers that be had overreacted by calling the police.

With her and Micah's coffees in hand now, she was surprised to find he still wasn't at the elevators when she returned. Maybe he'd arrived and gone up to the lab, in which case he'd take care of calling to get the medallion brought up. Avery had one quick stop to make first.

She'd been in the administrative wing only twice, but she found Goldie Brennan's office easily. It was the largest. She knocked once on Goldie's open door, and the older woman smiled widely at her and motioned her in.

"Oh, you're an angel! They weren't open yet when I passed by on my way in. Thank you so much, Avery!"

Avery set Micah's coffee on Goldie's desk. "Of course! We have to have our coffee—believe me, I know! Goldie, I stopped by because I have a quick question for you."

"Will I need my coffee first?"

"Oh, I doubt it. I was hoping you'd tell me about the museum closure Friday. Was there really some sort of break-in? We arrived to work in the lab, and the police were keeping everyone out."

Goldie sighed. "I'd hoped it wasn't true. My grandson found evidence that someone might have used the museum ductwork to get to the records department. We called the police, of course, but I think we were both hoping the heating duct cover had just fallen off or been run into by a hi-lo, or something like that. But if you're here about what happened, then I assume you already know?"

Avery sat in the chair opposite Goldie's desk. "Know what?" She shook her head. "I know nothing."

Goldie raised her eyebrows. "Oh. In that case, I'm sorry to be the one to tell you this. Your friend at the party, the detective? He's been moonlighting here, part of some case he's working on, I'm told. I'm sure that's not news to you. He happened to be patrolling the lower level when Nate discovered that duct cover broken. It's a good thing he was down there, as Nate was able to show him exactly how he'd found the cover. Your friend—our guard—had recently requisitioned the original certificate of authenticity for the Emperor's Twins. We keep the original here, and as you know, the yellow and pink go to the certifying parties and the collector. I'd told him we'd have it ready for him to look at by today, but it's gone. It was the only thing taken, so far as we can tell."

Avery closed her eyes. "And our yellow copy was stolen from the home office last week. I can't help thinking this has something to do with my mother signing the certificate early. Was that normal? Had she ever done that before?"

Goldie frowned. "I don't believe so. Getting the paperwork squared away was a bit nerve-racking as it was. I didn't think much about the date she'd signed."

"Nerve-racking because my parents were gone but the report was due? She was pretty organized. I'd figured whoever got it to you just took it from her open assignment files."

"It took some doing to locate it, that's all. I remember Sir Robert brought it to me in person. It had been misplaced on Micah's desk or something like that. With what happened to your parents, there wasn't even any rush to get it to me that Monday. I'd have accepted it late. I know your partners were devastated, as we all were."

"Yes, that makes sense," Avery said. She'd hardly given the business a thought the first few weeks after the accident. "Well, Micah is bringing in anything he had from the initial notes on that case. So at least we'll be able to learn more from that end— where the collector came to acquire it or how he chose MOA to submit to." She stood.

"Let me know if I can be of any help, Avery. With our charity gala this Friday, I still hope to have this all wrapped up. I've got our best antique-fine-jewels repairman on standby to return the dragon's missing eye to its rightful place in the medallion, if you find it's a fit." She lifted her coffee. "And thanks for this!"

Avery's mind was spinning as she headed up to the lab. She so hoped to find something helpful in the papers Micah had gathered, and now she had to ask him about that Monday after the accident. Had Anne signed the document and then left it on Micah's desk? It didn't seem like something her meticulous mother would have done.

She pushed through the lab door, resigning herself to handing over her untouched coffee to her partner, since she'd given the other one away. "I brought you a—" She stopped short, realizing she was talking to no one. The lab was empty.

Chapter Seventeen

Avery set her phone down after leaving a voice mail for Micah. It was completely unlike him not to show up, but maybe he was stuck in the subway without a signal or something. He was only a few minutes late. She called to have the medallion as well as the new ruby brought up, and ten minutes later Art and another guard were in her lab.

"Hi!" She smiled at him. It was strange that a week ago he'd probably been one of the guards in her lab and she hadn't even known. His visor was still pulled low over his brow, and now Avery knew that was by design; he'd probably been trying to stay incognito on the small chance she'd remember him from the few times they'd crossed paths during the accident investigation; she obviously hadn't. Dr. Singh said Avery had likely remained in latent shock for a number of days. Avery thought that was probably true for both her and Tilly. They'd been inside the car, and she'd never be able to erase those moments from her memory; they were still as clear as when it had happened.

Art nodded at her, unsmiling. "Let us know when you're ready to go to lunch, Ms. Ayers."

She stood up straighter and gave him a little salute, regretting it instantly. He was only doing his job. He clearly didn't want his coworker knowing anything about his outside work. "I'll do that," she said, keeping her expression serious.

He held the door open for his coworker, then glanced back and gave her a quick wink as he left.

Avery's heart jumped, making her smile again. He was a good guy. She was glad he was in her corner, with all the crazy stuff going on. She was learning his serious demeanor didn't mean he was a stick-in-the-mud. He just had a dry sense of humor.

Avery donned her cotton gloves, opened the case that held the dragon medallion, and got to work. Without Micah, the going was a little slow, but she made decent progress. By lunchtime she was nearly certain that the jewel Oliver Renell had submitted was the missing ruby eye of the dragon. She'd taken measurements of every angle of the void where the jewel belonged, then converse measurements of the ruby. It appeared to be a perfect fit, down to the micromillimeter. But the perimeter of the eye socket was another story. When she compared the existing right eye of the dragon to the void on the left and examined the way the inlaid ruby sat, flush to the perimeter of the gold, the measurements came out skewed differently for the new ruby. She'd run a computer simulation of the new ruby being placed into the empty eye socket, and she couldn't quite get the two dragon eyes to be perfectly symmetrical.

Avery growled in frustration and stepped back from the lab counter, removing her gloves and her Miltex magnifying loupe glasses and rubbing her eyes. Was it possible the problem wasn't a problem at all and it was simply the way the medallion had been poured when it was cast in eighteenth-century China? Or was it that the existing ruby eye wasn't seated correctly? In which case, had it been loose and repaired at some point? Or . . . she could hardly bring herself to entertain the idea, but in light of all the red flags with the certificate her parents had submitted, was the current eye not the original, authentic ruby? Was it indeed a spinel? It would certainly explain her father's scribbled calculations.

God, she wished Micah were here. She tapped her phone, but no calls or messages had come through. She used the phone in the lab to call for Art and his partner to come and lock everything back up. She'd get back into this after lunch.

Avery rode down in the elevator with them, Art just as quiet and professional as he had been this morning. Avery headed toward the front of the museum and Art went with his coworker in the other direction to Acquisitions Pending. Avery popped into the cafeteria just long enough to grab a sandwich to go. The line at the register seemed long today, but it was probably only because she was in a hurry. She'd planned to walk the handful of blocks to Bennington Bank and clear out whatever was in the safe-deposit box, but now she also wanted time to go by Micah's house and make sure he was okay. The lengthy line meant she had longer than she liked to decide between the subway and her car. If she took her car, she could hit the bank, the office to see if Sir Robert had seen Micah, and then run up to Harlem and knock on his door. She was beginning to get worried. She'd texted him and it had gone through, so she didn't think there was anything wrong with his phone.

In the parking garage, Avery pressed her remote start button, getting the air conditioning going so the car was beginning to cool when she got in. She wrapped up her half-eaten sandwich and set it on the passenger seat and pulled out of the MOA parking garage. She called Sir Robert on her way to the bank.

He picked up on the first ring. "Is it the eye?"

"What?" Avery asked.

"Sorry. I figured you were calling with an update on the medallion. No good news yet?"

"Oh," she said, chuckling. "It's looking good, sort of. I mean, the new ruby does seem to be the missing dragon eye." Should she get into the rest? There was too much up in the air. And she knew the science end of their job tended to go a little over Sir Robert's head at times. She'd seen his eyes glaze over while she and Micah were explaining the intricacies of authentication. "I found a, um, discrepancy with the other eye, though. It may be nothing; I just have to work through it. We're getting close. I hope to have a firm answer by tomorrow at the latest."

"Fantastic!" Sir Robert exclaimed. "Goldie will be thrilled when you tell her she can include the complete restored Emperor's Twins piece in her announcements at Friday's gala."

"Right, Nate said so too. *If*, Sir Robert. Just keep your fingers crossed. There's still an *if* to this. I really could use my other lab rat to take a look. My eyes were crossing by lunchtime today. Has he been in? Did he just forget his phone at home or something?"

"Micah? No. I thought he was meeting you there."

"He was supposed to," she said, disappointed and now more worried. "I don't like it. Micah's Mr. Reliable. It's not like him."

Sir Robert was quiet for a moment on the other end of the line. "Didn't you say he had to take his son back to school last night?"

"Just to the train station."

"Ah. He wouldn't have just gone along with him, would he? They're pretty close since Cicely died."

Would he have? "No, I don't think so. At least, not without letting one of us know he wouldn't be at work today."

"Hmm. Well, we've been here for a couple hours and he hasn't called or been in. I'll keep trying him, if you want. I'm sure he's fine," Sir Robert said.

Avery had a flash of irritation at him; he couldn't be sure Micah was fine. But he wasn't being callous, he was just Sir Robert. He and Micah were friends, but Avery and her parents had always been closer to Micah and his family. Sir Robert cared, but he probably truly believed it wasn't a big deal that Micah was unreachable.

"Yes, please, if you don't mind," she said, quelling her irritation. "That'd be good. Let me know when you get him."

She found a parking spot around the corner from the bank, and moments later she was in the bank lobby. Her heart raced with anticipation as she waited for the bank manager to meet with her. She should have let Art in on what she and Aunt Midge had figured out last night, but she'd tell him as soon as she got back to the museum. By then, she hoped to have something from the safe-deposit box that would knit together some of the pieces of this chaotic puzzle.

A pretty, middle-aged blond woman approached Avery in the lobby, holding out her hand. "I'm Mrs. Samson. You're Avery Ayers?"

"Yes."

"Come with me." The manager led Avery to her office, motioning for her to sit. "I understand you have the key to one of the safe-deposit boxes moved from the other branch last year?"

"I do," Avery said. "I don't have the vault number, unfortunately. I assume it's in one of my parents' names, Anne or

William Ayers. I know you'd normally have to verify identity, but I'm not sure if you're aware—they've . . . they've both passed away. All of their legal and financial holdings are now in my name. I can show you my ID." She reached for her purse.

Mrs. Samson looked sympathetic. "We are so sorry for your loss, Ms. Ayers." She tapped the keys on her computer, reading something. "Both Anne and William passed?"

"Yes. Last year in June."

"I see." She tapped the keys again, frowning. "One moment. I have to access a separate page, and this portal . . ." She appeared to be reading, her fingers momentarily frozen above the keys. "All right then. I see right here it's no problem to give you access. Your name is on the account."

Avery stared wide-eyed at the woman. "My name's on the account?" she repeated.

"Yes. Sometimes clients take that precaution, in the event it's necessary. Your parents did." She slid Avery's driver's license across the desk and checked it. "All set. Shall we?" She ushered Avery out and down two long hallways.

Avery had expected more difficulty in convincing the bank to grant her access to the safe-deposit boxes. Her parents had only ever used the small Springfield County Fidelity Bank, at least as far she knew. An unpleasant chill settled around her shoulders at the thought that they'd predicted the unpredictable, using a different bank for whatever was locked up and adding Avery's name to the account.

Mrs. Samson opened a heavy steel door and checked the note she'd made before leaving her office. "Let's see. We need vault five-seven-four." She moved to the far wall. "Here we are." She inserted her bank key and directed Avery to do the same.

Avery had never seen this process outside the movies. She helped Mrs. Samson pull the long metal box from the compartment once the small vault door was open. She stood looking down at it on the granite counter top. "Do I just open it?"

Mrs. Samson smiled. "I'll leave you in privacy to do that." She pulled the door closed behind her, and Avery was alone.

Avery took a deep breath, summoning her nerve. Much as she'd tried to imagine what could be in here, she really had no idea what to expect. Her parents' attorney had handled everything smoothly after the funeral, sitting with Avery, Tilly, and Aunt Midge and going over each item one by one, the bulk of which were now in Avery's or both girls' names: the bank accounts, the deed to the house, both their cars, their retirement account and annuities. Midge had been named as guardian to Tilly, and there was a trust fund with enough to cover the cost of a four-year university almost anywhere. Avery recalled being completely overwhelmed and confused, but the attorney had been infinitely patient and met with her and Midge a few more times until she felt she had a handle on things. She'd known then that her parents' planning had kept her and Tilly in their home and comfortable. But this. This was something else entirely. She was a little afraid to learn what they'd felt was so precious or controversial that it had to be separated out and hidden.

She lifted the lid, peering inside the red cloth-lined box. She blinked, making sure she wasn't missing anything. A lone black-and-silver key-chain flash drive lay at the bottom of the box. That was all.

Avery pulled on the chain she'd kept under her shirt since Saturday. She opened the clasp and threaded the necklace through the key chain hole on the flash drive, then tucked it back inside her top. Not positive she believed that was really all there was, she ran her fingertips over the entirety of the cloth-lined box, then turned it upside down, but there was nothing else.

Outside, lost in thought, she headed toward the corner. She almost wanted to take the rest of the afternoon off so she could get the flash drive home and see what was on it. She supposed she could check it out on her work laptop, but that just seemed like a bad idea. Without knowing what information this little piece of metal and plastic around her neck held, she really didn't want to risk inserting it into the laptop she and Micah had been using in the lab. Maybe she was being paranoid, but what if it somehow corrupted their files and all of the work they'd done?

She stopped to wait at the light before crossing, glancing toward her car half a block down on the right side. *Okay, yes, that does sound completely paranoid.* The flash drive had come from her parents. It had been in a safe-deposit box with all three of their names on it. Why on earth would her parents leave her something that would damage her work? Of course they wouldn't. Maybe it'd be fine to see what was on it when she got back to the lab? Otherwise she'd have to wait until tonight. She crossed with the light and dug around in her purse for her key fob.

She should have started the car already; her leather seats were going to be hot in this weather. From ten feet away, Avery pressed the remote start button.

She felt and saw the explosion before she heard it. Flames burst from the underside of her Jeep Cherokee, followed almost simultaneously by a deafening boom, and Avery was knocked backward off her feet, her vision filled for a moment with blue sky and skyscrapers rising around her. Stunned, she sat up and leaned forward, gingerly touching the elbow that had struck the pavement hardest. A car alarm filled the air and then was joined by others, though the high-pitched ringing in her ears was louder. Someone was shouting, but it sounded like they were underwater. A pair of hands slid underneath her arms and lifted her to her feet, dragging her back and then scooping her up and running with her. Her car was on fire. The flames reached up in wide, smoking tendrils onto and over the driver's side door and front end of the Jeep.

A smaller explosion blew the hood open, flames now coming from the engine. Avery saw Art Smith's worried face as he set her on the concrete and crouched down, pulling her with him.

"Get down now!" He hunched his body over hers, a much louder explosion shaking the ground beneath them.

Chapter Eighteen

"It got the fuel line," Art shouted, but he wasn't talking to her. He straightened up, and Avery saw his Bluetooth earpiece. He waved his arms, still in his security guard uniform, which looked enough like a police uniform that the scattered pedestrians listened when he shouted to get back and clear the area. Fortunately, most people had taken off quickly with the first explosion, but there had been a couple fender benders directly in the vicinity of the Jeep as drivers swerved to avoid the fire. No one seemed to be hurt.

Avery couldn't tear her gaze from her car. Her poor Jeep. It was her first car, bought with waitressing money way back when she was twenty. Cherry red and already three years old when she'd purchased it, it had a sunroof and bike rack and was her dream car. When her parents died, they'd left a nearly new Expedition and a metallic-blue Prius. She'd told Aunt Midge to take her pick, but Midge was too attached to her '57 Thunderbird. So they'd designated the Expedition as Tilly's, knowing William would have wanted his teenage driver safely ensconced in a big vehicle, and Anne's Prius stayed parked in the garage.

Avery had never been able to bring herself to sell it. She guessed she was now the owner of a Toyota Prius.

"—hurt?" Art had asked her a question, his face close to hers. Behind him, a fire engine wailed down Fifty-Seventh Street toward them.

She shook her head. Her ears were still fuzzy; he sounded partially muted. "I think I'm all right. Who did this? Are *you* okay? Why are you *here*?" It had just hit her that he was not at MOA but here, with her, at the perfect moment to pull her back from her car before she could get hurt.

He started to reply, but two police cars pulled up near them, followed by the fire engine. She watched as firemen extinguished the flames and first responders began dealing with the after-math—angry drivers with dented cars, people asking questions.

Art led Avery over to an ambulance that had just pulled up and directed the paramedic to check her over. Once she'd had a light shined in her eyes and answered questions about who the president was, they bandaged up her bloody elbow.

Art had left her to go talk with one of the police officers. The officer looked over at her, then at the foamy, smoking mess that used to be her car. He wrote something down, asked Art something and wrote some more, then headed over to the Jeep.

"What happens now?" Avery met him in the street, looking up at him.

"Did they say you're good? You don't need to go to the ER?"

"Yes. I swear." She showed him her bandaged elbow. "Minor injury. What did the officer say?"

"Just getting a few details about what happened. Was there anything in there you need?"

Everything inside her car was probably either burned or soaking wet. Besides Aunt Midge's sweater in the back seat, there really wasn't much. Sunglasses, a few CDs. "Nothing of value. I have my purse. Are we allowed to leave? I mean, am I? Oh jeez. I'll need to call someone." Her mind raced. Who could drive her all the way home to Lilac Grove? Micah. But not Micah. "Oh my God."

"We can go. They agreed to speak with you later. It's all right; I can drive you home."

"No, Art. We have to go to Micah's. I don't know if this is connected or not, but I haven't been able to reach Micah all day. And he never just blows off work."

He stared at her. "When did you last talk to him?"

"Last night, around dinnertime. But he was supposed to meet me in the lab this morning, and I can't get him on his phone, not even his house phone. This is not like him at all. He doesn't take sick days, and if he did, he would let me know."

He nodded. "Let's go see. You can tell me why the hell you were running around on a secret mission and keeping me in the dark while we drive."

Avery began to speak, but Art's expression stopped her. He wasn't simply giving her a hard time. He was angry.

In the passenger seat of his Dodge Ram truck, Avery fished the flash drive out of her blouse and showed him. The silver-and-black rectangle was about the same size as the safe-deposit box key. "I have no idea what's on it. Aunt Midge figured out the key must be to a box at some bank that had a Lexington Street address."

He looked at her sharply. "Why did it not occur to you to tell me? We *just* talked about this, Avery."

She raised her eyebrows. "Art, I am really sorry. For real." She rested her good elbow on the console and leaned toward him, waiting, so he'd have to look at her.

He finally did, scowling. "It was reckless. I'd say stupid too, but I know you're not."

"I'm sorry," she repeated. "Midge learned that the address of Bennington Bank used to be 1073 Lexington, which matched the key's inscription. But that branch moved over here to Third last fall. I didn't update you because, honestly, I thought I was going to get some more papers from a safe-deposit box. Who could have done this to my car? How would someone have been able to follow me?"

"I did. Anyone else could have too. You could have been killed," he said. "What if you'd started your car after you were in it?"

Avery blinked. That thought hadn't occurred to her. She felt the blood drain out of her head and heard a roar in her ears. What if she'd gotten into her car, buckled, and turned her key in the ignition instead of trying to get the AC going ahead of time? She took a breath, ready to defend herself, irritated at Art's irritation, but an abrupt wave of nausea hit her at that image, at what could have happened. She could have been inside her car. "I feel sick."

Art jerked the steering wheel and got the truck over to the curb. He reached around in the back, handing her a plastic bag. She rolled her eyes at him but kept it, putting her face near her open window. The cool breeze helped.

"Take some deep breaths," Art said. "In through your nose, out through your mouth."

She did as he instructed. It helped. "Sorry. I'm sorry." She turned her head toward him, resting it on the headrest. "Why would someone have tried to kill me?"

His eyebrows were furrowed, a deep crease between them, but this time not because he was angry with her. "To get you out of the way."

"Why?"

"I'm still working that out. The break-in at MOA Friday was part of this. Someone stole the original certificate of authenticity your mother signed. And yours is gone too."

"Someone doesn't want me to see the original signature," Avery blurted out. "That has to be it. She never would have signed two days early; I can't make that make sense. I don't think she ever actually certified the Emperor's Twins as genuine. There was a problem, and I think they knew. My dad left Micah a voice mail, saying he wanted to talk to him about the medallion before they turned in the report. And there's this." She pulled out the scrap of paper with her dad's numbers scrawled all over it.

Art had put the truck in park. He took it from her. "This doesn't mean anything to me."

She pointed. "These are specific gravity and chemical composition readings for a spinel. A man-made ruby. The real Emperor's Twins dragon is known through legend to have two natural Burmese ruby eyes. I think my dad knew. Maybe the medallion is real—I have no reason to believe otherwise; it's too intricate not to be," Avery said slowly. "But maybe the ruby eye is a spinel. Maybe they weren't going to sign the certificate at all. They would have had to tell Goldie, and she wouldn't have acquired it."

"And someone who needed the deal to go through made sure the signed certificate made it to Goldie and your parents never had the chance to do anything with what they knew."

"Yes." She was quiet, staring at the floor, trying to put herself into that investigation last year, to imagine what her parents had been thinking. "Art, they had to have known they were in danger. Why else would they have left me a trail of clues, a safe-deposit box key? Though I can't for the life of me fathom how they planned ahead for someone to plant those notes. And what about the phone calls? How could they have known that there'd be a need to put me in touch with you? They wouldn't have even known back then that I'd have this new ruby assignment and you'd be moonlighting at MOA. They . . . they couldn't have known anything. You didn't get involved until they were killed." Avery frowned, trying to unscramble the pieces and make them make sense. "But the note told me to find you for help." She stared at him.

Art was still, studying his hands on the steering wheel. A muscle in his jaw pulsed. He cleared his throat and then finally spoke. "I have to tell you something, Avery."

She held her breath without meaning to.

"It might be hard for you to hear. I want you to know, I haven't told you until this point because protecting you was more important than you knowing the truth. It still is. But I'm afraid if I don't tell you, not knowing will continue to compromise your safety even more."

"Art." She wasn't sure she was ready to hear what he was about to say.

"You've got to promise to take what I'm about to say only for what it is: a change in course to save your life. Yours, Tilly's, and Midge's. You cannot tell them." He looked at her, his intense gaze boring into hers. "That'll just undo any good there is to be gained by telling you. I'm going to lose my job over this," he muttered.

Avery bit the inside of her cheek, her hands clasped tightly in her lap. She knew she should tell him to drop it; nothing was worth his job. But she couldn't do it.

Art turned toward her in his seat. "Your father is alive."

Avery frowned. She shook her head slowly. "He can't be. I remember . . . at the hospital that night . . . the surgeon came out and talked to us himself. He said my dad's internal injuries were too severe. He couldn't save him." That was real. Her mind had worked against her for months, in her dreams, in her unpredictable anger, to twist what had happened and make it anything other than her parents both being dead, but they were.

"Avery."

"We went to the funeral."

Art reached over and took her hand, loosening her fingers, which were clenched tightly together. He held her hand between both of his, not speaking until she finally made eye contact with him. "The FBI made a decision that night."

Avery felt her pulse pounding in her temple. Even though her hearing had begun to normalize, now everything grew distant and far away: the sounds from the street outside the truck, someone's music farther down the block, a car horn. They were enclosed in a bubble, the two of them. Art's hands were warm, and his fingers felt rough on her skin. The brown stubble on his jaw and chin was a few days' growth; he must have been too tired or too busy to take the time to shave. His dark eyes never moved from hers, and she could see him weighing what to say next.

"Your parents were targeted because of the Emperor's Twins medallion. We found evidence of an explosive attached to the engine cradle of their car. None of you were meant to survive that night. I'm so, so sorry your mother didn't. But, Avery, your dad did."

He paused, letting that sink in, and then rushed forward. "By the time your father was in surgery, the FBI field officers were already in contact with Springfield PD and the highway patrol. The senior field officer strongly felt that if it became known that William had survived, not only would a second attempt be successful, but you and your sister would be used to get to him. Their director agreed. When your father woke up from surgery three days later, he was already in a different city with a new identity."

Avery was shaking her head before he even finished. "I don't believe any of this. If he was alive, he'd never have stayed away. He'd never have let us go through the worst pain imaginable, thinking he had died."

"He stayed away so that you could live. So that he could eventually have his family back. The moment he was well enough, he began pushing the Bureau's operatives to move on their plans to bring your mother's murderer to justice. But they needed proof. And your father didn't make it easy to protect him while he was chasing down answers on the Emperor's Twins and doing everything in his power to make sure he didn't compromise your and Tilly's safety."

She couldn't breathe. She could hardly swallow around the lump in her throat, and her eyes were hot with unshed tears. She covered her face with her hands, trying to gain control, but she was shaking; her entire body was shaking.

"Avery." Art put a hand on her shoulder, keeping it there and not moving at first.

She turned her face into his forearm, drawing in a hitching breath, and in one motion he wrapped his arms around her as she leaned into him. She let go, tears streaking down her cheeks, and she could finally breathe, her eyes closed and her cheek pressed into his chest. She didn't know how long she stayed that way. It could have been minutes or an hour.

Art held her, not speaking.

Avery's breathing began to slow. She felt her heartbeat slow too, leaving her head, leaving her throat, until she couldn't feel the heavy thudding anymore. She opened her eyes but didn't move. She couldn't yet. Art's chest was soft but firm, and his navy-blue uniform shirt smelled like fabric softener. Finally, she drew in a slow, steady, deep breath, feeling calmer. "Art, my dad . . ."

"Your dad is fine. He'd want me to tell you that he'll see you soon."

Chapter Nineteen

A very sat up, sniffling. She patted Art's uniform shirt where it was damp from her tears. "I don't, uh . . . I don't know what's wrong with me. My dad's alive. You just told me the best thing I've ever heard in my life. I didn't mean to get so . . ." She met his gaze and then looked away. She had no explanation for why she'd reacted that way.

"So human? So normal?"

She looked back at him.

"You almost died in an explosion and then learned that your father, who died a year ago, is alive. I think your reaction is completely normal."

"When can I see him?"

"Not yet. He's already broken protocol too many times. Right now would be the worst possible time for anyone to know he's still alive. But we're close. Whoever is behind this is getting nervous, and that equals careless. Let's go make sure Micah Abbott is all right."

He pulled out into traffic while Avery tried to process everything she'd just heard. "Whoever is behind this, whoever killed my mom, they had to have stolen the real ruby eye out of the medallion last year. Before my parents ever even began the process of certifying it. Right?"

Art nodded. "That's the working theory. They may have assumed the fake they made—what did you call it?"

"A spinel."

"They may have assumed their spinel was a good enough substitute that it'd slip right past your parents. They could have planned on it slipping right through with no one knowing the ruby eye wasn't real."

"Any good anthropologist with a gemology subspeciality would know it was fake. I haven't been able to finish evaluating it yet, but it's all about the math."

Art smiled at her. "You make it sound so simple, when it's honestly too complicated for me to really grasp. But, if the plan had worked, your parents would have certified the medallion in its entirety as genuine, MOA would have an authentic three-hundred-year-old artifact with a fake jewel in it, and the thief would have pocketed a sixteen-carat natural ruby. I assume that size ruby would be worth a small fortune."

"It depends what you call a small fortune," Avery said. "A flawless natural Burmese ruby that size would go for roughly fifteen million."

"Dollars." Art said it as a statement, but his expression was incredulous. "Fifteen million dollars?"

"Yep. That medallion, without either of the ruby eyes in it, would be worth around four million, given its relevance to history and the smaller inlaid jewels. The Emperor's Twins medallion, if it had both ruby dragon eyes intact, is estimated at a value of about forty-two million dollars."

Art shook his head, silent.

"You're properly speechless," she said, laughing. "It's seriously wild, isn't it? I don't spend much time thinking about the monetary value of these items. But with us thinking the existing ruby eye is fake, even if the one Oliver Renell submitted is real, that significantly diminishes the worth of the medallion."

"You're talking about tens of millions of dollars. Until now, I'd never heard any actual numbers. Jesus, Avery. Have you and your partners ever considered setting up some outside security for assignments like this?"

She sighed. "We should. My parents should have. I can see why we never have, though. Anytime we're handling an item with a high value like this, it's in a controlled setting. Like the MOA lab. MOA has its own security. That should have been enough."

"Not when you're dealing with an item that's been tampered with before it gets to you. It's something to think about going forward; that's all I'm saying." They were now on Micah's street, and Art found a parking spot out front. "Is this it?"

"Yes. You'll come with me?" She started to open the truck door and looked over her shoulder at him.

He was already out and shutting his door. "No, I'll let you come with me. Hang back some." He climbed the steps to the brownstone ahead of her, one hand on his gun in the holster at his hip.

She'd never even noticed before that he carried it. The other MOA guards had Tasers on their utility belts. "Do you carry that at the museum? They let you?"

He glanced at her, his hand outstretched to ring the bell. "I'm a cop. I always carry."

That fact made her feel safer and more worried at the same time. She was gripped with a bad feeling about Micah. She reached past Art and rang the bell and then knocked loudly.

"You've tried calling him more than once?"

"Several times, on his cell and his house phone, and so has Sir Robert."

Art waited a full minute, then pounded on the door and called loudly. "Micah Abbott, open up. It's Art Smith with Springfield County Police." He looked up and down the street, which Avery had also seen him do when they were approaching the house.

Behind him, Avery dialed his phone one more time, clinging to hope that he was fine and just not home. The house phone rang and rang on the other side of the door until the answering machine came on.

"Micah Abbott, I'm coming in. I believe your life is in danger." He turned to Avery. "Please tell me there's a hidden key somewhere?"

"Um, no. Not that I—" She gasped. "Wait!" She ran down the steps to the truck and returned with her purse. She rummaged inside the zippered inner pocket and produced a house key on a yellow-duck key chain.

"Perfect." He put his arm out, motioning her to stand behind him and away from the window. "Stay right there." Art turned the key in the lock and threw the front door open, stepping inside and calling Micah's name again.

Avery leaned forward on the porch, peering inside and seeing Art dart to the right toward Micah's dining room. A moment later she heard him speak on his phone. He gave Micah's address in Hamilton Heights. "I need backup and an ambulance. I have an injured resident, Micah Abbott, midfifties, Caucasian male, gunshot wound to the left shoulder. Premises not cleared yet."

Avery was inside the house in an instant at those words. She found Art kneeling over Micah, one hand pressed over his left chest. Her friend was breathing but unconscious. There was a lot of blood.

He looked up at her. "You shouldn't be in here!"

She dropped to the floor on Micah's other side, putting a hand on his arm. She cringed, seeing the blood. A gunshot wound to the left chest—had he been shot near his heart? The lung? How long had he been like this? Her friend's skin was ashy and gray, his lips a pale purplish blue. He had to live. He had to; she couldn't think about any other outcome. "I'm not leaving!"

He glared at her, then grabbed her hand, lifted his off the bloody bullet-entry wound, and replaced it with Avery's. He pressed on her hand with the flat of his palm, demonstrating. "Constant pressure, both hands. Don't let go. Don't take your eyes off his chest. Yell if he stops breathing." He stood.

"What? Don't leave me!"

"I've got to secure the house. The gunman could still be here. Pressure and breathing, got it?" He pointed at Micah's rapidly rising and falling chest.

Avery applied pressure. Art went through the dining room into the kitchen, gun drawn. Avery's gaze darted around wildly, seeing movement in every corner and behind every piece of furniture. *Be empty*, she thought. Let him find an empty house, no gunman, no danger. Whoever had done this could easily still be here. Micah's brownstone was an eclectic mix of the elegant old-world decor Cicely had strived for layered with single-dad functionality. Micah and Cicely had lived here since they married nearly thirty years earlier, and a decade or so ago they'd moved Cecily's mother in too. Every room exuded a lovely, tasteful, if slightly neglected feel. Though his study was upstairs in the spare room, Micah had a workstation down here too, taking up half the dining room table. It looked like a tornado had blown through. Papers and file folders were scattered everywhere—floor, kitchen sink, the back of the couch in the front room. Kitchen drawers stood open along with a few cabinet doors, reminding Avery of her own kitchen after the break-in.

She looked toward the ceiling, able to follow Art's progress through the house from doors being flung open and hitting the walls of rooms he was checking. It sounded uneventful so far, thank God. She kept returning her gaze to her stacked hands on Micah's chest, watching his breathing. She hadn't visited her friend often enough after his wife died. She should have. She could have brought him dinners for longer than the few weeks she'd done so. She should have helped him clear out Cicely's things when he was ready. She should have helped him get Noah ready to go away to college last summer. She'd first been gone in Philly, and then, when she was back, she'd been immersed in her own loss.

When Micah was better, when he was better and back home and fine, she'd fix her should-haves. She'd help him choose some new drapes, help clear the layer of dust, brighten up the place for him. When he was better. Avery bent at the waist and pressed her lips to Micah's forehead, her tears wetting his skin. "You have to be okay. Micah, do you hear me? Listen to me. You'd better hold on. You have to get through this. I can't lose one more person. Especially not you."

Avery's head jerked up at the sound of the second ambulance in her life that day. "See? They're coming to help you. Hang in there, Micah, please. You have to, for Noah and me and Tilly and all of us."

Avery didn't move until the paramedics surrounded her and Micah and one of them swiftly swapped a thick sheaf of sterile bandages for her hands, keeping his hand in place now. Another paramedic put an oxygen cannula in Micah's nostrils and started an IV. When they raised the stretcher onto its wheels to take him out, Avery followed, surprised to see a few of his neighbors on the front sidewalk. The one she'd exchanged pleasantries with in the past, coming and going, motioned her over. Avery racked her brain for the woman's name and finally came up with Vera Washington.

"Is Micah all right? What happened?" The woman's gaze followed her neighbor as he was loaded into the back of the ambulance.

"We don't really know what happened. I came to check on him when he didn't come to work today."

Vera's husband spoke. "You were right; we should have called the police." He shook his head. "My wife thought she heard something early this morning. A loud crack, like the one last winter when that big branch came down on our roof," he said, pointing up at the enormous maple tree that towered overhead.

"I made him go look." Vera picked up where he left off. "Our tree seemed fine this time, so we came right over and knocked on Micah's door, making sure he was okay."

Avery's eyes were wide. Art was going to want to hear this. She turned briefly to call him over, but he was already approaching. "And was he? Did he come to the door?"

Vera shook her head, her mouth turned down. "We should have known. Fred said he must be sleeping and we should leave him be, but I know he's always up early. We have our morning coffee on our back porches together most mornings. We're all early risers." She looked up at her husband. Her tone was sad rather than blaming.

"You were right," Fred told Vera, putting a hand on her shoulder. "I just thought—we know how hard he works, plus with his boy home all weekend, I figured he needed his sleep. We waited a while, but when he didn't answer the door, we left. Figured it was a car backfiring or someone around the block got hit with one of these big old branches. We could have called for help hours ago if we'd known something was wrong."

"Was he shot?" Vera leaned toward Avery, her voice a whisper. "Is that what we heard? That man is the sweetest—who on earth would do something like that?"

Avery nodded. "He was shot." She was aware of Art standing behind her now and unsure of what she was allowed to share about the scene inside the house, but she knew this couple cared deeply for Micah. They'd all lived here ever since Avery could remember. "You didn't see anything strange? No sign that someone had broken in?" She knew it was a dumb question as soon as she'd said it.

"Oh no," Vera replied. "I wish we'd seen something. Then we'd have called the police right away. But everything seemed normal, except him not answering his door. Fred thought he must be sleeping in, but I figured he'd already left for work."

The detective Art had been speaking with, a James Graham, had joined them as well, and he handed Vera and Fred Washington his card. "Thank you, ma'am. It's obvious you folks are good neighbors. If anything else comes back to you, give me a call."

Vera had tears in her eyes as she looked up at Avery. "We'll go visit him as soon as we can. Micah will be all right," she said, taking Avery's hand in hers. "We know he'll be all right; he's got to be, for his boy. Will you call and let me know as soon as you hear anything? Fred, go get me a pen," she said to her husband. "I'll write down our number."

Avery stepped away, wanting to catch the ambulance to see where they were taking Micah, but the vehicle was already backing out of the driveway. Before she could say a word to Art about wanting to follow, he shook his head.

"No. We need to get you home. Too much has happened. I've got another officer doing a sweep at your house, just to make sure everything's fine, but we need to go."

"But—"

"Avery, my only priority right now is protecting you. You're smack in the middle of too many pieces of this puzzle, and I'm not confident you or your family is safe. Detective Graham here has already sent someone to talk to Noah at his school, and I promise you, as soon as I can guarantee you aren't a target, I'll take you myself to the hospital to see Micah."

She gave up. Art let her go back into the house to collect a few things she thought Micah might want when he woke up. When she came back downstairs, the forensics team was already at work, marking areas in the dining room and snapping pictures.

Art had already given a detailed account to Detective Graham, but Graham had a few questions for Avery before they left. When he asked if Avery had any idea who might have done this to her colleague, she replied, "He was shot because of me."

Graham frowned, looking over at Art and then back at Avery. "How so?"

She began to go into detail about how Micah had promised he'd search through his copies of work-related documents for anything regarding the collector who had submitted the medallion so she could try to connect the dots on what was happening, but Art stopped her halfway through.

"I've told Detective Graham that I overheard you and Micah discussing that Saturday night. I'm sure the whole little group we were sitting with did too. Sir Robert, Nate, Francesca, and Wilder."

Avery took a step back, staring at him. "You're not suggesting any of them would hurt Micah over whatever he'd planned to give me?"

"I'm not sure of anything at this point. Do you really think it's a coincidence that whoever shot your friend happened to come upon him while he was in the middle of gathering old records on the assignment?" He spread his arms out to encompass the papers scattered around the dining room and kitchen.

"I . . . um . . . I mean, some of this is just Micah. He normally kind of has stuff everywhere."

Art turned to the other detective. "Will you keep me updated on anything you find referencing the medallion or an Edward Johnstone? Even if it seems like nothing, Ms. Ayers may be able to shed light on it."

Graham nodded. "My sergeant already verified you're still working the original homicide case. I'm sure you're aware the FBI field agents have been coordinating efforts between us, them, and Springfield County's PD. Keeping everyone in the loop isn't a problem. To me, this looks like that couple next door might have interrupted the shooter and made him run off, hopefully before he found whatever he was after."

Two black unmarked sedans arrived as Avery and Art were pulling away from the curb. In the rearview mirror, Avery saw three men in dark suits on their way up to Micah's front door. "Wow. FBI too, huh?"

"It's a collaborative effort. A field agent arrived to check out your car, too, just after we left. All those old movies that show the feds showing up and kicking local law enforcement to the curb perpetuate the idea that it's us versus them. More often than not, now, it's pretty widely accepted that a coordinated approach usually works best."

"I'm learning more than I ever wanted to know about law enforcement," Avery said.

On the drive back to Lilac Grove, Avery checked in with Tilly and Aunt Midge. Halston had chewed off part of his cast and they'd had to take him in that morning for a new one, but otherwise all seemed fine. She tipped her head back on the headrest of Art's truck and closed her eyes, feeling the beginnings of a headache. Her elbow was throbbing, too, under the bandage.

Avery's mind had Sir Robert, Francesca, Nate, and Wilder in a rotating queue; she couldn't stop thinking about what Art had said. Her parents had worked with Sir Robert for nearly a decade. It was true that Francesca had started dating him only a year or so ago, but she seemed to be genuinely into him. And Francesca also held a great deal of respect for Goldie Brennan in her MOA position. Nate was a bit of an outlier, as he'd been at MOA only since last year, and all Avery knew about him was what he'd told her—and that Goldie loved him enough to trust him with a lot of responsibility in his job. And Wilder . . . Wilder as someone who'd be driven to forge a jewel for millions or kill to cover up the evidence made absolutely no sense at all. Avery couldn't remember a time when he hadn't been in their lives. He'd never seemed to care much about money one way or another. And he was crazy about Aunt Midge, who would literally murder him if he ever tried to hurt Avery or Tilly.

She threw Wilder out as a suspect. She didn't care what Art might have to say about that; he didn't know Wilder. Avery tried to imagine any of the other three having an intricate plan to swap a fake gemstone with a real one and then killing the collector to keep him quiet. But how would Renell have known anything? If he truly was just a collector who'd found the Emperor's Twins ruby, he'd have easily discovered that the one-eyed dragon was at MOA and he'd have submitted his find. But why all the secrecy, the refusal to meet in person or by phone? And why on earth had he been killed?

She couldn't accept that any of the three people who'd over-heard her at the fire talking with Micah could have wreaked the havoc of the past week and a half. There had to be another explanation, another culprit. Her mind went to that one-time date with Tyler Chadwick. He'd been such a flirt right off the bat, and she'd been so flattered when he had asked her out. She hated to admit the possibility that her date with a Hollywood actor had been about anything other than him being attracted to her, but . . . why had he asked her so many questions about the value of the ruby? And he'd actually had the nerve to try to talk her into taking him to see it that night. Avery had thought at the time that he was just being pushy. Now she wondered if it was more than that.

Her eyes snapped open, and she scrolled to his number in her phone. Art looked curiously at her as she left a voice mail for him, saying it was urgent and to please call her back. She followed it up with a text, asking him to call her.

"What's that about?"

"Hold on," she said. "I can explain in a minute." She made another call, this time to Goldie. She filled the curator in on poor Micah, trying to offer reassuring words; she could hear from the woman's voice how upset she was. "Goldie, I'm sorry to ask you to do this, but it's vital that I reach one of the actors from the studio filming at MOA. It may help the detective figure out who hurt Micah."

"Of course. I have the assistant producer's phone number. I'm sure I shouldn't give it out, but could I call her and ask her to phone you right away?"

"That would be wonderful," Avery said.

"Is there anything I should tell her before she calls you back?" Goldie asked.

"You could let her I'm trying to reach an actor in production there. His name is Tyler Chadwick. I've tried calling him, but maybe she can have him call me. I'm with the detective now, and it would help a lot."

"I'm on it," Goldie said. "Assuming I can get her, expect a call from her or your Mr. Chadwick shortly. The assistant producer's name is Mallory Fein."

Art cleared his throat when Avery had hung up. "Care to explain?"

"I went on a date with this actor I met at MOA. He was a little obsessed with the medallion. He asked me a trillion questions about the dragon and the new ruby. I didn't think much about it then, but he even wanted us to go back to MOA and see if we could get a guard to bring us the ruby so he could get a look at it. Of course I told him that was crazy. And—oh my God." She gasped as something else occurred to her.

Art was staring at her.

"Um. Expressway," she said, pointing ahead. "Eyes on the road, Art Smith."

At that, he gave her a quick one-eyebrow-cocked glance. "Oh my God what?"

"The Firefly movie is filming in the south wing and part of the lower level—the basement. Tyler has access to the basement, where the medallion's certificate went missing. Did you ever run into him down there?"

He shook his head. "No. The only one I ran into down there was Nate. But this actor, Tyler Chadwick. I'm glad you told me about him."

Art took the Lilac Grove exit off the expressway. Avery could hardly believe it was only four thirty in the afternoon. Her Monday had been so long, she could have sworn she'd leaped into Wednesday by now.

Her phone rang as the truck pulled into her driveway. She grabbed it on the first ring, putting it on speaker.

"Ms. Ayers? Mallory Fein with Action Entertainment. I'm unfortunately not able to release any contact information for persons affiliated with the studio. I can have our legal department get in touch with the detective you mentioned to Ms. Brennan, as it seems there are some questions needing to be answered; they'll be able to help with reaching out to Mr. Chadwick. But I can tell you that Tyler Chadwick is no longer in production for our Firefly sequel. His manager notified Action Entertainment yesterday that he had a conflict and is no longer available."

Chapter Twenty

Avery couldn't believe she'd been tricked by someone as pushy and elitist as that jerk Tyler Chadwick. If that was even his name. And for what? A few scraps of information about the ruby? She couldn't see how or why any of that had benefited him. She and Art would need more time later to talk, since they'd just parked outside the house, but there was one thing she was certain of after hanging up with Mallory Fein. Francesca was up to something.

"Tilly, I'm home!" she yelled up the stairs from the foyer, Art standing behind her and Halston wagging and vying for pets and attention from both of them in his brand-new hot-pink cast.

Her sister slid into view at the top of the stairs in fuzzy purple kitten socks paired with orange-and-yellow plaid shorts and one of William's old Christmas sweaters. "Oh my gawd!" She galloped down the steps and threw her arms around Avery, then pulled back and looked her up and down. "Are you okay?"

"I'm fine. My personal bodyguard saved me."

Tilly threw her arms around Art. "Thank you!"

Art's shocked expression was priceless. He put his hands up in surprise, looking down at Tilly hugging him. Several inches shorter than Avery and a full foot shorter than Art, she made him look like a giant. He finally settled for patting her on the back. "You're welcome."

Tilly let go and stared up at him. "It's a good thing you've been stalking my sister."

"I haven't—"

She cut him off, smiling sweetly. "I'm just messing with you. Come on, Auntie has dinner ready. She's been all twitchy since your friend knocked on the door to search our house for killers and bugs and bombs, since Avery was almost blown up."

"Um." Avery looked back at Art as they started toward the kitchen. *Sorry.* She mouthed the word, giving him a helpless shrug. She had no control over what came out of Tilly's mouth. Passing Tilly in the doorway, Avery paused and motioned from her sister's head to her feet with a flick of her wrist. She understood the fuzzy socks, but the rest of her outfit was just confusing. "This is a nice look on you."

Tilly curtsied. "Thank you, I know."

"You could take this stuff a little more seriously, you know," Avery said. "Micah was shot this morning."

Tilly made bug eyes at Avery, her hands on her hips. "I know that. You told me. And whoever rigged your car almost cost me my sister on top of my parents. What should I do, A? You won't let me in on anything, Auntie wouldn't let me help even if you did, and now my nightmares are even weirder since all this mysterious note stuff started. How would you like me to act? Should I get scared and cry every time Halston barks at a leaf? 'Cuz I'm almost at that point, and I can try to rush it if it'd seem more appropriate to you."

Avery took a step back. "No." She shook her head. "I'm sorry. You're right. Maybe you're handling this better than any of us."

"Maybe I am."

Aunt Midge was at the kitchen island grating fresh Parmesan cheese over a steaming casserole that must have just come out of the oven. The table was set with a fourth place for Art and already held a large platter of garlic bread, a salad with three dressing choices, a heaping bowl of mixed vegetables, and three dozen chocolate chip cookies piled high in a cookie tin. Midge grabbed Avery and pulled her in for a tight hug. She didn't say a word, which was a little frightening. She finally let go, holding on to Avery's arms, and still didn't speak. Her gaze went to Art and then back to Avery. She took a deep breath, yanked her apron off, and carried the chicken Parmesan with potholders over to the table.

Tilly made eye contact with Avery. "Told you," she murmured.

They joined Aunt Midge at the table without being asked. The silence was painfully awkward. Tilly took a piece of bread and passed the platter to Art.

"Auntie, this looks so—" Avery stopped abruptly as Midge set the spatula down on the table with a smack.

"This assignment"—she chewed the words and spat them out as unpalatable—"is over." Her stare burned a hole right through Avery. "I won't tolerate it. Give it to another company. Let them die over it. I'll tell Goldie Brennan myself if you won't."

Avery folded her hands in her lap, sucking in her lips between her teeth. She had never, ever seen Midge like this.

When Avery didn't speak, Aunt Midge went on, her pitch rising along with her ire. "I lost my brother and your mother over this cursed medallion. How can you even think of persisting in this? Do you want your sister to have no one? Should Noah be left parentless too? What's it going to take for you to leave it?

Because, clearly, your parents dying, my dog being hurt, Micah being shot, and you nearly being blown up is not enough!"

Avery swallowed hard, her eyes burning. At the other end of the table, Midge was perfectly still, but she might as well have been vibrating, her distress was that palpable. To Avery's left, Tilly was uncharacteristically quiet, staring at the salad dressings. To her right, Art sat frozen with his hand still on his fork. Avery stood and walked around the table. She knelt by Aunt Midge and wrapped her arms around her. She could have been hugging a post, the tiny woman was so completely unyielding and stiff. Avery could barely feel her breathing. She held on. "Okay."

Midge drew in a deep breath, her posture softening in Avery's arms. "I don't believe you."

Avery loosened her grip so she could see her aunt's face. She expected tears but found only resignation and defeat. "Auntie. I didn't know until today that I was involved in something this dangerous. I'd never intentionally put you or Halston or Tilly in harm's way."

Midge nodded. "I know that."

"I'm sure my parents never expected they'd end up being targeted either."

"I know."

"If you really want me to terminate the assignment, to have Goldie get someone else to finish it, I will. But there's more at stake here than an artifact. Auntie," she said, hesitating and looking over at Art. She knew he had risked his livelihood telling her about her dad. She couldn't break his confidence, but she didn't know how else to make her family understand why it was so important that they get to the bottom of what was happening with the medallion and the new ruby. If they didn't, it would never be safe for William to return to them.

Art's eyebrows were furrowed, the crease between them deeply indented. He closed his eyes and then reopened them, giving her a single nod. As he did, he rested his elbow on the dining room table and covered his mouth and jawline with one hand, and Avery could see how conflicted he was.

"Auntie," she said again. "Tilly. Someone did cause the accident that night on the way home from Bello's. Art says there was explosive material found on the engine cradle. Mom and Dad's notes point to the existing ruby eye in the medallion at MOA being a fake, but someone needed MOA to believe it was real. If authorities aren't able to catch whoever's responsible, then we'll never—"

"Never what, A?" Tilly leaned forward, intensely focused on her sister. "Never what?"

"This can't leave this room," Avery said. She dropped her voice to just above a whisper, looking from Tilly to Aunt Midge. "This staying between us is a matter of life and death, and also Art's job. I'm serious."

"We understand," Aunt Midge said, sounding almost like herself again. She nodded, saying it again to Art. "We do. It won't leave this room."

"Dad is alive." Avery held her breath, watching her family.

"I knew it!" Tilly's chair tipped backward onto the floor as she stood and pointed across the table at Avery. "I knew it." She picked up her chair and sat back down. "I told you guys. Just saying."

"He's under protection, then?" Midge asked, her tone hopeful. "Is that what happened? What about Anne, Detective?" she asked Art.

He shook his head. "I'm sorry. Your sister-in-law truly didn't survive the accident. William is considered a federally protected witness in an ongoing case. He was transferred to a safe medical facility after extensive surgery for internal injuries from the accident. Once he regained consciousness and understood, he agreed to stay in hiding until the responsible party or parties could be caught. He was afraid they'd go through his family to get to him if they knew he'd survived."

Aunt Midge clapped her hands together. "Oh my goodness. Oh my. But now Avery's in danger until this is all wrapped up."

"You're all in danger," Art said, "the moment the killer realizes William is alive. It's imperative no one else knows." He looked at Avery. "No one. Not Wilder. Not your boyfriend Hank. Not Goldie. Not even Micah or Sir Robert. Do you understand?"

"Okay, but FYI, Hank's *not* Avery's boyfriend anymore," Tilly said.

Art raised his eyebrows at that but didn't comment.

"Is my brother all right now? He's recovered from the accident?" Midge asked.

"I'm told he's fully recovered. I'm not privy to any other information."

"When can we see him?" Tilly asked.

"I can't answer that either; I'm sorry. The best chance at getting him home is if we do our part to tie this case up." He nodded at Avery, his gaze going to the portion of chain visible at her neck. "I'm hopeful there'll be something significant in the papers at Micah's house, and we need to see what's on that flash drive."

The mood in the kitchen when Avery and Art left Midge and Tilly to do dishes was night-and-day different from when Avery had walked through the door earlier. In Anne and William's office, Avery set her laptop on her mother's desk, glancing over at her dad's empty one. God, she hoped to see him sitting at it soon. The idea of it made her smile—she and her dad here in the home office, working side by side.

Art tipped his head, giving her an appraising smile as he carried a chair around to sit beside her. "Feeling better, I see."

She nodded. "I can hardly believe it's true. But I know it is. I wanted to believe Tilly was right when we got that first note. I can't wait until he's home." She plugged the flash drive into the USB port.

Less than a minute later, she and Art had their pick of files to choose from. "Start with the first one," he suggested.

She clicked on the first file, and a copy of the intake form for the Emperor's Twins medallion appeared, with two sections starred. "Okay, this is the initial form that's filled out when we take an assignment. It gives information on the submitting collector—Edward Johnstone, right there; location of origin when it was originally acquired; initial contact person—the star there, next to Francesca Giolitti's name; whether there have been any prior appraisals and by whom—the other starred item, Rizzolo Fine Jewelry; and then this space where you can write whether an outside appraisal has been declined; and finishing with the last section, MOA's intention of acquiring the piece, pending the results of our process."

"Edward Johnstone is the one who called you, right? What was it he said? I can go get my notes," Art offered.

"It's all right. He said not to let the ruby or medallion out of my sight. And trust no one—I remember that."

"Hmm."

"I know." Avery looked at him. "Makes it sound like he felt something shady had happened with his submission." She went back to the flash drive contents and chose the next file.

The screen filled with a photo of Francesca and a hand-some dark-haired man. They were in front of some type of shop. The man's hand was on Francesca's waist, and her fingers were touching his upper arm as she leaned toward him. It looked like she was either telling him something in confidence or about to kiss his cheek.

"Well, that's interesting," Art said. "Look at the date stamp. Whoever put this photo on the flash drive went to the trouble to make sure the date was visible."

"This was two days before my parents died. The day before my dad left that voice mail for Micah saying he wanted to talk about the medallion." She left the photo file open and clicked the next item.

Another photo appeared, this one with the light fading, as if it was late afternoon or early evening. It was the shop Francesca and the dark-haired man had been standing in front of. The man was alone in this photo, just inside the glass front door, which bore the words *Rizzolo Fine Jewelry* with lettering under-neath: *JITA, ENAGO*. The man appeared to be locking up, as the store looked empty.

"What is that? What are those letters?" Art pointed.

"JITA is the Jewelers International Trade Affiliate and ENAGO is the European–North American Gemology Organi-zation. I'm a member of ENAGO. JITA is a designation some international shops will take on as a way of letting customers know they're worldwide." She frowned, putting her face closer to the screen. "How do I make this bigger?"

"Zoom." Art pointed to the small plus and minus signs in the corner.

"Oh," she said. "Duh." Zooming in, she rolled the cursor over the screen near the top. "I recognize this. Isn't this below the High Line? So we know right where this jewelry shop is. And we know Francesca's friendly with this man who works here."

"Francesca's friendly with lots of folks," Art commented.

"Sure seems like it." Something was jabbing at her memory. Something to do with Aunt Midge's Prince Ivan. How did that even make any sense? Maybe it was something vague that had been said the night of the party.

"Next one?" Art asked.

"Sorry." The next file was a photo as well. It was of a scrap of floral stationery with a string of letters and numbers written on it in two rows. Avery reached across the desk to the little clear plastic cube her mother kept to corral her blank note papers and held up the same exact floral paper.

"Aha," Art said. "What were your parents trying to tell us with this?" He took a small notepad from his pocket and jotted down the digits carefully. He glanced at Avery. "Could you read them to me while I double-check myself?"

"Sure." She recited the letters and numbers on the screen, pausing where there were spaces. Art stopped her at the ninth digit.

"Hold on." He erased two numbers and switched their order. "All right, once more from the beginning."

Avery threw a look at him in her peripheral vision. He was intently focused on the notepad, pencil poised to make any further necessary corrections. Odd. Why didn't he just look at the screen and check them himself? She read them aloud, slowly.

"Thanks."

She half expected him to say something about why he'd needed her to double-check him, but he didn't. "Okay, last file," she said. "Ready?"

He nodded once.

The photo that filled the screen was of a slightly blurry Francesca, but with a different gentleman this time. They stood in front of what looked like a hotel. The man was shorter than Francesca, dressed in a brown suit and wearing round-framed glasses. Avery squinted and peered more closely at the screen. It was obvious that the shot had been snapped from a distance, and the quality left something to be desired.

She gasped. "Oh my God." Avery covered her mouth. She stared a moment longer at the screen and then turned to Art.

His attention was on the screen, but he appeared unimpressed. He frowned at the image. "Right, Francesca again. With yet another man."

Avery shook her head. "No, look closer. Not just another man."

Art used the zoom feature, staring at the screen. "Is that . . . ? I'm not sure; I only saw the postmortems. Wait, look at the date stamp. Is that Oliver Renell?"

"Yes. I'm sure of it."

Art frowned, keeping his eyes on the image. "I thought you'd said no one had met him."

"That's what Nate told me. He said Renell wouldn't even meet him in the lobby of his hotel so he could hand off the contingent contract." She checked the zoomed-in photo. "That looks like the front of Beckworth Suites, doesn't it?"

Art nodded. "It sure does."

"In his emails, Renell told me exactly who he'd had contact with." Avery racked her brain. "Hold on." She opened a new window on her laptop and searched her email inbox. She pulled up the first email reply from Oliver Renell, skimming through what he'd said. "Yes, I knew I remembered right. This is what he wrote:

'Following my initial discussion with acquisitions liaison Ms. Giolitti, my only point of contact at Museum of Antiquities has been Mrs. Goldie Brennan. Mrs. Brennan did utilize the services of her grandson Nate, who I understand works in acquisitions, to deliver the contingent contract to me, though we did not meet in person. I had the gem couriered to MOA, care of Mrs. Brennan, on Wednesday, June 2nd, at which time it was signed into custody by Mrs. Brennan herself. I respectfully request to limit my communications strictly to Goldie Brennan and yourself. Ms. Brennan is aware and has agreed to honor this request. It should be stated on record that the gem never left my sight between Munich and the moment I gave the package to my private courier. Suffice it to say, I guarantee you are working with the gem I acquired in Munich.'"

Avery stopped reading. "There's more, but that's the relevant part I remembered. I guess Nate didn't know Francesca had gotten to meet Renell in person—at least someone did. He's so adamant that he only communicate with Goldie and me. He never says why, but don't you think the way he's so specific with all of this is a little strange?"

"I wish I'd had the benefit of meeting the man. He definitely sounds concerned about getting all the details on record here," Art said. "Maybe something about Francesca rubbed him the wrong way? Have you ever known that to happen with any of the other jobs you've had through MOA?"

She shook her head. "No. If anything, people seem to love working with her. She's well-spoken and sharp, and she sort of has this way of making whoever she's with feel special. It's not just Sir Robert, though I admit he's totally obsessed with her."

"It seems she wasn't successful at making Renell feel special," he said. "What's this?" He pointed at another email in the same thread between Avery and Renell.

"He was replying to my request asking if we could meet in person. Of course he said no."

"Not that part. Here."

She read aloud. "'*There is an important matter we should speak about after the authentication is completed.*'"

"I take it you never had a chance to speak with him about whatever he's referencing?"

"No. This is so maddening. I wish he'd been more forthcoming. I'm sure he felt it wasn't safe."

"I know the investigation's still in process for Renell's murder," Art said. "I haven't heard yet whether anything helpful was found in Renell's hotel room. I'd love to know what his aversion to Francesca is."

"She's somehow in the middle of this," Avery said. "Dad and Mom wouldn't have put these photos on this flash drive without good reason. I don't know this man." She pointed to the dark-haired man Francesca was with in the first photo. "But Francesca does. These photos are significant; we just don't know in what way. Especially since Dad risked his safety—and, by extension, ours—in order to add the most recent photo of Francesca and Renell. That must be why the bank manager reacted so strangely when I said both my parents had passed; he'd been in recently to add to the flash drive."

"Definitely important."

Avery pointed at the screen. "Renell met with Francesca on June second, the same day he had the ruby couriered to Goldie. He didn't waste any time after this meeting. Art." She swiveled in her chair to face him. "I know who we can ask."

Chapter
Twenty-One

Avery made it to the Manhattan office early Tuesday morning and had coffee brewing when Sir Robert arrived.

"Oh, it smells delicious in here! Where's your car? I didn't see it outside. Thought you'd be at MOA today," Sir Robert said.

"The Jeep's in the shop," Avery said, her first lie to Sir Robert. She and Art had vehemently disagreed on several points. Art wouldn't budge on his stance that Sir Robert was not to be told about the explosion or the visit to the bank. Avery had tried to convince Art that no matter what was going on with Francesca, Sir Robert couldn't possibly be in on it. But Art's cop brain didn't see it that way. "I have a rental. And I'm heading to MOA in a bit but had some things to work on here this morning."

"Any word on Micah?" Sir Robert asked. He set his briefcase at his desk and moved through the shop to the back, turning on the rest of the lights.

"I talked to Noah on the way in. Micah's in critical but stable condition in the ICU. I hate how that sounds."

Sir Robert nodded. "That's a non-update. It tells us nothing. And how are *you*, after your day yesterday?"

"A little shaken up from finding Micah on my own that way. But nothing I won't survive."

"Now, I didn't quite catch all of it. You decided to use your lunch break to go and check on Micah, and when he didn't answer, you used your key? And he'd been shot? It's just so hard to believe!"

She nodded. "The police are pretty sure it has something to do with our assignment. The ruby and now the medallion." The coffeemaker finished, and she poured them each a cup. She looked at Sir Robert over her shoulder. He appeared to be texting someone on his phone. "Are you still three sugars, no cream?" she asked.

"Absolutely. Leopards don't change their spots, you know. Thank you, Avery," he said as she set his coffee on his coaster.

She set hers down next to his at his desk and then dragged her chair over, sitting near him. She tried not to think about her phone in her pocket. She'd dialed Art on arrival this morning and kept the line connected while he muted his end. "I need to talk to you about something, Sir Robert."

He raised his eyebrows and gave her a small grin. "Of course. Oh no. Is this about your turkey sandwich in the refrigerator that went missing?"

She smiled. "Nope, though I suspect Micah."

"Good. Yes. It was definitely Micah."

"I need to ask you about a few things concerning Francesca."

"Oh? She's stopping by in a bit; shall we wait? Then you can ask her directly."

"No. I'd like this to stay between us, please." Avery took a deep breath. "Were you aware that she met with our collector who submitted the ruby? She met Renell in person."

Sir Robert's expression didn't change. "No, but that's her job."

"It's just . . . he was extremely reclusive with me and Nate and even Goldie. None of us was ever able to actually meet with him, though we tried. Nate said none of MOA's team had ever seen him in person."

"Nate must not have been aware of Francesca's meeting with him, then. Or . . . and maybe I shouldn't suggest this, but it should be said . . . perhaps Nate has something to gain by twisting information."

"Like what?"

Sir Robert shrugged. "Who knows? But I've seen the rivalry there. Francesca has put her time in, she travels looking for good opportunities, she's got all the contacts, she's responsible for bringing in many more acquisitions than Goldie's grandson. But you've met him. He's just waiting for his next step up that corporate ladder."

"I do see that," Avery admitted. Art had told her not to push. There was always the chance that Sir Robert was in cahoots with Francesca in some way, though she was still having trouble wrapping her head around that possibility.

"All set then?" Sir Robert sipped his coffee.

"Almost." She leaned back in her chair. "Sir Robert, you know I've been going through my parents' notes from the Emperor's Twins case. I noticed that my mother signed the certificate of authenticity two days early. It was turned in to Goldie June eighth, but Mom signed June sixth."

"Yes. Micah asked me about that too. It does seem odd." Sir Robert's brows were drawn together in puzzlement.

"So you don't know what compelled her to sign early? It was the day of the accident."

He shook his head. "I wish I could help you with that one. I'm sorry."

Avery pushed on. "I thought perhaps if I got a look at the original instead of just our fuzzy yellow copy—which has since been stolen—then maybe I could at least verify that it really was her signature on the front page. It'd be so much clearer to read. Then I'd know for sure that it was just an anomaly, she signed early for whatever reason, and it'd stop nagging at me."

"That's a good idea. Goldie would have the original. I'm sure she could show it to you."

"Ah, good idea. I'll have to ask her." Avery bit the inside of her cheek. Careful, careful. Art had warned her not to give anything away, and to their knowledge, Sir Robert might not know about the original being stolen. "I've got to ask: how did Goldie receive the certificate that Monday? My parents were gone, obviously. And I'm told Micah was out that day, as he was too distraught to work."

"That was an awful day. An awful time. The work seemed so much less important in light of the loss. I wasn't involved in that assignment, but I did know of it, as high profile as it was. We found the certificate on Micah's desk, complete and ready to be submitted. I believe your mother must have left it there for him in case he came in before she did Monday morning. Your parents would typically go straight to MOA when they had a case there, and then Micah would meet them later to pitch in and discuss findings. Much the same as the two of you seem to operate now."

Avery frowned. "I wonder why she wouldn't have planned on taking it directly to Goldie herself on Monday," she mused.

"Oh, your parents and Micah always held a little quarter-backing session prior to submitting certificates or reports. I'm sure she wanted to make sure Micah reviewed it before it went to Goldie."

That made perfect sense, especially in light of William's message to Micah saying they needed to talk before the certificate was completed. Though that alone made it more unlikely that her mother had signed it early.

We. Sir Robert had said the word *we.* Art's voice in her head told her not to push, but she needed to know. "Who found the certificate on Micah's desk? You said *we,* but Micah wasn't here."

"Francesca did!" He smiled at Avery. "Good thing, too; I wouldn't even attempt to find anything in that organized chaos," he said, looking over at Micah's desk. "She always seems to be in the right place at the right time. So helpful." He smiled at the photo he kept on his desk of the two of them at a swanky fund raiser last Christmas.

"Oh! Good thing, for sure." She suddenly remembered what it was that had nagged her so since last night, concerning Prince Ivan. The couple had said they'd gotten their beautiful rings from a little shop below the High Line, and Goldie had remarked that she thought it was the same shop that handled some of their collector's independent appraisals. She hadn't been sure, but she'd said Nate would know for certain. Avery was almost positive the place Prince Ivan's husband Colin had mentioned was Rizzolo's. "I'm off to MOA. Will you be here for a while yet?"

"I'm afraid so. I thought we had the Barnaby's auction house account in the bag, but I have one last meeting tomorrow and I need to prep."

"You're the best," Avery said, smiling. "I'm sure you'll convince them. Oh! I almost forgot. I noticed on the Emperor's Twins intake form that the collector agreed to take the medallion for a third-party appraisal before he submitted it to MOA." She'd indeed noticed, both when she and Tilly were browsing through the files at home that were later stolen and again last night on the flash drive, but Sir Robert didn't need to know that little tidbit.

"Yes," Sir Robert said. "Most collectors don't take that extra step, but Francesca feels it's always prudent to recommend."

"Makes perfect sense. I'm not surprised at all that she's so thorough," Avery said, buttering Sir Robert up. Any compliments aimed at Francesca were an indirect compliment to him. Avery could see it in the way his eyes brightened.

"You know," he said, "I've been in this line of work a long time, and I've never come across anyone in acquisitions who's as invested and passionate about their work."

Avery nodded. "I can see that too. Hey." She put a hand on the door and turned back, as if her next question was an afterthought. "Does she have preferred places she sends collectors for appraisals? I mean, I know we'd be a conflict of interest for the MOA jobs, since we look at the piece once it's submitted. I saw a jeweler called Rizzolo's on the medallion intake form. They must be good for her to recommend them."

"Never heard of them," Sir Robert said. He turned toward his computer and pulled the keyboard closer.

Avery groaned inwardly. She really couldn't tell if he was simply Francesca's clueless beau or her inside man. "Sir Robert."

He glanced up from typing.

"I wonder if Francesca pushed Oliver Renell to have the ruby appraised before he submitted it. His intake form says he declined an outside appraisal, but seeing as Francesca met with him—"

Sir Robert interrupted her, finally allowing his exasperation to show. "Avery. How would I know?"

"Renell refused to work with Francesca at all after she met with him," she blurted, her eyes wide.

"What?"

Avery let go of the doorknob and came back over to Sir Robert. "I should have just come out with it. I'm sorry. I had been emailing with Renell before he died, and after his initial meeting with Francesca, he specifically stated that he refused to work with anyone other than Goldie or me. He was adamant on that point. He seemed almost paranoid about the security of the ruby. If Francesca pushed a little too hard for him to have it appraised beforehand, that could be why."

Sir Robert sat back in his chair, staring at her. "You're saying Renell refused to deal with Francesca because he didn't trust her? Based on nothing but his own paranoia? You think she's running some kind of racket where she sends people for appraisals and, in return, what? She gets a kickback from the appraiser or something? Rizzolo's, right? That's what this whole conversation has been about?" He stood, leaning on his hands and glaring at her.

Avery was stunned at how quickly he'd gotten from point A to point B. She'd mentioned Rizzolo's only once. "I don't know. Honestly. I'm trying to make sense of things. You can't deny there's a lot of theft and death tangled up in these assignments."

He threw his hands up in the air. "And now she's a murderer too. Do you hear yourself right now, Avery Ayers?" His expression was twisted painfully; he looked as if he was about to either cry or explode.

Avery put her hands out in front of her in a calming gesture. She sat down in the chair opposite his desk, looking worriedly at him. "Yes. I hear myself, and I'm sorry. Sir Robert, please, calm down. I didn't mean to insinuate Francesca had anything to do with anyone dying."

He sat back down. He looked furious. "If you believe she had anything to do with any of what's happened, then you might as well accuse me too. Go ahead."

She shook her head, making her tone cajoling. "No. Listen, I adore Francesca. She's charismatic and vibrant and interesting, and I know you love her." She put her hand on the desk, trying to appease him. "I think I have too many small pieces of the puzzle, but I was never given the box, so I have no idea what the big picture looks like. If that makes sense. I'm just asking questions, that's all. I promise."

Sir Robert took a deep breath and let it out slowly. "I see."

"I'm sorry." She stood. "I really am. I never meant to upset you."

"Join us for dinner tonight," Sir Robert commanded. "If you had the opportunity to spend some time with Francesca, maybe you could put this line of thinking to rest. Eight o'clock at Mexicana Villa. We choose a different Mexican restaurant every Taco Tuesday. Just come, have a conversation, enjoy a taco. Maybe it will help."

"I'd love that," Avery said, relieved that his anger was short-lived. "I'll see you at eight."

Half an hour later in MOA's lab, Art came through the door with the other guard. This time, they each carried a locked case. Avery stood back while both were opened, revealing the Emperor's Twins medallion and the lone ruby from Oliver Renell.

Art stayed this time, and his partner left. "I don't care if there's only one way in and out of here; I'm not leaving you alone today. Especially with Micah gone," he said.

"Thank you," she said, looking up at him. "I always feel safer when you're around."

Something crossed his features—pleasure or embarrassment; Avery couldn't be sure which. He didn't reply but took a seat in front of one of the two lab computers.

"I'm finishing this today," Avery said, determined. "I was nearly there yesterday."

"Pretend I'm not here. I'm going to check in with a few people for some updates on Renell's case and your break-in."

They worked in silence. Avery picked up where she'd left off yesterday morning, which seemed like a lifetime ago. She set the scrap of paper with her father's handwriting on the counter top beside her for reference as she examined the dragon's existing ruby eye, pulling up her computer simulation of both eyes in place in the medallion for comparison. By early afternoon, she was starving but finally had conclusive results.

She straightened her back, stretching her arms up over her head. This job sometimes meant too many hours hunched over microscopes and dichroscopes and laptop screens. At the other end of the lab, Art had his back to her; he must have finished what he was doing on the computer. He leaned back in his chair, head down, and at first glance Avery assumed he must be on his phone. When she came around to his side, she saw he was sound asleep, his chin on his chest.

She perched on the edge of the workstation and cleared her throat. He awoke with a start, sitting up abruptly and looking up at her. "I wasn't."

Avery laughed. "You weren't what?" She smiled at him. "I get the feeling you find artifact appraisal boring."

He removed his guard cap and scrubbed a hand through his hair. "Are you kidding? Wait'll I tell you what I know." He tipped his head toward the computer. "I heard from Detective Graham."

"Oooh, really? Tell me."

"You first," he said, standing. "I'm guessing you've figured something out with our dragon friend over there?"

She led him to her workstation, putting her cotton gloves back on, and carefully lifted the medallion. "The current eye in the dragon is a spinel. My father's calculations were accurate. This area around the perimeter of the eye socket"—she pointed—"was one of the giveaways. Watch how the real Burmese ruby seats into the empty socket." She set the medallion down, picked up Renell's ruby with her jeweler's tweezers, and angled it into the void.

"Oh," Art said. "The upper edge has a bit of an overhang, doesn't it?"

"Just enough. And you can see here, on the upper lid of the other eye, the spinel is nearly flush. The ruby is safer, more protected, in its original position, the way the creator probably intended. It's not meant to be level with the surface of the dragon's face. Whoever made the spinel did a good job with the jewel, honestly. The quality and clarity are striking, but the chemical composition and refractive index of the spinel are indisputable. It's impossible to know the exact specific gravity without taking the spinel out of its setting, and I think that'll probably have to be done by some kind of specialist the FBI decides on. It'd be easy to damage this fellow in the process of trying to restore him. But the spinel will have to come out. It's a fake. And I'll tell you something else, Art."

His gaze was glued to her. "Tell me."

"My parents would never have certified this medallion. *Never.* My dad had figured it out. He was obviously wary of who he could trust, which must be why he began looking into how the genuine Emperor's Twins medallion—and the medallion is genuine, I've verified it—was submitted to MOA with a fake ruby."

"Which explains him connecting Francesca to Rizzolo's and snapping those photos."

"And if Renell had gone along with Francesca's recommendation, we'd likely be looking at two fakes right now. His genuine dragon-eye ruby wouldn't have made it to MOA."

"All right. Check this out; come here." They returned to the computer Art had been working on. "First, those numbers on your mother's stationery paper? They're routing numbers for two offshore bank accounts my team traced to the Cayman Islands. We're working on identifying who owns them. My money's on Francesca Giolitti."

"Oh wow," Avery said. "So she sent Edward Johnstone, the collector, to Rizzolo's for an appraisal before he submitted the medallion to MOA. Francesca's contact at Rizzolo's, the man on the flash drive, replaced the existing ruby with the fake and probably planned on it slipping by my parents. And when it started to look like it wouldn't, they made sure my parents weren't a problem. Francesca had to have forged my mother's signature on the certificate. It's the only explanation. I couldn't tell from our fuzzy yellow copy, but I'm sure I would have caught it if I'd been able to see the original."

"Which was pretty easy for her to get rid of," Art said.

"Not necessarily," Avery argued. "She doesn't have access to those records here. Only Goldie does."

"Or possibly Goldie's grandson? He was down there when I made my rounds. Maybe I caught him right after he'd taken the original? He said he was passing through and spotted the heating duct cover on the ground. He could have done it and lied to cover his tracks."

"I guess." Avery frowned. "I mean, it makes sense, but those two . . . I'm not sure Francesca would bring Nate in on something like this. He is Goldie's grandson. He seems to care what his grandmother thinks of him."

"We can feel things out tonight at dinner." Art glanced at her. "I'm your new boyfriend and we already had plans tonight, so you're bringing me along for Taco Tuesday with your friends."

She smiled at him. "I am? They're both going to recognize you, you know. Not just from the museum but from the party last weekend."

He shrugged. "Can't see how that'll hurt. And it cements the boyfriend cover story, right? Besides, even as a museum guard, I'd have no reason to know anything about fake jewels and murdered collectors. Listen, I got a couple updates from Springfield County Evidence. The DNA results of the blood sample we took from your hallway floor came back without a match in the system. But I requested the final composite sketch our artist made from the description your aunt and sister gave. Look." He tapped a key, and the sketch appeared on the screen.

"Oh wow," Avery said again. "Just a sec." She fetched her phone from her purse. "I saved the photos in my Drive; I can access them on my phone." She pulled up the picture of Francesca and the man outside the High Line shop and held her phone up next to the composite sketch.

Art nodded. "That sure looks like the same guy."

"Oh! I know. Hold on, I've got to text Tilly." She zoomed in on the man and sent a screen shot to her sister, then realized too late she probably should have told her what she was sending. "Oh jeez." She called her.

Tilly picked up on the first ring. "Dude! Warn me first before you send a creepy pic to me—what the heck! How do you have his photo?"

"You recognize him?"

"Of course I recognize him. He was a super pushy jerk. This is the guy who broke into the house later when Aunt Midge and I were gone, right?"

Avery glanced at Art, who looked triumphant. "Yep. Definitely."

"Um." Tilly quieted her voice. "You promised Auntie you weren't going to be putting yourself in any more dangerous situations, remember? What are you doing?"

"Nothing. Really. Art and the people he works with are closing in on catching the guy, that's all. I'll be home late tonight, okay? Let Auntie know I'm with Art and everything's fine. I promise."

"So now what?" Art asked when she'd hung up. "As far as your assignment, I mean. Are you able to wait until tomorrow to tell Goldie about the fake ruby in the dragon?"

"I can do that. Are you going to have your NYPD friends stake out Rizzolo Fine Jewelry to get this guy?" She nodded at the sketch on the computer screen.

"I don't think that'll be necessary. We know who he is. Sometimes Google is a great tool in police work." He bent over the keys, typing, and the website for Rizzolo Fine Jewelry opened. He chose the tab that read *About*.

Avery gasped, leaning in to read. " 'The Rizzolo family owns and operates seven fine jewelry stores worldwide, each personally managed by a family member. Meet your region's store owner below.' " She pointed to the black-and-white thumbnail photo beside the New York location. "Carlo Rizzolo. That's him."

Art nodded. "Now we just need to prove Francesca's connection to him."

Chapter
Twenty-Two

With a couple hours left to kill before meeting Sir Robert and Francesca for dinner, Avery decided Aunt Midge's Fifth Avenue apartment would be the best place to wait. They left Avery's Prius in MOA parking and made a brief detour to the Thirtieth Precinct, where Art was able to pick up the equipment they'd need later. When he came back out to his truck, he informed Avery that forensics was working on a few sets of fingerprints from Micah's place that didn't match Micah's or Noah's. "I'm betting they're a match for the prints that were lifted from Renell's hotel room. Probably the same weapon too."

"Every little piece brings us closer to getting my dad back," Avery said.

At Midge's building, Art followed her through the door and paused, looking around and whistling.

"This is your aunt's place? And it just stands empty?"

"Not really," she said. "We use it quite a bit. To spend the night in the city after dinner or a play, to host get-togethers with friends, and I use it at least a few times a month when I'm too tired to drive back to Lilac Grove after work."

Art moved the massive windows in the living room. "Incredible." He turned around, looking up at the enormous chandelier. "Your aunt has a very . . . unique style. I really like it. Bold but elegant."

"Yes!" Avery exclaimed. "I've never heard her taste put that way, but yes. You're right. How about something to eat? I'm not sure we'll actually get to eat tacos later, depending on how things go." She moved to the kitchen.

The refrigerator held a few stray beers, a bottle of Pellegrino, a six-pack of Coke, and one petrified bagel that had been there God knew how long. Avery cooked the only thing in the freezer, a boxed pepperoni pizza. They sat at a corner of the extravagantly long dining table, sharing cardboard-flavored pizza. "We should have gotten takeout," she apologized.

"Hey, I'm impressed you even found food in there. Besides, if you're hungry enough, it doesn't taste half bad."

She shook her head. "I'm definitely not hungry enough. Want to sit outside?" She grabbed them both a Coke and led the way out onto the terrace.

Looking out over Central Park from the seventeenth floor, Art asked, "Is there any news on Micah?"

"Only that the bullet missed his heart, which I sort of figured. Noah said he'll have to have reconstructive surgery for his shoulder, but they need to make sure he's stable first."

"That makes sense. I'm sorry that happened. He's a great guy."

She nodded. "He is. He and my dad were—are—a lot alike. Oh, that's such a strange feeling. If the police can make arrests and be positive my dad is safe, how soon could we see him?"

"I don't know. Really. I've not been privy to his whereabouts. But I'd think relatively soon."

"Art. I've never asked you this, and I should have. Do you have someone at home, worrying about you, when you're doing all this work, running back and forth between Springfield County PD and working at MOA?"

"No one."

"No one? Do you have family in Lilac Grove? Or did you just choose it for the lilacs?"

He gave her a sideways glance. "I've got three sisters in Springfield County. I chose Lilac Grove because it's pretty much in the middle of them all."

"Oh!" She laughed at herself. She didn't know why she'd thought of Art as an island, a loner. "Three sisters! My goodness. And no brothers? You're the only boy?"

He nodded. "I am."

"Where are you in the lineup? I'm curious. No, wait." She changed her mind, scrutinizing him. "Don't tell me. John Arthur Smith, you are the baby of your family. You have three older sisters."

He stared at her. "How did you know that?"

She shrugged. "Anthropology major, remember? It's not a key focus, but I definitely was fascinated when we covered birth order and psychological traits."

"I don't believe that's how you knew I'm the youngest. It was a good guess."

She shook her head. "Nope. I bet I can guess your sign too."

Art laughed, making her smile. He rolled his eyes at her. "I don't even know my sign."

"When's your birthday?"

"December twenty-second."

"Oooh, right before Christmas. That . . . makes . . . you . . ." She tapped his arm with her fingertip three times, once for each word. Who was she kidding? "Nope. I've got nothing, sorry."

He leaned toward her, grinning. "I knew you were bluffing."

"Yeah, Aunt Midge is our family zodiac expert. We'll have to ask her."

Art stretched his long legs out, crossing them at the ankles. "Or not. I don't think I'm her favorite person. You know, we could skip this dinner with Sir Robert and Francesca. Between what we know and whatever else the feds have gathered, there may be enough to get a warrant for Rizzolo Jewelry."

"But what if there's not? And what about Francesca's role in all of it?"

He sighed. "That's tough. I'm still waiting on updates from Detective Graham on the fingerprints, though I doubt that'll give us anything concrete on Francesca. From a sheer size-and-trajectory standpoint, we know she wasn't the shooter."

"We need to do this," Avery said firmly. "Even if Francesca doesn't slip and say something during dinner, it's still the chance we need to carry out the rest of your plan."

"All right. I should go change." Art had fortunately been able to scrape together something that wasn't a uniform from the dry cleaning he'd never brought into his house after his last pickup.

"Follow me." Avery led Art up the wide, curving staircase and sent him down the hall to the room Tilly used when they stayed. "There's a connected bath through the closet in case you want to shower. We have time."

He gave her a funny look. "Do I smell?"

She stepped as close to him as she'd allow herself. She sniffed near his neck, meeting his eyes. "Not at all." He smelled like soap, a clean scent with an undertone of mint or pine.

Art's gaze dropped to Avery's lips, and her breath caught in her throat. Then he abruptly stepped back and turned away from her, heading down the hall. "I'll meet you downstairs."

She exhaled, her heart racing for a moment. For Pete's sake. What was the man's issue? She'd never been a natural flirt. But she and Art had such an easy rapport, and to her, it felt obvious that she really liked him. Was it not mutual? Or was he just oblivious to her signals?

Trying to shake her disappointment, Avery pinned her hair up and took a steaming-hot shower. She dried off and liberally used one of Aunt Midge's many delectable scented lotions. She closed her eyes and inhaled, then tossed the bottle in her purse to take home with her. Midge wouldn't mind. She believed nice things were to be enjoyed, not coveted and preserved.

Avery pulled her slim, curve-hugging black pants back on but chose a filmy black-and-red blouse with a wide neckline that bared her collarbones and enough decolletage to be sensual rather than sexual. She hoped. She finger-combed her long brown hair, sweeping it forward over one shoulder, and touched up her lipstick.

Art was waiting for her when she came downstairs. He sat on the oversized round peacock-patterned ottoman near the foyer, looking dapper and out of place. His crisp white dress shirt and gray plaid Ralph Lauren pants made him look like neither the detective nor the security guard she was used to. She saw from the damp edges of his hair that he had showered after all. Avery swallowed hard, trying not to think of him as handsome. Art was functional. An ally. Here to help her get her father back. That was all.

He stood. "Avery, you look . . ."

She raised her eyebrows, resisting the urge to glance down at herself.

He cleared his throat and left the thought unfinished. "Are we ready?"

She moved through the apartment turning off lights, and they headed downstairs to Art's truck.

Sir Robert and Francesca already had a table when they arrived at Mexicana Villa. The couple stood, and they exchanged greetings all around.

"I hope it's all right that I brought a date. We'd already made plans for tonight, but this sounded like so much fun," Avery told Sir Robert and Francesca. Putting a hand on Art's arm, she said, "I'm not sure you've all officially met? Sir Robert, I think you and Art may have played a mean game of croquet at my party the other day. Art Smith, Francesca Giolitti and Sir Robert Lane."

"Of course," Francesca said. "You're the MOA security guard who helped my colleague Nate Brennan last week when he discovered the heating duct issue."

"That was me," Art confirmed. He shrugged. "Not sure it was worth shutting the whole place down for that. Did they even find anything had actually been stolen?"

Avery could have kissed him. Smart, to play clueless and gain Francesca's trust. He wasn't an eagle-eyed security guard intent on raising alarms; he was just there to do his job and assume all was well.

"No. It turned out to be a waste of time for the NYPD and a loss of two days' revenue for MOA." She flipped her hair over her shoulder and sipped her red wine. "*C'est la vie.* You two need a drink—where is our server?"

Sir Robert flagged down one of the staff and Avery and Art put their drink order in, Avery requesting exactly what Francesca was drinking and Art getting a coffee. Francesca frowned at him. "That's no fun. Coffee with tacos?"

Art smiled, and it looked completely forced and fake to Avery. Francesca seemed to buy it, though. "Night shift," he said. "I'm working later; I moonlight over at the Met. Crazy hours lately."

"Ugh," Sir Robert said. "That's brutal. I'm completely useless if I don't get nine full hours of sleep at night."

"I can confirm that's true," Avery said. "You're unbearable to be around in the mornings if you haven't slept."

Francesca was nodding too. "Too true. Everyone pays for it if Sir here doesn't get his beauty sleep." She slipped her arm through his and gave him a peck on his cheek.

Avery was surprised to find that the conversation flowed smoothly through dinner. She made a mental note to remember the restaurant. The food was delicious, and the combination of little twinkle lights everywhere and authentic music gave the place a warm, inviting ambience. She'd need to come back another time when she wasn't stressed and playing a part.

After dinner, when they'd ordered three more coffees to join Art with his, Sir Robert broke the illusion of an easy, amicable evening out with friends.

"So, Avery was asking me a few things this morning that I just don't have answers to. I suggested she go straight to you, darling," he said, addressing Francesca.

Avery's cheeks burned. She should have known that Sir Robert and his love for drama wouldn't make this easy. She'd hoped he'd be discreet and just let her work her way around to her queries naturally. She smiled at Francesca, knowing she couldn't conceal the worry she felt. She'd have to use it. "I hate to talk business. This is all so nice. Honestly, I can catch up with you at the museum tomorrow, Francesca."

The woman returned Avery's smile minus the worry. "Oh poo. Don't worry about it. I never let business ruin a nice evening; nothing you can ask me would do that. What's on your mind?"

Avery's thoughts raced as she tried to assemble an inquisitive but inoffensive sentence. Under the table, Art's warm hand covered hers, folding it into his much larger one and giving it an encouraging squeeze. She felt instantly calmer. "You know Micah and I were finally able to verify for certain that Oliver Renell's jewel is indeed real, a sixteen-carat natural Burmese ruby. Quite amazing in itself."

"Oh, absolutely," Francesca agreed. "And how's the progress with the Emperor's Twins?"

"Almost there," she lied. "I'm a little slower with Micah in the hospital. But how wonderful if the dragon could be restored with both his ruby eyes by the gala this Friday! That's my hope." She shoved away the pang she had, knowing it wasn't at all possible.

"Oh, wonderful!" Francesca clasped her hands in front of her chest.

"I was asking Sir Robert about some of the minutiae involved in the certification process. One thing I'm a little fuzzy on is the whole reclusive thing Oliver Renell had going on. Did you ever actually get to meet him?"

She nodded. "I did, surprisingly. Just once, to go over details of him submitting the jewel to MOA."

Sir Robert chimed in. "Apparently, Nate made it sound like you rubbed Oliver Renell the wrong way and he refused to work with you after that."

Avery gritted her teeth. "I'm not sure he—"

Francesca waved a hand in the air. "It's fine. Avery," she said, reaching one manicured hand across the table and turning it palm up, waiting.

Avery took Francesca's hand.

Francesca squeezed it, patting it with her other one. "I'm going to sound like a horrible person when I say this, so please remember, my heart is in the right place," she said. "I'm worried about Nate Brennan. I've debated saying something to Goldie; maybe I need to. I don't know if you're aware, but Nate struggles with a gambling addiction."

Avery widened her eyes. "No. Nate Brennan? I had no idea."

Francesca nodded sadly. "Yes. He lost a fortune in Monte Carlo, and Goldie took him under her wing when his own parents were too disgusted to deal with him. Goldie trusts him to stay strong and keep working to beat his problem. But what you're telling me isn't even the first red flag I've seen with him." She paused. She looked at Sir Robert, then Art, then back at Avery. "This should stay between us until I have a chance to let Goldie get him some help. Honestly, I even wondered if he was attempting to break into the records room below Goldie's office the day you found him with the broken heating duct, Art. I don't know what he's up to, but his addiction seems to be controlling him. It's all about getting his next high—in his case, money allows him to chase the high."

Avery was quiet. Holy hell. This woman was good. If Avery hadn't seen all the incriminating photos and files, she'd totally have believed that Nate was behind the mayhem and there was no Carlo Rizzolo or Francesca as an accomplice. "Oh my," she said aloud.

Francesca nodded. "Yes."

Sir Robert spoke. "You see? Always best to be direct. Does that clear things up, Avery?"

"Completely," Avery said. "Thank you, Francesca."

Francesca picked up her purse. "Would you all excuse me? I'm off to the ladies' room before we call it a night."

"I'll come with you." Avery took her purse from the back of her chair, holding it near her lap while she pretended to dig around for something. Art opened his hand and dropped the listening device disguised as a pen into Avery's purse before she stood.

Soon she and Francesca were standing at the vanity, Avery washing her hands and Francesca reapplying her lipstick. She just needed an opportunity. Francesca's large Louis Vuitton purse should make it easy, but so far, she'd have been caught if she tried. Aside from planting the bug, there was one last thing that had been poking at Avery's thoughts since she and Art had come up with their plan in the lab. What if they gained the ability to eavesdrop on Francesca but she simply went home and went to bed and then went to work the next day, and so on? What if they had to wait weeks or even months before she said or did something incriminating, something that linked her with Carlo Rizzolo?

Avery missed her dad. And she could hardly imagine how he'd been away from them this long; it must be awful for him to remain in hiding. How much longer could he be expected to stay that way? She hated to push, but she had to.

She offered Francesca a mint from the tin in her purse. "This has been so much fun. We should do it again."

Francesca paused in applying her lipstick. "It's been lovely. Sir Robert and I need more couples friends to do things with. Will you be bringing Art to the gala on Friday? You two are so cute together."

"No, Micah and I . . ." Avery's voice trailed off. "Oh. I can't believe I hadn't even thought of that. Micah and I were going together, since neither of us had a plus-one when I bought the tickets. I guess I could ask Art now."

"Poor, dear Micah. Such a sweet man. Any news on him?"

Now they were getting into dicey territory. If Francesca's connection Carlo truly had been the one to shoot Micah, Avery couldn't share anything. Carlo probably wanted him dead, like Renell. She shook her head. "No, no updates yet. It seemed bad." And then she saw her chance—not to plant the bug, but to plant a seed she hoped would grow. "It's awful, too, because Micah was shot right before we were set to talk about some concerns he had about the Emperor's Twins medallion. He had a few files he wanted to give me, and he said he'd found a letter my dad had left in his desk. It must have been from a year ago."

Francesca finished her lipstick and put it away. "What do you mean?" She didn't look at Avery.

"I'm not exactly sure, but he seemed really worked up about whatever was in the letter. I mean, you've seen Micah's desk; I'm not even surprised it took him a year to come across it. I can't imagine what my dad would have needed to tell him. He said he was keeping it locked up in his desk at the shop and he'd show me when we met yesterday. But he never came to work. And now, with him in the hospital, who knows when I'll find out what it was about."

"Oh my." Francesca's complexion had definitely gone paler. "That's horrible. All of it—Micah being shot, and now this mysterious letter. God willing he'll recover and you'll get to the bottom of things."

Avery nodded. "As soon as I hear anything, I'll make sure to update you and Sir Robert. As you said, he's such a sweet man."

Francesca threw her bag onto her shoulder, and Avery held the door for her as they left the powder room, slipping the small, unassuming-looking blue pen into the woman's purse as she followed her down the hall toward their table.

Sir Robert and Art stood as they approached.

"The check's taken care of. This fellow's got to get to work," Sir Robert said of Art.

Outside on the sidewalk in front of the restaurant, the foursome exchanged quick hugs and kisses on cheeks in parting. "Definitely doing this again," Sir Robert said, nodding at Art.

"Call us," Art said. He held out an arm for Avery, putting it around her shoulders. They were parked in the opposite direction.

In Art's truck, Avery spun in her seat to face him. "Turn it on!"

He grinned. "I believe Detective Graham and the federal field agents are probably already listening. Excellent teamwork, partner. No trouble getting the pen into her bag?"

"Easy peasy. Can we listen too?"

Art pulled his phone out and opened a secure, restricted site, typing in some information. A map appeared on his screen, with a little blinking dot that wasn't moving. He put the phone in its cradle on the dashboard. "We can listen, but you might want to lower your expectations. It could be a while before we hear anything of value."

"I think we'll hear something very, very soon. Like, now. Or as soon as Francesca and Sir Robert part ways for the night." She filled Art in on the seed she'd planted, expecting him to be thrilled that she'd sped up the process.

"You realize that was not part of our plan, right?" He looked the opposite of happy.

"Well, yeah, but—"

He grabbed his phone from the holder on the dash and dialed, giving the address for Artifacts and Antiquities Appraised to his contact at the Thirtieth Precinct. "I realize it's not your— yes, I'll hold." He groaned. He turned and spoke to Avery while he waited. "If your plan works, Francesca's going to show up at the shop and break into Micah's desk, which isn't going to help at all in connecting her to Rizzolo."

"Art, she won't—"

"Graham? Listen." Art barked orders into the phone, the gist of which was that a car was being sent to keep an eye on the shop. He ended the call and switched back to the secure channel they'd be able to monitor Francesca on.

Art put the truck in gear and pulled out into traffic, keeping an eye on the flashing dot on the screen. Through the speaker, Francesca and Sir Robert chatted about whether to get a town car or a limo for transport to Friday's gala.

"Art. She's not going to the shop," Avery said quietly.

"Why wouldn't she?"

"Because Francesca doesn't get her hands dirty. She's going to get Carlo Rizzolo. We know they're in this together. I'm telling you, that's where she's headed, and from the sound of it, Sir Robert isn't part of this at all."

Art was quiet, listening again. Francesca was describing her gown to Sir Robert. She sounded completely unflustered. If she was concerned at all about a mysterious letter a dead man had left for Micah Abbott, it wasn't discernible from her tone.

"You're right about Sir Robert," Art conceded. "He's in the dark."

"What do we do now?" Avery asked.

"We follow them. If you're right about Francesca, we'll be headed to the High Line once she's on her own."

Chapter
Twenty-Three

"Okay, Sir Robert's building is coming up on the right," Avery said, pointing. The cab a ways in front of them had its blinker on to pull over.

Art moved over into the right lane, slowing as much as he could as Sir Robert exited the cab.

Avery and Art listened in uncomfortable silence as the couple said good-night, Sir Robert trying to convince Francesca to come up with him for a cocktail and Francesca saying she was exhausted and couldn't wait to have a bath. That led to Sir Robert offering to help. Art's hand shot out and he hit the mute icon, making Avery giggle.

"Gross. It's like listening to your parents' pillow talk," she said.

Art cocked an eyebrow at her. "Ahem. I'm about seven years younger than your friend Sir Robert. Hardly old enough to be your parent."

"No! That's not what I meant at all." Avery laughed. "We're just not meant to hear that. Besides, you're about seventeen years younger than Francesca. She's technically old enough to be both our parents."

Now Art chuckled. The dot on the map began to move, and he tapped the screen to unmute.

Rustling noises came through the speaker, and Avery imagined Francesca changing position in the back of the cab, perhaps setting her purse beside her. "Could you please drop me at Twenty-Fourth near Tenth? The Getty Building would be fine."

"Yes, ma'am." The cabby's voice came through, and then a sliding sound followed by a click. Francesca or the cab driver had closed the partition.

And then pure gold came through Art's phone. Francesca's voice was low, probably in case the cab driver might still overhear, but it was clear enough in Art's truck for them to catch Francesca's side of a phone conversation. Avery wished they could hear the person on the other end of the line.

"We have a problem. I'm coming to you," Francesca said. There was a pause as she listened.

"I've got a new find." Francesca spoke again. "I planned to bring you the details this week, but we've got something to take care of first." Another pause. "Look, this has to be handled tonight. We've got to get something from Micah Abbott's desk that William Ayers left him last year. Something to do with the medallion."

A moment of silence passed. "He's still alive, Carlo; I don't know any more than that." Francesca's tone betrayed her frustration with the person on the other end, who Avery assumed must be Carlo Rizzolo. "I wouldn't do that," she snapped. "It's only going to stir up more suspicion. He may never even wake up; just leave it alone."

After a beat, her voice rose in anger. "For Christ's sake, Carlo, he's got a kid!" More silence. "No, you're not." Her voice became abruptly calmer. "Oh, this one's a small job, a five-carat perfect-cut diamond. He'll probably contact you in the next day or two."

There was a longer pause. "I realize that," she said. "God, you're such an ass. They can't all be the Hope diamond." Another lull, and then Francesca ended her call with Carlo. "About five minutes; almost there."

Silence filled Art's truck. Avery began to speak but stopped; she didn't know where to start.

"Give me your phone, please," Art said, holding out a hand. She did.

He quickly dialed, keeping his eyes on the road and checking the GPS tracker now and then. "Graham, you heard that? Can you beef up security at the hospital for Micah Abbott? And send someone to his house too. I think his kid might be there."

"Noah's staying there?" Avery's eyes were wide.

Art glanced at her and nodded. He hung up and gave her phone back. "Don't worry. They've already got officers in the area in Hamilton Heights; Noah will be fine. Graham said they'll assign one to stay at the house."

"This guy—Francesca's guy—is going to try to finish the job of killing Micah. And you think he'd go for Noah too? Oh my God." She shook her head. "I mean, we've been talking this all through all day, but I guess some part of me didn't want to think Francesca could be part of this. Until now."

"I'm sorry."

"Oh! Jeez." Avery cringed. "I'm sorry for Sir Robert."

"There is one thing," Art said. "Not that I'm defending any of her actions, but she did try to call Carlo off. She told him to leave Micah alone."

Avery sighed. She knew there were countless ripple effects that would come from blowing this whole thing wide open, but for the moment, all she could think of was poor Sir Robert.

Art parked so they could see into Rizzolo Fine Jewelry and turned off his lights. Francesca had already paid the cab and was waiting on the sidewalk as Carlo Rizzolo came through the shop to let her in.

Avery narrowed her eyes, trying for a better look, then thought to use her phone. She set her camera to the video setting and zoomed in, sucking in her breath. "That's him. From the pictures and the sketch." As she watched, Carlo grabbed Francesca by the waist and pulled her into an embrace.

His voice was a low growl. "How are you even more gorgeous now than when you divorced me? That's what I want to know."

Francesca put both hands on his chest and shoved him, hard. "It's been years, Carlo. Knock it off."

Carlo put his hands up. "Whatever. So tell me how you've managed to screw this whole job up. I did my part. I even made sure the Ayers' car was basically ash by the time the explosions finished. There was no way to trace any of it back to us."

Avery clapped both hands over her mouth, her eyes huge. Francesca had even been involved in her parents' murder!

Francesca jabbed a finger into Carlo's chest. "And I told you that was a mistake! Your little fireworks stunt launched an investigation instead of it being written off as a car veering off the road. Their girls were with them! Do you know how many other opportunities you had to take them out? Your recklessness is going to be our downfall, Carlo."

"I'm going to throw up." Avery bent at the waist, putting her head between her knees.

"Deep breaths," Art said. He put a hand out and lightly stroked her back. "Slow, deep breaths, in through your nose and out through your mouth."

Avery did as he said, breathing through it. She forced her head up. She couldn't miss what was happening, as awful as it was.

Carlo's size and body language looked menacing, even from across the street in the safety of Art's truck. "The deal was, you get Renell to bring the ruby here before submitting it, so we'd finally have both. Did you do that? Let me think. No, you didn't. Did you get your movie-star boyfriend to fly under the radar and make the medallion certification disappear without a fuss or actually get the new ruby out of the museum for us? Oh wait. Also no. Now you're telling me that a guy who's been dead for a year left a note for Micah Abbott about the medallion and I'm supposed to rush over and break in to steal it. Do I have that all right?" He'd paced back and forth as he raged, and now Carlo stood over small, slight Francesca, daring her to argue. For a fraction of a second, Avery was frightened for her.

Francesca didn't move, didn't step back. She remained in Carlo's space, looking up at him. "Renell was intractable. It was almost like he had been warned somehow. And Chadwick did get rid of the original. Tell me how it affects you that the museum closed for a couple days. Oh wait," she said, clearly mocking Carlo's rant, "it doesn't. Your idea of having him wine and dine the appraiser so she'd sneak him in to see the ruby and take it was idiotic to begin with; it was never going to work. I told you Avery would see through him. And yes. Unless you want police to find out from Micah or Avery Ayers or whoever the hell else knows about this letter that we swapped out the medallion's ruby for a fake, you'll go over to their shop and take everything from his desk. That's literally all. You have. To do."

"Dang," Avery whispered, glancing at Art. "She's terrifying."

Carlo moved through the shop, turning out display case lights. "This had better be worth it. All *you* have to do is keep your promise. I'll have the spinel ready for you tomorrow. Get us the ruby before the gala."

"Not a problem. And this time, make sure your spinel is actually good enough to pass off as the real thing. I still think if you'd done a better job with the last one, none of that mess last year would've happened."

He turned quickly and looked back at her. "What the hell do you know about fabricating a fake?" His volume rose with his anger. "You think you could do better? You hold up your end of our arrangement, keep sending me the goods, and I'll do my part. I don't need your advice."

"Are you going to their shop or not?" She stood watching as he turned out the last of the lights. He disappeared into the back of the store and the overhead lighting went out as well, except for the lights by the entrance.

"I'm going. I'm not promising to leave Abbott to die on his own, though. And I want you to think about something, love."

"Don't call me that," Francesca said.

Carlo shrugged, pulling his keys from his pocket. "Whatever. I've been wondering. How much of a liability is Robert Lane? Because I think—"

Francesca smacked Carlo hard across the face. As he reeled back, she looked down at her hand, shaking it. She stepped toward him. "Don't you dare." She spun and stormed out, not looking back.

Carlo exited too, pulling the door closed and locking it behind him. Avery thought he would go after her, but he headed the opposite direction. Down Twenty-Fourth Street, Francesca hailed a cab and was gone. Carlo got into a sleek black Jaguar opposite his shop and peeled away from the curb in a cloud of burning rubber and squealing tires.

Art's truck jerked to life, and he took off in pursuit. "Buckle up," he said to Avery. She let go of the door handle long enough to do so, then held on for dear life as Art's truck took the left onto Tenth Avenue, following Carlo's Jaguar. She watched the speedometer digits climb into the forties and fifties, the world flying by in a blur as Art dodged traffic to stay behind Carlo.

Beside her, he spoke into his phone. He'd bypassed Graham this time, and he'd stopped tracking Francesca. "I'm in pursuit of a late-model black Jag, license plate Frank-Nora-Larry-five-two-four-five. Suspect is armed and dangerous, heading north-bound on Tenth Avenue approaching Thirtieth Street."

Art dropped the phone to wrestle with the steering wheel. The low body of the Jag took the lane changes and turns much easier than Art's pickup truck. Avery grappled under her seat but couldn't find his phone.

Sirens screamed through the air nearby. Carlo's car turned left onto Thirtieth Street and Art stayed with him, slowing his truck for the turn.

"Suspect heading toward Hudson Yards," Art shouted. Avery shot a glance at him, but she knew he was yelling in hopes that he'd be heard through his phone, wherever it had landed.

Carlo's Jag looked as if it hadn't yet recovered from the sharp turn onto Thirtieth at high speed; it wove back and forth wildly. Up ahead, three police cars converged as the Jaguar appeared to attempt the turn onto Twelfth Avenue, but it had lost too much control.

The Jag's taillights swung hard to the left, tires skidding on the pavement as the car at first headed straight for a building. Carlo tried to brake and instead spun out, catching a curb with the front end of the car. The Jaguar's headlights veered crazily upward, and then a sickening clap struck the night air, a grotesque crunching noise amid the sound of screaming metal and tires skidding into stops on the pavement. The Jag was on its roof at Thirtieth and Twelfth, wheels spinning, flames spiraling from the back of the car.

Art braked hard, throwing an arm out to steady Avery and stopping at a safe distance. They watched through the windshield as the aftermath of the chase played out like a movie that was far too real.

Police officers cautiously moved toward the car, weapons drawn, none of them getting too close. Gunshots filled the air, and it took Avery a moment to realize they were coming from the Jaguar as officers darted behind their vehicles. Then the night fell silent, so quiet for a few seconds that the only sound was that of the growing flames coming from the car. Officers' shouts broke the silence, demanding that Carlo exit his vehicle peacefully.

She saw the flash inside the upside-down car that ended it. Carlo fired one last shot into the cluster of law enforcement, and the Jaguar ignited and burst into flame. She shielded her eyes from the bright flames reaching for the sky. She could feel Art watching her. She finally turned and faced him, her heart racing from the roller coaster of everything she'd just seen and heard.

"Avery. Are you all right?" His brow was furrowed in worry as she met his gaze.

She blinked at him, swallowing hard. "I think so. Are you?"

The corner of his mouth rose in a half smile. "I'm fine. Let me get you home. The police have it from here; there's nothing more we can do."

Before he could move away from her and start the truck and take her home, Avery put her hand on his scruffy cheek. "Thank you, Art." She leaned in and kissed him. She'd completely surprised him; she felt it in his hesitance. She sat back, moving out of his space. She had no clue how he felt about her. As kind as he was, as magnetic as the pull between them seemed, she was probably just part of his job, one that had begun a year ago and was now over.

"That wasn't fair," Art told her. He hadn't moved; he looked slightly dazed. The glow from the flames outside the truck's window cast his face half in a soft, warm light and half in shadow.

"I'm sorry," she said. "We can go now."

"Avery." She loved the way he said her name. Like a statement, not a precursor to one. "Do you know how long I've wanted to kiss you?"

She stopped breathing. She shook her head.

"For about the last year. Or at least the last two weeks. Definitely since you found me at MOA and yelled at me and demanded I help you."

"Then why haven't you?"

He shook his head. "Too complicated. This had to be about the job. I knew, once I did, my judgment would be clouded. It had to stay about getting your dad back to you. But now—"

Avery's heart pounded at his words. She leaned into his arm that was stretched out along the backrest. She ached. She needed him to touch her, to stop talking and just kiss her. "Art." She said it the way he said her name. "I get it. Could you—"

Art pulled her against him, his strong arms around her, and kissed her, and she didn't care anymore that she couldn't breathe. She didn't need air when she had Art.

Chapter
Twenty-Four

When the doorbell rang Wednesday morning in Lilac Grove, Avery and Tilly beat Halston to the front door.

William Ayers was nearly knocked off his feet by his daughters throwing their arms around him. A big man, he laughed and wrapped them in the tightest hug he could, one arm around each of them. In khakis and a blue plaid shirt, their dad looked thinner and a little paler than his usual robust, healthy self, but his smile reached his eyes and made them crinkle at the corners. "Oh, my girls." William turned his face into Avery's hair, and then he kissed the top of Tilly's head, and still he didn't let go of them.

Aunt Midge appeared in the foyer, her fingertips covering her mouth and tears welling up in her eyes. William slowly loosened his grip, and Tilly and Avery let go so he could hug his sister. He dwarfed Aunt Midge. When she finally released him, she smacked him in the chest. "You could have told us you were alive."

"He really couldn't." Art spoke from the doorway. Behind Art was William's handler with the federal WITSEC program, a balding middle-aged man with a tired face.

Aunt Midge filled coffee cups for everyone around the dining table. The handler, who introduced himself as Agent Miller, placed an envelope on the table in front of Avery.

"What's this?" She pulled out a white form. It was the original copy of the forged certificate for the Emperor's Twins. "This looks nothing like Mom's signature," she said, assessing it and then turning it around for her family to see. "The *As* are too rounded instead of sharp, like Mom's were, and this stupid loop under the *Y* isn't at all right. I couldn't even make that out on our yellow copy. How did you get this?" She looked up at Agent Miller.

"Our agents found it in the safe at Rizzolo's, along with bullets that match the casings we found at Micah Abbott's and near Oliver Renell's body. We also took possession of several pieces of jewelry we believe are stolen as well as a few large gemstones we've got specialists working to identify. One does appear to resemble the ruby eye of your medallion—"

Avery interrupted. "You found it? The real ruby that was stolen last year? He still had it?"

Agent Miller shook his head. "No. I'm sorry. This appears to be a spinel, based on our team's evaluation; we assume it's the one Rizzolo was creating for Francesca to swap with Renell's ruby."

"Oh." She sighed heavily. "I guess it was crazy to hope he still had it. And this?" She tapped the certificate in front of her. "Does this mean Tyler Chadwick really was part of this? Was he working for Francesca? He had access to the basement through the film set. Was he responsible for stealing this?"

"That's the working theory, especially since we've had no success in reaching him using the contact information we were given. Not sure it'd matter if we did find him. So far, there's unfortunately no actual proof of Chadwick's involvement," Agent Miller said.

"There's a little good news, though," Art said. "Agents did recover receipts. Rizzolo was a thief, but he was still a business-man. He had documentation of each and every sale he and Fran-cesca collaborated on."

"What?" Avery asked. "What does that mean?"

"We've got the buyer for the Emperor's Twins ruby," Miller explained. "Based on the listed purchase price, we doubt the buyer was aware he was purchasing a stolen jewel. Operatives are already in Versailles with the goal of bringing the ruby back to the museum. I can't say much more, but the fake that Rizzolo was making to replace Renell's was just one of several he had in the works. Francesca Giolitti doesn't seem to be the only person he was working with. This is much bigger than you know. You and Art Smith here probably saved inestimable fortunes, per-haps even other lives."

Avery had no response to that.

"Nice going, A!" Tilly had a response for everything. "Double A, actually." She nodded at Art. "High five, Art Smith."

"Detective," Aunt Midge corrected her. "Impudence, my dear. You know better. It's Detective Smith."

Art smiled. "Or how about Art?"

"That'll work," Tilly said.

"What about Francesca? Did you catch her?" Avery asked. "And how did Renell know he shouldn't get his ruby appraised at Rizzolo's?"

"I'll take that one." William spoke up. "I was able to connect the collector who submitted the Emperor's Twins, Edward John-stone, with Oliver Renell." He glanced at Agent Miller. "I was forbidden to get involved. But I did get a message to Johnstone that he had to tell Renell not to trust Francesca. Johnstone was pulled into the case by law enforcement a week or so ago when it became apparent that the medallion itself might have been tampered with."

"Oh wow. That makes so much sense," Avery said.

"Francesca is gone," Art interjected. "When I made the decision to follow Carlo, I lost Francesca's signal, and Detective Graham was too far away to pick it up. We can't find her."

"What do you mean," Avery asked. "She's, like, gone gone?"

"Her apartment is cleaned out," Agent Miller said. "Her car is still in its spot in the parking garage. She left a note addressed to Sir Robert, which of course we opened."

"And?"

"It's just a good-bye letter. No word or hint about where she was heading. Interpol has her profile. We'll get her sooner or later."

"I don't want to be around when Sir Robert reads that note," Avery said. "Poor guy."

Aunt Midge went to the refrigerator and began pulling out items. "We're having pancakes. William, you've lost weight, and I don't like it. Are you here to stay? You're not going anywhere?" She turned and addressed him sternly, hands on her hips.

"Yes, Midge. I'm here to stay. I promise."

* * *

On Friday, Art arrived ahead of schedule to escort Avery to the MOA charity gala. Upstairs and nearly ready, Avery heard Tilly invite him in, telling him she liked his penguin suit before Aunt Midge chastised her.

Avery was halfway down the stairs when she caught part of the conversation between Art and her dad. William's deep voice carried up the stairway.

"I'd go ahead and grill you, ask what you do for a living and what your intentions are with my daughter, but I don't think I need to do that," he told Art.

"No, sir, probably not," Art replied.

"I hope you know how grateful I am that you never gave up. A different man, a lesser detective, might have slacked or passed it down the line. Thank you."

"It was my pleasure," Art said. "Getting you home to your daughters was the most important thing."

Avery stepped into the foyer, tears in her eyes. "Guys, stop." She swiped under one eye. "This stuff isn't waterproof!"

Art stared at her, his lips parted, dumb struck.

Tilly slid through the foyer behind the two men, slowing to whisper to Art, "Get a grip, man. It's just a dress."

He blinked and closed his mouth. "Avery. You look beautiful."

"She always does," Tilly said sweetly from the doorway. "She just doesn't normally look this girly."

Avery's simple black gown for the gala was a silky, shimmery sheath that skimmed and clung to her curves. The sequined spaghetti straps, generous slit up one thigh, and plunging back were a little much for her typically tailored taste, but she'd caught sight of this dress at Rachel's Mixed Bag in town and had to have it. Rachel had asked her to stop by the store yesterday, as she hoped to hire Avery to appraise a stunning jeweled tiara she'd found at an estate sale. Avery had happily agreed to help, and then she'd spotted this vintage 1920s gown on her way out.

Tilly was cheeky about her look tonight, but she wasn't wrong. Avery was stepping out of her box, and she loved the feeling. She'd have preferred her running shoes to the bejeweled heels she wore, but there was time enough for that. She'd missed her runs lately. The marathon was still months away, and she figured all the adrenaline of the last twenty-four hours had to count for something.

Avery and Art had one stop to make before the gala. Walking through the hospital hallways toward Micah's room, Art took Avery's hand. "We're getting some looks," he told her. "Actually, I should say, you're getting some looks."

She glanced at him. "It's all you."

Micah smiled at them from his hospital bed. Avery was surprised to see Sir Robert already here visiting, dressed in his tux for the gala.

Noah stood as they entered the room, gathering his backpack and jacket. "I'm heading out to see Tilly before I catch the train. Wow, you two look great." He gave Avery a quick hug and shook Art's hand and was gone.

"He couldn't get out of here fast enough," Micah said. "Something's going on between him and your sister, you know."

Avery bent and carefully hugged him. "I noticed. Tilly's been waiting." She went around the bed and greeted Sir Robert, keeping her hands on his arms after they'd hugged. "How are you?" She searched his expression.

He couldn't hide the effect losing Francesca had had on him. His sadness shone right through the small smile he gave her.

"I'm doing okay. Really," he stressed. "Or I will be eventually. She left me a letter, you know."

Avery nodded. "I did hear that. Was it . . . did it help ease any of this for you? I know how strongly you felt about her. I can't even imagine how difficult this has been for you."

He nodded. "She did love me. It's the one thing I don't doubt. She said as much in the letter. I may have started out as a simple pawn in her plan with her ex-husband, but Francesca sounded tortured over having to leave me in order to save her own skin."

Avery squeezed his arms and finally let go. "I believe she loved you too. We all saw the way she looked at you. I'm so sorry, Sir Robert."

He cleared his throat, pushing the painful subject aside. "Tell us about your dad. Does he feel all right? What the hospital told us about him being in surgery for so long the night of the accident—I take it that part wasn't a lie. How is he?"

Avery sat on the edge of Micah's bed. "He seems to be doing fine. He's lost some weight, I'm sure the past year was as hard on him as it was on us. And he's quiet. But mostly he's just so happy to be home."

Micah covered her hand with his. "And you girls have your dad back. We've all missed him so much. It's a wonderful miracle."

She nodded. "He can't wait to see you both. He's coming to visit you tomorrow, Micah. And I'm sure he'll be back at work next week."

"Oh!" Sir Robert said. "We got a bit of good news. The Barnaby's account is ours if we want it."

Avery looked at Micah, who was still smiling, and then back at Sir Robert. "We want it! Don't we?"

He nodded. "I've already accepted," he admitted.

"Perfect. That'll be fantastic for business. Which means you need to hurry this up," she said to Micah, waving a hand over his hospital bed.

"I'm working on it, I promise. After making it through this past week, I'm just happy to be here."

* * *

As the MOA gala began to wind down, Art asked Avery for one last dance. His hand was wide and warm at the small of her back, and she felt his heartbeat under her palm on his chest.

"I know what's different," she said, meeting his gaze. She nuzzled his cheek with hers. "You shaved." She tipped her head, stroking her fingertips along his jawline, sharp enough to cut glass.

He grinned. "A rare occurrence. Do you hate it?"

She closed her eyes and pressed her lips against his bare cheek. "So much." She'd started and then stopped herself so many times in suggesting they extend their evening, as the time had flown by much too quickly. Aunt Midge's apartment was empty and only minutes away; the thought of spending more time with Art in a cozier setting was almost irresistible.

But Art was working the next day, and Avery had made a promise to Dr. Singh. She'd come a long way since the trauma of last year, but she had more work to do before she'd trust herself to dive into another relationship. She wasn't about to sabotage whatever was happening with Art before it even got off the ground. He meant too much to her. She wanted to get this right.

Art drew back a bit, his gaze searching hers and then dropping to her lips. "Avery."

Her breath caught in her throat. He was deliciously close. "Art."

He didn't loosen his hold. "How about tomorrow?"

"What's tomorrow?"

"A date," Art said. "You and me. Without any bad guys or car bombs or missing priceless jewels. Just a boring, excitement-free date with just the two of us."

"I don't think so," Avery said.

Art's brow furrowed. "Why not?"

"Because I could never be bored with you," she said, smiling. "Tomorrow sounds perfect."

The song ended, and Avery realized they'd danced over to the focal piece of the gala: the Emperor's Twins medallion, newly restored to its original glory. The FBI had been successful in recovering the stolen ruby from Versailles and had gotten it back just in time. Displayed in a high-security, lighted glass case, the ferocious dragon gleamed under the spotlight, the large twin rubies sparkling in their multifaceted brilliance.

Goldie Brennan sought Avery out as she and Art were leaving. "I wanted you to be the first to know," Goldie said. "We have a rare imperial Russian vase arriving from London on Monday. It comes to us amid some disturbing rumors surrounding its history, but it is uniquely stunning. I'll send the paperwork over."

Avery smiled. "That era is one of my father's specialties. We can't wait to get started!"

Acknowledgments

A note from literary agent Fran Black:

When discussing some of the characters for this book with Tracy, I came up with the initial ideas for three of her characters, people I've known personally much of my adult life. Of course, I took some liberties. I would like to thank the real Francesca (Francesca Giolitti), who is an American of Italian descent and is such a terrific friend that she would give me the Prada off her back and try on a million lipsticks with me to get that perfect red; Robert (Sir Robert Lane), who, while not an actual knight, does carry himself with an air of distinction and really is Francesca's beau; and Midge (Aunt Midge), the heartbeat of Tracy's story and my heartbeat, my own Auntie Mame. My world would be different without these friends, and this story would not live without Tracy having created the wonderful world in which they live. These characters were so much fun to develop with Tracy. When you meet Francesca, Sir Robert, and Aunt Midge, you'll see why they add so much to the story. Thank you, Tracy.

Acknowledgments

From the author:

RUBY RED HERRING was a labor of love in many ways. This story came together as a result of the spark of an idea, a few characters floating around in my literary agent's incredible mind, and my own love of a good mystery. The fact that I am eternally grateful to Fran for the doors she's opened for me made it easy to create Avery Ayers's world and her quest to uncover the truth in both her personal life and the portion of her professional life filled with priceless jewels and artifacts.

I'm also so thankful that Faith Black Ross took the time to consider the project and wanted to see it take form. I'm thrilled to be able to accompany Avery and her close-knit circle of family and friends into the next story, which Faith has made possible.

My amazing husband has been my partner on the journey to publication since day one. He's weathered all the angst, joy, impostor syndrome, heartbreak, frustration, triumph, and satisfaction of this process right along with me, always supporting me and knowing that when I feel like I've had enough and say *I quit*, I don't really mean it. He knows that I can't *not* write. Thank you, Joe, for being my own constant and forever leading man.

Thank you, Katy, Joey, and Halle. My kids are the light of my life and bring me laughter and fulfillment every day. Thanks so much for all the times you step in and take care of everyday things so that I may have another hour or two of writing time, and thank you for your unfailing support of this thing your mom loves to do so much!

As always, major thanks to my mom for showing me as a kid that there is always time to create stories; thank you to my dad

Acknowledgments

for cultivating in me a deep love of reading; thank you, Julie, for being my favorite sister and wonderful cheerleader! I'm also fortunate to have fantastic reading friends in Ann, Rocsana, Sandy, Suzette, and fabulous cousin Jimmy.

Finally, to every reader out there, thank you so much! I hope you enjoy Avery's adventures!

21982319916528